This Angel Has No Wings

Charles Tindell

Charles Tindell

HILLIARD HARRIS
PUBLISHERS

Published by

HILLIARD  HARRIS
PUBLISHERS

P.O. Box 3358
Frederick, Maryland 21705-3358

This novel is a work of fiction. Names, characters, places and incidents either are the product of the author's imagination or are used fictitiously. Any resemblance to actual persons, living or dead, events, or locales is entirely coincidental.

This Angel Has No Wings Copyright © 2004 by Charles Tindell

All rights reserved. No part of this book may be reproduced or transmitted in any form or by any means, electronic or mechanical, including photocopying, recording, or by any information storage and retrieval system, without the written permission of the Publisher, except where permitted by law.

First Edition

ISBN 1-59133-080-7

Designed by **HILLIARD**  **HARRIS**

Cover Illustration © S. A. Reilly
Release Date: August 1, 2004
Manufactured/Printed in the United States of America
2004

Dedicated to:

My wife, Carol.

My son, Scott, his wife, Jennifer,
and his children, Julia, and Alexander.

My son, Andrew, his wife, Lisa
and his children, Benjamin, and Joshua

My son, Robert.

Acknowledgements

A story seldom comes to fruition by the author making the journey alone. In my journey in writing *This Angel Has No Wings* there have been many along the way whose guidance and support made the completion of the journey possible.

Acknowledgement must be made to those whose reading and critiquing of my manuscript proved invaluable. The following individuals' support and encouragement greatly helped me in my journey: Brad Albien, Mary E. Bergquist, Ann Boerth, Jean Boerth, Jonay Gilbertson, Rosie Grossman, Mary Halvorsen, Claire Johnson, Judy Kocher, Susan Lestina, David Osborne, Sharon and Bert Rothnem, Verna VanSickle, and Kim Walker. Thanks to Lisa Thorp for taking my photograph for the book.

Special thanks is to be given to Deb Cutsinger and Jean K. Mattson whose editing proved to be very valuable and reminded me that I should have put more effort in learning the rules of grammar and punctuation during my years in school.

In addition to the individuals mentioned above, I also want to acknowledge the staff, residents, and volunteers of the Minnesota Masonic Homes/Bloomington for their ongoing support and encouragement in this process.

A word of appreciation is also expressed to the members of the South Side Writer's Group whose feedback every Saturday morning in the meeting room at the Eagan Library proved to be very helpful. I always took their suggestions into consideration.

Finally, I wish to express my gratitude to my publisher, Stephanie Reilly, who asked me to take a leap of faith and to join partnership with them in publishing this book. For her guidance and encouragement, I am grateful.

Chapter 1

HOWIE CUMMINS HAD a hunch the brunette with the diamond earrings wasn't from the North Side as soon as she entered his office. Wearing enough jewelry to start her own store, she looked as if she had just come from one of those up-scaled shops on Nicollet Avenue. She had to be from one of the rich suburbs. Either that or a high-class hooker. Maybe both. Whatever her background, she looked troubled.

Her emerald eyes flickered as she glanced around the sparsely furnished office. She paused at the framed movie poster advertising Humphrey Bogart starring in *The Maltese Falcon*. The poster, Howie's *pride and joy*, hung prominently on the wall opposite the door she had come through. "Is...this the MAC Detective Agency?" she asked.

"It sure is." Howie discreetly tossed the old tee-shirt he used as a dust rag behind the file cabinet; cleaning the office could come later. "Can I help you?"

She looked past him as if he was invisible causing him to wonder if she expected someone to come through the door behind him. *Hey, Lady, that only leads to my living quarters and I'm the only one who lives here.*

"I would like to speak to Mr. Mac, please," she said, her eyes still fixed on the door.

"Mr. Who?" he asked, and then realized for whom she was asking. "There's no such person."

She acknowledged him now, scanning him up and down; her face registering disappointment as though she had just been told there was no Santa Claus. "You mean to tell me there's no Mr. Mac?"

"That's right. MAC is an acronym."

"Pardon?"

"An acronym. Each of the letters stand for something." Her eyes remained fixed on him. "The first two are for my partners, Mick Brunner and Adam Trexler. They're not here right now. The C stands for Cummins." He offered her a winsome smile that usually won over people, especially women. "That's me. Howie Cummins."

Her lips parted, but no words came out. Several moments ticked by before she spoke. "You're a detective?" A hint of a blush appeared on her high cheekbones. She cleared her throat. "Excuse me, I'm sorry but you look so...so young."

"I know. Everybody tells me that." He wondered if it would make a difference if she knew he graduated from high school in '59, over seven years ago. Probably not. Dimples accentuated whenever he smiled along with baby-blue eyes and a face that never showed a five o'clock shadow didn't help his case either. "Please, Miss... ah... Mrs.?"

"Hammond." Her voice, gentle and soft, came across like silk flowing over a bare arm. "Jodelle Hammond, and it's Miss."

He gestured to the less worn of two leather chairs sitting in front of a reconditioned mahogany desk. "Well, Miss Hammond, why don't you have a seat?"

"Thank you." She sat down and crossed her legs, her skirt rising above her knee. "And you may call me, Jodelle."

"It'll be my pleasure," Howie said as he sat down, being careful not to stare at her shapely legs too long. He hadn't dated on a regular basis since he and Sheri departed nearly a year ago. She claimed that he wasn't spending much time with her. That was true, but he was busy trying to start his agency, and that came first. "Now, Jodelle, what can I do for you?"

When she didn't respond, but seemed transfixed on his chair, he knew he had to explain. "This used to be a dental office. When I moved in, Doctor Anderson was retiring and he asked me if I wanted the chair. I took it and modified it. I thought it would prove to be a conversation piece."

She glanced around the room, her eyes coming back to rest upon him; there was a hint of amusement on her face. "Quite eclectic," she offered.

Howie nodded, but preferred his description of his office as free spirited. Besides, his furnishing reflected a little problem called cash flow, but he hoped that was about to change. "As I was saying, what can I do for you?"

"What sort of cases do you investigate?"

He wasn't about to tell her that they had only been open for three weeks and that she was their first client. What he and his partners lacked in experience, however, would be made up by tenacity and hard work. When many of his friends first heard that he planned to open a detective agency, they were skeptical. "But you were voted the class clown in high school," a former classmate quipped. "Wouldn't you have better luck being a comedian?" Howie brushed off such remarks, determined to prove that he could handle any case that crossed his desk and that he should be taken seriously. Besides, he had made a promise to himself when his father died two years ago that he would make a successful go of it. When he had initially thought about becoming a private investigator, his father had encouraged him to pursue his dream. Now, as his dream was becoming a reality, he was determined. "We work on everything," he said.

"JoJo is missing," she blurted out. "I think she's been kidnapped." She paused and bit her lip. "Or, dead."

This Angel Has No Wings

IT HAD BEEN nearly two hours since Jodelle Hammond left. Howie was sitting at his desk, leaning back in his chair, and paging through one of his collector's issues of *Police Gazette* when the office door swung open. He peeked over his magazine; his partner, Mick, had paused at the doorway. "What's so interesting out there?" Howie asked.

"I'm admiring this sign Kass made for us; it's just as classy as the one downstairs."

"I won't argue with that." The sign, advertising MAC Detective Agency, had black stylized lettering against a light gray background; a similar sign hung downstairs next to the street entrance door. Kass had insisted on having both signs made for them. "After all," he said with obvious pride, "it's not everyday that three of my young friends open a detective agency above my drugstore." As owner of the building, he had Howie's apartment remodeled so they could use the front room for an office. "It's a beginning," Kass said. "Maybe someday you'll be famous. Then you'll tell people that it all began at my drugstore."

"How're you doing, buddy?" Mick asked as he walked in, closing the door behind him. His tone, as usual, was light and upbeat. "Solve any crimes, yet?"

Howie lowered his magazine. "Where's Adam?"

"He should be here any minute." Mick sniffed the air and looked around. "I think his last class gets out at four." He sniffed again. "Say, who's been here?"

"Our first client."

"No kidding! So who is she?"

"You're just going to have to wait." Howie set his magazine on the desk. "I'll tell you all about it when Adam gets here. That way I won't have to go over it twice." He motioned toward a chair. "So take a load off your feet and relax."

"Okay, okay, so you're not going to tell me now." The amusement in Mick's eyes complimented his smirk. "You know that you haven't changed since junior high; you still like to stretch things out for dramatic effect, don't you?"

"So, how were the rug rats today?" Howie asked as Mick sat down. As far as Howie was concerned, anybody under the age of fifteen was a rug rat. While Mick came from a large family with scores of nephews and nieces always underfoot, Howie grew up in quiet surroundings as the only child of parents who were nearly forty when they had him. "Did you keep those little eighth graders under control?"

"I tried, but they got pretty wild. I had to lay down the law during sixth hour Social Studies." Mick stretched his legs out and slouched down in the chair until he could comfortably rest his head against the back of it. "We're barely into the school year; it's going to take them a while to settle down."

"Don't worry, you're big and tough enough to handle them."

"I sure hope so." At six-two and weighing in at nearly two thirty-five, Mick presented an imposing presence. Black curly hair that never looked fully combed, a broad sloping forehead, and a nose that had been broken twice during his high school football days only added to his menacing appearance. His intimidating looks, however, didn't fool anyone once they got to know him. Although Howie often kidded Mick that he hired him for his muscle, the big guy proved to be the most tender and kindhearted and easiest going of the three.

Howie picked up his magazine and was about to open it when he noticed Mick sniffing the air again. "What's the matter?" he asked. "Are you afraid what Mary might think if you came over smelling like Chanel Number Five?" Mick and Mary had gone together ever since high school and, after eight years, were getting married next year. He wagged his finger at him. "You better be careful; now that you're getting married, she might not like that."

Mick gave him a quick exaggerated smile and then got up and sat in the other chair.

"That's better," Howie said, grinning and giving him a knowing wink. No sooner had he leaned back in his chair, propped his feet up on the desk, and resumed reading his magazine than the downstairs entrance door banged. "That must be Adam," he announced. He cocked his head and listened to the creaking of the stairs; he took pride in identifying people by their footsteps. "Yep, that's him."

"About time." Mick straightened up in his chair. "Now I'll get some answer about this case."

Howie just smiled as the two of them listened as the footsteps reached the top of the staircase. Within moments, the door opened.

"Well, you two sure are working hard," Adam said. "Here we've been in the detective business for nearly a month now and you guys look like you're on vacation."

"How did school go?" Mick asked.

"Always the teacher, aren't you?" Adam closed the door behind him. He appeared pleased that Mick had asked about school. In his first year at the seminary, he had struggled, wondering whether he had what it took to be a minister. In spite of his self-doubts, Mick had encouraged him to stick with it. Howie suggested that if being a preacher didn't work out, he could always try his hand at modeling. "With your brooding bedroom eyes, thick dark brown hair, and athletic built; you could make it big. Women would go crazy over you. You've got your height going for you also." At six feet, Adam was only a couple of inches shorter than Mick.

"So how did it go? Mick asked again.

"It went okay. I've got a quiz coming up."

"Yeah, what subject?"

"Eschatology."

"Escha-what?" Mick exclaimed. "It sounds like a disease."

"All right guys," Howie said, "let's cut the chitchat and get down to business. We've got our first case to handle."

This Angel Has No Wings

"We do?" Adam said. "Great! I've been looking forward to this ever since I signed on to help." He nudged Mick. "Who is it? What's it about?"

"I don't know," Mick replied, throwing up his hands while nodding at Howie. "Ask him. He hasn't said a word to me about it. He's been waiting for you to show up."

Adam quickly settled in the chair next to Mick. He sniffed the air and gave Mick a puzzled look. Mick shrugged his shoulders and pointed to Howie. "Okay, lets hear it," Adam said. "What've you got?"

Howie licked his thumb as he flipped through his pocket-sized notepad. "A couple of hours ago, this gorgeous brunette comes in. I tell you, this woman looked like Betty Grable. I--"

"Wait a minute; Grable was a blond," Adam said.

Mick snickered. "Hey, buddy, maybe you're not the expert on old time movie stars like you think you are."

"I know Grable was a blond, but imagine her being a brunette."

"Okay, we get the picture," Adam said. "So, what did she want?"

Howie first looked at Adam and then at Mick; he took his time in answering. "She hired us to find JoJo."

"Wow!" Mick whacked the arm of his chair causing both Adam and Howie to flinch. "That's great. Who's JoJo? A relative?"

"Hey, guys, do you think we're ready for a missing person's case?" Adam asked.

"Why not," Mick replied. "We have to start someplace." He arched his bushy dark eyebrows. "This could prove interesting."

"I know but it might--"

"Wait, you two," Howie interrupted. Dealing with Adam's cautious one-step-at-a-time approach along with Mick's carefree, full-steam-ahead one could present a challenge. "Let me explain something." He brushed back a shock of reddish blond hair. "JoJo's a cat."

"A cat!" Mick glanced at Adam and began to laugh. "You mean to tell us that our first case is looking for some lost cat? Why doesn't the woman just put an ad in the paper or tack up posters on telephone poles like everyone else?"

"I agree," Adam said. "Maybe I didn't think we were ready for a missing persons' case, but looking for a cat isn't my idea of detective work. We've got better things to do with our time."

Mick nodded. "When we agreed to help out on a part-time basis, you promised that we'd get involved in some interesting cases." He turned to Adam. "Do you remember what *Sam Spade* here said to sell us on the idea?"

"He said, and I quote, 'It'll be an opportunity for you guys to get some excitement into your otherwise boring and pathetic dull lives.'"

Howie leaned back in his chair and clasped his hands behind his head. His desire to become a private investigator came about when the three of them were seniors in high school. At the time, he confided to them that his role model was Humphrey Bogart in the movie, *The Maltese Falcon*. His dream was realized when he got his certificate from a correspondence school; it didn't matter to him that he had found the school's name on the back of a matchbook cover. Nor did it matter to Mick and Adam; they kidded him that since he and Bogart were the same height, which was good enough for them.

"How's this for excitement?" Howie asked. "What would you two say about splitting a G?"

"A what?" Adam asked.

"Come on," Mick said, "speak English. We didn't go to detective school."

"A G is a thousand bucks."

"A thousand bucks!" Mick slapped the arm of his chair again and then gave Adam a playful punch in the arm. "Tell me, he's kidding. Wait a minute. What am I saying? He's not kidding; is he?"

Adam shrugged. "Don't ask me."

"A thousand dollars for finding some cat." Mick shook his head in disbelief. "Who is this woman, anyway?"

"Jodelle Hammond."

Adam leaned forward. "You mean Hammond of Hammond's Department Store in downtown Minneapolis?"

"One and the same."

"Why is someone like her coming to a rinky-dink operation like ours?" Mick asked. "She could hire the best kitty-cat detectives in town."

Howie shot Mick a stern look. "She said that since we grew up on the North Side--"

"Hold your horses," Mick said. "How did she know that? What did she do; hire a detective?"

"Let's get serious," Howie said. "She knows we're from this area. That's one reason she hired us. And the second reason is because we're the only detective agency listed on the North Side."

"We're listed in the Yellow Pages?" Mick poked Adam. "Did you know about that?"

"No, it's news to me."

Mick turned his attention back to Howie. "So, what has that got to do with this MoJo?"

"It's JoJo," Howie emphasized through gritted teeth. "Jodelle Hammond's sister lives here on the North Side. Her name is Maureen." He reached into his shirt pocket. "Jodelle gave me her address and this photo of her. She suspects that her sister may know something about JoJo's disappearance."

"Let me see the picture," Mick said.

After Mick finished with the photograph, Adam looked at it and then gave it back to Howie. "How old is she?" he asked.

"In her late twenties."

"How about Jodelle?" Mick asked.

Howie slipped the picture back into his shirt pocket. "She didn't tell me, but she did say that she was older than her sister."

"Let's back up for a moment," Adam said. "This isn't making sense. Why doesn't she just call her sister and ask her?"

"Yeah, it'd be a lot cheaper," Mick pointed out.

Howie flipped through a couple pages in his notepad, "According to Jodelle, about eight months ago the two of them had a dispute and her sister moved out. Apparently, she has lived in a couple of different places, but always in this area. Jodelle told me that if she tried to call her, her sister would hang up."

"But why would her sister even know about the cat?" Adam asked.

"She gave me the impression that her sister may have taken the cat. When I asked her why Maureen would do that, she was very vague about it." Howie turned a page in his notepad. "That's all I have. I guess I should've pressed her more."

"You were just thinking about that thousand bucks," Mick said.

Howie nodded. "I have to admit that I just about croaked when she mentioned it. She made it sound like it was petty change to her."

"Probably is," Adam said. "I remember reading that the Hammond family is among the top ten wealthiest in the Midwest."

"Really?" Howie said. "Tell me more."

"I read an article about them a few months back. It's seems like old man Hammond started with a small clothing store on Lake Street and within five years relocated in downtown Minneapolis. He invested his profits in the stock market where he hit it big. He earned his first million within six months."

Mick let out a low whistle. "I wonder what he thinks of his daughters' feud?"

Howie scribbled a note to himself to ask. "We'll have to talk to him about that."

"I don't think that's going to happen," Adam said.

"Why's that?" Howie asked. "Is he a recluse or something?"

"You might say that."

"What do you mean?" Mick asked.

"Well, the guy's dead."

"What!" Howie exclaimed.

"He died nearly a year ago. According to this article, it was a heart attack." Adam paused. "I can't remember how old he was at the time. His entire fortune was left to his two daughters. The downtown store still has the family name but they're not involved with it anymore."

"No wife?" Howie asked.

"Divorced years ago."

Howie leaned back in his chair and took a sip of lukewarm coffee. "Here's what I think we should do." He leaned forward and set the cup down on the desk. "Why don't we go and check out the address?"

"You mean now?" Mick asked.

"Yeah, why not? We might get lucky. What do you say?"

"Okay, I'm game," Mick replied. "Where is it?"

Charles Tindell

"It's not that far away," Howie said. "It's over on Twenty-fourth and Girard. Are you going to come?" he asked Adam.

"Oh, sure, why not? I didn't want to study, anyway." Adam got up from his chair. "Let's find the cat and be done with it."

After locking the door, Howie put up a sign. *Not In. Be Back Later.*

Mick shook his head and pointed to the sign. "That has got to go. It reminds me when Doctor Anderson was here. I used to go to that guy all the time."

"It was sure nice of Kass to let you have this place after Anderson left," Adam reminded Howie as the three of them walked down the steps to the outside entrance.

"I know, but it works out for both of us. He gives me a break on the rent and I'm always available to work whenever he needs me." Howie snapped his fingers. "That reminds me. I have to work for a couple of hours this evening."

Mick turned to Adam. "Hey, do you think Sam Spade ever had to work at a soda fountain while he was ridding the world of cat-nappers?"

"I wouldn't know."

"Look, I've got an idea." Mick paused. "We should stop and get some catnip. That way JoJo will find us."

Adam patted his partner on the back. "That's a good idea, but I suppose then we'd have to split the reward with JoJo."

"Naw, we'd just let her keep the catnip."

"Alright, guys," Howie said, "how long am I going to hear about this? Let's not forget that the Hammond woman was very upset."

"Okay, okay," Mick said, putting up his hands in mock defense. "We're just having a little fun."

"Who's driving?" Adam asked.

"I'll drive," Mick volunteered. "Since you're a fledging student and Howie's...say, how would you characterize our boss?"

"I think he's a Sam Spade want-to-be."

"Just watch it, wise guys," Howie said, feeling good about finally getting their first case to work on. Even though the case only involved a missing cat and possibly some kind of dispute between two sisters, he saw it as opportunity to prove his ability. Once he finished this minor case, he could go on to more important ones that would give him the needed confidence and prove to the skeptics that he had what it takes to be a detective.

In the car, Howie sat in the front seat as Adam opted for the back. On the way, they tried to figure out how any cat could be worth a thousand dollars. Adam suggested that perhaps, it's one of those blue ribbon felines. "You know, rich folks like that kind of stuff." Mick offered the idea that maybe the cat did TV commercials.

Adam tapped Howie on the shoulder. "Did she give you a picture of JoJo?"

"No, she said she didn't have any with her."

"That's too bad. How are we suppose to identity it, then?"

Mick laughed. "That's easy. Just look for something that has a tail and says, meow." He glanced over at Howie. "What street did you say it was again?"

"Take a right on Girard, and it should only be a couple of blocks." Howie shot a quick glance back at Adam. "And as far as the cat is concerned, she said it's gray and has blue eyes."

The houses on Girard were small and cramped together. A couple of the front lawns looked as if they hadn't been mowed for a month. On the curbing in front of one house sat a dilapidated gas stove with a hand-scrawled sign advertising that anyone willing to haul it away could have it.

They drove past a heavy-set older man working on his car engine as another guy looked on while drinking a bottle of beer. Finding a parking space across the street from the address, Mick parked the car and they got out.

"That's it," Howie said as he pointed to a white-framed house.

"Are you sure?" Adam asked. "It's got a *For Sale* sign in front of it."

"I see it, but that's the address she gave me."

"Man, check out the porch," Mick said. "The thing looks like it's going to fall off."

Howie looked up at the threatening sky. "Let's go and check this place out before it starts raining. And keep your eyes open for JoJo."

"Like I asked before," Adam said. "How are we going to know JoJo if we don't know what she looks like?" He glanced around the neighborhood. "There's probably lots of gray cats roaming around."

"It should be a piece of cake," Mick said. "We just find a cat that doesn't look like it belongs in a low-rent area like this. It'd probably be wearing a diamond studded collar."

As they walked up to the porch, Howie noticed some kind of marking on the sidewalk leading around to the back of the house. He was going to point it out but Mick and Adam were already at the front door and were waiting for him to join them.

While Howie knocked, Adam stepped over to the front window and peeked in. "That's not going to do much good."

"Why's that?"

"Come over here and take a look." Adam moved away from the window. "Whoever lived here has moved out, and they took everything except the rug."

"Really? Jodelle didn't say anything about her sister moving again."

Mick walked over and looked in the window. "Well, maybe she didn't know about it."

"I want you guys to look at something," Howie said as they walked down the porch steps. He led them around to the side of the house. A triangle, three feet long and nearly as wide as the sidewalk, had been crudely spray painted in black. Inside of the triangle were three F's.

"What do you think that is?" Mick asked.

"At first glance, I thought it was a religious symbol," Adam said. "The triangle is symbolic of the Trinity." He shook his head, "But I don't know about this."

"What do you mean?" Howie asked, aware of the uneasy look in Adam's eyes.

"I can't put my finger on it. It's just a feeling." Adam continued to stare at the triangle. "It looks like whoever did this went over it again and again, like they wanted to scorch it into the cement."

"Maybe it was the gas company," Mick said. "They're always marking up lawns and sidewalks with strange symbols." He knelt down and ran his fingers over one of the F's. "How long do you think this thing has been here?"

"I can't tell, but it doesn't look new," Adam said.

Howie felt a drop of water on his head and then looked up at the dark clouds. "Come on, let's go; it's going to pour any second." As they walked away, he took one last look. He didn't know what that symbol stood for, but he decided he better draw a sketch of it in his notepad for further reference; just in case.

Chapter 2

HOWIE AND HIS two friends jumped into the car just as the first rain drops spattered down. He looked back at the house, wondering why a woman with the kind of money Maureen Hammond must have would live in a neighborhood like this. *And why would she bother with a cat, even if it was worth a thousand bucks? What's really going on between her and her sister?* There were still too many questions and he had no answers. "Well, what do you guys think?"

"Beats me," Mick said as he rolled up his window. "Are you sure you got the right address from her?"

"Yeah, I repeated it to her after I'd written it down." Howie took out his notepad and double-checked the address he had written against the numbers on the house. "You can see for yourself. It's the same address."

Adam leaned forward and rested his arms on the back of the front seat. "Maybe Maureen did live here, but when the owner decided to sell, she had to move."

"But why?" Howie asked. It made no sense to him.

Mick started the car and turned on the wipers. "Maybe because JoJo wanted to live in a higher class neighborhood."

"What I mean is that she wouldn't have had to move until the house was sold," Howie explained. "It takes a couple of months for that whole process. And the agent would want her to stay while he showed the house."

"How do you know so much about that?" Mick asked.

"Because I've got a friend who's in the business and he says that it's always better to show a house that has furniture in it. She didn't have to move out because the house was for sale. My guess is that something else was going on." As Mick put the car in gear and pulled away, Howie wrote down the name of the real estate agency listed on the *For Sale* sign. He would contact them to get some information on the owner. *Maybe the owner knows where Maureen moved.*

Adam tapped him on the shoulder. "So, where do we go from here?"

"Give me some time to think this through," Howie replied. It was important to demonstrate to his partners that he knew what he was doing.

Charles Tindell

He had gotten them to come into the business and now that they had a case, he had to show them he could handle it. For the next couple of blocks, he chewed on the eraser end of his pencil and reviewed his notes. By the time they turned onto Broadway he had decided upon their next step. "What are you guys doing tomorrow afternoon around three?"

"Why?" Adam asked. "What have you got in mind?"

"I think we should go over and talk to Jodelle." Howie replied, convinced that she was hiding something from them. "Can you guys go?"

Mick shook his head. "I can't."

"Why not?" Howie asked.

"Because after school, I've got to prepare some assignments for the coming weekend."

"But tomorrow's only Wednesday." Howie pointed to a car pulling out from its parking spot. "Watch out; that guy isn't looking."

"I see him." Mick slowed the car as the driver pulled out without bothering to check traffic. "I know tomorrow's only Wednesday," he said as he stepped on the gas, "but I've got to keep a couple of steps ahead of the kids. If I give them enough work for the weekend, maybe it'll drain off some of their energy come Monday morning."

"How about after you get done with that?"

"Can't do it then, either." When Mick agreed to work with Howie, he made it clear that his first priority were his students. Last year the kids at his school voted him as their favorite teacher. "I'm going to meet with one of the student's mother. She'll be in around four-fifteen."

"You can do those assignments later," Howie suggested. "And can't you reschedule your meeting?"

"I better not. When she called me, she sounded pretty upset. Her son's involved in some things that she wants to talk over with me in person." Mick switched lanes. "She's afraid it's going to affect his grades. From my contact with the kid, I think she's got her hands full."

Howie looked back at Adam. "How about you, then?"

"That depends. I have classes until two. Then I should do some studying."

"You'll have time for that later on in the evening. We won't be out too late."

"Why can't you go by yourself?" Mick brought the car to a stop for a red light and then turned to Howie. "You're not scared of being alone with a beautiful, older woman, are you?" he asked with a twinkle in his eye.

"Of course not." Howie wasn't about to admit that he was attracted to Jodelle Hammond the minute she walked into his office. He reminded himself, however, that she was a client. Once the case was over, though, then he might pursue a different kind of relationship. "I just want to get someone else's opinion of her. You know, just to make sure I read her right that first time."

"I'll go," Adam said, "but just as long as it doesn't run too late. What time do you want me there?"

"Meet me up at the office around three." Howie glanced over at Mick. "What time are you done meeting with that kid's mother?"

"Hopefully by five. Why?"

"How about if you go back to that house on Girard and check with the neighbors on both sides. You might get some leads from them."

"Sure, what do you want me to ask?"

Howie flipped open his notepad. "Find out how long Maureen lived there and when she moved out. And ask if any of the neighbors know the owner." He flipped the page. "Also, ask them about what they thought of her as a neighbor."

"You mean things like if she was quiet and kept to herself, or if she had wild parties every night?"

"Yeah, something like that."

"Don't forget about asking if they've seen any cat around," Adam said.

"And if they did," Howie added, "if she had it when she moved in. Neighbors notice things like that."

"Got it; anything else?"

"Yeah," Howie said, "the light's turned green. Let's go."

THE NEXT DAY, as he waited for Adam, Howie drew up a list of questions he would be asking Jodelle. He was especially curious why she was offering so much for the cat; a question he now realized he should have asked. He was checking over his list when there was a faint knocking on the door.

"Come on in, it's not locked."

The door slowly opened and a little boy peeked in. Howie guessed his age to be eight or nine. "Come on in, kid."

The youngster shut the door quietly and took a few steps toward the desk. "Are you the detective?" he asked timidly as he clutched a brown paper sack in his hands.

"Yeah, I'm Howie Cummins. What's your name?"

"Joey."

Howie looked at the clock on the wall. It was two-forty five. "How come you're not in school?"

Joey's mouth dropped open and his brown eyes doubled in size. "You're not going to report me, are you?"

"You don't have to worry, I wouldn't do that." Howie stifled a grin. "What can I do for you?"

"I want to hire you."

"Joey..." Howie paused and ran his fingers through his hair. He didn't have time for this. "I don't know who sent you, but--"

"Mr. Kass sent me."

"You mean, Kass from downstairs in the drugstore? A short guy? Looks like Santa Claus without the beard? He sent you?"

Joey nodded as he looked around. Howie couldn't tell if the kid was awestruck by being in a detective's office or disappointed. "Why don't you come over and sit down. You can tell me why Mr. Kass sent you."

Charles Tindell

The boy slid onto the chair, still clutching his paper sack with both hands. "Mr. Kass said you could help me."

"He did, huh? What do you need help with?"

"My cat's missing."

Oh, no! Not another one. "Your cat? Why did Kass think I could help?"

"When I told him about my cat being lost, he said that he knew of a good detective that could find him."

Howie recalled how last night, while working at the soda fountain, he had shared with Kass that their first case involved finding a cat. "How long has your cat been gone?"

"Nearly a week." Joey sniffed, and a tear appeared in the corner of his eye. Howie could picture Kass melting over such soft brown eyes. Over the years Kass always helped out kids in any way he could. Howie, himself, owed a lot to the guy. "He's been gone before, but never this long."

"What's his name?"

"Midnight." Joey pointed his finger toward Howie's chair. "Is that a dentist's chair you're sitting in?"

"Yeah."

"Cool."

"Thanks. Now, Joey about your cat; since his name is Midnight, I suppose then his color is black?"

"Huh, huh, except he has a little white mark." Joey raised his head and touched a spot under his chin. "Right here. You wouldn't notice it unless you were looking for it."

Howie took out his notepad. "Where do you live?"

"Over on Lowry right across from the park." Joey pointed again. "Behind that door? Is that where you keep the crooks?"

"No, that's where I live."

The brown eyes grew even larger. "You live here?"

"I sure do." Howie knew that he couldn't turn the kid away. He would, however, have a talk with Kass. Two cat cases were enough. "Let me get some information from you, okay?"

After he took Joey's phone number and address, Howie put down his pencil. "I've got to make something clear to you, Joey. I can't promise you that I'll find Midnight, but I'll give it my best shot."

Joey's eyes glowed as he smiled for the first time since he had come into the office. "You'll find him. I know you will."

"Okay, we'll see." Howie hoped that the cat was living it up in the park chasing squirrels and birds. When he had time, he'd check out the park, maybe ask around the neighborhood. It'd take a few hours, but he owed Kass for all the times the guy had helped him over the years.

Clank! Joey set his sack on the desk.

"What's that?" Howie asked.

"Two dollars and seventy-seven cents, but I'll be earning more." Joey bit his lip; his brown eyes grew anxious. "Will it be enough for now?"

This Angel Has No Wings

Howie cleared his throat. "Ah, let me check something." He turned to a blank page in his notepad, making sure he shielded it from Joey's sight. "Oh, yeah, here it is. You've got more than enough. The charge for a missing cat is exactly two bucks." Joey reached into his sack and pulled out a handful of change. "Hang on there," Howie said, "I only get paid if and when I find Midnight. Is that a deal?"

"Deal." Joey's face exploded into a smile. He slid off his chair to leave, but then stood quietly.

"You got another question for me, kid?"

Joey nodded.

"Let's hear it."

"Do you carry a gun?"

"No. Some detectives do. I don't." When Howie decided to become a detective, he told Mick and Adam that he would never carry a gun. "That's good," Mick quipped, "Because you'd probably shoot yourself in the foot if you did." Both his partners knew, however, the real reason Howie didn't like guns. A grade school friend of his was accidentally shot and killed by an older brother who had found their father's gun hidden in a closet. Also, Howie's police detective friend, JD, shared that he had never once used his gun in seventeen years. "A good detective doesn't outgun the bad guys," JD said, "He outsmarts them. We have too many guys on the force who think they're John Wayne."

No sooner had Howie's young client left, than Adam walked in. "Who was the kid?"

"His name is Joey."

"What did he want?"

"Remind me to tell you about it on the way; let me finish this first." Howie hoped that Adam would forget about it. He was afraid that his partners would razz him, especially Mick.

Adam sat and waited while Howie wrote down the description of Joey's cat. "I've got tons of reading to do for an early morning class tomorrow," Adam said. "I hope this thing with Jodelle doesn't take too long."

"It won't." Howie glanced over the list of questions he had prepared. "Okay, I'm ready." He slipped on his sports coat, and straightened his tie. "Let's go. We'll take my car."

Traffic was light. The drive took less than a half hour. Jodelle's house, a two-story Victorian, was fifteen minutes south of the downtown area near one of several small lakes located within the city limits. Although her home was in an upper class neighborhood, both Adam and Howie agreed that her house was modest in comparison to the others. Howie parked around the corner, nearly a block away.

"How come so far away?" Adam asked as Howie turned off the ignition.

"Just in case she doesn't want to explain to the neighbors why an old clunker was parked in front of her house."

Adam rubbed his finger across the dashboard. "At least, it's clean."

Howie laughed. "Yeah, and paid for."

"You want the windows rolled up?"

"No, it's too hot out. Leave them open." Howie looked at the houses across the street and down the block. "The people who live around here are rich. They wouldn't think of touching this heap with a ten-foot pole."

Walking toward Jodelle's house, an albino squirrel darted across their path and scampered up a large oak. "Hey, did you see that?" Adam asked, "Maybe that's a sign of good luck."

"Let's hope so." Howie watched the squirrel for a moment as it sat on a lower branch, chattering at them. "I have a feeling that with this case, we're going to need some."

As they turned onto Jodelle's front walk, they found themselves skirting a torn-up section of sidewalk. The cement chunks lay in a pile off to one side. Howie pointed to the pile. "Wonder what's going on here?"

"Beats me," Adam said as they approached the front door.

Howie rang the doorbell. "Do you think a butler will answer?" He was about to ring it a second time when the door opened.

If Jodelle Hammond was surprised to see them, there was no indication. Dressed in beige slacks and a short sleeve wine color sweater, she greeted them in a friendly tone. "Good afternoon."

Howie took the lead. "Hi. I hope you don't mind us dropping in on you like this, but there are some things we need to talk about."

"That's quite alright."

"Great." When Adam cleared his throat, Howie got the hint. "Oh, and this is Adam Trexler, one of my partners."

She extended her hand. "Hello."

"Hi, it's good to meet you." Adam gestured toward the sidewalk behind them. "It looks like you've got some problems."

"Yes." Her smile momentarily faded. "The workers are coming back tomorrow to finish."

"May we have a few minutes of your time?" Howie asked.

"Of course, forgive me. Please come in. I was just in the sitting room having a cup of tea. I've been expecting you."

As they followed her, Adam tugged at Howie's coat. *Expecting us?* He mouthed. Howie just shrugged and shook his head. He was more curious about the troubled look he saw in her eyes when the sidewalk was mentioned.

They were led into a spacious room tastefully decorated in predominately pastel colors. Large bay windows on two adjacent walls gave the room an airy, outdoor feeling. They sat on cushioned, white-wicker chairs around an oval-shaped glass coffee table. In the center of the table sat a bouquet of fresh flowers.

"May I offer you something to drink? Tea? Lemonade?"

"Nothing for me," Howie said.

Adam shook his head. "No, thank you," and then added, "The flowers are beautiful."

"Thank you. I have a garden in the back. I so enjoy working with my flowers. It relaxes me."

"You said you were expecting us?" Howie asked, wanting to bypass the pleasantries and get down to business. "What did you mean by that?"

"I thought you would want to see me again, and soon." She hugged herself, rubbing her arms as though suddenly chilled. "It's about the address I gave you for my sister. The house was vacant, wasn't it?"

"You mean you knew that?" Howie said, exchanging glances with Adam.

"Yes," she replied, avoiding eye contact.

"Why didn't you tell me that to begin with?"

"I don't know...I guess..." She seemed to be searching for words. "I guess I was confused... and afraid."

"Afraid? Of what?"

She took a deep breath. "This may sound silly, but I was afraid that you perhaps wouldn't take the case."

As she sat with her hands in her lap, Howie noticed her left forefinger twitching. "Why would you think that?"

"I don't know." When Jodelle went to pick up her teacup, her hands trembled. With two hands, she moved the cup to her lips and took a sip. "I'm sorry, but this whole thing is making me so nervous. You need to find my sister."

Adam glanced over at Howie, giving him a puzzled look. "Your sister? I thought we were looking for your cat?"

"You are." Jodelle tugged at her pearl earring. "I just mean that if you find my sister, I'm sure you'll find the cat too."

"What kind of relationship do you and your sister have?" Howie asked.

"What do you mean?" she quickly asked, sounding offended.

"I mean were you close? Did you get along? Did she ever--"

"I love Maureen," Jodelle blurted out. "She's the dearest sister in the world. I'd do anything for her. She's the only real family I have left."

"Your mother's still living, isn't she?" Adam asked quietly, as though instinctively knowing she needed to settle down.

"Yes, but the woman remarried after she and our father were divorced. She never showed any interest in us." Jodelle's voice took on a chilled tone. "I haven't had any contact with her for years. It was our father who raised us. He made sure we were a very close-knit family. When he died, Maureen and I became even closer as sisters."

"So you never had any disagreements over anything?" Howie felt like he was talking to a completely different woman than yesterday.

"Like most sisters, we had our differences and little misunderstandings every now and then, but nothing major."

Adam leaned forward slightly. His expression and voice showed a compassionate interest. "Why then would she take the cat?"

Jodelle looked at Adam with a puzzled expression. "I..." she began, and then stopped. She rubbed her arms again.

Charles Tindell

"Are you okay?" Howie asked.

"I'm sorry, I'm just not myself today." She looked at Adam. "What did you ask?"

"I was asking about JoJo, your cat," Adam replied quietly, patiently. "What makes you think your sister knows something about its disappearance?"

"I just do." Jodelle massaged her forehead. "Now, please, you must excuse me. I'm feeling ill. I didn't sleep well last night."

"I'm sorry to hear that," Howie said, "but if we could just ask a few more questions."

"No, please. Just find my sister, and I'm sure this whole matter will be cleared up."

Before Howie or Adam could say another word, Jodelle stood up, signaling that the conversation was at an end. At the door, she thanked them for coming, and asked to be notified immediately if they found out anything.

"Something's screwy here," Howie said as he and Adam walked to the car. "Her story isn't jiving with what she first told me."

"You mean about the relationship between her and her sister?"

"Exactly. Yesterday when she came into the office, she said that the two of them had some kind of falling out."

"Didn't you say that's why her sister moved out?"

"Right. And not only that, she gave me the impression that her sister may have taken the cat out of spite or revenge." Howie glanced up at the tree for the squirrel they had seen earlier; it was nowhere in sight. "But now, she seems to be more concerned about her sister than the cat. This isn't making sense."

"Hey, it looks like we've got a visitor," Adam said when they turned the corner. Up ahead a dark haired young man was leaning against Howie's car; he was dressed in slacks, a black turtleneck sweater, and a navy blue blazer. Howie guessed him to be in his late twenties or early thirties. Arms folded, his smug smile remained fixed as he watched them walk toward him.

"I wonder who he is?" Howie asked.

"You got me, but he has that look like he could own this neighborhood."

"Maybe he does, but I don't like his shifty eyes," Howie whispered as they got closer. "Can we help you?" Howie asked as they walked up to him.

"No," he sniffed, "but I believe I can help you." His tone was smooth and mellow, but had a hint of arrogance.

"Yeah, how's that?" Adam now had an edge to his voice that hadn't been there when he had talked with Jodelle.

"It would be in your best interests to drop this case."

Howie didn't like the superior expression written all over the guy's face, nor his condescending attitude. He especially didn't like the stranger leaning on his car. "I'm not sure what you're talking about."

"We both know I'm referring to Jodelle Hammond, whose house you just came from." He waited as if he expected a response. "Oh, yes, I know that you and Adam here are partners in a small-time detective agency over on Broadway on the North Side. I'm surprised that your other partner isn't here. Mick, that's his name, isn't it?"

Adam folded his arms and cocked his head; his dark brown eyes unflinchingly locked upon the stranger. "Why don't you, first of all, tell us who you are."

"Of course. How rude of me." His thin lips formed a smile. "I'm Damien, Jodelle's brother."

"Her brother?" Adam shot a glance over at Howie before turning his attention back to Damien. "I don't remember her saying anything about having a brother."

"Let's just say that I'm... a long-lost brother. The black sheep of the family."

"So what do you want?" Howie asked, chastised himself for not having asked Jodelle if she had any other siblings.

"I'm here to tell you that you should forget all about this case."

"Sorry, but we were hired by Jodelle."

Damien moved away from the car. "Look, I'm warning you."

"Warning us?" Adam's eyes narrowed.

Howie felt his neck muscles tighten up. "By any chance, are you threatening us? Because if you are, we don't take kindly to threats."

"Gentlemen, who says I'm threatening you? You should consider it a friendly suggestion—one that is in all your best interests. It's up to you if--"

"You said it," Howie cut in, "it *is* up to us."

"Why don't we go and talk this over with your sister," Adam suggested.

"I don't think that's necessary." Damien smiled. "Everything that needs to be said has been said. I believe we understand each other's positions quite clearly. Good day." Without saying another word, he left, walking in the direction that Howie and Adam had come from.

"What was that all about?" Adam asked.

"Don't ask me. I just wonder why Jodelle never mentioned him."

"Maybe because he's the black sheep."

As they drove away, Howie looked in the rear view mirror. Damien was nowhere in sight. "I wonder why he wants us off the case? What does he have to do with JoJo?"

"Do you think he had anything to do with the cat's disappearance?"

"I don't know. The more we get into this case, the more unanswered questions there are."

"Well, you said detective work would be interesting."

They got back to the North Side shortly before five. Howie parked on the side street across from Kass'. "Thanks for coming. Roll up the windows on your side, will you?"

After doing his window, Adam turned to roll up the back seat window. "Hey, what's this package back here?"

"What are you talking about?"

"There's a package wrapped in brown paper and tied with twine."

"What?" Howie turned around; the package, the size of a shoebox, sat in the corner on the passenger's side.

"Isn't it yours?" Adam asked.

"No, I've never seen it before."

This Angel Has No Wings

Chapter 3

"So, what do you think?" Adam asked as he and Howie studied the package laying on the back seat of Howie's car.

"I don't know." Howie leaned over the front seat to get a better look. "I don't see any writing on it, do you?"

"No, but it could be on the bottom."

"Maybe." Howie thought about reaching back and turning the package over, but decided he would wait until they considered the possibilities of what it could contain.

"And you're sure it wasn't there before?"

"Pretty sure. I think I would've noticed it."

Adam looked over at Howie for a moment. "So, it had to be put there some time between after we left the car to visit with Jodelle Hammond and when we came back."

"That's the only time the car was left unattended. And the only person we saw by the car was Jodelle's brother. What was his name? Damien?"

"Yeah. Do you think it was him who slipped it in?"

"In my book, he's the likely suspect." Howie massaged a knot forming in the back of his neck. "There's something though that I can't quite figure out."

"What's that?"

"If it was him, why did he stick around and talk to us?"

"I know what you mean. You'd have thought that he would've just slipped it in and then taken off so he wouldn't be connected with it. Unless..." Adam paused.

"Come on, unless what?"

"Well, all the time he was yakking, I got the feeling he was looking down that long pointed nose at us. You know, like he thought he was superior."

"I had that feeling, too. That guy came across as being so arrogant that he probably thought he could get away with anything." Howie recalled the smirk on his face and how it stayed there during the whole time he was talking. "If he left it, maybe he was daring us to find it while he was still there."

"You mean like he was playing some kind of game with us?"

"Exactly."

"I wonder what he would've said if we had discovered it?"

Howie shrugged. "He probably would've claimed he didn't know anything about it."

"Okay, let's assume it was him. He did threaten us." Adam gestured toward the package. When he spoke, his voice carried with it a note of concern. "I know I'm being paranoid, but are you sure it's not some kind of bomb?"

"Yeah, I'm sure," Howie replied. That the package could contain a bomb had passed through his mind. At first, he was going to suggest that they should perhaps get out of the car. Maybe even stand across the street for a while. He dismissed that, however, as being over melodramatic. Besides, if Damien wanted to kill them, the package would have exploded by now. "If it was a bomb, there would be some kind of ticking noise." Howie paused. "You don't hear any, do you?"

Adam cocked his head and listened. "But don't you think we should call the police anyway?"

"No," Howie snapped. He had no intention of everybody on the North Side witnessing the new detective calling the police for help. *What if it turned out to be nothing but some kind of prank? I'd be the laughing stock of the neighborhood.* "We can handle it."

"So, what are we going to do with it?"

"We'll bring it up to the office and open it there."

"Whatever you say."

"Okay, you get it. I'll open the door for you."

"Me?" Adam's eyebrows rose. "I tell you what. I'll open the door. You can get it."

Howie rolled his eyes. "And to think you're studying to be a minister." He got out of the car and joined Adam on the sidewalk; they stood for several minutes looking through the window at the package. Only after two young girls walked by and asked what were they looking at did Howie decide it was foolish to stand there any longer. Adam agreed, and then cautiously opened the door. Howie carefully placed his hands on both ends of the package, lifted it a couple of inches, and then slowly set it back down again.

"What are you doing?"

"Just checking to see how heavy it is."

"How heavy is it?"

"Feels like it's a couple of pounds." Howie didn't tell Adam that just as he was about to lift it, his mind flashed to a scene in some old gangster movie he had recently watched on television. In the movie, an unmarked package exploded as soon as the detective's partner moved it. Taking a deep breath, he picked it up again and slowly backed away from the car. "Okay, I got it." To his surprise, trickles of sweat cascaded down his back.

Carrying the package up the stairs to the office seemed like an eternity to Howie. At one point, he stumbled. The package tilted and as it did, he felt something inside slide across the bottom of the box. The movement sent chills down his back. Adam opened the office door and let him go in first. Moving quickly across the room, he set the package down in the middle of his desk. After slumping into his chair, he wiped the perspiration off his forehead, took a deep breath and blew it out slowly. The two of them sat for a long time, not saying a word.

Adam finally broke the silence. "Now what?"

Howie leaned forward and studied the package for a moment. "We open it."

"Go ahead, be my guest."

Howie rummaged through the desk drawers, found a pair of scissors, stood up, and bent over the package. Adam looked on as his partner carefully cut each strand of twine. At one point, Howie looked up and offered a smile. "You think that with all this twine he could've at least put a bow on it." After he cut the final strand, he put the scissors back in the drawer, and then folded back the wrapping paper to reveal a shoebox. "What have we got here? Black Oxfords. Size nine. "At first, he was hopeful that he could trace the box to where the shoes were purchased. His hopes faded, however, when he didn't see any markings of any kind on the box.

"Are you going to open it?" Adam asked.

"Yeah, I was just checking the box for clues." Howie leaned forward, placed his hands on both ends of the box's lid, and carefully lifted the cover. "Oh, man!"

"What is that?" Adam cried, his eyes recoiling at the contents of the box.

Howie took another look. "I'm not sure, but if Damien's behind this, he's one sick person."

MICK GLANCED AT the clock and wondered if his partners had gotten anywhere with Jodelle Hammond. They had to be back at the office by now, probably sitting around and having a Coke and something to eat. For the past hour, he had been meeting with the mother of Robby Davis. Even though these conferences with parents took time, he would have it no other way. He remembered his parents coming home from teacher conferences concerning his older brothers and how highly they spoke of the teachers. Those meetings helped his parents deal with one of his brothers who wanted to quit school at age sixteen. Because of the teacher's involvement, his brother stayed in school and even went on to college. Teachers played an important role in shaping the lives of young people, and Mick loved that challenging aspect of his job. As he sat and talked with Mrs. Davis, he knew he had another challenge. The picture she painted of her fourteen-year-old was of a son whom she feared was going off the deep end.

Charles Tindell

"Mr. Brunner, like I told you, it started with those comic books about witches and in just the last couple of weeks, Robby's gotten into playing with a Ouija board."

Mick was familiar with Ouija boards. They weren't that bad. When he was younger, he used to fool around with one. "I wouldn't be concerned about it if I was you."

"How can you say that?" Robby's mother's eyes reflected her disbelief. "Those things are used to communicate with spirits and ghosts."

"That may be true, but I think most of the kids just play around with them." Mick spoke calmly. "They just want to know if they're going to get married and stuff like that. I think they're harmless, but I suppose too much of anything can cut into school work."

"That's exactly what I'm talking about. Robby doesn't seem to have any interest in school. And then he started hanging around with some weirdos." Mrs. Davis' voice rose to a higher pitch. "They wear such disgusting clothes. And the music they listen to is terrible. I tell you, ever since his father left two years ago, Robby has changed so much."

"Mrs. Davis, I tell you what, I'll talk to him my first available opportunity."

After Robby's mother left, Mick spent a few minutes reviewing the next day's assignments and then tidied up the stack of papers on his desk. It was nearly five-thirty before he got in his car and drove to the address on Girard. He would check the neighbors on either side, starting with the one on the right. He walked up the steps to the front porch and rang the doorbell. After a short time, he rang it again. Someone was home because he noticed the curtain moving in the front window. He was about to ring the doorbell again when an elderly man opened the door part way.

"What do you want?" the man shouted. "If you're selling something, I don't have any money."

"I'm with the MAC Detective Agency. My name--"

"You say your name is Mac and you're defective?" The old man cocked his ear as his bushy white eyebrows rose sharply.

After finally hearing who Mick was and why he was there, the old gentleman opened the door further but did not invite him in. When Mick asked about Maureen Hammond, he gruffly shot back that he didn't know the woman. "Didn't care to, either." After a couple of other questions, Mick decided that the guy wasn't going to be of any help. He was about to thank him for his time when the bushy eyebrows rose again.

"Do you want to know why she left?"

Mick nodded.

The old guy tugged at a tuft of wiry white hair growing out of his ear. "Because of that triangle on the sidewalk."

"You know about that?"

"Darn tooting, I do. Ain't blind you know. I can see that thing from my kitchen window. Mighty strange with those letters inside of it."

"You said she left because of it. Are you sure?"

This Angel Has No Wings

His eyes narrowed to the point where all Mick could see was his humped nose and bushy eyebrows. "Sure, I'm sure! I got eyes and ears, ain't I? That triangle thing appeared one morning, and the next day she moved out and the house was put up for sale." The old man knotted his eyebrows and motioned for Mick to come closer. "I know who put that thing there."

"You do? Who?"

"Martian aliens. I know about those UFO's; I read about them in one of those newspapers you buy at the supermarket." His eyes narrowed. "That's why I keep my door locked. Don't let anyone in."

Mick assured him that he would definitely report that to his partners. That seemed to please the old guy. As Mick walked to the next house, he chuckled to himself. *I wondered what this neighbor is going to be like.* He rang the doorbell. As he waited, he thought about what Howie had said about detectives meeting all sorts of people. That was one of the reasons Mick agreed to help out. He enjoyed people and felt that every individual had a story to tell. He also believed deeply that every person had something worthwhile to offer. One of his favorite quotes was from Will Rogers, the American humorist. *I never knew a man I didn't like.* He rang the doorbell again, wondering what kind of interesting person he would meet now. When the door opened, the aroma of freshly baked bread greeted him.

"Yes, what can I do for you?" A heavyset woman asked, eyeing him suspiciously. She appeared to be in her early forties.

"Hello, I've a few questions about the house next door that's for sale. I wonder--"

"Call the number listed on the *For Sale* sign."

"I'm not interesting in buying it." Mick spoke rapidly, sensing the woman was about to close the door in his face. "My name's Mick Brunner and I work for the MAC Detective Agency over on Third and Broadway."

"Oh, my!" she exclaimed, her eyes turning friendly as she smiled. "You're a detective? Are you really?"

Mick nodded.

"Goodness, gracious; this is so exciting. I must tell you, I love to read mysteries, especially Agatha Christie. Are you working on a case?"

"Yes, I am. I'd like to ask some questions about the woman who lived next door. May I have a few minutes of your time?"

"Certainly. Please come in. It's not every day I get to talk to a real live detective." She led him into the living room, asked him to sit down, but then excused herself. "I'll be right back. I'm sorry, but I've got bread in the oven."

Mick sniffed the air and listened to the sounds coming from the kitchen. The thought of warm bread with a slab of butter made his stomach growl. The smell reminded him of going to his grandmother's house when he was a young boy. Grandma had a woodburning stove and she always baked bread for him. As he breathed in deeply now, he hoped the woman would offer him some. When she returned empty handed, he was disappointed.

Charles Tindell

"Now about your neighbor, Maureen Hammond, are you--"

"Did she commit a murder or something?" the woman asked as she sat down on the edge of her chair.

"Oh, no; nothing like that. I'm just trying to locate her. There's, ah, some insurance money coming to her." Mick didn't like lying, but he sided with Howie that there were times where the end justified the means—a position that usually pitted the two of them against Adam, however. "She has to sign some papers," he added. "That's why I need to locate her."

"Is that all?" The woman, her eyes not being able to contain her disappointment, settled back in her chair. "I'm afraid I can't tell you too much about her."

"What can you tell me?"

"Well, she kept to herself. I seldom saw her out in the yard. She always paid to have the lawn cut. Little Tommy Lanesburrow down the street did it. He does it for me, too. You see, my husband has a bad back and--"

"Excuse me, Ma'am, but I don't have a lot of time. Is there anything else you can tell me about Miss Hammond?"

"There's not much else to tell. She lived in that house for nearly four months. It was a surprise to me when the *For Sale* sign went up. I didn't even see the moving truck come."

"How long ago did she move?"

"Let me see." She put her hand up to her mouth and tapped on her lips with her forefinger; her eyes turned upward, as if the answer was written on the ceiling. "I think it was about a month ago, now."

Mick was trying to remember what other questions Howie would want him to ask, but the bread smell was distracting him. "Did you ever see a cat?"

"A cat?" Puzzled, the woman shook her head.

"Thank you, Ma'am. I don't have any further questions. I do appreciate your time." Mick got up to leave.

"It was nice talking to you," the woman said as she went with him to the door. "Wait until I tell my husband that a detective visited our house."

"Oh, that reminds me," Mick said as they stood at the door. "I do have one last question. Did Miss Hammond have many visitors?"

"Not really, I only remember seeing one. A woman in her thirties."

"Do you know who it was by any chance?"

"No, but the reason I remember her is because she reminded me of one of my favorite movie stars." The woman paused. "She was a little before your time, so you may not know her. Her name was Betty Grable."

Chapter 4

HOWIE PLACED THE cover back on the shoebox, not wanting to look at its contents anymore. For the next couple of minutes he and Adam sat and stared at the box until the ringing of the telephone abruptly broke the silence. He let the phone ring several times before answering.

"MAC Detective Agency." *It's Mick,* he mouthed to Adam. "Yeah...yeah...really?" He listened with interest as he occasionally glanced at Adam. "So the old guy thought it was Martians, huh? How about the other neighbor?" Howie took out a pencil and scribbled some notes in his notepad. "What! Are you sure she said, 'Betty Grable'?"

"What are you talking about?" Adam whispered.

Howie signaled Adam to be quiet. "Yeah, he's here. Sure. I'll fill him in. Can you come over tonight? No, huh? Tomorrow then? Good. What time? That's okay with me. Wait a minute. Let me check with him." He put his hand over the receiver. "Mick can meet tomorrow around four. Can you make it?"

"Sure, no problem."

"Four is okay with him. Yeah, I know. We'll have to talk about that. Listen up now. We got something here for you to see. I don't know what it is, it's hard to describe." Howie went on to share his and Adam's meeting with Jodelle, their subsequent encounter with Damien, and finding the package in the backseat. He described the contents of the shoebox the best he could. "Well, that's what we think it looks like." He listened as Mick expressed his disgust. "Yeah, I understand. We had the same reaction. It makes me sick to my stomach just to look at it. Sure. Okay. We'll see you tomorrow."

"What's this about Betty Grable?" Adam asked even before Howie had a chance to hang up.

"One of the neighbors told Mick that she'd only seen one visitor at the Hammond house. It was a woman in her early thirties who looked like Betty Grable."

"You're kidding? Do you think that could've been Jodelle Hammond?"

"More than likely. And that means we have to have another talk with her and get some straight answers this time."

"What did he say when you described that thing in the box?"

"He didn't know what to think."

"Well, neither do I." Adam glanced at the clock, stood up, and stretched. "I've got to go home."

"But, it's only a little past eight."

"I know, but I still got studying to do."

Howie opened his mouth to say that he didn't have to study so much, but knew he'd go home and spend more time brooding about whether to become a minister. As far as Howie was concerned, Adam's moral standards went far beyond both his and Mick's combined. He and Adam had discussed his struggle before, but nothing was resolved. "Well, I'm going to go over my notes," Howie said. "I have to see if I can make some sense out of this case." He felt tired, but doubted if he'd make it to bed before midnight. "Say, will you do me a favor?"

"Sure. What?"

"Call me in the morning around seven just to make sure I'm up. I've got a lot of things to do and I don't want to oversleep."

"Okay." Adam pointed to the box. "What are you going to do with that?"

"I don't know. I'll think of something."

"Just be careful and watch yourself."

"What do you mean?"

"I don't know exactly; I can't put it into words." Adam glanced at the box. "It's just a bad feeling I have about that thing in the box. There's just something... evil about it."

WHEN THE PHONE rang the next morning, Howie was still in bed. He groped for the receiver, nearly knocking over the lamp. "Hello, MAC Detective Agency," he mumbled, trying to focus his eyes on his alarm clock. "Oh, hi, Adam." Howie rubbed the sleep out of his eyes. "What time is it? Okay. No, I didn't sleep all that well. Yeah. Thanks, for calling. See you at four."

Howie washed and dressed. After breakfast, he sat down at the desk and reviewed his notes of the past couple days. When he came to the phone number of the real estate agency he had gotten from the *For Sale* sign at Maureen's house, he decided he needed to call them. Since it was still too early to call, he spent the next hour drinking coffee and thumbing through some issues of *Police Gazette*. It was ten after nine when he picked up the phone and dialed the number of the agency. The woman who answered informed him that the agent selling that particular house would be in the office around one that afternoon. He took their address and the agent's name, having decided that it would be worthwhile to pay him a visit in person. You could pick up more clues interviewing someone in person than over the telephone.

This Angel Has No Wings

It was five minutes after one when Howie walked into the *Good Neighbor Real Estate Agency* on Penn and Broadway. An attractive young woman sitting at the front desk, filing her nails, greeted him.

"Hello, may I help you?"

Howie recognized her voice as the same as he had talked to earlier. He also made a mental note that since she wasn't wearing a wedding ring, he might call upon her once this case was over. By then, he would be ready for some companionship of the opposite sex. "Yes, I called this morning about the house on Girard. You told me that Gary Sherman would be in by now."

"Yes, he is. Let me tell him you're here. Your name?"

"Cummins. Howie Cummins."

He watched as she pushed the intercom and informed the husky male voice who answered that there was someone here to see him. "Please, Mr. Cummins, have a seat. He'll be right out."

Howie had no sooner sat down, when a booming voice greeted him. "Hello, there, Mr. Cummins. I'm Gary Sherman, but everybody calls me Sherm. Why don't you come back to my office and we can talk there."

The office was just large enough for a small desk and two plastic tan chairs. It had a musty odor mixed with stale coffee and cigarettes. Its only window looked out onto the parking lot.

"Can I get you a cup of coffee?"

"No, thanks."

"How about a can of pop? We've got a machine in back."

"Mr. Sherman, I--"

"Hey, call me Sherm."

Howie nodded, and then wondered if the stain on *Sherm's* tie was from breakfast. "The reason I'm here is because I have a few questions about the house you have listed on Twenty-fourth and Girard."

"Oh, yes. The white one with the front porch. It's a gem isn't it?"

"It's a gem all right."

"Great location, also. Let me tell you, it'd be a great place to live. It's an old established neighborhood with fine upstanding neighbors."

I wonder if he knows about the old guy and the aliens?

"And best of all, the price is right. You can't go wrong with it."

Howie cleared his throat. "Look I'm sorry, but I'm not interested in buying it."

"You're not?"

"No, I'm not." He felt bad about letting the air out of Sherm's enthusiasm.

"So, how can I help you?"

Howie explained that he was a detective working on a case. "I need to contact the owner." He figured that from the owner, he might find out where Maureen Hammond moved.

"I see. Well, that shouldn't be too much of a problem. I have the file right here in my drawer." Howie watched as Sherm pulled out a manila folder. "Okay, here it is. Her name is Maureen Hammond."

Charles Tindell

"Who did you say?"

"Maureen Hammond."

"She's the owner of the house?"

"That's right. Would you like her phone number and new address, also?"

At ten minutes past four, Mick walked into Howie's office. "Sorry, guys, but I got hung up at school." He went over and sat next to Adam. "Okay, where is it?"

"He's got it stored away."

"Just a minute. I'll get it." Howie got up and opened the door leading to his living quarters. Within a short time, he came back and placed the shoebox on the desk. "Here it is. It's all yours."

"Where did you have it?"

"He kept it in the refrigerator," Adam said, and then added. "You'll understand why when you open it."

Mick looked at Adam and then at Howie before opening the box. "Oh, man, that's gross!" he muttered after he had removed the cover. He looked the object for a few moments and then put the lid back on. "I see what you mean. Are you sure it came from Jodelle's brother?"

Howie moved the box onto the floor. "He's the most likely suspect. We didn't see anyone else around the car."

"And he threatened us," Adam added.

"I know, you told me." Mick wrinkled his nose while pointing to the box. "But that? What does that all mean?"

"Don't ask me," Howie said. "That's what we have to figure out. I think we need to go over what we have so far." He looked at his notes and then held up his index finger. "Number one. Jodelle Hammond comes in and offers a thousand bucks to find her cat named JoJo." He held up a second finger. "Two. She thinks either her sister, Maureen, has it or knows something about it. Three, she gives me the impression she and Maureen are on the outs. Four, then she sends us on a wild goose chase to a house she already knew would be vacant. And number five, we go back and talk to her, and it's like night and day. She loves her sister." He looked at Adam. "Isn't that the impression you got from her?"

"Oh, yeah. What I don't get is why she was so vague when we started asking about why her sister would even take the cat."

"What did she say about that?" Mick asked.

Adam shrugged. "Nothing. She just said find her sister, and that was it."

"You mean she didn't even mention a word about having a brother?"

"No," Howie said. "But Damien told us that he was a long lost brother. So maybe she doesn't consider him as part of the family. That doesn't surprise me because I got the impression she feels the same way about her mother."

This Angel Has No Wings

Adam tapped Mick on the arm. "Howie filled me in about the visitor who looked like Betty Grable; tell me about the old man who thinks aliens drew that triangle."

"Okay, like I said on the phone, this old guy thought the triangle was the work of aliens. I think he said, Martians. He's so convinced that little green men drew it that he stays in his house most of the time. He wouldn't let me in, but I did get a piece of the puzzle from him."

"Hang on for a sec." Howie turned to a blank page in his notepad and picked up a pencil. "Okay, go ahead."

"He said that Maureen moved out the day after that triangle appeared on the sidewalk."

"Was he sure about that?"

Mick laughed. "Oh, yeah."

"This whole thing is becoming more bizarre as we get into it," Adam said. "What are we going to do with that thing in the box?"

"Maybe we should take it to the police," Mick offered.

"No way," Howie snapped, wishing his partners would stop making that suggestion. "How would that look? We're barely into our first case and we go running to the cops. Who would want to hire us after that? We'd be just a big joke."

"So, what are we going to do?" Mick asked.

"Just keep our cool and go slowly. I spent some time this afternoon thinking about a plan." Howie picked up the box and set it in front of Mick. "I want you to take this and do some checking on it."

"And where do you suggest I begin?"

"I knew you'd ask that." Howie leaned back in his chair. "You can start at Jack's Meat Market."

Mick opened his mouth to respond, then paused for a moment. "Hey, that's not such a bad idea. And while I'm doing this, what are you going to be up to?"

"I'm going to check out the address I got from the real estate agency. I'm anxious to talk with Jodelle's sister."

"What do you want me to do?" Adam asked.

"You can come along with me."

THE MEAT MARKET was not very crowded when Mick walked in. The owner, Jack, was just finishing waiting on a customer. "Hi there, Mick," he yelled out.

"Hi, yourself." Mick liked Jack. He had known him since Mick played football in high school. Jack's son, Ken, was a second-string tight end. Although Mick was an all-conference guard, he never let it go to his head. He befriended Ken, and for that, Jack said he was eternally grateful, calling Mick a good kid. Mick waited until Jack was finished with his customer and then waved him over.

"What can I do for you?"

Charles Tindell

Mick glanced around. Even though the other two customers were being helped, he wanted to have as much privacy as possible. "I've got something for you to look at. Can we go in the back room and talk?"

"Sure." Jack led him through swinging double doors. "So how's teaching suiting you?"

"It can be challenging, but I like it a lot."

"That's what I want to hear. I always knew you'd make a good teacher." He pointed at the bag Mick was carrying. "You got something to show me?"

Mick nodded, asking if he could set it on the cutting table.

"Sure, but just hang on." Jack ripped off a piece of white wrapping paper and laid it over the table. "There you go."

"Thanks." Mick took the shoebox out and set it on the paper.

"What's this?" Jack laughed. "You want to show me a pair of shoes?"

"No, no. Open it. You'll see."

Jack wiped his hands on his apron, and lifted the cover. "Where did you get this?" he asked, chuckling, and showing no sign of surprise.

"Why, what is it?"

"What is it, you ask?" He chuckled again. "You city boys don't know anything, do you? It's a cow's tongue."

This Angel Has No Wings

Chapter 5

HOWIE PULLED UP to the address he had gotten for Maureen Hammond from Sherm, the real estate agent. The neighborhood proved to be a vast improvement from where she had previously lived; here, lawns were cut, homes well cared for, late model cars instead of clunkers parked on the street. "That's it," he announced to Adam.

"The apartment building, you mean?"

"Yup." The two-story brick building had minimal but attractive landscaping. The front entrance appeared as if it had been recently painted.

"Why do you think she moved here?"

"Maybe because it's only a couple blocks from Broadway and shopping." Howie pointed out a corner food market down the street, doing so as an example of how important the power of observation is in their line of work. "She can even walk to the grocery store." He opened the car door. "Come on, let's go pay Miss Maureen Hammond a visit before she moves away."

They walked up and opened the door to the entryway. Howie checked the mailboxes and found one labeled, M. Hammond. "At least, the mailbox says she's still here." He was about to push the buzzer for her apartment when he paused. "You know, I've got a feeling that she wouldn't answer even if she was home."

"So what are you going to do?"

"Let's try this." Howie pushed the button for Fred Meyer, Apartment Manager. "Stick with me," he said as he winked, "and you'll learn all the tricks of the trade."

Within moments a not-so-friendly voice crackled over the intercom. "Yeah, what do you want?"

"I'd like to talk to you, if I may."

"You're not selling anything, are you?"

"No, sir."

"And you're not one of those religious do-gooders, are you? A couple of them came around last week and preached to me about my poor lost soul."

Charles Tindell

"You don't have to worry about me doing that. I'm a detective and I need to ask you some questions."

"You're a detective?" There was a long pause. "My ex-wife didn't send you, did she?"

"It's has nothing to do with you or your ex-wife; it concerns one of your renters." Howie waited for a reply, but when none immediately came, he spoke up, inserting a note of urgency in his voice. "It's really important that we talk."

"Well...okay, I'll be right out."

Howie and Adam looked through the glass partition into the hallway as they waited. Soon, one of the apartment doors opened, and a short, stocky man with graying hair appeared. He eyed the two of them through the glass before opening the door.

"You didn't tell me there were two of you; so what do you want to know?"

"We're from the MAC Detective Agency down on Broadway and Third." Howie reasoned that if people knew they were from the area, they would be more open to answering questions. "We'd like a few minutes of your time."

"I guess I can give you that, but come on into the hallway so we don't block the entry."

"Thanks. I'm Howie Cummins. This is my partner, Adam Trexler." The smell of a pot roast baking in an oven permeated the hallway, reminding Howie of how his father used to make one every Sunday. "We're trying to track down Maureen Hammond. There's a M. Hammond listed on your mailboxes. We assume it's her, but we want to make sure." He took out a photograph that Jodelle had given him of her and Maureen. It had been taken at a St. Paul restaurant. The occasion was Maureen's birthday, and the two of them were holding up wine glasses and offering a toast toward the camera. Both appeared as if they were laughing. "This is a picture of Miss Hammond taken about two years ago. She's the one on the right. Do you recognize her?"

The manager took the picture and studied it. "Yeah, it's the woman up in 4C, alright. She has a different hairstyle now, but it's the same person. Who's the other woman?"

"Her sister," Howie said.

"Is that so? I got to tell you she looks a lot like that movie actress who was popular back in the forties and fifties." He took another look at the picture. "Can't think of her name right now."

"Betty Grable?" Adam offered.

"Yeah, that's it." He handed the picture back. "My buddy had a crush on her. Thought she was the most gorgeous woman he'd ever seen. He even had a pin-up of her on his locker when we were in the army. I don't see her much in pictures anymore, do you?"

Howie shook his head and then offered a polite smile. "Ah, getting back now to the person we're looking for. You said she does live here?"

"That she does, but she's not here right now."

"Are you sure?"

"What day is today?"

"It's Thursday," Howie replied.

"Then I'm sure."

"When will she be home?" Adam asked.

"Not until Saturday afternoon." The man must have caught the questioning look Howie gave him. "I know that for a fact because she asked me to collect her mail. I don't know why, though. She doesn't get anything other than junk mail."

"How long has she been gone?" Howie asked.

"Let's see, now." He scratched the stubble on his chin. "It was last Friday she talked to me. Or was that Thursday? No, I'm sure it was Friday. Said she was leaving the next day. So it'll be a week come Saturday."

The meowing of a cat immediately caught Howie and Adam's attention. They looked past the man and saw a black cat with white markings cautiously coming toward them.

"What's the matter? You guys act like you've never seen a cat before." The manager knelt down and the cat came running to him. "Her name is Kit-Kat," he said as he stood up cradling the ball of purring fur in his arms. "I've had her for nearly eighteen years."

"So you allow pets here?" Adam asked, giving Howie a sideways glance.

The man flashed a toothy grin. "When the owner offered me the job as manager, I told him I wouldn't take it unless my cat could come with me. The day I came was the day this place changed its policy from no pets to one where cats were allowed." He stroked the ball of fur. "Isn't that right, Kit-Kat? Yeah, nice kitty."

"Do you know if Maureen Hammond has a cat?" Howie asked.

"I don't know. Maybe. I never asked. Since she moved in, I've never been up to see her. Of course, she's never asked me to come up, either." As the man talked the cat rubbed its face against his hand. "Only seen her a couple of times. She stays pretty much to herself. Keeps a very quiet apartment. No trouble. That's what I like."

Howie wanted to take out his notepad, but was afraid that taking notes might prove too intimidating. "How long has she lived here?"

"A little over a month. Rented the apartment one day and moved in the next."

"By any chance, did you see who helped her move in?"

"She didn't need much help."

"What do you mean?"

"The apartment she moved into was completely furnished already, even dishes and silverware. She only needed to bring in clothes and some other personal items like towels and bed linens. The man paused to scratch his cat under her chin. She brought that stuff in herself. I know, I held the door for her."

Charles Tindell

"Are all your apartments furnished?" Adam asked.

"Nope, just that one."

Howie reached out and petted the cat. She let him rub her under the chin, lifting it up for him and purring.

"She likes you," the guy said, nodding his head and smiling. "That's a good sign. Cats are good judges of character."

"She's a nice kitty." Howie continued to stroke the cat. "By the way, I'm just curious. Did Miss Hammond sign a lease?"

The guy cocked his head, his eyes shifted back and forth between Adam and Howie. "I suppose I can tell you that; you two being detectives and all that." He scratched his chin again "That's just like telling the police, isn't it?"

"Oh, yes," Howie said quickly as he glanced at Adam, giving him a half smile and catching the disapproving look in return. His partner didn't approve of lies; not even half-truths.

"Well, in that case, I guess it's alright." He glanced around and then lowered his voice. "At her request, no lease was signed. She gave me three months rent in advance and offered to pay fifty dollars more a month if I'd waive the one year lease." He glanced around again—this time lowering his voice to a whisper. "Money didn't seem to be a problem for her. She paid me in cash."

"Anything else?" Howie asked.

"Nope, that's about it, I reckon."

"Thank you for your time. We'll be back but we'd appreciate it if you didn't mention this visit to Miss Hammond. People get jittery when they find out that detectives have been asking questions about them."

"Is she in some kind of trouble with the law? I don't want those kind of people living here, even if they do keep a quiet apartment."

"She's not in any trouble. You don't have to worry about that." Howie decided to try the tactic Mick had used with Maureen's former neighbors over on Girard. "Miss Hammond has to sign some papers on an insurance claim. That's why we're here."

"Is that all?"

"Yes, sir," Howie said as he reached out and stroked the cat's head. "Not all detective work is like you see in the movies."

The manager laughed. "Yeah, I guess so." He stroked his cat a couple of times before setting her down, telling her to go home. She, however, just stretched out by his feet. "Do you mind if I ask you two something?"

"No, go ahead," Adam replied.

"You two are mighty young for being private detectives, aren't you?"

"We're always being told that."

"I guess so, but when you get as old as me and Kit Kat here, everybody looks too young to be doing what they're doing."

"Thank you again for your cooperation," Howie said. "And remember, we'd appreciate it if you kept this visit to yourself."

This Angel Has No Wings

"Sure," the man said as his cat meowed. "Okay, pumpkin, I hear you." He smiled at Howie and Adam. "She's telling me she's hungry." He sniffed the air a couple of times. "She wants some of that roast beef that Mrs. Larson is making. Come on, pumpkin, we better go and pay her a visit."

Howie and Adam said their good-byes to both the man and his kitty, and then headed back to their car. "I wonder what Maureen did with all her furniture?" Howie asked.

"If she was in a rush, she probably just had it stored. Don't you think?"

"You're probably right. And if you want to know what I think, she probably got that furnished apartment just in case she decided to move again in a hurry."

"I agree," Adam said. "Say, you were pretty clever back there."

"Me? What are you talking about?"

"Don't give me that innocent look. You made up to that guy's cat so he'd be open to answering more questions, didn't you?"

"Can I help it if cats love me?" Howie pulled out his keys and tossed them to Adam as they approached the car. "Why don't you drive? I need to write down some notes on our conversation with that guy."

As soon as Adam pulled away from the curb, Howie took out his notepad and began jotting down a record of their conversation with the apartment house manager. They rode in silence for quite some time before he put away his notepad. "Okay, I'm done."

"You mean I can talk now?"

"You have my permission."

"Gee, thanks. Now that we have that settled, are you still coming over to the seminary to have lunch with me on Saturday?"

"I'm planning on it. The timing should work out pretty good since I'm going to try and catch Maureen Hammond at home on Saturday afternoon. Do you want to come with?"

"No, I've got some research to do in the library."

"That's okay. Over lunch you can give me your suggestions as to what kinds of questions I should be asking her." Howie already had a list of questions, but he wanted his partners to start thinking like detectives.

Adam glanced over at Howie. "As Mick would say, just ask her if she knows anyone by the name of JoJo."

"Hey, that reminds me." Howie took his notepad out and paged through it. "Here it is. That apartment manager said that Maureen has been gone for nearly a week."

"So?"

"Don't you see? If she's been gone that long, who would take care of JoJo? Either she has an accomplice, or she doesn't have the cat, or she took the cat with her."

"There's a fourth option."

"What's that?"

"I've a friend who has a cat. She lives in an apartment by herself. Upon occasion, she has gone away for a week." Adam slowed down for a car turning in front of them." She tells me that 'she just leaves the cat enough water and food, and makes sure she puts out two litter boxes. Cats are not like dogs. They can take care of themselves without a lot of trouble."

"Well, that eliminates that theory."

"Don't worry, I know you'll come up with more. You always-- Hey, there's Mick," Adam said, as they turned the corner by Kass' Drug Store. Their friend was standing in front of the entrance to Howie's apartment pacing back and forth. When he saw them, he waved.

"Wonder if he found out anything?" Adam asked as he parked across the street from Mick.

"Let's hope so." Howie took his car keys from Adam. "What do you say that we lock this baby up? I don't want to find any more packages in here."

"Sounds good to me." Adam turned to check the back seat before getting out and heading across the street with Howie.

"Hi, guys," Mick said as they walked up to him. "Any luck?"

"Yeah," Howie replied. "Maureen Hammond is staying in an apartment a couple blocks off Broadway. Over on Logan and Twenty-first."

"So, what did she say?"

"She wasn't home, but we talked to the apartment manager. He said she'd be home this weekend. I'm going back on Saturday afternoon."

Adam pointed to the bag Mick held. "How about you? Any luck finding out what that thing is?"

"Let's go up and I'll fill you in." Mick handed the bag to Howie. "Here, you can have it back. I'm tired of carrying it around." Once in the office, Mick shared what he had found out from his friend, Jack, at the meat market.

"A cow's tongue!" Howie exclaimed. "Is this Damien's idea of a joke?"

"If it is," Adam said, "I don't appreciate his sense of humor." He ran his hand through his hair. "I just can't figure this out. If it was Jodelle's brother who gave it to us, why did he do it?"

Mick shrugged. "Maybe he thought you guys looked undernourished."

"What are you talking about?" Howie asked.

"According to Jack, there are people who think tongue of cow is a delicacy. They eat it all the time. In fact, he said we should try it some time. You should've been there when he picked it up and sniffed it."

Howie couldn't imagine anyone wanting to even touch it, let alone smell it. "What did he do that for?"

"To see how fresh it was. Jack said it wasn't more than a couple days old. He even offered to cook it up for us."

"I don't think it was given to us with that in mind." Howie said. "The question is what do we do now."

Mick grinned. "I suggest we go around asking cows to stick out their tongues. When we find one that is tongue-less, then we've got a witness." He paused. "The only problem is finding cows around here. There can't be too many of them."

"But that's an idea," Howie offered.

"What?" Adam said. "Come on, you're not serious, are you?"

"What I mean is finding out where that tongue came from." Adam and Mick gave him a questioning look. "Don't you see what I mean?" Both shook their heads. "Answer me this, where would someone get a cow's tongue?"

"You can go down to Jack's," Mick answered. "He said he'd gladly order one for us."

"That's what I mean," Howie said, shaking his finger at Mick to emphasize his point. "All we have to do is go around to the places that would sell them. There can't be too many of them. We go and give them a description of Jodelle's brother, Damien. If we can connect him with buying a cow's tongue, then we know, for sure, that it was him who left that package. At least, it'll be a piece of the puzzle."

"That's a good plan, except it's not going to work," Mick said.

"And why's that?"

Mick's grin faded. "Because Jack told me that whoever cut that tongue off did a sloppy job."

"He said what?" Adam asked.

"That it was a sloppy job. It wasn't the whole tongue. It was like someone reached into the cow's mouth and cut as much out as they could. Jack says that they left the meatiest part. That's the back part. If you look in the mirror and stick out your tongue, you'll know what I mean. The tongue we have is something that Jack said he wouldn't sell."

Howie put his elbows on the desk and buried his face in his hands for a few moments. "That brings us back to square one," he said as he looked up. He rubbed his temples and closed his eyes for a moment. "I can't think straight anymore. What do you say that we call it a day? We can meet again tomorrow."

Mick got up out of his chair. "Same time? Four o'clock?"

"Yeah, if that's okay." Howie looked at Adam. "Is that a good time for you?"

Adam nodded.

"I'm sure glad it's Friday tomorrow," Mick said as he stretched. "I need the weekend to rest my brain from all this crazy stuff."

"Are you going out with Mary this weekend?" Howie asked, already knowing the answer—Mick and his finance, Mary, usually reserved Saturday nights for each other.

"I sure am. We're going out to eat and see a movie. I got to get my mind off cow tongues for a while. How about you guys? Doing anything special?"

"I'm going to have lunch with this guy on Saturday over at his school." Howie flashed Adam a smile. "You're still treating me, aren't you?"

"Only if you go to that lecture with me."

"What's he talking about?" Mick asked.

"Oh, he wants me to hear some dry old dusty professor."

"It's not some any old professor. It's Professor Franklin Lewis. And he's very interesting to listen to. You're going to enjoy him."

Mick stretched again, this time yawning as well. "So, what is the old professor going to talk about?"

"I don't know, but it doesn't matter," Adam said. "Whatever subject he covers, he'll give us something to think about."

MICK'S SIXTH HOUR class on Friday was quieter than usual. He told himself it was because he had kept his students' interest most of the hour. And it was true. He had challenged them to never stop learning. "No matter what the cost," he admonished them, "it's important to get an education and to do what you really want to do in life." He felt he got his point across and was especially pleased with the response he had given when Stu Larson, the class clown, had asked a question that gave him a chance to expound his philosophy even further.

"Mr. Brunner, how does a person really know what he wants in life?"

"Stu, that's a fair question, and a good one. I have to admit, though, there's no easy answer to it. You have to know it within yourself." Mick leaned back against the front of his desk. "It's got to be something you know that you want to do more than anything else in the world." He walked over and stood in front of Stu's desk. "Use your talent to become a clown in the circus, or a stand-up comic, or a football player, or even a teacher. Whatever you want in life; go for it."

"Yeah!" Stu shouted as others in the class hooted and laughed. "Thanks, Mr. Brunner, I will."

Several of the kids came up to Mick after class and thanked him for his words. "Man, that's what teaching is all about," he muttered once all the kids had gone. Teaching gave him a high that he never could achieve in any other profession. He didn't mind working part-time as a detective, but he took the job only because of Howie. Mary had objected at first, but came around to support him. "I just don't want anything happening to you," she said. He was lucky to have her and looked forward to their wedding a year from now. Unlike his partners, he liked the idea of settling down and coming home to a wife. Howie was too focused on his work to settle down. Adam, on the other hand, was too much of a loner; a brooding personality who felt he didn't need anyone in his life. Mick needed Mary, though. Since he came from a large family, he hoped they could have at least four children. She had smiled when he told her about how many kids he wanted. "As long as you're willing to change diapers," she said. That wouldn't be a problem since he loved kids.

Mick glanced at the clock in his classroom and decided to call it a day. He was just about to leave when a student came in to tell him that he was to stop in the office before he left. Whatever it was, he hoped that it wouldn't take too long. It was not uncommon for Waite, the principal, to tie up a teacher on a Friday afternoon to discuss some issue that could easily have waited until Monday. He packed up his briefcase and headed for the administration offices.

"Hi, Charlotte, what's going on?" Mick asked as he walked into the office. Of the three clerks, he knew Charlotte the best.

"It's not your birthday, is it?"

"No. Why?"

"Because a package showed up for you this afternoon." She reached below the counter. "Whatever it is, it's heavy. I thought it might be a box of candy."

"Don't we wish."

"I know, but it doesn't have the shape of a candy box. It has more of a shape of a...a shoe box." She sniggered. "Maybe someone is sending you a pair of shoes. Do you need a new pair?"

Mick forced a smile. "Nope, I just got myself a pair." A cold chill ran up his spine as he took the package, wrapped in brown paper and tied with twine. It could have been the identical twin to the one Howie and Adam found in Howie's car, except this one had his name on it, neatly printed in black ink.

"Do you know who brought it in?"

"I'm afraid I don't. It was on the counter after I came back from my afternoon break. I assumed someone delivered it." She paused. "Are you okay? You look a little peaked."

"I'm fine. It's Friday and I'm just tired."

She nodded. "I can understand that. Anyway, I asked the other girls about the package, but they didn't know, either. They said when they came back from the workroom; it was just sitting there. And they were only gone for a minute or two."

"Well, don't worry about it. Thanks." Picking up the package, Mick felt the same uneasy feeling he had gotten when he had handled the one containing the cow's tongue. When he got to his car, he set the package on the passenger's seat, and sat there debating whether to open it. Curiosity got the best of him. Again, a shoebox. Black Oxfords. Size nine. He took a deep breath before opening it. What he saw made him nearly gag. Quickly putting the cover back on, he took the box and placed it on the floor in the back seat. There was no way he was going to have it next to him. Before he went up to Howie's, he had to stop at Jack's Meat Market again.

AFTER HIS VISIT with Jack, Mick headed for Howie's. He parked the car, grabbed the box, and ran across the street to the entrance door. Letting the door bang behind him, he sprinted up the stairs, taking two at a time. As soon as Adam and Howie saw what he carried in with him, their conversation halted in mid-sentence. They watched in silence as he slowly walked up and set the box on the desk.

"What's in it?" Howie asked.

"A cow's heart," Mick replied, emphasizing the last two words. "It was anonymously delivered to school."

Howie blew out a puff of air and shook his head. "Guys, this is getting too weird."

"If you mean by weird, something evil," Adam said, "Then, I agree."

"I hate to say this," Howie said, hesitating for a moment, "but I think there may be one more package coming."

"Why do you think that?" Mick asked.

Howie nodded at Adam. "Because there's still one person in this room who hasn't received a package yet."

Adam's eyes darkened at Howie's prediction.

"Man, I need to sit down," Mick said.

The three of them sat without saying a word as the ticking of the wall clock filled the silence. "Do you guys want a cup of coffee?" Howie finally asked, hoping it would help beat off a headache he felt coming." Both of his partners declined.

Mick pointed at the box. "If you're going out into the kitchen, take that thing with you. I'm tired of looking at it."

"What did you do with the contents of the other box?" Adam asked.

"I wrapped it and put it in the frig. And I kept the box for evidence." Howie picked up the shoebox. "I'll be right back." Within a short time, he returned, carrying his cup of coffee. He sat down and set the cup on his desk. "Okay, what do we have so far?"

"The heart and tongue of a cow," Adam said.

"A missing cat," Mick added.

"Yeah," Howie said, "and Jodelle's brother, Damien, who has a strange sense of gift giving."

"And all this adds up to what?" Mick asked. "What's the connection?"

He took a sip of coffee, hoping that the aspirins would soon take effect. "Good question. I wish we had some answers. Maybe we just need the weekend to sort through things. If I can see Maureen Hammond on Saturday, we just might get some of those answers."

"Let's hope so," Mick said.

"Are you still coming over to school tomorrow?" Adam asked Howie.

"I'll be there. Believe it or not, I'm actually looking forward to it. It might be a nice diversion."

THE LECTURE room was nearly filled on Saturday morning. Even though Howie and Adam had arrived early enough to have a choice of seats, Howie insisted on sitting in the back. "Just in case he's boring," he explained. "I don't want to be stuck up front. This way, we can slip out anytime we want." He looked on with interest as the room filled up. "What's this guy's name, again?"

"Professor Franklin Lewis. You'll like him. He's even shorter than you."

Howie gave Adam a half smile. "Hey, don't knock it. Don't you know? Good things come in small packages." The image of the cow's tongue flashed through his mind. "Well, not always. If you know what I mean."

Adam nodded. "Professor Lewis, however, is one of those good things that do come in small packages. He's one of the best things that have happened to this place."

"Oh, yeah, why?"

"The rumor has it that when the president of the seminary asked Lewis what subject he'd like to teach when he came a couple of years ago, he replied he'd be willing to teach any class they requested. His wife died of cancer and since he doesn't have family, he said he wanted to keep busy. The guy's a Hebrew scholar and an expert in Old Testament theology."

"Hmmm, sounds pretty good."

"You're telling me. And he's in his late sixties. Can you imagine being that old and still being so active?" Adam gestured toward the side exit door. "Here he comes now."

Howie and Adam watched as two men walked in and took seats by the podium. When Adam pointed out Professor Lewis, Howie was surprised at how short he really was, and how frail he looked. His glasses rested so close to the tip of his nose that they appeared as though they could slide off any moment. His clothes were rumpled—his white hair, unkempt.

"What time is it?" Howie asked.

"A few minutes to eleven."

"Your Professor Lewis looks like he already fell asleep in his chair."

"Don't let that fool you. In chapel, he always looked like he was asleep." Adam waved to another student who had waved at him. "One day, one of my classmates asked him what the sermon was about. He thought he had caught Lewis sleeping through the service. My friend was speechless when the guy nearly repeated it word for word."

"Wow."

"You can say that again. And another time when Lewis was leading chapel services, he stumbled over the words of the Lord's Prayer. Afterwards, in class, we asked him what happened? Do you know what he said?" Howie shook his head. "He said he was mentally translating the Hebrew into Greek into English as he led the prayer at the time, and that was why he had stumbled over a couple of words. He was genuinely embarrassed and apologized to us for his miscue."

"I'm impressed."

"We all were."

At precisely eleven, the other gentleman sitting up front with Professor Lewis rose and went to the podium.

"That's Carlson," Adam whispered. "He's professor of New Testament Greek."

"Ladies and gentlemen, I have the privilege of introducing to you my colleague, Professor Franklin Lewis. As all of you know, Professor Lewis has been with us over two years now. I must confess that I, indeed the whole faculty, have been impressed by his long list of credentials. If I were to list the books he has written, the journals he's been published in, and the honorary degrees he's been awarded over the past forty years, I'm afraid we wouldn't have time for his remarks." Professor Carlson paused, waiting for the smattering of polite laughter to subside. "So without further ado, I want to introduce him to you as our esteemed and beloved colleague. He is more than my peer and my friend; he is also my teacher and mentor. Professor Franklin Lewis."

Howie watched with interest as the frail old man suddenly came to life. As Professor Lewis walked up to the podium, the guy had a grace and dignity about him that commanded respect.

"Thank you, Professor Carlson, for not boring these students with things about myself that I have long forgotten." When Lewis paused and looked over his audience, Howie could feel his charisma. "I begin with a question. How many of you believe in the Devil as someone who dresses all in red, has horns, a long tail, and walks around carrying a pitchfork?" Professor Lewis scanned the audience and then smiled. "Good, neither do I. But let me tell you this, I have great respect for this adversary of ours. I respect his cunning, his ability to lead people into great falsehoods, and his cleverness into deceiving people to think of him as one who is concerned about their welfare."

"I like this guy already," Howie whispered.

"I am here to tell you today that Satan is alive and well. And while we here in the Midwest may think that we are safe from his wiles, I need to tell you that followers of Satan are quite active here in the Twin Cities of Minneapolis and Saint Paul."

Both Howie and Adam leaned forward in their seats as Lewis described satanic activities, citing a case study he was involved in. "Several years ago, I had the opportunity of talking with a young man who had been heavily involved in satanic rituals. He related to me how new converts were inducted into the group. As part of the initiation ceremony, they were required to wear the tongue of a cow around their neck."

A collective audible gasp rose up from the audience as Adam and Howie stared at each other with their mouths open.

"Yes, you heard me right; a cow's tongue." Lewis paused as if to let his audience fully absorb his words. "After the cow's neck was slit open, its tongue would be cut out while the poor creature was still struggling for life. They would gather its blood and..."

Howie nudged Adam. "Let me have a pencil and paper." For the rest of the lecture, he took notes. They were getting another piece of the puzzle.

HOWIE TOOK A sip of coffee. It tasted bitter, but at least it was hot. He and Adam sat at a corner table in the school cafeteria discussing Professor Lewis' lecture. "I have to tell you, we've gotten ourselves in something weird with this case." He stirred a spoonful of sugar into his coffee, mesmerized for a moment by the swirling black liquid. "Did you hear Lewis when he said that they not only use cows but other animals in their rituals?"

"I sure did."

"Maybe that's why Maureen took the cat."

"You mean she could be involved in this stuff?"

"It would explain why Jodelle was so vague about it. Maybe she's too embarrassed about her sister, and maybe she's trying to protect her." Howie paused. "And don't forget about the brother. He's the guy that sent us those packages."

"Do you think he and Maureen are in it together?"

"I don't know, but there's got to be some connection. After all, he said he's the black sheep of the family. Maybe that's why." Howie took another sip of coffee; it tasted weaker than the stuff he made. "Do you think you could talk to your Professor Lewis about our case?"

"Oh, sure, I don't think there would be any problem."

"Good, but let's keep that in reserve for now." Howie looked at his watch. "I've got to go and see if Maureen Hammond is back."

IT TOOK HOWIE a half hour to get to Maureen Hammond's. He didn't want to ring her apartment number because he still figured she wouldn't answer. When he buzzed the manager's apartment, however, there was no response. Just as he was trying to figure out what to do next, the door from the outside opened and a pizza deliveryman came whizzing in. The aroma of pepperoni pizza came with him as he balanced the box on one hand and buzzed an apartment number with the other. Other than giving Howie a nod, he paid no attention to him. "Who is it?" the voice over the intercom asked. "Pizza delivery." The door buzzed and when the pizza guy opened the door, Howie followed him in. While the guy went straight ahead, Howie took the stairs to the right. When he found apartment 4C, he knocked and waited, and then knocked again with a persistence that signaled he was not going away.

"Who is it?" a female voice asked.

"Maintenance man." Howie stepped aside, hoping she hadn't looked through her peephole yet. "The manager asked me to look at the plumbing in all the apartments."

"I don't have any problems."

"Ma'am, I'm just doing what I was told to do." Howie thought he picked up a note of fear in her voice. "If you want, I can get the manager up here and he can tell you himself."

It was several seconds before she replied. "That won't be necessary. Just a minute." Howie kept glancing up and down the hallway as he waited. He wet his lips and swallowed as he listened to the rattle of a door chain being unhooked, and then the door itself being unlocked. It opened slowly. It was Maureen Hammond, all right. He recognized her from the photograph. As soon as she saw him, however, fear flashed across her face. "You're not--"

"I'm Howie Cummins from the MAC Detective Agency," he said quickly, afraid she would slam the door. "We need to talk." He was prepared to put his foot in the door if she tried to close it. "It's about your sister, Jodelle. She's in trouble." It wasn't exactly the truth but it was the only thing he could think of to say at the time.

"Did something happen to her?" Maureen asked, her voice trembling.

"No, not yet." Howie felt he needed to go with whatever her fears were for Jodelle; it was the only way she was going to let him in. "Can we talk inside? I think that might be better."

She stood in the doorway, blocking the way for several moments before finally stepping aside. "Okay, come in." After she let him in, she locked the door and slid the chain lock in place. "This building has had a break-in recently," she explained.

"When did that happen?"

Maureen seemed unprepared for his question. "When? Ah, let's see. I believe it was Wednesday when the manager came up to caution me about keeping my door locked. He also told me to be careful of strangers. That's why I was so hesitant about letting you in."

She was lying but he didn't say anything. She led him into the living room. As he glanced around for any evidence of JoJo, he noticed a picture of Jodelle on a bookcase.

"Please sit down." Maureen motioned toward the couch. As he sat, she moved a cushioned chair closer. "Tell me, has anything happened to Jodelle?" she asked, her hands locked together as if in prayer.

Howie was confused. If there was any animosity between the two sisters, Maureen certainly wasn't showing any. "Your sister's okay. In fact, she was hoping you could help out with a problem she has. She's missing--"

"I already told her I took it and I wasn't giving it back until I decided what to do."

"But don't you think JoJo belongs--"

"Who's JoJo?" Maureen got a puzzled look on her face.

"Why, it's her cat."

"You must be mistaken. You can't be talking about my sister."

"Miss Hammond, I'm confused. Why wouldn't I?"

"Because she's never owned a cat in her life. She's allergic to them."

Chapter 6

AFTER HIS VISIT with Maureen Hammond, Howie didn't feel like working. He had, however, promised Kass that he would put in a few extra hours behind the soda fountain. It was a promise he would keep. After Howie's father died, he couldn't afford the rent on the duplex he and his father were living in. It was Kass who came to him and offered the space above the drugstore, assuring him not to worry about a little thing like rent. "We can work things out," Kass said with a broad smile and a firm handshake. Even though Howie worked for Kass as a way of reducing the rent, he knew that the man could have rented out the apartment for a lot more than he was paying.

When Howie walked into the drugstore, though, he was glad to see that it wasn't very busy. All six stools at the fountain were unoccupied, unusual for a Saturday afternoon. Kass was at the register chatting with a customer.

Howie said hello to Kass and then went over and straddled the end stool. He chastised himself for handling the visit with Maureen the way he had. She had caught him completely off guard when she informed him that her sister never owned a cat. He had been stunned by that revelation.

"Are you absolutely sure your sister never had a cat?" he had asked.

"Mr. Cummins, I already told you that Jodelle hates cats because of her allergies. Don't you think I know my own sister?"

Without giving him a chance to reply, she had abruptly stood up and announced that there was no need for any further questions. She showed him the way out and he left with the sound of the door clicking behind him. It was only when he was driving back to his apartment that it dawned on him that Maureen had admitted taking *something*.

What had she said? Something about already having taken...it? Why didn't I catch that and try to find out what she was referring to? He considered turning the car around, but decided going back wouldn't do any good. *She won't talk to me, now. Besides, Jodelle only hired me to find a cat. She didn't mention anything else, and she didn't accuse her sister of taking anything else.*

He drummed his fingers on the counter as he tried to figure out Jodelle's angle. *Why had she lied about the cat? Was it an excuse to track down her sister? If so, why? And what was Maureen referring to by it?* He sat silently, staring at the swirl patterns on the countertop. The next time he talked to Maureen he would get some answers; he wouldn't be brushed off so easy. He may not have had much experience being a detective thus far, but he was a fast learner and he wouldn't make the same mistake twice.

"Ah, my boy, you look like you're deep in thought."

"What? Oh, hi, Kass. Sorry, I didn't realize you were standing there." Howie looked at the clock above the hot fudge dispenser. It was nearly three. "Is it okay if I sit for a few minutes more before I begin?"

"Of course. We haven't been all that busy, anyway." Kass got a glass and filled it with ice and water. "Here, you look like you're thirsty."

"Thanks." Howie gulped it down.

"See, what did I tell you? Kass knows." He picked up the glass. "Do you want some more?" Howie shook his head "You look tired," Kass said as he wiped the counter.

"It's been a frustrating day."

"Maybe you shouldn't work this afternoon." Kass gave him a worried look. "Take some time off. Get some rest."

"Oh, no. Thanks, anyway. Just let me sit for a while and then I'll be okay." Howie glanced around the store. "So, it's been slow, huh?"

"Slow enough." Kass got a box of straws from under the counter and began to fill the dispenser. "Oh, I almost forgot. That kid, Joey, was in this afternoon."

Howie nodded. He didn't want to tell Kass that he had forgotten all about Joey. "Did he find his cat, I hope?"

"No, he was hoping you had. I told him it's only been a couple of days and that he should be patient."

"Was he okay about that?"

Kass smiled. "As okay as an eight-year-old little boy with a missing cat could be. He's so worried about his pet. I sure hope you can find it."

Howie made a mental note to drive up to the park by Joey's and do some scouting around tomorrow afternoon. He wasn't hopeful, but he didn't want to face the kid again without having made an effort. "The next time he comes in, you can tell him that I'm working on his case."

"Good, I'll do that."

Even though Howie had a client, he had to get a few more to help pay the bills. He didn't mind working at the drugstore, but was eager to build up a clientele and establish a reputation on the North Side. The sooner he could devote full time to the business, the better. He liked Kass, but working behind a soda fountain didn't fit his image of being a detective. "Anybody else come in looking for me?"

"As a matter of fact, there was."

"Really? Who?"

"It was right after Joey left. A man came in and started asking questions about you. He wasn't exactly looking for you. I mean he didn't seem like he was interested in talking to you in person." Kass paused, stroked his chin, and then glanced toward the front of the store at a customer who just came in. "It was more like he was just pumping me for information."

"Do you know who he was?"

"To tell you the truth, he never did give me his name."

"What kind of things did he want to know?" Howie asked, wishing that Kass would have asked the guy's name.

"Let's see, now." Kass scratched the top of his baldhead. "He inquired about what hours you worked here at the soda fountain; how long have you been in the detective business; if--"

"What did you tell him about how long I've been a detective?"

"I told a little white lie." Kass' round face flashed an impish grin. "I made it sound like you have been doing this for quite some time. You know, like you're a seasoned private eye. That's okay, I did that, isn't it?"

"Of course, and thanks." Howie smiled. It was great that Kass was such a supportive friend. "I appreciate you looking out for me."

"You know, this guy seemed very interested in your work. At first, I thought he might be a potential client, but then he started going on as to how exciting and dangerous your work must be. I wasn't sure what he was getting at." Kass looked toward the front before leaning over the counter. Then he spoke in a hushed tone. "He asked if you carried a gun."

"What did you say?"

"I told him I didn't think so, but I wasn't sure. His question, however, got me thinking and I got worried about you and Mick and Adam." Kass hesitated as if he was afraid to ask his question. "You boys don't carry a gun, do you? Tell me you don't."

"You don't have to worry, we don't."

Kass raised his hand to his chest and took a deep breath. "Oh, I'm so glad to hear that. I'm proud to have you boys being detectives, but I wouldn't like the idea of you having guns. I don't know why, but the thought never occurred to me until this guy mentioned it."

"Well, you can rest assured, we don't. I wouldn't even want to carry one; it's not my style. But let's keep that between you and me. Okay?"

"Certainly."

"Now, tell me, what did this person look like?"

"Hmmm, let me see. He had jet-black hair, cut short. He was nearly six feet tall, and I'd say he was in his late twenties to middle thirties. Dressed nice, smooth talker, and his eyes..."

"What about his eyes?"

"His eyes were the same color as his hair, and they were so penetrating, like he could see right into your soul." Kass shuddered. "I can't explain it, but they made me feel uncomfortable."

"Did he have a long slender nose and come across as arrogant?"

"Yes, that sounds like him. Do you know him?"

"We've crossed paths." *What was Damien up to now?* Howie was already convinced that it was Damien who had sent the packages. What he couldn't figure out was why Damien wanted them off the case when there didn't seem to be a case in the first place. Something else was going on and he was determined to get to the bottom of it. "Anything else about him?"

"No..." Kass paused. "Well, yes, one other thing. It's my opinion, of course. His looks were striking, but not the leading man type."

"What do you mean?"

"You know, how in movies the male lead is usually played by handsome leading men types? This guy was good looking, but in a menacing kind of way. He was a slick talker; so slick that you wouldn't want to trust him." Kass laughed. "I don't know if I'm making any sense but he'd make a good-looking villain. You know, someone sinister. Someone you wouldn't want to meet in a dark alley."

Howie hadn't thought of Damien in that way, but now that Kass mentioned it, he had to agree. "Thanks, I appreciate the information."

The clanging of the cowbell over the entrance door drew Kass' attention. "Oh, oh, here comes Mrs. Molander. She's going to want to talk to me about her arthritis. I better go."

After Kass left, Howie took his napkin and started ripping it into small pieces as he thought about Damien. *The nerve of that guy coming around here and sticking his nose into my business. He thinks he can send those packages and just walk right in as if nothing happened. I don't know what his game is, but I'm going to find out.* Howie vowed to pay Jodelle a visit the first chance he got. *Let's see what she says when I confront her about the imaginary JoJo and her very real, long, lost brother.* He scooped the pieces of the napkin up and wadded them into a tight little ball; he didn't like being played for the fool and he looked forward to meeting up with Damien again, even if it was in a dark alley.

ADAM HAD GONE to the library to do some studying once Howie left to pay Maureen Hammond a visit. "Hope you find her at home," he had told Howie. It was now nearly seven and Adam told himself that it was time to call it quits and head for home. Not having eaten since lunch, he decided to stop where his mother worked at Andy's Sandwich Shop on Broadway. The place was a half block up from Kass' Drugstore. Not much bigger than a matchbox size hamburger joint, it was squeezed in between a movie theater and a clothing store. When he walked in, only three of the eleven stools at the L-shaped counter were taken. As usual when business was slow, his mother could be found at the pinball machine, either watching someone play or playing it herself. Tonight, she was looking on as a short redheaded guy played.

"Hi," his mother yelled as soon as she saw him come in. She laughed. "I bet you haven't eaten, have you?"

"That's right, and I'm hungry." Adam sat down at the opposite end, next to the wall. During high school days, he ate at Andy's on a weekly basis. He and his mother had always been close. She raised him after his father walked out in their first year of marriage. Working as a waitress, she helped put him through college and was so proud when he started seminary.

This Angel Has No Wings

She wasn't aware of his personal struggle and he saw no need to share it at this point. She would be disappointed enough if he decided to drop out of seminary.

"Hey, Sam, I've got to go and fix something for my kid. Keep the machine hot and don't tilt it. Okay? When I get back, we'll go double or nothing."

"Ah, Virg," Sam said, not taking his eyes off the ball he was playing, "are you trying to take all my money?"

"As much as I can." Virg went behind the counter and walked over to where Adam was sitting. "So what will you have?"

"The usual."

"Chocolate malt and hamburger. Right?"

"You got it." Adam looked on as his mother went to the grill and slapped on a hamburger patty; its sizzling could be heard even over the clanging of the pinball machine.

"Put some onions on it, also," Adam yelled. His mother turned and nodded. While he waited, he looked over the sports section of a newspaper somebody had left behind. The combined aroma of fried onions and hamburger made his mouth water.

"So how did school go today?" his mother asked as she brought him his food.

"Pretty good." He took a bite of his hamburger, and had to use a napkin to wipe the juices from dribbling down the side of his mouth. The hamburgers were greasy, but Andy's had the reputation for having the best burgers on Broadway. "I managed to get some good studying in for the test next week and I've got all my research done for my paper"

"That's great. I'm so proud of you. It's hard to believe that you're in your first year of seminary."

"You're telling me," Adam mumbled while taking another bite. He washed it down with a couple sips from the malt. His mother bragged every chance she got to any customer who would listen to her brag about having a son who was going to be a preacher. It was something he wished his mother wouldn't do. When it came to God, he had more questions than answers.

"Hey, Virg," the other waitress shouted, "don't forget to tell him about the package."

"Oh, that's right."

Adam took another bite of his hamburger. "What are you talking about?"

"There was a package delivered here for you this afternoon."

"What! A package? For me?"

"It has your name on it so it must be for you." She laughed. "And whoever printed it did such a nice job. The other waitresses were even talking about the fancy lettering."

Adam set his hamburger down, a knot formed in his stomach as he thought about what Howie had said earlier.

"Is there something wrong with the hamburger?"

Charles Tindell

"No, why?"

"The look on your face."

"I'm just a little shocked at getting a package down here." His back and neck muscles tightened. "Where is it?"

"It's in the back. Just a minute, I'll get it for you."

While his mother was gone, Adam thoughts went to the two other packages that he and his partners had received.

"Here it is," his mother announced as she placed it on the counter.

As soon as he saw the shoebox-size package with the brown wrapping paper, he knew that Howie's hunch had been right. What troubled him was how anyone knew where to deliver it unless they would have been checking up on him. The fact that it had turned up at his mother's workplace made him angry. "Thanks." He took the package and placed it on the stool beside him. "Do you have any idea who delivered it?"

"No, Blanche gave it to me when I came in. She said that some guy dropped it off during the noonday rush."

Adam intentionally kept his voice calm. "Did she say what he looked like?"

"Not really. It was so busy that she just took the package and barely looked at the guy. All she said was that he was tall and had dark hair." His mother glanced at the package; her eyes glistened with anticipation. "Well, are you going to open it?"

Adam shook his head. "No, this is some stuff for Howie." He hoped his mother wouldn't press him, and when she did, he found himself lying. "I'm sorry, but I can't tell you what it is. All I can say is that it's something he wants to use for surveillance." He felt like a hypocrite lying since he had recently told Howie about not wanting to compromise his ethics while working with him. "Remember, I'm suppose to be studying to become a minister, not a detective." Part of his internal struggle, however, came from the dilemma that he found detective work exciting and more suited to his personality.

"Oh, that Howie." His mother chuckled. "He's always trying some newfangled ideas. It must be interesting work. Aren't you glad that he asked you and Mick to help out?"

"Yeah, it's interesting work, all right." Adam forced a smile. "You know, with Howie, there's never a dull moment."

"Have you gotten any cases yet?"

He was going to say no but since his mother and Kass were good friends, she would probably hear about it from him. "We got a case the other day. It's no big deal. Some woman hired us to find her cat."

His mother grinned. "For goodness' sake, a cat? Well, it's a beginning anyway."

If you only knew. Adam glanced at the package. He couldn't help but wonder what part of the cow this box contained. It was lighter than the last package. Having it next to him gave him a sense of dread. He had to talk with Howie. "I have to go."

"You haven't finished your hamburger."

"I'm sorry, but my stomach feels a little queasy," he said truthfully. When his mother glanced at the hamburger, he quickly explained. "Don't worry, it's not the food. It's just nervous tension from studying so much and being worried about all the work yet to be done."

His mother cocked her head, but said nothing. It was a lame excuse, and she probably didn't believe him. He couldn't help that. After promising his mother he would eat something later at home, he left.

Adam hurriedly walked the half block to Howie's. As he crossed the street he looked above Kass' and saw that the lights were on in the office. That was good. It meant that Howie was there. He ran up the stairs and threw open the door, causing it to slam into the wall.

"What the--" Howie cried. "Don't do that to me. You scared me." He took a deep breath. "At this time of night, at least, knock or--"

"Look at this!" Adam held out the package. "I just got it. It was delivered down at Andy's this afternoon. Down where my mother works!" he shouted. "Can you believe that?"

"Take it easy. Calm down."

Adam nodded and took a couple of deep breaths. "I just can't believe the nerve of that guy, Damien." He dropped the package on the desk, went back and closed the office door, and then came and plopped down in the chair. He felt exhausted.

Howie leaned forward, picked up the package and set it down. "It's not too heavy."

"So what do you think?"

"I think we should open it." Howie took out some scissors. "Do you want to or should I?"

"Go ahead." As Adam watched, he became aware he was chewing on his lip. It was a nervous habit he thought he had broken a couple of years ago. He looked on as Howie carefully removed the wrapping paper. The box was identical to the first one; black Oxfords, size nine. His eyes narrowed as Howie lifted the cover.

"Will you look at that," Howie whispered, tilting the box so Adam could see.

"It reminds me of a communion chalice," Adam said, feeling surprised and relieved at the same time. The cup was silver and about eight inches tall. Its base was nearly as large in circumference as its mouth.

Howie reached in and picked it up. "This thing is pretty light." He tipped the cup to look at its bottom. "It can't weigh much more than--"

"Look at that!" Adam cried as a drop of thick reddish-brown liquid plopped into the bottom of the box.

"Is that what I think it is?" Howie's asked.

Adam nodded. "I think so."

Howie tilted the cup upward and looked inside. "Wait until you see this."

"What?"

Charles Tindell

"The inside is coated with blood, and it looks fresh." He showed Adam and then set the cup down. "You don't think someone..."

"I don't know what to think," Adam said, staring at the cup. "What bothers me is where did that blood come from?"

"What do you mean?"

"I mean did it come from what we got in those other two packages."

"You mean from the cow?"

Adam nodded. "I can't look at that, anymore; there's something ominous about all of this." He picked up the cup, laid it back in the box, and put the cover back on.

Howie rocked in his chair a couple of times before leaning forward. "What if it's not cow's blood?"

"You don't mean..." Adam stared at Howie for several moments. "Man, what have we got ourselves into here? His tone took on a sense of urgency. "Don't you think we should go to the police?"

"No," Howie replied brusquely as he moved the shoebox aside. When he hired Mick and Adam, he told them that he wanted to prove that his agency had what it takes to get the job done. "Like I've told you, I'm not going to do that. Not yet."

"Okay, but what if someone was murdered! What if Damien is some lunatic who gets his kicks from drinking the blood of humans like Dracula?"

"Wait a minute," Howie cautioned. "Let's be rational about this. I can't be positive, but my bet is that it's not human blood."

"Oh, that's fine, then. We're just dealing with something more normal. Some guy who cuts out a cow's tongue and heart, and then drinks its blood." Adam paused for a moment. "Why don't you at least talk to Davidson?"

"I'll think about it." Jim Davidson, a seventeen-year veteran police detective worked out of the Fifth Precinct at the North Side Station. Howie had first been introduced to the man through a mutual acquaintance over a year ago. He and the detective hit if off immediately. After their first encounter, Davidson, who preferred to be called JD, slapped Howie on the back and told him that if he had any questions or needed any advice, to just give him a call. Both Mick and Adam took an immediate liking to Davidson when he stopped in one day at Howie's and had coffee with the three of them.

"We got to let Mick in on this," Howie said, counting on Adam to calm down in the meantime. "I'm going to call him." He had also thought about contacting JD but was reluctant to ask for his help on their first case. He respected Davidson, but also wanted to prove to him that he could handle detective work on his own.

While Howie dialed Mick's number, Adam took the cup out of the box to have a closer look.

"Mick wants to know if he should come over," Howie asked.

"It doesn't matter with me. Tell him it's up to him." As Adam slowly rotated the cup, he noticed a small symbol engraved on its base. It looked like a crow with its wings outstretched. The crow was holding something in its beak. There was printing underneath the crow but he couldn't make out the tiny letters, his eyes were too tired from studying all day. He wondered what Mick's reaction would be when he saw the chalice. "Is he coming?"

Howie held up his hand to signal he wanted to hear whatever Mick was saying. "Okay, I agree. Yeah, you don't have to tell me it's strange. Just a minute, Adam wants to know if you're coming." Howie looked at Adam. "He says he'll be here in fifteen minutes."

"Ask if he's got a magnifying glass." Adam pointed to the tiny printing.

Howie nodded and then asked Mick. "Good, bring it. Okay, we'll see you soon."

"What did he say when you told him what was in the package?"

"He didn't say much at all other than agreeing that we have gotten ourselves into some strange stuff here."

Adam held the cup up and pointed to the markings. "I'm pretty sure that's a crow. But what do you think he's holding in his beak?"

Howie took the cup and held it under a desk lamp as he squinted at the design. "I can't tell what that is, but those letters underneath look like FFF."

Charles Tindell

Chapter 7

Mick closed the office door quietly behind him and put his finger to his lips. "Shhhh." As Howie and Adam looked on with baffled expressions, he moved to the window and looked out.

"What in the world are you doing?" Howie asked.

"I think I was followed."

"What!" Adam got up and joined Mick at the window. "Are you sure?" he asked as he looked out at the street below.

"No, maybe I'm just paranoid, but who wouldn't be with this crazy case." Mick went over and sat down. He saw the shoebox on the desk, but disregarded it for the moment. The possibility that he could have been followed from his own home had unnerved him. "I thought for sure this Buick was following me."

Adam looked out the window again and then sat down next to Mick. "What made you think it was tailing you?"

"I happened to notice this car in the rearview mirror. It came down the street just as I left home." Mick cracked his knuckles; a habit he did whenever he became edgy, which was not very often. "At first, I didn't think anything of it. What made me suspicious was that it stayed the same distance behind me. When I turned, it turned."

Howie leaned back in his chair, clasping his fingers behind his head. "It could be just a coincidence."

"I know, but it happened a couple of times. I even slowed down, thinking it'd pass, but it never did." Mick gestured toward the window. "And then when I turned off Broadway to come here, it also turned."

"I only saw a couple of cars parked down there," Adam said. "Yours and a white Ford."

Howie leaned forward and took out his notepad from his shirt pocket. "So where do you think this Buick is now?"

"I don't know. When I pulled over to park, it drove past me." Mick got up and looked out the window, hoping to see some sign of the Buick. After watching a couple of cars drive by, he sat back down. "I tried to get a look at who was driving but it was too dark to see, and I didn't get the license number either."

"Did you notice how many were in the car?"

"There was only one person, and I can't be sure, but I think it was a man." Mick took in a deep breath and let it out slowly. "Man, I tell you, during the whole time, I had this feeling that whoever it was, purposely wanted me to know that I was being followed. The whole thing is spooky if you ask me."

"Talk about being spooky." Adam pointed to the shoebox. "Just wait until you examine Dracula's cup."

Mick rolled his eyes. "Yeah, I can hardly wait." He reached into his pocket. "Here's the magnifying glass you wanted." After he handed it to Howie, he leaned forward and looked at the chalice nestled in the box. Having heard Howie's description of it over the phone, he had no desire to handle it. "So, you actually think that somebody drank blood out of that?"

Howie nodded as he lifted the chalice, making sure it was upright. When Mick asked to see the blood, Howie tipped the cup toward him. "Ugh!" Mick cried. "That's enough, take it away. I sure hope that isn't human blood."

"It could be cat's blood," Adam suggested. "From what Professor Lewis said, the people in satanic cults sacrifice not only cows, but cats and other animals as well."

"You mean it could be JoJo's blood?" Mick asked.

"It could be," Howie said as he continued to examine the chalice, 'but in my book, I don't think so."

"Why do you say that?"

"Because Maureen told me that Jodelle never had a cat in the first place. So no cat, no blood."

Adam's mouth dropped open. "She never had a cat!"

"That's right." Howie gave his partners a wry smile. "Makes for another interesting twist in the case, doesn't it?"

Mick leaned back and closed his eyes for a moment. He needed to make some sense out of all of this. The past half hour seemed liked a blur. When he had received the phone call from Howie, he was just about to leave to pick up Mary to go to a late movie. He called her immediately, explaining the urgency in Howie's voice without giving specific details, and promising they would go to the movie tomorrow night. She understood since they had previously talked about confidentiality when working on a case. "Maureen could be lying," he said to Howie. "I suppose Jodelle could be lying, also, but she's the one that put up a thousand bucks."

"Let's suppose that Jodelle is lying," Howie said. "Then the question is why did she want us to find a cat she never had, and why did she make it sound like Maureen knew something about it?" He paused as if to let them reflect upon his words. "She knew all along where her sister lived on Girard, and even visited her at least once. But why didn't she know where she had moved to?"

"What are you getting at?" Mick asked.

"Maybe Maureen was involved in something Jodelle didn't think she should be and was taking it upon herself to stop her."

"You mean, like a big sister watching out over her little sister?"

"Exactly. It could be that Maureen decided to move because she didn't like big sister interfering with whatever she was doing."

Adam glanced at Mick before turning his attention to Howie. "So are you saying that Jodelle wanted us to find her sister all along?"

Howie nodded. "I think that's a reasonable assumption."

"But why lie to us? Why not just tell us she was looking for her sister?"

"Perhaps because Maureen somehow got involved in Satanism along the way, and if she did, Jodelle didn't want anyone to know about that. Maybe Maureen and her black sheep of a brother have the same interests."

"You mean like sharing a cup of blood every now and then?" Adam asked.

"It could be. Maureen could've lied about her sister not having a cat just to throw me off track. If that was her plan, she did a pretty good number on me." Howie set his jaw. "But I won't be fooled again."

Mick realized what Howie was getting at. "You mean to say that there still might be a JoJo and that Maureen took the cat for some kind of satanic ritual?"

Howie shrugged. "It's a possibility."

"That's sick," Mick said.

"You don't have to tell me that." Howie resumed examining the chalice. Mick and Adam watched as he focused on the markings at the base. "Oh, yes," he said with a note of triumph. "Just as we thought, that figure is a crow with outstretched wings." He squinted. "But I can't make out what it has in its beak."

"Can you see what those letters are?" Adam asked.

Howie looked up. "I was right, those are three F's. And do you remember where we saw those before?"

"I sure do," Adam replied. "On the sidewalk at that house on Girard."

Mick asked now to see the chalice; his curiosity had gotten the best of him. After peering through the magnifying glass, he looked up at Howie. "I wonder what those letters stand for? Do you think they could be someone's initials?"

"I doubt that. That would be too obvious. Maybe--"

The phone ranged. Howie let it ring a couple of times before answering it. Within a few seconds Mick and Adam knew something was wrong by the look on his face.

"Who is this?" Howie winced as he held the phone away from his ear. "Listen, whoever this is...hello...hello?" He shook his head as he hung up the phone. "That was a strange one. Some woman just screeched at me and then slammed the phone down."

"She really must have yelled," Mick said, "because I could hear her."

"What did she say?" Adam asked Howie.

"It sounded like she yelled, 'Take heed of Bea Lyle.'"

"Bea Lyle?" Mick said. "Who's she?"

"Don't ask me."

"Halloween is coming up," Adam offered, "maybe it was someone's idea of a pre-Halloween prank call."

Mick gave Adam a nervous half smile. "That's sort of far fetched, isn't it?"

"Yeah, I know. I guess I was just hoping."

"I know what you mean, but I've got a feeling that phone call has something to do with this case. Don't you?" he asked Howie.

Howie ran his fingers through his hair a couple of times. "I don't know. I hope not. We've got enough crazy stuff going on already."

"Are you sure Bea Lyle was the name that was said?" Adam asked.

"I can only tell you that's what it sounded like."

"Do you think she's connected with Damien?"

"Maybe she's his girlfriend," Mick suggested, wondering what kind of girl would fall for Damien.

Howie looked up at the clock. "Hey, guys, I don't know about you, but I'm tired. It's late and so much has happened in the past twenty-four hours that my head is spinning."

"That goes double for mine." Mick was ready to call it a night. He needed to go home and get some sleep. First, he would call Mary and let her know that he's home. He wished she wouldn't worry so much, but it was a nice feeling to have someone who did. "What do you suggest?"

"Tomorrow's Sunday. Why don't we all take a breather from this 'til Monday? What do you say we just mull this over in our heads for a while? Okay?"

"Sounds good to me."

Adam pointed to the chalice. "What are you going to do about that?"

"I'm not sure."

"Talk to Davidson, will you," Adam pleaded.

"Hey, that's a good idea," Mick said. "He said he would help us out."

Adam continued to plead. "Come on, you don't have to tell him everything about the case. Just find out about the blood."

Howie drummed his fingers on his desk as his eyes shifted back and forth between Mick and Adam. "Okay," he finally said. "I'll give him a sample of the blood and ask him to have it analyzed in their police lab."

"Great," Adam said, a note of relief in his voice. "That sounds good. At least, then, we'll find out what kind of blood it is."

"I'm betting that it's cow blood," Howie said. "I'll see JD Monday morning. We should have an answer in a couple of days."

"Is it okay if I talk with Professor Lewis about that cup?"

"Sure." Howie took the chalice from Mick and laid it back in the box. "He might be able to give us a few pieces of the puzzle. Just don't mention names, okay?"

"I won't. Are we going to meet on Monday?"

Charles Tindell

"We better, and one more thing, give some more thought to who this Bea Lyle might be."

Mick stood up, he was ready to go home and call Mary. "I agree with Adam. She's probably connected with Damien in some way."

"Whoever she is," Howie said, "just remember, we were warned. So, be careful."

This Angel Has No Wings

Chapter 8

AFTER ADAM AND Mick left, Howie spent another hour examining the chalice and jotting down notes. Using an eyedropper, he managed to suck up a couple drops of the brownish-red liquid that was now beginning to coagulate. He sealed the end of the eyedropper using a Band-Aid, placed it in a plastic bag, and stored it in the refrigerator. He thought about rinsing the chalice out, but decided against it in case his police friend needed more samples. The shoebox containing the chalice was also stored in the refrigerator. "I'm going to have to get a bigger frig," he muttered as he shut the door, and went to bed.

HOWIE WOKE UP later than usual the next morning. Surprisingly, he had slept well and had not dreamt about the case. As he lay there, he reluctantly looked at the alarm clock. *Nearly nine. Time to get up.* After a mid-morning breakfast of toast and cold cereal, he went downstairs to help out in the drug store. From ten until shortly after one, he served banana splits, malts, and cherry phosphates, to the after-church crowd. Kass invited him to share a sandwich and a Coke before he left. While they ate, they discussed general things, but nothing about the case.

"I better be going," Howie said as he finished the last of his sandwich.

"You eat too fast," Kass observed.

"I know, but I've got things to do."

"And you have a beautiful fall day to do it. It's sunny and the radio says it's going to reach a high of seventy-three degrees. Enjoy this day while you have it." Kass took Howie's plate, and wiped the counter. "So what are you going to do on this Sunday afternoon? Are you going to be with Mick and Adam?"

"No, they have their own plans. I'm going to spend some time looking for Joey's cat."

"Oh, that'll be nice." Kass smiled. "You'll find his cat. I know you will. You're a good detective."

"Thanks for your confidence. See you around."

Charles Tindell

Howie drove to the park near Joey's, figuring that was his best bet to find the cat. After parking by the baseball diamonds, he locked the car, and started his search. He wasn't all that hopeful of finding the animal, but he had promised Joey, and making the effort was important.

For the next hour he crisscrossed the park, climbing up and down the massive hill that rose in the middle of it. Although in the shade of the trees it was cool, he had managed to work up a sweat. The thought crossed his mind that the cat could have been run over by a car while crossing the street. *Naw, I don't think so. Joey would've found out about it.* As he walked down the hill toward the playground, he saw some kids on the swings. Thinking that they might be regulars to the park, he decided to go over and inquire. He had nothing to lose by asking a few questions.

"Hi," Howie said to a boy no older than nine or ten who was watching the other kids swing. "I'm looking for a lost cat."

"A cat? What color?"

"Mostly black, has a little white under its chin, but you wouldn't notice that unless you were looking for it."

"Didn't see any, Mister." The boy yelled at those on the swings. "Come on, you've been on there long enough. It's my turn," he whined before turning back to Howie. "I saw a dog running around about a half hour ago."

"Sorry, kid, but I'm just in the market for cats today."

"You can ask my sister, she comes here a lot to play with her stupid friends."

"Where is she?"

"Over there by the drinking fountain." There were two young girls talking and giggling about something. "She's the goofy-looking one with the jeans and red sweater."

"Thanks."

"Hey, Mister, is there a reward if I find the cat?"

Greedy little rug rat. Howie smiled. "Sure."

The rug rat's sister eyed Howie suspiciously as he walked up to her and her friend. "Hello. Your brother back there told me that I could ask you about a lost cat."

"Oh, poor kitty. I love cats." She looked at him with sorrowful eyes. "Can we help you look?"

Howie wondered how she and the rug rat could be even remotely related. "Thanks, but I've already looked. I'm just wondering if you've seen a black cat running loose in the past week or so. Your brother says you and your friends come to the park all the time."

"No, I haven't seen one. I hope the kitty's okay."

"I think I saw the cat," the other girl said.

"Really? Where?"

"In a cage."

"What do you mean in a cage?"

This Angel Has No Wings

"Last week I was playing here after school." She turned to rug rat's sister. "I called your house but nobody answered. So I called Sue, and she came with me. Is that okay?" After being reassured that she hadn't betrayed their friendship, she finished her reply to Howie. "Me and Sue saw this man walk by carrying a cage. It was like a birdcage, almost, but it was bigger. Inside was a kitty. The poor thing was meowing and meowing."

"And it was black?"

"Uh, huh."

"Do you remember what the guy looked like?"

When she shook her head, her long blond hair whipped in front of her face. "No, but my friend said she'd seen him in the park lots of times."

Howie looked around. "Is your friend here?"

"No, she's sick today. She called me and told me about throwing up on her mom's new carpeting."

"Yuck!" the rug rat's sister exclaimed.

"I know," her friend squealed, making a face, "it was gross listening to her talk about it."

Howie wanted to get going. "Did she ever say anything about what that guy was doing those other times when she saw him at the park?"

"He was just walking around carrying that cage, but it was always empty. We thought he was going to trap squirrels or something. Then we saw the cat." She stuck out her lip like she was going to pout. "I just felt so sorry for the poor kitty cat."

Kid, don't start crying. It'd wreck my day. "Was it hurt or anything?"

"I don't know, but it sounded like it didn't want to be in that nasty cage. I don't think it liked that man. Poor kitty."

"Poor kitty," the rug rat's sister echoed. She looked up at him. "I bet you miss him."

"I do, thanks." Howie thought about telling them that he wasn't the owner, but was afraid that they would ask who he was then. Once they found out that he was a detective, there would be no telling the questions they would have, and he didn't have time for that. Besides, he didn't think it was a good idea that a lot of people knew about what he was doing. If these two found out, the whole neighborhood would know, and he didn't need any more cat cases. He took the name and phone number of the girl's friend, hoping that when he called her he would get a description of the guy. When he walked past the swing set on his way back to his car, the one girl's brother was pushing another kid off a swing, telling him that it was his turn now. When he saw Howie, he yelled, "Hey, Mister, if you want some help finding your cat, you can hire me."

"I'll think about it, kid."

When Howie got back to his apartment, he decided he would go for a long run, take a shower, make himself some supper, and catch up on his reading. He would get to bed early, and then call JD the first thing in the morning.

Charles Tindell

On Monday morning, Adam was also planning to see someone concerning the case. He was hoping to talk with Professor Lewis about the chalice. Following the mid-morning daily chapel service, he tracked down Lewis and asked if he had some time to see him that day. The professor peered over his wire-rimmed bifocals, smiled, and replied that he would be delighted to have a visit with him.

"I'll be in my office after my one o'clock class, and will be there until four. I can meet with you anytime between two and four."

"I'll stop by around two fifteen, if that's okay?" After Lewis said that it would be, Adam felt relieved. "Thanks. I appreciate this. I'll see you then."

During lunch, Adam sat by himself at a corner table. With his book opened and a sheet of notebook paper in front of him, he hoped that others would think he was engaged in study, and wouldn't bother him. Other than someone briefly stopping to ask about a class assignment, his ploy worked. He didn't want to explain to anybody why he was pondering a drawing of a triangle with three F's inside of it. He was as much puzzled with it as the first time he saw it, and wondered if it had any connection with the phone call they had received on Saturday night. *Bea Lyle? Who is she, and why were we warned about her?* He had casually mentioned the name to his mother on the chance that the name had surfaced among the customers down at Andy's. If there were a Bea Lyle on the North Side, his mother would know. He was disappointed, however, by her reply. "I never heard of her," she said.

It was ten minutes after two when Adam arrived at Lewis' office. The door was open. His professor was hunched over his desk reading a book that had to be four inches thick. Reluctant to disturb him, Adam stood at the door and waited. It wasn't long before he decided to intentionally clear his throat.

Professor Lewis looked up and offered a friendly smile. "Oh, come in, come in," he said cheerfully as he put a marker in his book and closed it.

Adam sat in a cushioned chair next to the professor's desk. It was the first time he had been in Lewis' office, and was amazed at the number of books. Three of the four walls had bookshelves reaching up toward the ceiling. In addition, there were stacks of books on the floor. He wondered how his professor could move about, let alone work in such a cramped space. "I'm really glad you've given me this time to come in and talk."

"Quite alright. It's always my pleasure to talk to students." Professor Lewis noticed Adam looking at the stacks of books. "Have you ever been in here before?"

Adam shook his head.

"I tell you a secret." With a sweeping gesture of his arm, Lewis pointed around the office. "I haven't read all these books, but they certainly look impressive, don't they?" He chuckled as he slapped his knee. "They make me appear wiser than I am."

Adam knew that his professor was down playing his reputation. If he hadn't read all of the books, Adam was sure he had read most of them. It was well known among the faculty and students that Lewis had a habit of reading two books a week. It was rumored that he had started that practice when he was a young graduate student over forty years ago.

"My friend and I attended your lecture on Saturday."

"I remember. You two sat in the back." Lewis pushed his glasses up on his nose a bit. "I think your friend had reddish blond hair and was shorter than you. He looked quite young, more like a teenager, but I would surmise he's in his mid-to-late twenties. Am I right?"

"Yes, sir, you are. And both of us enjoyed your lecture. You said some very thought provoking things that morning."

"Thank you, that's always nice to hear. We, professors, can be quite dusty at times."

"We were very interested in what you had to say. It especially made me stop and think about Satan." Lewis nodded but gave no verbal reply. "I guess I'd never thought of Satan as being real. You made it sound as if he practices his evil in every day life."

"Ah, he does. We read about our sly adversary within the pages of ancient writings, and think of him as the product of mythology." Professor Lewis took off his glasses and laid them on his desk. "But, it has been my experience that his spirit and teachings are very much alive. It's something that each generation has to contend with."

Up until they had received the packages, Adam had never seriously considered Satan as being part of the modern world. Whenever the subject was discussed in class he held the position that evil had its origin in societal injustices and that Satan was just a convenient metaphor. When one of his classmates told him that he sounded like a social worker, he had wondered if that was his calling rather than being a minister. He had never shared that struggle with Professor Lewis, but now wasn't the time to do so. Perhaps he would talk to him once this case was resolved. Of all the professors, he had the deepest respect for him. He was hopeful that Lewis could help him sort through his struggles. "I'd like for you to look at something my friends and I received, that is, if you have the time."

"I would be glad to."

Adam told him about the chalice without giving any explanation of how he had received it. He also decided not to mention the other two packages or anything about the blood. It wasn't so much that he didn't trust his professor, as it was that there were still too many unanswered questions. Besides, Howie had reminded him that they had to keep client confidentiality. "This cup looks like a chalice and has these strange markings on it."

"What kind of markings?"

"We think it's a crow with outstretched wings, and it's carrying a banner in its beak." As soon as Adam mentioned it, he noticed Lewis' eyebrows arch slightly.

"I'd very much like to see this chalice."

"Do you think from what I described, it could be one that's used for communion in a church?"

"Oh, no." Lewis' face-hardened and his eyes reflected a steel intensity. "It has nothing to do with what we know as a church."

"One more thing. There are tiny letters inscribed on the base of the chalice. Three of them."

"And what, may I ask, are they?"

"FFF."

Lewis' eyes narrowed causing his wiry gray eyebrows to come together. "Yes, by all means, bring it in. I don't know where or from whom you got it, but if it's what I think it is, I wish to caution you to be careful."

Adam stayed for another ten minutes as Lewis expanded on that part of the lecture he had talked on Satanism. When he got up to leave, his professor again cautioned him to be careful and talked briefly about the powers of the Prince of Darkness. By the time Adam left, he was more convinced than ever about the personal presence of evil and that perhaps Satan wasn't just a metaphor.

HOWIE STOPPED AT the drugstore that Monday afternoon to see if Kass wanted him to work that evening. He poured himself a cup of coffee and sat at the soda fountain waiting while Kass finished with a customer. He had just come from meeting with JD, his contact at the police department. He envied JD. Davidson fit the image of the stereotypic seasoned detective. At six feet tall, his ruggedly attractive looks showed evidence of his occupation; a nose that had been broken twice, a small scar on his chin, and another larger scar above his right eye. A square jaw and shoulders complimented his solid built, and his steely blue eyes could stop you cold. Although in his early fifties, Davidson had the moves and mannerisms of someone fifteen years younger. Old enough to be Howie's father, Davidson said that he reminded him of himself when he was just starting out chasing the bad guys. "Young and inexperienced," he said with a laugh. When Howie opened the detective agency, JD sent a note, congratulating Howie and his partners; he also included a bottle of aspirins. The next day Howie called to express his appreciation to his new police friend. It was then Davidson casually mentioned that if he could be of any help in any way, to just let him know. "And call me JD," he added.

When Howie had handed JD the plastic bag containing the eyedropper, he wasn't ready to share what they were working on; it was a matter of pride more than anything else. *I might be young and inexperienced, but I need to prove I can do this on my own.* "Can you check this out for me?" he asked.

Davidson chuckled. "I see you're up to par with the latest equipment in gathering blood samples."

"We do what we can with what we have," Howie said. "When do you think you can get this analyzed?"

"Officially?"

"I appreciate it if it stays off the record."

This Angel Has No Wings

JD nodded. "I can get it back to you in a couple of days. Do you want your Band-Aid back, also?"

"Keep it as a souvenir."

Now he waited for Kass, Howie took a napkin and began scribbling notes on it about his meeting with JD that morning. He was still writing as Kass walked up to him.

"Using my napkins again to take notes, huh?" Kass laughed. "Now that you're working on a case, you should get yourself a little notebook you can carry around."

"I have one." Howie folded up the napkin and stuffed it in his shirt pocket. "But I left it on my desk."

"You must be keeping some pretty late hours," Kass said. "You've been drinking a lot of coffee."

"It's this case we've been working on." Howie watched Kass wipe the counter. He knew that Kass wouldn't inquire about the case, but was waiting for him to say more. "Do you believe in the Devil?"

Kass immediately stopped what he was doing and looked up. He seemed surprised by the question. "I don't believe in a personal devil, but I believe in the concept of evil. I know that such a thing exists."

"What do you mean?"

"You're too young for this, but during WWII, there were unspeakable acts done to others. No one would've dreamt that human beings could have done such things to other human beings." Kass sighed. "But things were done. You know about the concentration camps, don't you?"

"A little. I remember as a kid going to a movie house and watching newsreels of how they had to use bulldozers to bury the dead in mass graves." Howie had nightmares for days after seeing those films. "That was awful. I was only about eight or nine, but I'll never forget those pictures."

"That's good. No one should ever forget." Kass' solemn tone matched the expression on his face. "Everyone should see those pictures. Those pictures remind us that evil exists."

"I know, but that was a long time ago. Do you think it still exists?"

"Certainly. I have no doubt about it. Evil is evil. It rears its ugly head in every generation." A hard edge crept into Kass' tone. "It's like a snake with seven heads. While you're cutting off one head you have to keep an eye on the other six. And while you're watching the other six, it re-grows the head you've just cut off."

Howie wondered what Kass would say if he knew about the packages they had received. He was also curious as to what Adam's professor had said about evil. Not wanting to get into a heavy discussion, he was glad that Kass didn't ask him what this had to do with his case. "Say, you know a lot of people around here, don't you?"

"I've been here on this corner for over thirty years. There's very few people I don't know, and very few who don't know me."

"By any chance, then, have you ever heard of a woman by the name of Bea Lyle?"

Charles Tindell

"Bea Lyle?" Kass shook his head. "I knew a Beatrice Olson, but she died about ten years ago. Does this Bea Lyle live around here?"

"I don't know." Howie felt he better offer some kind of explanation. "Her name came up the other day when I was talking with Mick and Adam."

Kass looked at Howie with a puzzled expression. "Is this another case? Maybe a missing person's case now?"

"You might say that." It wasn't exactly the truth, but Bea Lyle was a person Howie wanted to find.

"You and your partners are going to be so busy with detective work that you won't have time for anything." Kass grinned. "That's good. You become famous detectives like your hero, Sam Spade." He pointed to the wall behind him. "Then I get your autographed picture and hang it on the wall over the malt machines."

Howie laughed. "Well, don't make a space for it yet." He got off his stool. "Thanks for talking. If you want me to work later, I will, but right now I'm going to meet with Mick and Adam."

"You tell them I'll save a spot to hang a picture of them, also." Kass smiled. "Now, go do your detective work and become famous."

"Thanks...and Kass? If Mick or Adam come in looking for me, tell them I'm upstairs." Howie left and went up to his office. He had a good hour to relax before Mick and Adam showed up. Getting a couple of magazines from his bedroom, he made himself comfortable at his desk. During that hour he did some reading, drank three cups of coffee, but mostly reflected upon his life. He felt good about finally being able to be doing detective work; it was a long time coming. After high school, he worked two jobs to help his ailing father with the bills. That was okay. Both Mick and Adam had gone on to college. His two friends had definite goals in mind as to what they wanted to do with their lives—Mick more so than Adam. Howie's dream resurfaced one evening while he and his father were watching a detective show on television.

"Son, didn't you always say you wanted to be a detective?"

"That's right," Howie replied, not having forgotten his dream, but had put it aside.

"Then why don't you go for it? I've seen too many people let their dreams slip away." His father put his hand on Howie's shoulder and gently squeezed. "You know what your mother always said."

Howie's mother always told him that people should strive to help others and thereby leave a positive legacy in the world. She was a fine Christian woman. Too bad she died when he was still in grade school; he was still angry with God about taking his mother away from him. As he finished the last of his third cup of coffee, he glanced at his movie poster.

"Bogie, being the best detective I can be is going to be my legacy. That's how I'm going to honor the memory of my parents."

Shortly after four, Howie's office door opened and his partners walk in. "Have you come up with anything about Bea Lyle?" Mick asked as he and Adam sat down.

"Not a clue." Howie lay his magazine down.

"Neither have I," Adam said. "How about the blood sample? How soon did Davidson say we'd find out?"

Howie flipped open his notepad. "He said to give him a couple of days. I figure it might take longer."

"What if it's human blood?" Mick asked. "What do you think he'll say about that?"

"If it's human blood, knowing him, he'll want to know more, and probably recommend that the police get officially involved."

"I have to agree with him," Mick said.

Howie looked at Adam. "What about you?"

"Oh, yeah, I agree."

"Well, I disagree, but we'll argue that point then," he said, his tone firm. "Anything else?"

"I had a conversation with Professor Lewis today," Adam said. "He told me that he'd like to see the chalice. That isn't a problem, is it?"

"No. Let me clean it up first, though."

"What if you need more samples?" Mick asked.

"JD said that what I gave him was enough." Howie wanted to hear more about Adam's meeting with his professor. "Did Lewis give you any ideas?"

"No, but when I mentioned the markings and the letters, he became very interested. He told me to be careful."

"Of what?" Howie asked.

"He said that even though we live in the modern world, there are still the Powers and Principalities to contend with."

"What's that?"

"That's preacher talk. Powers and Principalities come from Romans, one of the books of the Bible. What it essentially means is that there are forces of evil that the forces of good have to contend with. I think--"

The ringing of the phone stopped Adam in mid sentence. He looked at Mick and Howie. "Do you think it's another warning?"

"We'll find out." Howie took a deep breath. "MAC Detective Agency. Howie Cummins speaking." *It's Jodelle Hammond*, he mouthed. "Wait a minute, slow down. Just be calm. Yes, yes." He listened without saying anything for a few minutes. "Okay, just hold still. My partners are here with me. We'll be right over."

"What's going on?" Mick asked as Howie hung up.

"She found a package on her doorstep. And guess what? It was wrapped in brown wrapping paper and tied with twine."

Adam leaned his head back on the chair. "Oh, man, here we go again."

Charles Tindell

"You're telling me." Howie felt the adrenalin surging through his body. "And listen to this. There was a note attached to the package, and the note says that the package is only to be opened when one of us is there."

"What!" Mick exclaimed.

"Yeah, and not only that, on the front of the package there is a triangle with three F's inside of it."

Chapter 9

"Slow down," Mick pleaded as Howie sped south on Lyndale on their way to Jodelle Hammond's.

Howie glanced over at his friend. "Relax, will you?" he said and then checked the speedometer. "I'm barely going forty-five."

"But the speed limit is only thirty," Mick said.

"Howie!" Adam yelled from the back seat. "The light's red!"

Howie slammed on the brakes as Mick braced himself against the dashboard. The car came to a screeching halt just as it reached the intersection. Once the car stopped rocking, he looked in the rearview mirror. Adam was settling back in the seat, brushing a shock of hair from his eyes. "You okay back there?"

"I think so, but my guardian angel's a little shook up."

"Pass her up here, will you?" Mick pleaded. "The way this maniac's driving, I'm going to need her."

"Sorry, guys, but Jodelle sounded frightened on the phone." Howie recalled how her voice had quivered when she described the markings on the package. Although he felt sorry for her, he was hoping that she was sufficiently shaken to start giving them some answers. And maybe if they got lucky, they would spot Damien in the area. "The poor woman sounded like she might go off the deep end."

"Hey, we understand that we need to hurry," Mick said, "but don't kill us in the process. Remember, we're your partners. We're the good guys."

"Okay, okay, I'll watch it."

For the rest of the way, Howie, for the most part, kept his promise. Only twice were hints given to him to slow down. The first time was when Mick shouted back to Adam to send his guardian angel up front. "And make it fast, will you!" The second time occurred when Adam warned him that there was a police car following them. When Howie looked in the rearview mirror, he didn't see any cop car, but he got the message. "

When they got to Jodelle's, Howie decided to park around the corner just as he had last time. He glanced around, but there was no sign of

Charles Tindell

Damien. Thinking that all three of them going up to her house would draw too much attention, he was about to suggest that one of them stay with the car when Mick spoke up.

"You guys go in. I'm going to wait out here just in case our friend, Damien, decides to drop off another one of his packages."

"Okay," Howie said, "but, if you see him, come get us. There are a few questions I'd like to ask him."

"I've got a few questions for him, myself," Mick said.

"Just be careful," Adam warned. "You may be bigger, but he looks the type that would pull a knife or something. I wouldn't trust him if I was you."

"Don't worry, I won't."

As Howie and Adam walked up to Jodelle's front door, Howie took note that the repair of the sidewalk had been finished. The pile of cement chunks was gone and rolls of sod had been laid where the lawn had been damaged during the repairs. *That was quick. I wonder what was the big rush?* A fragment of a remark flashed through his mind. It was something he thought Adam had said when the three of them were driving back from the house on Girard. "Do you remember what you said about those markings on the sidewalk over where Maureen used to live?"

"I'm not sure. Refresh my memory."

"On the way back to the office, you said something about that triangle being so scorched into the cement that it'd be impossible to remove."

"Oh, yeah. I remember, but it wasn't me who said that. It was Mick. He said that in order to remove it, they're probably going to have to tear up the..." Adam stopped and surveyed the sidewalk. The look on his face was that of someone who had just uncovered the secrets of the ancient pyramids. "Are you thinking what I think you're thinking?"

"Well, it's a possibility. If there was a triangle on the package Jodelle just received, she could've had one on her sidewalk, also. That would explain why the sidewalk was all torn up that day."

Adam nodded. "You know, now that I think about it, she appeared anxious when I asked her about it."

"If we get the chance, let's bring it up," Howie said just as they reached the door. He was about to ring the buzzer, when the door opened.

"Please, please, come in." Jodelle looked past them toward the street, her eyes darting back and forth. Once inside, Howie heard her lock the door behind them. She led them into a room with a large stone fireplace and dark oak paneling on two of the walls. The other two walls accommodated built-in floor-to-ceiling bookcases. In front of the fireplace was an oversized chocolate colored leather couch and two matching chairs. An oval-shaped, pearl-white marble table sat in front of the couch. There were two items on the table. One, a silver ashtray containing the crumpled remains of three cigarettes, and a fourth that was lit, sending faint curls of white smoke into the air. The second item was a shoebox-size package wrapped in brown wrapping paper and tied with twine.

This Angel Has No Wings

Jodelle offered them the couch while she curled up in a chair. "This was my father's study. He spent a lot of time here." She looked around the room with a hint of a smile upon her face. "My sister and I used to come in and play quietly while our father sat working at the desk over there."

Howie glanced around. He liked what he saw. A massive oak desk. Lush dark-red carpeting. Oil paintings of old-time sailing vessels. Brass lighting fixtures. Everything in the room presented a solid and secure feeling.

"Sometimes, our father would pretend that he didn't know who we were. We would cry, 'Daddy, we're your daughters!'" Jodelle paused, closing her eyes for a moment. "'Are you sure?' he would ask. 'My daughters always sit on my lap and give me a kiss on the cheek.' We would giggle and run over and sit on his lap, and kiss him until he exclaimed, 'Hooray! Hooray! You are my daughters!'"

"He sounds like a great father," Adam said.

"Thank you, he was." Jodelle looked toward the fireplace. "And during the winter months we always had the fire going. He would sit with us in front of it and read us stories. It was so nice." She reached over and picked up her cigarette. "I quit six months ago," she said, offering them a nervous smile.

"We need to talk about the package," Howie said quietly.

"I know," Jodelle replied in a tone barely above a whisper.

"Do you know who it's from?" Adam asked.

Jodelle shook her head as she brought the cigarette to her lips with trembling fingers. She avoided looking at the package. Although she seemed calmer than when she had called, Howie saw the fear in her eyes. He didn't want to press her at the moment, but he didn't believe her when she said she had no idea who could have sent the package. *She knows because she knows what those symbols mean. She would have to know that. Why else would she be so frightened? What is she trying to hide?* "Do you know when the package came?"

"No," she answered sharply. She took a puff of her cigarette before snuffing it out in the ashtray amongst the others. "It was on the front doorstep when I came home this afternoon around three-fifteen. I thought a delivery man had left it, that is, until I saw...the markings on it."

"You mean, the triangle?"

Jodelle nodded.

"You said there was a note. May I see it?"

She reached into the pocket of her sweater and handed Howie a folded piece of paper. *This is to be opened only in the presence of someone from the MAC Detective Agency.* The note had the same stylized printed letters as had been on the last two packages. Howie showed it to Adam, and then reached for the package. "We might as well open it and see what's in it." He asked Jodelle if she had something to cut the twine with. After she got up and went to her father's desk, he leaned over and whispered to Adam, "If this is another part of a cow; it's going to freak her out."

Charles Tindell

"Here you go." Jodelle handed Howie a pair of scissors. She curled back up in her chair, and watched as Howie cut the twine and unwrapped the package. Like the others, it was another shoebox. Black Oxfords. Size Nine. "Does the box or the shoe size have any significance to you?" he asked her.

She shook her head. Howie was aware that she was now intently watching as he lifted the cover. "It's some kind of knife," he announced. "It reminds me of a shiv," he said to Adam and then became aware of the puzzled expression on Jodelle's face. "When we were in junior high, kids called these things shivs. It's street lingo for a homemade knife."

"May I see it?" Adam asked.

Howie reached in and picked the knife up. As soon as Jodelle saw it, she gasped. She dug in her pocket and produced a pack of cigarettes. Her hands trembled so bad she had trouble getting one out.

"Here, let me," Adam said as he took the pack from her, and shook one out. He gave the pack back to her, and then took the knife from Howie. "Remember, how some of the kids made these things in shop?"

Although Howie nodded, he was watching Jodelle. When she wasn't puffing on the cigarette, she was chewing on her lip.

Adam continued to examine the knife. "This took some time to make," he said with a note of awe. "Look at this handle; it's so elaborately carved." He touched the blade, and then quickly drew back his thumb. "Better watch out; the blade is razor sharp."

"Why would anyone want to send you this?" Howie asked. When Jodelle didn't reply, he decided that he was done playing games with her. "If you want us to stay on the case, you've got to come clean, and start giving us some answers. Now, why was it sent and what does it mean?" When she still didn't reply, he got up. "Lets go, Adam. We're done with--"

"Wait!" Jodelle cried. She took another puff from her cigarette and then pointed to Adam. "That thing you're holding. It's called an athame."

Howie sat back down. He glanced at Adam, but his friend just shrugged. "What did you say it was?"

"An athame."

"Just exactly what is it for?"

Jodelle's eyes darted back and forth between them. She took several puffs off her cigarette.

"It's used in certain...rituals."

"You mean, satanic rituals?" Adam asked in a tone of voice filled with disdain.

Jodelle closed her eyes and took a deep breath. "Yes."

"Let's back up for a moment," Howie said. It was time to get some straight answers. "Let's go back to the time you first walked into my office." He waited until her eyes were focused on him. "There was no missing cat by the name of JoJo, was there?"

Jodelle looked at Adam and then back at Howie. "I'm sorry, but I had to tell you *something*. I needed to find my sister, but I was afraid you would ask too many questions so I made up a story."

"Why didn't you just tell us you were looking for your sister instead of leading us on?" Adam asked.

"You have to believe me when I said I was afraid that you would ask too many questions." She set her cigarette in the ashtray. "I was counting on you just tracking her down and giving me her address. When I had the address, I would have paid you and said you were done with the case."

Howie believed that Jodelle was telling the truth, but sensed that she wasn't telling the whole story. "You said that you and your sister had some kind of falling out."

"Yes, that's also true."

"So, tell us about the atha-- whatever you call that thing. What has that got to do with your sister?"

"I can't tell you that. Let me just say that she has something in her possession that puts her life in great danger."

"What are you talking about? What does she have?"

Jodelle swallowed and shook her head. "I can't tell you. I'm too afraid." She picked up her cigarette and took a quick drag. "All I can tell you is that it's a notebook."

"A notebook?" Howie and Adam exchanged glances. "What's in it that's so important?"

"I can't tell you!" Jodelle cried. Her body shuddered as if she was suddenly freezing.

Howie had more questions to ask about the notebook, but realized the woman could go off the deep end if further pressed.

"Ask her about her brother," Adam whispered.

Howie nodded and turned back to Jodelle. "Okay, for now, I won't ask you anything further about that notebook."

"Thank you. I appreciate that."

"Don't thank me too much. I'm only finished for now. If you want us to stay on the case, we're going to have to talk about it again." He didn't wait for any response as he followed up on Adam's suggestion. He was done playing Mr. Nice Detective. He'd let Adam speak to her in gentle tones. "Now, what about your brother? Why did he warn us to stay off the case?"

"Brother? I don't have a brother."

"Wait a minute." Howie tried to tone his voice down, so as not to reveal his frustration. "You mean to tell me that you don't have a brother by the name of Damien?"

"That's right."

"How do we know that you're telling us the truth?" Adam asked with obvious bewilderment in his voice.

"I swear to you I'm not lying. If you don't believe me you can ask life-long friends of our family." Jodelle eyes darted back and forth between the two of them. "I'll give you their names and numbers. You can call and talk to them. It has only been my sister and me." She paused. "What in the world makes you think I have a brother?"

Howie described how, when he and Adam left her house last time, this guy was waiting for them at their car. "He said his name was Damien and that he was a long-lost brother, like the black sheep of the family."

"The man's obviously confused. What did he look like?"

"He was about six feet and slender built. Black hair, cut short. Dark eyes." As Howie went on with the description, Jodelle's eyes grew agitated. He had believed her when she said she didn't have a brother, but there was some connection between her and Damien. "You know who he is, don't you?"

She sat unmoving as if in a trance. Howie had always been told by his father never to raise his voice to a woman, but this situation called for an exception. "Don't you?" he shouted.

Jodelle's body jerked. She blinked her eyes a couple of times and then swallowed. "Ye...yes, but he's not my brother."

Howie's throat went dry as he and Adam exchanged glances. "Well, who is he then, and what does he have to do with you and your sister?"

Jodelle stared at the barren fireplace for several moments before answering. "He's some one from the past that I thought we were done with." She shut her eyes for a moment as though trying to erase the memory. "I can't tell you, anymore. All I can do is to plead with you to find my sister. It's more important than ever, now."

"We know where your sister is," Howie said.

"You've found her?" Jodelle rested her head on the back of the chair for a moment and breathed a sigh of relief. "Thank goodness. Is she alright?"

"She appears to be."

"Where is she?"

"She's on the North Side still, living in an apartment." Howie wasn't about to give her the address quite yet. He would use it as a bargaining chip the next time she decided to withhold information. "It's off Broadway a couple of blocks."

"Oh, please, will you talk to her about returning the notebook?" Jodelle's voice was frantic. "You have to convince her it's important."

Adam leaned over and gently touched her on the arm. "Is the athame some kind of warning?" Jodelle nodded. "And does it concern your sister?" She nodded again as she reached for her pack of cigarettes and curled up even tighter in the chair.

"I think she's had enough," Adam said.

Even though Howie had more questions, he reluctantly agreed. He felt exhausted, and could only imagine what the person now curled up in the chair in a fetal position was feeling.

This Angel Has No Wings

ON THE DRIVE back from Jodelle's, Howie and Adam filled Mick in while he examined the contents of the latest package. Keeping the knife in their possession had been Jodelle's idea. When Howie had asked if they could bring the knife back to the office for a few days, her response was immediate. "Take it," she pleaded. "I don't want that thing in my house. I never want to see it again."

"So, she got pretty shook up when you started to describe Damien?"

"You can say that again." Howie glanced in the rearview mirror at Adam. "Wouldn't you agree?"

"I sure do. I don't know by what name she knew Damien by before, but she definitely knows him. When you were describing him, she looked like she just wanted to go and hide someplace."

Mick held up the knife. "What did she call this thing, again?"

"An athame," Adam said.

"And she said it was used in satanic rituals?"

"She didn't exactly bring it up herself," Howie answered. "Adam did."

"But when I did, she didn't deny it." Adam leaned forward, resting his arms on the back of the front seat. "Say, you don't suppose?"

"What?" Howie asked.

"Well, you know those other things we've got?"

Mick turned to face Adam. "You mean you think this thing was used +to do that?"

"Maybe."

Howie brought the car to a stop for a red light. He agreed with Adam. All the items they received in packages were connected in some way. *Damien's sending a message. But what?*

"Look, we've got to get going on this. If what Jodelle said is true, her sister could be in danger. I'm going over to Maureen's now. Can you guys come?"

"Sure, I can," Adam said.

"How about you?" Howie asked Mick.

"I'd really like to, but I've already taken too much time off now. I still have to work up a test for my students. And then tomorrow, it's going to be a late night at school. You guys understand, don't you?"

"Sure we do," Howie said, identifying with Mick's dedication to his work. "Don't worry about it."

Once Mick was left off at his car, Howie and Adam drove on to Maureen's. Only once did Adam remind Howie to slow down. After parking in front of her apartment building, they got out and hurried to the door. "I'm going to buzz her," Howie said as they went into the entryway.

"What if she doesn't want us to come up?"

"I'll tell her I've got a message from her sister. She'll let us in." Howie pushed the button. After several seconds, he pushed it again.

"Maybe she's not home."

Howie didn't know what kind of trouble Maureen was in, but he had a gut feeling that it was serious. He rang the manager's apartment number.

"Yeah," a voice answered gruffly.

"Hello, Mr. Meyer, this is Howie Cummins from the MAC Detective Agency. My partner and I were here the other day. Do you remember us?"

"Sure I remember." Meyer sounded like he didn't want to be disturbed. "So, what do you want?"

Howie was afraid that if he made his request over the intercom, it would be too easy for the guy to turn it down. "Could you come out and talk to us for a minute. It's important."

"Can't you come back later? I'm right in the middle of watching my favorite television program."

"Please, it's very important."

There was a long pause. "Okay, but this better not take too long; I don't want to miss the ending of my show."

Howie gave Adam a half smile as they waited. Within moments, the manager's apartment door opened.

Meyer walked up, opened the door, and invited them to step inside the hallway. "Okay, what's so important?" he asked Howie.

"It's about Maureen Hammond. We're here to see her but she's not answering her buzzer."

"So, maybe she's not home."

"Oh, she is," Howie said. "We had called and told her we were coming. She told us she'd be waiting." When Adam cleared his throat, Howie glanced at him and gave him a knowing smile before turning his attention back to the manager. "She couldn't have gone anyplace. We talked to her only fifteen minutes ago."

The manager stood there for a moment eyeing the two detectives. "What exactly do you want from me?"

"It's vitally important that we check on her," Howie said. "I wonder if you'd let us in to her apartment?"

"What!" The manager looked at Howie as if the young man was crazy. "I can't let you in. That's against the law. You ought to know that; you're a detective."

Howie gave Adam a questioning look. "Should we tell him?" As though receiving an affirmative answer, he continued. "We didn't want to share this because it's confidential, but under the circumstances we have no choice." Howie made a show of looking around as if checking to make sure they were alone. "Miss Hammond is a diabetic and we're afraid that she may have gone into a diabetic coma. Isn't that right?" he said to Adam, expecting to be back up. "Isn't that right?" he asked again when his partner hesitated.

Adam nodded.

"In fact, it's happened once before," Howie said. "If we don't raise her blood sugar level immediately, she may die." He glanced at Adam. "You brought her medication, didn't you?" Adam nodded again. "So you see, Mr. Meyer, we're not entering illegally. This is a possible medical emergency. If she's in a coma, and you don't open the door, she could die, and you could be liable."

This Angel Has No Wings

The colored drained from the manager's face. "Just a minute," he stammered. "Let me get my keys."

Howie winked at Adam as they waited for the manager to return. "Just stick with me and you'll go far."

"But I wonder what Professor Johnson would say about that?"

"Who's he?"

"He teaches ethics at school."

"Is that so?" Howie paused. "Well, just tell him that a little white lie is sometimes necessary to obtain a greater good."

"I'll bring that up in class the next time. He may just want you to come in for show and tell."

After the manager returned, they followed him up the stairs. "Are you sure this isn't illegal?" he asked while fumbling with his keys as he stood in front of Maureen's apartment door.

"We wouldn't lie to you." Howie pointed to Adam. "Just ask him. He's studying to become a minister."

The manager's eyes widened. When Meyer turned to unlock the door, Howie felt a hard tug on his sleeve. It was Adam; his lips were tightly pursed and his eyebrows knotted. Howie got the message; his partner didn't like using the fact that he was going to be a minister to back up a lie. *I guess I'll just have to inform Professor Johnson that he better keep his teaching job because he wouldn't make it as a detective.*

"Holy smokes!" the manager cried as he swung the door open. "It looks like a tornado went through here."

Howie and Adam moved from room to room while the manager stayed in the living room staring shell-shocked at overturned furniture. In the bedroom, dresser drawers were pulled out, their contents strewn about. The closet door was wide-open, clothes still on hangers lying in a pile. The blanket and sheets were ripped off the bed, and the mattress was half on the floor.

"Hey! Come in here!" Adam yelled from the bathroom.

When Howie went in, he froze in his tracks. On the bathroom mirror was scrawled a triangle with three F's inside of it; an opened lipstick tube lay on the counter.

Charles Tindell

Chapter 10

DAMIEN WAS PLEASED. Having left the city early Monday afternoon, he had gotten a head start on any traffic heading north. The five-hour drive gave him a chance to settle down. He had been furious that he didn't find the notebook at Maureen's apartment that morning. As he drove he tried to figure out what his next move should be. The answer came to him quite by accident. An hour into the trip, he noticed a billboard advertising a certain product. What caught his attention was the product's slogan: *Take It To The Next Level.* "That's it!" he yelled. "Thank you, Lucifer!" Having decided his course of action, he relaxed and looked forward to the ritual planned for later that night. He stopped and had a pleasant meal at a small town cafe along the way. It was a family-style restaurant where they served home cooking and real mashed potatoes. He lingered afterwards, sipping coffee, watching and listening to the people around him.

A family sitting at a table to the right of him talked about this being their last trip up to the cabin for the fall. At other tables, he overheard snatches of conversations - a middle-age couple discussing how they should celebrate their upcoming anniversary; a woman sharing with a friend the details of a recent operation; a family with little kids. *Ordinary people with ordinary lives. How boring.* The family with the kids had stopped to eat while on their way to spend a few days at a hotel in Duluth. The two children could barely contain their excitement about the hotel's indoor swimming pool. After Damien got up to leave, he stopped momentarily at their table.

"Sounds like you kids are going to have a lot of fun swimming," he said with a smile.

"We sure are, and we're skipping school," a little blond-haired boy piped up.

"Bobby," his mother scolded, "that's not true." With a look of embarrassment, she explained, "We got permission from their teachers."

The little boy asked Damien. "Do you want to come along?"

Damien laughed. "Maybe next time," he replied. "Tonight, I'm afraid I have other plans." As he walked away, he heard their mother comment, "Oh, what a nice young man." He just chuckled to himself.

This Angel Has No Wings

The night was clear and still pleasantly warm when Damien finally drew near to his destination three hours later. He turned off the main highway onto a gravel road, making sure he checked his mileage so he wouldn't miss the dirt driveway. After four and nine tenths miles, he began looking for his turn off. Even in the daytime, the driveway was difficult to spot because of it being nearly overgrown by weeds. It looked more like an old wagon wheel trail with two tracks separated by a growth of weeds. "Ah, there it is," he said as he checked his mileage. "Five miles exactly," he announced as he turned off the gravel road.

He was nearly a hundred yards in before his headlights reflected off the boarded-up windows of the farmhouse. Damien stopped the car for a moment. The place looked the same. The front door was still barely clinging to its hinges, and the roof still showed evidence of the chimney fire. He had first discovered the place nearly a year ago after getting lost while trying to find a country cemetery. As he drove down the gravel road, he spotted the dirt driveway leading off into the woods. Thinking it might prove interesting to see where the driveway led, he turned onto it, and soon came upon the abandoned farmhouse. He later found out that the house had belonged to a retired bachelor farmer. The old guy had apparently valued his privacy because the house could not be seen from the road. It was his quest for privacy, however, that probably contributed to his death. The local sheriff speculated that there had been a chimney fire some time during the month of January. How he came to that conclusion, nobody knew. The fire had burnt itself out before doing much damage to the rest of the house. In the spring, two kids came upon the farmhouse while looking for their lost dog. They saw the blackened roof, and even though the front door was wide opened, they were afraid to enter because of the horrible stench inside. "It smelled like a dead skunk," one of them told the sheriff. The old man's body was hardly recognizable. Animals had gotten to it. The coroner listed the death as being due to unknown causes. The only heir was a third cousin who lived down South, and had only seen the property once. It had been for sale for years, but nobody wanted it nor came near it. It was rumored that the ghost of the old farmer roamed the woods. It was the rumors surrounding the place that convinced Damien it was the ideal spot for their gatherings.

Damien drove past the house up to the barn. Letting the car idle, he got out, stretched, and then walked over and pulled open the barn doors. The creaking of the door hinges echoed in the night, sounding like someone scratching their fingernails across a chalkboard. He wasn't concerned about the noise since the nearest neighbor was nearly two miles away. After parking his car in the barn, he took his satchel containing the items he would need for later on, and started down the pathway behind the barn that led into the woods. He had no trouble keeping on the path since he had traveled it many times before, and on nights much blacker than tonight.

After moving through the shadows of the trees for nearly fifteen minutes, he came upon the clearing. He stopped, put his satchel down, and gazed into the starry sky. It was ideal weather, certainly much more to his liking than the last time the group had gathered. Two weeks ago when they had come together, it had rained. *Rained? It had been a steady downpour.* He had thought about postponing at the time, but didn't dare. The others would question his decision, and he could not appear weak before them. He was their master, and as such, if he wanted their continued allegiance, he could not show any weakness. He had stuck it out and led them through the entire ritual. Some of the others had shed their robes and stood naked as the two cowans were brought into the circle. The two, a young man and his girlfriend, had been caught up by the moment, and Damien actually saw a smile on their faces. By the time their initiation was over, however, any trace of a smile had disappeared. Damien remembered that night well. His wet robe had clung to his skin like icy fingers. The next day he woke up with a high fever and chills. He stayed in bed for the next two days. *Tonight, though, will be different.* "It will be glorious!" he shouted, as he held his outstretch arms to the stars above. He drank in the night air and then sat down next to his satchel. Glancing at his watch, he knew he would not have to wait long for the others. The others would not dare be late.

"Are all here and robed?" Damien asked as he walked up to a young man who was straightening out his garment.

"Yes, Damien."

"And did you bring the animal?"

The young man called to another person who came over carrying a wire cage. The creature inside huddled against one corner. With its ears back, it spit and hissed at Damien.

"That's good my little one," Damien said. "The more life force you have, the better it will be for us." He turned and spoke to the group who had now gathered around. "It's time to begin." He instructed them to face inward, hold each other's hands, and form a circle. At his direction, the twelve robed figures positioned themselves. They stood silently, silhouetted by the light of three campfires. It had been Damien's idea to have the fires as part of their ceremonies. The fires were strategically located so that if one connected them with lines, the resulting figure would be a triangle.

Once the group had created the circle, Damien then instructed them to widen the circle by slowly stepping backwards until their arms were extended as far as possible with only the tips of their fingers touching the fingertips of those on either side of them. "Perfect," he said as he took a leather pouch from inside his robe. Walking around the group, he poured white powder upon the ground. When he had finished, the outline of a circle was completed, and the group stepped inside. Damien was ecstatic when he measured the circle's diameter and found it to be nearly nine feet.

It was close to midnight when Damien glanced at his watch. It was time to call upon the Prince of Darkness to send his cohorts amongst their group. "I beseech you, O Great Lucifer to bless us with your presence. Do what thou wilt shall be the whole of the law." After pausing for a moment, he took from inside his robe an athame. It had taken him nearly two months to construct it. On it's handle was carved the head of the Goat. It had been difficult to carve, but he was pleased with the results. It was more elaborate than the one he had sent to Jodelle. That one had served its purpose. This one will serve its purpose even better. He held the athame with both hands high above his head.

"God and Goddess; Lord and Lady,
Father and Mother of all Life.
Here do I present my personal Tool for your approval.
From the materials of nature has it been fashioned;
Wrought into the form you now see.
I would that it henceforth may serve me
As a tool and weapon, in thy service."

Damien placed the athame on a makeshift altar in the center of the circle and then knelt before it. As he kneeled, the others did as well. When he was finished paying homage to the athame, he stood. The others, however, remained kneeling. "Before we begin, I am pleased to say that we shall celebrate Samhain this year in a way we have never celebrated it before. For the special occasion, I shall have black robes for all of you to wear and--"

"Damien, isn't black only for--"

"Silence!" Damien bellowed.

The speaker prostrated himself. "Forgive me, I--"

"Silence!" Damien screamed. The young man who had spoken had only been in the group for a month. *The fool should know better than to offer words of contrition.* Such utterances were frowned upon and seen as signs of weakness. He would have to be dealt with and Damien knew exactly how he would do it. During the ritual, each member was to sip from a goblet containing a mixture of bodily fluids and wastes that Damien had prepared. Tonight, however, this young fool would be commanded to drink the entire cup himself. He chuckled at the thought of watching him gag. "We have worn brown robes for nine years now," he said as he addressed the group. "They have served their purpose well. But now we will bring our celebration to the *next* level." In the past they had only used animals. He knew that they understood what he meant by the next level. "That is why, my brothers and sisters, we shall wear black."

Damien drank in their nervous excitement. The flames of the fire illuminated their faces, twisting them into grotesque shapes. "Let us begin."

The group responded in unison, "Let us begin this night. Damien, our Master, lead us... lead us...lead us...lead us," they chanted.

Damien raised his hands and the voices grew silent. He lifted his arms toward the stars and spoke in solemn tones. "Amen. Ever and forever glory the and power the and kingdom the is thine. For. Evil from us deliver and...."

Charles Tindell

Chapter 11

IT WAS A visitor that Mick hadn't planned on. Ten minutes after his final class ended on Monday, the door opened and Robby Davis strolled in. "My mother says I've got to talk to you or else she'll send me to a shrink." He tossed his notebook on Mick's desk. "Can we get this over with?"

Mick motioned to the chair next to his desk. "Why don't you sit down?"

"I'd rather stand," Robby snarled, looking at the ceiling and then at the floor, anywhere but at Mick.

Mick was tired and he didn't feel like having to deal with this kind of crappy attitude right now. He still had the weekend's homework assignments to read and grade, and he wanted to prepare some new material for next week's class. If he were lucky, he would be done and out of there by seven. He had neither the time nor the patience to deal with a smart-mouth kid. "Please sit down, and do it now!"

A pained expression swept across Robby's face as he eyed Mick and then plopped down on the chair with his legs sprawled out in front of him and his arms crossed. "This is about me playing with the Ouija board, ain't it?"

"That's only part of it." Mick had to consciously tell himself not to let the kid get to him. He got along with most kids, but Robby was going to be a challenge. "You're here because your grades are slipping. Your mother feels you're spending too much time reading other stuff."

"What other stuff?"

"Come on, Robby, you know darn well what I'm talking about." Mick intentionally put an edge to his voice. "Don't play around with me."

Robby shifted uneasily in his chair. "You mean the stuff about witches and Satan?"

"Yeah." Mick hoped his voice hadn't revealed his surprise. *His mother never anything about Satan. Does she even know?*

"It's just comic books." Robby's lip curled. "Didn't you read them when you were a kid, Mr. Brunner?"

Mick smiled. "Sure, I did, but it was more like Archie and Superman." When Robby rolled his eyes, Mick felt like the kid probably thought of him as somebody who lived in prehistoric times. He was trying to figure out what direction he should take in the conversation when he noticed a three-dimensional cross drawn on Robby's notebook. "That's some cross you drew," he said hoping to find something positive to connect with. "Does that--"

"That ain't what you think." Robby grabbed the notebook and turned it around so that Mick was now looking at the cover right side up.

The kid was right. It wasn't what he had thought. If it was a cross, it had been drawn upside down. "How come you drew it that way?"

"I thought we were talking about comic books?" Robby glanced around the room. The expression on his face was one of sheer indifference.

"Why do you read about witches?"

"Because they're cool."

"And in these comic books, you read about Satan, too?"

Robby smirked, but didn't reply. When Mick asked again, Robby said that he didn't want to talk about it. "My grades are down because of Mrs. Whitmore. It's her fault."

"Oh, how's that?"

"She doesn't like me because I told her that she and her stupid class was boring."

Robby had a valid point about Mrs. Whitmore, the English teacher. One evening, Mick had sat in on a talk she was giving to the Parent's Association on the importance of correct grammar in one's life. He had all he could do to keep from falling asleep. Even though he suspected bringing up Mrs. Whitmore was a ploy on Robby's part to divert the conversation, he felt he had no choice but to deal with it. And so it went. For the next twenty minutes, it was a cat-and-mouse game. The kid may be reading some weird stuff, but he was no dummy, and he was very good in holding his own in the conversation. He slipped away from Mick's every effort to engage him in a discussion about why he was so interested in witches and Satan. The only positive note came toward the end when Robby said that he would work harder on his grades. Mick wasn't sure if he had said that only to get him off his back, or if he really meant it. He wanted to believe the latter so that he would have something positive to tell Robby's mother.

"Can I go now?" Robby sighed

"Okay, but if your grades don't improve, we'll talk again. Do you understand?"

"Yeah." Robby grabbed his notebook and was out the door before Mick could say another word.

MICK LEANED back in his chair and yawned as he glanced at the clock. It was a few minutes past eight. Other than a ten-minute snack break around six, he had been working steady ever since the Davis kid left. Pleased that he had finished what he had set out to do, he straightened out the papers on his desk, placed the exams he had corrected in the right-hand drawer, and then locked it. He put the lessons he had prepared into his notebook to take home with him. Leaving the classroom, he turned off the lights and walked out into the hallway. It was the first time he had stayed so late and it seemed strange not to see students rushing back and forth. Like many of the other teachers, he loved the everyday happenings of school life; even the noisy chaos between classes. But now, with the only sound—his own footsteps echoing off the tile floor, it was too quiet and eerie. *If they ever wanted to make a scary movie, they could do it using a school building at night. Imagine walking down a dimly lit school hallway and a locker door flying open to reveal--*

"Working rather late, aren't you, Mr. Brunner?"

The voice startled Mick and he dropped his notebook. Looking in the direction the voice came from, he was relieved to see that it was the school custodian. "Hi, Sam."

"Didn't mean to scare you."

"It's my fault." Mick bent down to pick up his notebook. "I guess I wasn't expecting to see anyone. I had forgotten that you work nights."

"Yep, the graveyard shift." Sam chuckled as he leaned on his broom. "Nobody else wants it, but me. I like it."

"Doesn't it spook you being alone here at night?"

"Nope. Me and the building are friends. I know every night sound there is." Sam looked around knowingly. "You don't hear those sounds during the day because it's too noisy. Too many people around, but they're there."

Mick smiled as he looked down the hallway he had just come from. He couldn't be sure, but he thought he had heard something.

"See what I mean?" Sam said. "Just the old building stretching after a days' work." He looked down the hallway and smiled. "It's telling me it needs a rest before tomorrow morning comes."

"And I could use some myself," Mick said. "I better get going."

"Mr. Brunner, I didn't see any cars out there." Sam paused, and then, as if he felt an explanation were needed, added, "One of my jobs is to check the parking lot. If I see anything
 suspicious, I call the police."

"My car's not out there because I walked. I don't live that far away, so it doesn't take long." Mick patted his stomach. "And besides, it keeps me in shape."

"Okay, have a nice walk home. Good night."

"Good night, Sam."

As Mick stepped out into the night, he breathed in the pleasant cool air. It had been stuffy in his classroom and toward the end he had a hard time concentrating. He hoped walking the eight blocks to his house would refresh him. In the eastern sky, a half moon shined brightly. The side streets he took were mostly deserted; occasionally he came across a person walking their dog. He wondered if he and Mary should get a dog after they got married. He'd want a big dog like Lucky, the Golden Retriever that his family had when he was as a kid. He loved Lucky and, even though the dog lived to be thirteen, he was heart broken when it had to be put to sleep. *I'll have to talk to Mary about getting a dog. We'll name it Lucky 2.*

To save time, Mick decided to cut through the park. The walkway through the park wound around a playground and a baseball diamond. A large hill rose in the park's center. As a kid, he had dared his friends to go to the top of that hill and ride their bicycles down. After a double dare, they all did it. Although he was scared, he didn't want to chicken out. Halfway down the hill, the front wheel of his bicycle came off. How he walked away with only a few minor bruises and cuts, he still didn't know. Now, as he walked the pathway around that hill, he looked up toward the top but it was too dark to see anything. The trees lining the walkway cast twisted shadows across it, and leaves crunched under his footstep. He knew it was silly but he consciously quickened his pace. He had been to the park many times at night before, but always with a group of friends. He was thinking about what Sam would say about the night sounds in a park when he heard the crunching of leaves behind him. Before he could turn, a blanket was thrown over his head and body, and he felt two, maybe three people grab him.

"Hey!" Mick yelled as he struggled to break free of their grip. He felt a needle in his arm. Before he blacked out, the last image he had was of falling head over heels as the front wheel of his bicycle came off.

Charles Tindell

Chapter 12

WHEN THE PHONE rang early Tuesday morning, Howie was still in his pajamas. He was sitting at his desk and having a cup of coffee as he read the morning newspaper.

"MAC Detective Agency. Oh, hello, Mrs. Brunner. No, you didn't get me up." Mick's mother was the last person he would have guessed to be calling at that hour. "No, Mick's not here." He went to take another sip of coffee but then stopped just as the cup reached his lips. "Say that again," he said nearly spilling the black liquid. "So, he didn't come home last night?" Howie tried to speak calmly and not let his own anxieties be heard. Mick's mother sounded worried enough. "Maybe he left before you got up." He set his cup down. "You checked, huh?" *Where would the big guy be?* "Okay, maybe he stayed overnight at one of his teacher friends. He's done that before. Yeah, I know he should have let you know. Sure, I'll do some checking on him. I wouldn't worry. Yes, I'll call you if I find out anything."

As soon as he hung up, Howie called Adam. If Adam was surprised at being called at that hour, there was no indication by the tone of his voice. "Listen," Howie said, "Mick's mother just called. She went up to his room to wake him thinking that he had overslept, but he wasn't there. His bed looked as if it had never been slept in." Howie picked up his coffee and took a sip. "She's not sure what to think." He listened as Adam suggested that he could have stayed at a friends'. "Yeah, I told her that." Howie looked at the clock. "Can you come over for a few minutes before you go to school? I don't feel right about this. Okay, thanks. See you in a half hour."

Howie quickly washed and got dressed. He thought about making the bed, but it was only Tuesday. Wednesday was the bed-making day. Tuesday was for washing dishes. He walked into the kitchen, scanned the sink full of dirty dishes, shrugged, and walked out. The dishes could wait for another week. Coming back to his desk, he decided to make a couple of phone calls before Adam arrived. The first call was to Jack Higgins, another teacher who taught the same subject as Mick. Maybe Mick had stayed with him. If not, perhaps Jack knew where he was. It was a long shot, but Howie felt he

88

had to try. After the eighth ring, however, he hung up. No luck. The next call was to Mick's school. He hoped he would find Mick there. When Adam walked in a few minutes later, he had just hung up the phone.

"Any news?" Adam tried to make himself comfortable in a chair, but seemed too restless.

"No. I just got done talking with somebody at the school office. Mick's not there and he never called in sick."

"That's not like him."

"You're telling me." Howie and Adam exchanged a knowing look. Both knew that Mick was such a responsible guy that if he was going to be five minutes late for his own funeral, he would call in.

Adam shifted in the chair. "Did you try Mary?"

"I didn't want to upset her."

"I think she should be called. She has a right to know."

"Look, I thought about calling her but decided against it. She would ask questions that we don't have the answers for; and if she asked about the case and Mick's involvement, I dare not say anything."

"But don't you think Mick would want her to know?"

"I don't think so." Howie was annoyed at Adam's persistence. "Mick is always saying that he doesn't want her to worry. Well, if she doesn't know, she's not going to worry, is she? It's not like he's been missing for days." He took a sip of coffee. "Do you want a cup?" he asked, hoping that the matter would be dropped for now.

Adam shook his head. When he spoke, his tone gave evidence of his concern. "Do you think this has anything to do with the case?"

"I've a sinking feeling it does." Howie was worried about Mick. *I wonder if Damien had something to do with his disappearance.* If there was any possibility of that, and he thought it very likely, he knew just the person they should be talking to. "I think we need to talk with Jodelle Hammond. Do you have some free time this morning?"

"I got a full class schedule today, but I'll skip the afternoon sessions. I can make it back here later this morning. I'm anxious to find out what's going on with this whole thing. If you ask me, I think both Jodelle and her sister have some answering to do." Adam chewed on his lip for a moment. "Maybe we should call JD."

Howie knew that Adam would suggest that he get in touch with the police detective. He had briefly thought about doing that, but decided that they had no hard evidence to tie Damien in with Mick's disappearance. Besides, he didn't want to go running to JD for advice every time something came up. "Look, for all we know Mick stayed with one of his teacher friends last night and maybe he overslept or his car broke down." He could see that Adam wasn't buying what he was saying. "Okay, if Mick doesn't show up after we get back from Jodelle's, I'll get in touch with JD."

"And you'll let Mary know then?"

"Yeah, I'll call her right after I talk to JD."

"That makes me feel better." Adam glanced at the clock. "I really got to get going. I'll be able to be back by eleven."

"Good, we'll go see Jodelle then," Howie said. "While you're gone, I'll check with some of Mick's other friends. I'll even call the hospitals, just in case." He checked his notepad for other ideas he had written down. "If you see Professor Lewis, will you touch base with him? I'd like to know if he has any more thoughts on what you talked to him about. His expertise could prove useful to us. You might even pick up a clue as to where we can find Mick."

"I'll make sure I see him, and I'm glad you mentioned his name. I'd forgotten about him asking if he could take a look at the chalice. Can you get it for me?"

"Just a minute." Howie went into the kitchen and got the box containing the chalice out of the refrigerator. When he came back, he handed it to Adam. "I got a call last night from JD concerning the blood."

"What did he say?"

"Just what we suspected. The police lab confirmed that it's not human blood."

"Did you tell him what we thought it was?"

"Yeah."

"And?"

"He made some wisecrack remark about us youngsters sticking to drinking milk; he said that it's healthier than that red stuff." Howie declined to mention that, on a more serious note, JD also inquired if he could be of any help with the case, but backed off when told that it was being handled. Adam was right, however; if Mick didn't show up by this afternoon, he would call JD.

AFTER HIS NINE o'clock class, and before mid-morning chapel services, Adam was able to track down Professor Lewis in the cafeteria. The professor sheepishly confessed that he needed to have a cup of coffee before chapel. "I better stay awake since I'm giving the meditation this morning." He grinned, and then winked.

"I won't take too much of your time then," Adam said. "I'm just wondering if you have any more thoughts on what I talked to you about last time." He waited until a couple of students walked past them. "Also, I brought the chalice I was telling you about."

"Very good. I have to stop at my office to get some notes. We can talk along the way." When Lewis started to walk away, Adam found himself hurrying to catch up as his professor continued to talk.

Adam was surprised at the professor's quick pace. "I really appreciate you giving me this time."

"My pleasure. Besides, I'm anxious to see this chalice of yours. Of course, I won't have any time to examine it now. May I keep it for a day or two?"

This Angel Has No Wings

"Sure." Adam didn't think Howie would mind. "When I mentioned before about those three F's engraved on its base, I got the feeling you knew what they represented. Am I right about that?"

"You certainly are. You'll understand in a couple of minutes."

After they got to the office, Adam waited as Lewis set his coffee down, and then watched with curiosity as his professor reached over and got a bible from the shelf above his desk.

"Let me read something to you," Lewis said.

Adam sat down as Lewis opened the bible toward the back. He licked his finger as he turned the thin pages. "Ah, here it is. The thirteenth chapter of the Book of Revelation, verse twenty-three: 'This calls for wisdom: let him who has understanding reckon the number of the beast, for it is a human number, its number is six hundred and sixty-six.'" Professor Lewis closed the bible, and looked at Adam with a knowing smile. "Are you familiar with that verse?"

"I'm afraid not," Adam said, feeling embarrassed.

"Don't feel bad, my boy. This verse comes from a book of the Bible that few people have read, and fewer still have understood."

Adam was one of those who didn't understand it. He had attempted to read the Book of Revelation once, but it was too confusing. He had thought about taking a course on it next year, that is, if he still was at the seminary. "Professor Lewis, I...I..."

"Yes?"

"Ah, I have to admit that I don't understand the connection between what you read and those letters on the chalice," Adam said, having decided that this wasn't the right time to talk about his own issues.

"Think of the letter, F." Professor Lewis' face glowed with a radiance that reflected his love of being a teacher. "What number is it in the alphabet?"

Adam mentally counted out the letters. "It's number six."

His professor smiled, and nodded his head, making Adam feel as if he had just passed final exams. "And three F's?" Lewis asked.

"Well, that would mean three six's." As soon as he uttered the words, it dawned on him what Lewis was pointing out. "Six hundred and sixty-six!" He wished Howie were here. If he had been, he'd be excitedly writing in his notepad as he drilled Lewis with questions. "But what's the significance of that number?"

"Permit me, if you will, to give you a short course on this last book of the Bible."

Adam nodded but then glanced at the clock. He was anxious to hear what his professor had to say, but was concerned about Lewis' commitment for the chapel. "I'd like to hear about it, but do you have the time?"

"For a student willing to listen and learn, I always have time." He pointed to the clock. "I'll tell you a secret. I purposely keep that thing five minutes fast. So, don't worry about the service. I've a good fifteen minutes before I have to be there." When Lewis chuckled, his eyes twinkled with mischief, giving him the appearance of a white-haired leprechaun. "They can't start without me," he announced. He took a sip of coffee, and then cleared his throat. "The Book of Revelation is what we call Apocalyptic Literature. What that fancy name means is that it was written in code so that if it fell into the wrong hands, specifically the Roman authorities, they wouldn't know what the numbers and symbols were referring to."

"It sure was confusing to me when I tried to read it."

Professor Lewis smiled warmly. "The first couple of times I tried to read it, I got so frustrated that I was going to quit seminary." He shrugged. "But I digress; let me continue. When I mention the number, seven, what do you think of?"

Adam thought for a moment. "Lucky number seven is all I can think of."

"It is lucky in a sense," Lewis replied. "In the Scriptures, seven is thought of as being a complete number. It's a sacred number and symbolizes perfection. So when you have the number, six, it's a number that falls short of perfection. Three six's then may be interpreted as imperfection carried to its highest power. Or to put it another way, it represents ultimate evil; an entity that's completely evil. That's why the Beast is referred to by three sixes."

"So three F's on that chalice is referring to the Beast of Revelation?"

"Perhaps, but more likely it's a reference to evil or to Satan, himself." Professor Lewis' eyes flashed a note of concern as he leaned forward. "That's why I warned you to be careful. I don't know what you're dealing with and I'm not trying to pry, but whatever it is, it certainly has an evil origin."

Adam didn't know what to say. He was thinking about Mick, but felt he couldn't share what had happened with his professor at this time.

Professor Lewis leaned back in his chair. "Now, is there anything else that has occurred that's a little out of the ordinary?"

"What do you mean?" Adam realized that Lewis probably suspected more than what he was letting on.

"Have there been other signs or symbols?" Adam shook his head. "Have there been any photographs?"

"No." Adam wasn't sure what kind of pictures his professor would be alluding to.

"Have there been unsigned letters; letters that were written using what may have appeared to be symbols or ancient alphabets?" Receiving a negative response, Professor Lewis continued. "Any unusual phone calls, maybe coming around the stroke of midnight?"

At the mention of phone calls, Adam thought of the one they had received several days ago. "There was this phone call one night, but it wasn't at midnight. We thought it was some kind of a Pre-Halloween prank."

"Describe the phone call."

"I didn't take the call. My friend did, but I was there. Whoever called warned us of some woman by the name of Bea Lyle. I suppose--"

"Wait a minute! Say the name again."

"Bea Lyle."

"Say it once more, only this time say it as one name."

"Bealyle?" Adam wasn't sure was his professor was getting at, but whatever it was, he saw the intensity in his eyes. "Does this mean something to you?" he asked. "Do you know this woman?"

"One moment, please." Professor Lewis got up from his chair and went over to a bookshelf. He ran his finger across the books until it stopped at a thick one whose blue binding was fading. Removing it from the shelf, he brought it over and set it on the desk. Adam watched as he turned the pages. "Here it is." He handed the book over to Adam as he pointed to a paragraph half way down the page. "Read this."

When Adam read the words, a chill ran down his back. Whereas, before he had been concerned about Mick, now he was scared.

> *Belial - one who plots evil; is uniformly regarded as the proper name of the Prince of Evil (alias Satan); the biblical name of the Devil or one of the fiends. One of the fallen angels in Milton's Paradise Lost.*

Professor Lewis looked at the clock. "I'm afraid I need to go, but let me say this. You've sat in my lectures so you know that I don't believe in the notion of a personal devil as is popularized by cartoonists, but I do believe in the existence of evil." His eyes narrowed. "And there are individuals who, by their words and actions, personify that evil. I believe that whoever you are dealing with has such an evil presence." He closed the book. "Now, you know why I warned you to be careful."

After he left Professor Lewis' office, Adam couldn't help but worry about Mick. If his professor was right, Mick's life could be in danger.

Chapter 13

Mick's head was floating, anchored to his body only by a long white piece of string. It was such a pleasant sensation that he wanted to find Howie and Adam, and tell them about how wonderful it felt. He looked for them but couldn't see them. It was too dark. Dark? It was pitch black. He tried calling their names but no sound came forth. He wondered what would happen if the string should break. No sooner had he thought it, it happened. He began to float away like a balloon rising above the crowd at a parade. He tried to grab his head before it got too far away, but he was so tired. His arms and legs felt so heavy that he didn't think he could move them. He was right; he couldn't. His head continued to float upward. He tried to see where he was going but the black void could not be penetrated. He wondered if he was floating into space. Maybe he would become the first head to land on the moon. Wouldn't that be a riot? He looked for the moon but couldn't see it. He tried to find even the faintest of stars, but couldn't. As he floated, he became aware of a sweet fragrance. It enveloped him like a fog. At first, he enjoyed breathing the sweetness in, but it became overpowering, and he thought he would become sick to his stomach. He wished his friends were there to help him. He was wondering who could take away the sickening sweetness when he was distracted by a choir of angels singing far off in the distance. He recognized the melody but couldn't remember its name. It was so familiar, that he hummed along with it. Just as quickly as the angels had begun, they came to a muffled end. He was still humming when he heard the buzzing. Bees? He hoped not. He couldn't see them but he could hear them. There was more than one bee and they were getting closer. Now, they were flying around him.

"He's still out of it," buzzed the one bee.

"Let's make sure," replied the other.

Mick tried to swat the pesky creatures but his arms were too heavy to lift. One of the bees stung him in the arm. The bees continued to buzz but he didn't care. His whole body was floating now. The bees lifted him and flew off with him, but he still didn't care.

He was lying on a soft mattress now. The bees were gone. Am I in my bed? No, this can't be my room. It's too cramped and stuffy. The walls had closed in on him.

This Angel Has No Wings

Within moments the mattress started to move with such a gentle, soothing motion that he didn't care whether he could turn over or not.

Charles Tindell

Chapter 14

"I SHOULD'VE KNOWN it wasn't some woman's name," Howie said as he and Adam drove to Jodelle Hammond's. For the past fifteen minutes, Adam had been going over what he and Professor Lewis had talked about that morning. He had just finished telling Howie about the name, Belial.

"Don't be too hard on yourself," Adam said. "Anyone could've taken that as Bea Lyle. They're pronounced the same."

"I know, I know." Howie appreciated Adam's support, but still was angry with himself. If they were ever going to get to the bottom of this case, he would have to pay attention to every possible clue. He couldn't allow himself another mistake like that. Too much was at risk, and now with Mick missing, the stakes were much higher. Earlier, he had shared with Adam that he had spent the morning calling Mick's friends and had even contacted the area hospitals. "I struck out on all counts, though," he lamented. Jodelle was his next hope. He was expecting to get answers from her, and from those answers, some clues into what made Damien tick and what he could have done with Mick. His mind was racing, and he wanted to make sure he understood what Adam had told him. "Okay, let me get this straight. Your professor thinks we're dealing with some kind of beast from the Book of Revelation?"

"Not literally. He said that the person who sent us the chalice probably feels that he represents Satan and wants to champion his cause on earth."

"Oh, man. What a way to begin; we get hired to find some non-existent cat and end up tracking down the Devil." Howie gripped the steering wheel so tight that his knuckles began to ache.

"We're not going after the Devil, himself."

"Thanks, that's reassuring." As far as Howie was concerned, if Mick was in the hands of Damien, it was the same thing.

"What Lewis was getting at is that it's just someone who thinks he's a fallen angel."

"A fallen angel? What's that? Some angel who's lost his wings and can't fly anymore?"

Adam nodded. "Yeah, I guess that's one way to put it."

This Angel Has No Wings

"If you ask me, this angel has not only lost his wings, but also his marbles." Howie brought the car to a stop for a red light. "We're dealing with a nut case here, and I'm pretty sure who the nut is."

"Damien?"

"You got it." Howie's back muscles tighten. "From the first time we saw him, I thought he was creepy." He looked at Adam, his voice reflecting the anger boiling inside of him. "What gets me is that he acts like he can get away with all of this. He's so arrogant that he thinks he's not going to be caught."

"So you think he had something to do with Mick's disappearance?"

"You bet he did," Howie shot back. "His fingerprints are all over this case."

"Maybe we should have called JD before we left."

"No, it's better that we talk to Jodelle first about Damien. That way I'll be better able to give JD a more complete picture." Howie still hoped they could track down Mick without calling JD.

The light turned green and for the next couple of blocks, they rode in silence. Howie wondered how involved Jodelle was in this whole thing, and how much she knew about fallen angels and beasts from the Bible. And if in some way, in all of this stuff, there was a clue as to Mick's disappearance.

"I hope Mick's okay," Adam said, the worry in his voice evident.

"Mick can take care of himself." Howie felt guilty about getting his friends into such a mess. He didn't know if he could continue in the business if anything should happen to Mick. *Stop thinking like that. You just have to take this one step at a time and--* "What did you say?"

"What are you going to tell Mick's mother?"

"I'm still working on that. I know I'll have to call her some time today, but I'm going to put it off as long as I can." Howie thought about Mick's family and how close knit they are. *It's going to be tough on them.* "Once she and the rest of the family finds out that Mick's missing, I wouldn't be a bit surprised if they went to the police." He glanced over at Adam. "I don't want that to happen. Not at this point. It'd blow our case, and I don't think Mick would want that."

"Are you sure?"

"Yeah, I'm sure," Howie said, trying to sound as confident as he could.

"Do you think we'll have any luck with Jodelle?"

"I don't think she had anything to do with Mick's disappearance, but we need to get a few more answers about Damien from her."

"If we don't get anything from Jodelle, maybe we can talk to her sister."

"That would be great if we knew where she was." Howie pulled around the corner from Jodelle's house and parked. "I went over to her apartment this morning."

"What did you find out?"

"Nothing. She wasn't there. I talked with the manager. He said that she'd stopped by his apartment early that next morning."

"You mean after we were there?"

"Yeah. She told him that she'd gotten another place to live."

"What? Where?"

"She didn't tell him. All she did was go up to her apartment, pack some boxes, and leave." Howie watched a kid ride by on a bicycle; it reminded him of a much simpler time in his life. "He told me she appeared nervous, and wanted him to go up to the apartment first to make sure it was empty. Whoever ransacked the place really spooked her."

"Did she say anything to him about what was on her bathroom mirror?"

"No, but she gave him fifty bucks to clean up the place for her." Howie took a deep breath; he needed to calm down. "She apparently didn't set foot in the bathroom."

"How does he know that?"

"Because when he went in to clean after she left, he found personal items. You know, stuff like her toothbrush and comb."

"Jodelle said that Maureen had the notebook, didn't she?" Adam's eyes narrowed. "I bet whoever went through her apartment had to be looking for that. I sure would like to know what's in it that's so important."

"That goes for me, too." Howie opened the car door. "What do you say that we go and find out?"

Jodelle answered her door the second time Howie rang the buzzer. As soon as they were led into the fireside room and were seated, he told her about Mick. "I suspect Damien had something to do with it," he said.

"Oh, no!" Jodelle buried her face in her hands as Howie and Adam waited in silence. "Just a moment, please." She excused herself, and went over to her father's desk. Howie heard a drawer slide open and then close. When she came back, she was carrying a pack of cigarettes; a lit cigarette was already in her hand.

"Is there something you should be telling us now?" Howie asked; it was more of a demand than a question.

Jodelle puffed on her cigarette as she stared at the fireplace. Howie was determined to get some answers. "Do you think Damien could have anything to do with my partner's disappearance?" When it became apparent that she wasn't going to say anything, he forced the issue. "Look, if we don't get some answers from you on this, and now, we're going to the police." He hoped she wouldn't call his bluff.

"I met him years ago." Jodelle spoke softly while keeping her eyes focused on the fireplace. "He went by the name of Luke at that time. I never did find out his last name. We met at a dance. He called me up the next night and we went out."

"Are you talking about the guy we described as Damien?" Adam asked.

She nodded.

Howie took out his notepad. He didn't care if his note taking intimidated her. "Is Damien his name or is it Luke?"

This Angel Has No Wings

"I don't know what his real name is, anymore." Jodelle took a puff from her cigarette; wisps of white smoke curled toward the textured ceiling. After putting her cigarette out in the ashtray, she offered a wry smile. "I suppose I should call him, Damien, if that's what he goes by now."

"It's up to you," Howie said. "Either way, we'll know who you're talking about." He wondered how many alias the guy had, having a feeling that Damien wasn't his given name, either. JD would have a tough time finding out anything on this guy unless he has a previous record.

"I think I'll call him, Damien," Jodelle said with a note of sarcasm. It'll make it easier for all of us." She paused. "The name, Luke, never seemed to fit him, anyway."

"Tell us what happened after you started dating." Howie tried to imagine someone like Jodelle going out with a creep like Damien.

"After a couple of months, I really fell for him. He was considerate and kind. We were so alike in our views of life. We both loved the outdoors and nature." Jodelle crossed her legs. "At least, he said he did. He told me that we were soul mates. I believed him, and then..." Howie and Adam waited until she lit another cigarette. "He wanted me to meet some friends of his, whom he said, shared a reverence for the natural world as much as he and I did."

"Was this some kind of a religious group?" Adam asked.

Jodelle nodded. "You're quite insightful. It was, but not in the traditional sense. Father always taught us to be open-minded and not to be afraid to experience new things." She flicked her cigarettes ashes into the ashtray. "The people were so accepting of me the first time I met them, and we shared many ideas in common."

"What kind of ideas?" Howie asked.

"That there's a powerful energy force that is spread throughout the natural world." She looked at them for a moment, her eyes asking if she should continue.

"Go on," Howie urged.

"There was also the belief that both animate and inanimate objects possess a spirit and this spirit forms part of the whole. That one is able to tap into this energy through certain rituals." She paused. "As I said, it tied in very well with my love of nature."

"Is there a belief in any kind of deity involved with this?"

"Yes," Jodelle answered. Howie looked at Adam and nodded his approval. His partner was more an expert in religious matters than himself. "Members of the group were unified by their belief in a dual divinity."

"Two gods?" Howie asked.

Jodelle nodded. "A god and a goddess."

Howie didn't consider himself overly religious, but thought he knew most of the religions because of the discussions he's had with Adam. He couldn't recall, however, any religion that had both a male and a female for gods. "Is there a name for this group?"

Jodelle shifted in her chair as she picked a piece of tobacco from her tongue. "Members call themselves Wiccans. They practice a religion called Wicca."

Howie jotted both names in his notepad. As he looked up, he noticed Jodelle's foot tapping rapidly on the rug. He kept his voice calm. "How did Damien fit into these Wiccans? Was he one of them?"

At the mention of Damien, Jodelle shuddered. "He was the leader of the coven."

"The what?"

"Coven. It's a name that Wiccans use to refer to the group of which they're a member."

"I've heard of that term before," Adam said. "Aren't covens made up of people who practice witchcraft?"

"Witches!" Howie exclaimed. "Are you telling us that this guy, Damien, runs a club for witches?"

"It's not what you think," Jodelle said. "There are various kinds of covens. Most are made up of ordinary people who are simply seeking a deeper religious experience than what they find in traditional churches."

"If that's true, how did some one like Damien get to be their leader?" Howie asked. "He's not exactly your typical altar boy."

"He deceived them like he deceived me," Jodelle answered, her words coated with bitterness. "After I joined, he began to make changes. There were many in the group who didn't like what he was doing."

"Why didn't they kick him out?"

"Because he did have some supporters, and those who were not, were afraid of him. He warned them that he was in touch with other spirits that gave him power." She smiled but it was contemptuous. "He dared them to challenge these spirits."

Adam's eyes narrowed. "Did they?"

"No, he was too intimidating, and so sure of himself, that no one ever challenged him. As people left, he brought in others who were more in agreement with his way of thinking and doing things."

Howie continued to jot down notes. There had to be something in this that would provide a clue as to where Damien might have taken Mick. "What kind of changes did he make?"

"He said he had a vision one night. After that, he started to talk more about Satan." Jodelle rubbed her arms as though chilled. "And then we began doing rituals involving the worship of Satan."

"And you were part of it?"

Jodelle rested her head on the back of the chair and shut her eyes. "Yes, he made me do it." She took a couple of deep breaths. "It was so horrible. It's a part of me that I want to forget. I have nightmares about it all the time."

"Why didn't you just get out?"

"I tried," she said, looking at Howie with pleading eyes. "Don't you understand that I couldn't? He wouldn't let me." She curled up in her chair and began sobbing.

Howie glanced over at Adam. The agony in her voice had unnerved Adam as much as it had himself. He let her be for a few moments. "I know this is painful for you, but I just have one more question. How does Maureen fit into all of this?"

As soon as her sister's name was mentioned, Jodelle looked up at Howie. "She has a notebook that Damien wants back."

"Did she take it from him?" Adam asked.

"No, I did."

Howie's head ached. His brain was on overload as he realized that blackmail now could be added to the growing list of things that were mixed in with this crazy case. "Let me understand this," he said. "If Damien gets the notebook back, he's promised to leave you alone? Is that it?"

Jodelle wiped her eyes with a tissue she had gotten from her pocket. "Yes, that's what he said."

"And you believe him?"

"I have no choice."

"What's in this notebook?"

"I don't know. He showed it to me a couple of times, but I couldn't make any sense out of it." As Jodelle talked, she kept glancing back and forth between the two detectives. "It's written in some kind of language I never saw before. All I know is that he referred to it as *The Book of Shadows*."

ON THE RIDE back to the office, Howie and Adam decided that they would call Mick's mother after calling JD and Mary. Howie wanted to reassure her that he had already talked to the police. Deep down, he secretly hoped that Mick would be sitting in the office waiting for them.

After Howie parked the car, Adam nudged him and pointed to a little boy standing in front of the entrance door to Howie's apartment. "Isn't that the kid who was up in your office a few days ago?"

"It sure is."

"What was his name again?"

"Joey, and he's probably here to check to see if I found his cat."

"What are you going to tell him?"

"I've got to tell him the truth. What else can I do?"

"Good luck." Adam glanced at Joey. "The kid looks like a lost soul standing there, and you're going to tell him that his cat is still missing. I don't envy you."

As soon as Howie and Adam got out of the car, Joey waved at them. He stepped to the curbing and was about to cross the street when Howie shouted for him to stay where he was. They waited for a car to drive by, and then walked over to him.

"Hi, Joey. Are you waiting to see me?" As Joey nodded, Howie noticed that his lower lip began to quiver. "Why don't you come up and we'll talk in the office." He would give the kid a few minutes of his time and then quickly send him on his way; he had more pressing matters at hand.

Joey glanced suspiciously at Adam and then looked at Howie.

"He's okay. He works with me."

"Hi, there. My name is Adam."

"My name's, Joey," he replied, nearly in a whisper. "I have a cat named, Midnight."

Howie winced.

Adam opened the door and they walked up the flight of stairs to the office. Once inside, Joey and Adam sat on the leather chairs while Howie made himself comfortable in his chair behind his desk. "Joey, I haven't found Midnight yet. Is that why you're here?" Joey shook his head, and his lip began to quiver again. "What's wrong?" Howie had a sinking feeling that Midnight might have been the victim of road kill.

Joey looked over at Adam and then back at Howie. He sniffed a couple of times. "The other kids at school don't believe me," he whimpered.

Howie was confused but relieved that Midnight apparently still retained one of his nine lives. "You mean they don't believe that your cat's missing?"

Joey shook his head. "About you."

"About me? What do you mean?"

"They don't believe I hired a detective."

"They don't, huh? Well, what do you expect from a bunch of rug rats!" Joey looked at him with a puzzled expression. "Rug rats is detective talk for kids that don't believe," Howie explained. "Isn't that right?" he said to Adam.

"He's right, Joey."

If that was Joey's problem, Howie figured that he must have come to have him write a note to his class, or maybe call his teacher as proof that he had hired a detective. "What do you want me to do?"

"You'll help me?"

"Of course."

"Promise?" Joey scooted to the edge of his seat. "Cross your heart?"

"Yeah, Joey, cross my heart." Howie reached into his drawer to get a sheet of paper. He would write something that would wow Joey's skeptical classmates. "Okay, just tell me what--"

"Next week is show and tell," Joey said, his eyes revealing a sparkle of excitement.

"Show and what?" Howie hoped he had heard wrong. "What are you asking, Joey?"

Adam cleared his throat. "I think Joey wants you to go to his school and tell the rest of the students that he hired you as his personal detective." He winked at the brown-eyed little boy whose quivering lips had been transformed into a bright smile. "Isn't that right?"

Joey nodded vigorously, rocking back and forth so much that he looked liked he would fall off his chair.

"Okay, Joey, I'll come, but I'll have to call you early next week about it. I'm pretty busy right now and I need--"

The office door opened and Kass came rushing in. "Oh, sorry, I didn't know you were with a client." As soon as Joey heard the word client, he sat up straighter in his chair and stuck out his chest. "Hello, Joey."

"Hi, Mr. Kass."

Kass walked up to the desk, smiled at Adam, and then turned to Howie. "I've got something for you."

As soon as Kass placed the white envelope on his desk, Howie's body tensed up. On the envelope, drawn in red crayon, was a triangle with three F's inside of it. "It was delivered to the drugstore about an hour ago," Kass said.

When Adam leaned over and saw what was on the envelope, he shot a worried glance toward Howie.

"I came up as soon as I got it, but you weren't here. I've been coming up every fifteen minutes."

"Who delivered it?" Adam asked.

"I don't know. Gretchen took it at the cash register while I was with some customers. She told me that it was a man in a dark suit, medium height."

"Did she notice anything else about the guy?"

"No...oh, wait a minute." Kass put his hand on his cheek for a moment and then shook his finger in the air. "Now, I remember. She said that when he handed her the envelope, she noticed that part of his forefinger was missing."

Howie got out his notepad. "Which hand?"

"I think she said it was his right. He gave it to her and said it was for the MAC Detective Agency, and then he left without saying another word."

"Thanks." Howie took the letter.

"Well, I better go and leave you to your detective work."

"Kass, why don't you take Joey and fix him a banana split. Put it on my tab." Howie was anxious to open the envelope. He was positive it had something to do with Mick. "Joey, I'll call you to find out what day and time to come to your school, okay?" Howie smiled. "I promise I will. Cross my heart."

"Okay." Joey hopped off his chair. As they left, Adam and Howie could hear Joey excitedly telling Kass that Howie was going to come to his school for show and tell.

Adam leaned forward. "What does it say?" he asked as Howie tore open the envelope.

"My dear detectives, Howie and Adam. Are you missing your friend? I suppose you are. Don't worry. You can have him back. We're done with him." Howie had to pause to get himself under control. All he could think about was getting his hands around Damien's neck. "Just look for the angel, for the angel cannot look for you."

Charles Tindell

"What do they mean that they're done with him?" Adam asked. "You don't think they..." his voice trailed off, but Howie knew what was going through his mind.

"They better not have done anything to him." Howie's gut felt like it was being tied in knots.

"What do you think that bit about the angel means?"

Howie stood up. He was ready to go. "I don't know, but he drew a map. By the looks of this thing, we'll find Mick somewhere south of the Cities."

"Anybody sign it?"

"No name but it's signed with a D. Guess who that is."

"Don't you think you should contact JD?"

"We don't have time for that now," Howie said as he headed toward the door, not giving Adam any time to disagree.

MICK STRUGGLED to open his eyes; his eyelids felt like window shades that didn't want to cooperate. When his eyes opened, it didn't matter. He still couldn't see anything. *Why is it so dark? Why doesn't mom come in and turn on the lights? She knows I have to get up and meet my friends at the corner. I told her that the three of us had made a pack. After all, this is our senior year. Mom, don't you remember that I told you we had agreed to walk to school together every day. Where is she? Mom, come in here.*

Muffled noises outside his room drifted into Mick's consciousness. *That must be Mom. She can call my friends and tell them I'm too tired to go to school today. Oh, Mom, my head feels like it's floating. Maybe I have the flu.* Beads of perspiration trickled down his forehead. *Why doesn't she come? Mom, I can't breath! It's so stuffy in here. If I could only get to a window.* He tried to get up but his body wouldn't budge. *When Mom comes in, I'll ask her to open the windows. Oh, my head. My brain feels like it's on a merry-go-round. I got to have some air. I wond-- Is that the door? Is that you, Mom? Turn on the light, will you? And open some windows.* He heard locks being snapped open. *Good, she's going to open-- Hey, what's going on?* Instead of the anticipated fresh air, his bed began moving like it was on roller skates. The rumbling echoed off the walls inside his room. He felt like he was inside a tank. *What are you doing, Mom? Where are you taking me?* The rumbling stopped and Mick felt his bed lifted and then set down. He lay silently in the dark, struggling to breath. *Mom, you got to open a window. It's too suffocating in here. I'm so tired. I... can't... keep my...*

MICK SLOWLY BECAME aware that the air he was breathing was fresh. It was cool and invigorating, and his whole being could not get enough of it. As he lay there, he thought he heard voices. He tried to speak, but his lips felt like they were glued shut. *Where am I?* Without warning, he felt himself being lifted. *What's happening? Who's carrying me? Am I hurt?* He opened his eyes but it was still too dark. *What's happened to me? Oh, yes, I remember now. The front wheel came off my bicycle and I wiped out. We're at the park, aren't we?*

This Angel Has No Wings

Howie and Adam must have come to help. Guys, take me home to Mom. She'll fix me up. Hurry up, will you, my head feels like it's going to float away again. Hey, Howie, did I tell you how I dreamt about my head being the first one on the moon? Isn't that funny? How come you're not-- Ouch! What did you guys drop me for? What's the matter, was I too heavy for you? He felt as if his head was spinning one way as his brain spun in the opposite direction. *Where am I? In bed again? Well, this mattress is too hard, guys. Where's Mom? She'll know what to do.* He felt himself being propped up against the headboard. *Mom, what are you going to do? What are you doing to my shirt? Careful, you're ripping it. Why isn't anyone turning on the lights? I want to see what's going on. Oh, I can guess what you're going to do, Mom. You're going to fix me up, aren't you? Hey, guys, did I tell you that whenever I'm sick or hurt, she rubs my chest with some thick, gooney stuff? I hate the stuff. It smells. Ouch, that stings. Mom, don't, that really stings. I'm not lying. Mom, stop! Mom!*

Charles Tindell

Chapter 15

AFTER READING THE note Kass delivered, Howie and Adam wasted no time. They rushed down the stairs, ran across the street to Howie's car, jumped in, and sped off.

"Watch it!" Adam yelled as Howie turned a corner, tires squealing, causing an older woman to drop her shopping bag as she hopped back on the curb.

Howie glanced in the rearview mirror. The frightened woman appeared to be okay, but the contents of her bag lay scattered in the street. He glanced over at Adam. "Don't worry; she's not hurt," he said and then explained, "Sorry, but we've got to get there fast. Mick needs our help.

"Okay, but it's not going to do him much good if we get pulled over by a cop."

"I know, but--"

"Look, I want to find him as much as you do, but let's not do anything foolish." Adam's tone softened. "I know we can't afford any delays, but let's not shoot ourselves in the foot."

Howie hated the thought of Mick being in the hands of some one like Damien, but Adam was right. Besides, he didn't relish the thought of wasting valuable time trying to explain to a cop why he was driving so fast. Delays could be costly. They, however, were delayed when they got stuck in a traffic tie-up on the freeway. A half hour later, having only traveled three-tenths of a mile, they finally came upon the cause - a three-car accident involving injuries. As they drove by the scene, Adam pointed to a young man lying on a stretcher by the side of the road. The man attended to by paramedics, appeared unconscious. Howie and Adam glanced at each other, and though neither said a word, both knew *who* the other had on his mind. Once Howie had driven a couple of miles past the accident, he stepped on the gas. "Nobody's around to stop us for speeding, now," he said. "All the cops are back there." He didn't get any argument from Adam, and it wouldn't have done any good if he had.

Forty-five minutes later, they turned off the freeway onto a paved two-lane country road. Howie pulled the car over on the shoulder, letting the engine idle.

This Angel Has No Wings

"What are you stopping for?" Adam asked.

"I just want to make sure we're on the right road." Howie looked back toward the freeway; he wanted to be positive that they had taken the right turn. For Mick's sake, they couldn't afford to make a mistake now. "Check the map again, will you?"

"As near as I can figure out, this is the road." Adam pointed to the map. "See, there's the Texaco Station we just passed. According to this, we're to take the first turn after that."

Satisfied, Howie put the car in drive and took off. Every couple of miles, they would pass a farmhouse. Occasionally, they met an oncoming car. The driver of the last one had shaken his fist at them. "Probably some farmer who thinks that us city slickers ought to slow down," Howie said.

"That's not such a bad idea." Adam looked at the map again. "This thing doesn't show any mileage between points, and we've got another turn off coming up." He turned and glanced in the direction from which they had come. "We don't want to speed past it."

Howie didn't want to slow down, and as far as he was concerned, he didn't need to. *I don't see any cops out here.* "What's the name of the road we turn on?"

"It doesn't give a name. It just shows a crossroads."

"How far do you think it is?"

"Your guess is as good as mine, but like I told you, I think you better slow down so we don't miss it."

"Don't worry, we won't," Howie said. Adam was being cautious, but this was a time to throw caution out the window. Mick was in trouble, and he felt responsible. For several moments he second-guessed himself as to whether he should have called JD. He, however, quickly shook the feeling off and concentrated on the road ahead. "Just tell me which way we turn when we come to it."

"We turn left, and then it looks like we take the first road to the right." Adam scanned the countryside. "I wish we had some landmarks to go by."

Howie looked toward the sun hanging low in the western horizon. "We better find him soon. It's going to be getting dark."

THE CHIRPING OF birds was the first sound that filtered into Mick's awakening consciousness; the second was the smell of freshly mowed grass. Both of these were quickly displaced by a stinging, burning sensation on his chest; all the nerve endings felt like they had been rubbed raw and then hot embers scattered over them. His slightest movement caused the fabric of his shirt to rub across his chest, and every time it did, his nerve endings screamed as though they were being scraped by jagged pieces of broken glass.

Mick was in a sitting position, propped up against something. *A tree? No. A rock? Maybe.* Whatever it was, he was thankful he could rest his throbbing head. His eyes flickered open, but there was only darkness. At first, he thought it was night. *Something's covering my head.* He tried to shake off whatever it was, but couldn't; it was too securely tied at the base of his neck, making him feel as if it was a noose. *Where am I? The park?* He vaguely recalled that a blanket or something had been thrown over his head. Arms had wrapped him and threw him to the ground. If someone were to ask him when that occurred, he wouldn't have been able to answer. As far as he was aware, it could have happened just minutes ago, or for that matter, hours, even days ago. He tried to lift his right arm to his chest, but couldn't. When he moaned, it came from deep within him. Something had a grip on his wrist. It was the same when he tried to move his other arm. His arms were stretched behind him so tightly that his shoulders felt as though they were being pulled from their sockets. He closed his eyes and tried to concentrate on the chirping of the birds.

Howie slammed the car to a skidding stop. They had come upon the crossroads, but he wanted to make sure. When Adam said that it had to be it, Howie wheeled left onto the gravel road. He had to slow down when the pinging of the rocks hitting the undercarriage sounded as if they were going to come through the floorboard. Ten minutes later, he and Adam had stopped, and were looking down a dirt road leading off to the right. The road gradually inclined until it disappeared over a rise. "Are you sure this is the turn?"

Adam looked at the map again. "It has to be."

"Let's go then." Howie hoped they would find Mick soon. They had to. The sun had set and twilight was rapidly fading. The thought of trying to find Mick at night unnerved him. "How in the world are we going to find him?"

"Maybe he'll see our headlights."

"Let's hope so." Howie scanned both sides of the road as he drove. There was nothing but open fields and trees. No buildings of any sort. "We're supposed to be looking for some kind of angel now, right?"

"That's right. The note said that we're to look for the angel because the angel cannot look for us." Adam reread the note and then put it in his shirt pocket. "Don't ask me what that means, though."

They drove up and over the rise and then drove for another fifteen minutes without seeing anything but trees and open countryside. Darkness had fallen, and Howie expressed concern that with only the headlights, they couldn't see very far on either side of the road. "We could pass him by without knowing it."

"We just have to hope we can spot something from the road," Adam said.

Howie slowed the car to less than twenty. He felt caught between going too fast and missing something, and yet, going so slow that it would take forever. *How long of a stretch of road is this, and where does it lead to?*

"How far have we gone?" Adam asked.

This Angel Has No Wings

"Nearly twelve miles." Howie was worried. *What if this was all a game, and Mick was someplace else?* Damien was the type of person who would get perverse enjoyment from steering them wrong.

Adam leaned forward. "There's something up ahead."

"What is that?"

"It looks like a cemetery."

"A cemetery? What's that doing out here in the middle of nowhere?" Howie's hopes rose. Where there was a cemetery, there had to be a church, and where there's a church, there's has to be an angel. He had been in churches in the cities where there were scenes of angels painted behind the altar area. A couple of the churches even had statues of angels. He stepped on the gas. *The church can't be too far away.*

"Stop!" Adam yelled after they had driven past the cemetery.

Howie slammed on the brakes. The car slid to a stop in a cloud of dust. "What's wrong?"

"I just thought of something. That cemetery might be what we're looking for."

"What are you talking about? We're supposed to be looking for an angel." Howie put the car in drive. "I figure there's got to be a church up ahead."

Adam grabbed the steering wheel. "Wait! Think about it! What do you find in cemeteries?"

"Dead people," Howie replied, not trying to be funny.

"I know, but what else?"

"What do you mean, what else?" Howie looked back at the cemetery. "Tombstones?"

"Exactly. And besides tombstones, cemeteries also have monuments and statues." Adam's voice flowed with nervous energy. "There may be a statue of an angel in there."

Howie whipped the car around and drove up to the entrance. A large half-moon-shaped sign hung over the twin iron rod gates: *Our Lady of Mercy's Garden of Peace*. "It's a pretty good size place for being out here in the sticks," Howie said.

"Look over there." Adam pointed to the right corner of the cemetery. Partially illuminated by the car's headlights stood a monument that reached nearly as high as the iron rod fence.

"I see it. Do you think that's an angel?"

"I can't tell from here." Adam rolled down the window. "Hey, I think I see another one."

"Where?"

"About twenty yards behind and to the left of that first one. See it? It's in the middle there. I can barely make it out."

Howie looked but couldn't tell what the dark shape was; it could have been anything. "I'm convinced. Let's go and see if we can find the angel."

"Have you got a flashlight?" Adam asked as they got out.

"It's in the trunk. Hang on; I'll get it." Howie got the flashlight and then rejoined his partner at the front of the car.

"What's wrong with that thing?" Adam whispered. "It's not giving off much light."

"I haven't used it for a long time." Howie whacked the flashlight against his palm a couple of times. "It probably needs new batteries." He anticipated Adam's next question. "And I don't have any spares."

"How about if we turn the headlights on?"

"I thought about doing that, but with my old clunker here, it wouldn't be advisable. We'd be stuck out here if the battery went." Howie looked around; he never realized the countryside could be so spooky. "I don't think we want to get stuck out here with a dead battery."

When they got to the gate, Howie held the flashlight as Adam lifted the latch and swung the gate open. "The hinges could use some oil," Adam whispered. Once inside, they found themselves on a one-lane gravel roadway that branched off in two directions. The roadway appeared as though it encircled the cemetery.

"What do you say we yell out his name and see if he answers?" Adam said.

"That's a good idea. Go ahead."

"Mick!" Adam yelled. "Can you hear us?" The two of them waited, listening. "Maybe this isn't the place."

"Let me try." Howie took a deep breath. "Mick! It's Howie! If you can hear us, call out." Howie was afraid to breathe, lest the sound of it prevented him from hearing if Mick answered. The chirping of crickets and the rustling of the wind moving through the trees were the only sounds they heard.

"What do you think we should do?" Adam asked.

"I don't know." Howie looked toward the car. There had to be a church up the road. If they took time to search the place and Mick wasn't here, they would have wasted a lot of time for nothing. *But if he was here...* "As long as we're here, we better check it out." He turned on the flashlight. "Do you want to split up?" he asked.

"Only if you let me have the flashlight."

"Sorry," Howie said, "dumb question." He thought about taking the pathway to the left, and circling the cemetery, but decided that it would be better to cut straight through the middle. It meant walking amongst the tombstones, but they had no other choice. The beam from his flashlight didn't reach very far, and if they stayed on the road, they wouldn't have enough light to see anything in the middle of the cemetery. Besides, there were large trees lining the edge of the pathway and scattered throughout the grounds, and he didn't want to take the chance of one obstructing their line of vision. He pointed the flashlight in the direction of the first statue that Adam had seen. As they moved toward it, they tried to avoid stepping on graves, but found being so careful took too much time.

This Angel Has No Wings

"That's not an angel, is it?" Howie asked as they approached the statue; it's face and body illuminated by the flashlight.

"I don't think so. I think it's the Virgin Mary."

They made their way toward the center of the cemetery, stopping to check out several monuments. Howie looked at his watch. They had been there nearly twenty minutes. He was about to call it quits when Adam nudged him.

"Shine your flashlight over there."

Twenty feet ahead of them stood a statue; its back was facing them. What caught their attention was that it appeared to have wings.

"That might be our angel," Adam said.

They ran toward the angel, looking for their partner on the way. When they reached the statue, Howie shined the light on its body. "Those are wings alright, but I don't see Mick around, do you?" He considered the possibility that Mick could still be back in Minneapolis and that Damien was playing games with them. The very thought of Damien being someplace else and smirking at sending them on a wild-goose chase made him furious.

"Shine the light on the face," Adam said. "Something's not right."

"What the..." A chill crept down Howie's spine. "The eyes. What--"

"Shhh," Adam said. "Did you hear that?"

"Hear what?"

"Listen."

The moaning came from behind them. "Shine your light over there," Adam urged. Twenty feet away was a body propped up against a tombstone.

"Mick!" Howie yelled as he and Adam ran to their partner. Howie untied the rope from around Mick's neck and removed the black hood. "Mick, are you okay?"

"Help me untie him," Adam said. A rope had been tied to one wrist, wrapped behind the tombstone, and then tied to Mick's other wrist. His arms had been pulled back so far that Howie was afraid that they had been yanked out of their sockets. Howie swore under his breath as he struggled to untie the knots. Adam got his untied first, allowing Howie to move Mick's arm forward.

Howie winced at the sound of his friend's moaning. "Take it easy, Mick."

"Can you hear us?" Adam asked, his voice shaking with emotion.

Mick's eyes flickered opened. He had trouble focusing in on the voices.

"Mick, it's me, Howie. Adam's here, too." Although Mick gave no reply, a hint of a smile formed on his lips.

Adam touched Howie on the arm.

"What?"

He pointed to Mick's shirt. "Did you see that?" he whispered.

Howie grimaced when he saw the pencil thin dark stains. "Mick, I'm going to open your shirt, okay?" He handed Adam the flashlight, and then slowly and gently peeled the shirt open while Mick moaned through gritted teeth.

"Oh, no!" Adam cried. "Who could have done--"

"Let's get him out of here," Howie said. "Mick, we're going to get you up and take you home. Okay?"

Adam and Howie helped Mick to his feet, telling him to lean on them. As they struggled to get him back to the car, they walked past the angel. Howie glanced at the angel's face, and wondered if Damien had chiseled her eyes out so she couldn't witness who had carved the three F's on his partner's chest.

This Angel Has No Wings

Chapter 16

HOWIE AND ADAM placed Mick in the back seat for the return trip to the city. They decided that they would take him to Howie's, clean him up, and then determine whether he should see a doctor. From what they could tell, whoever had cut him had used something like a razor. The cuts were paper-thin. Whoever did it knew what they were doing, and had made the incisions with the finesse of a surgeon. The three-inch letters had been cut just deep enough to draw a small amount of blood. Blood had coagulated on the puckered reddish-pink skin around the cuts, effectively accentuating each of the letters. While obviously disturbing, the cuts didn't appear as serious as they first thought.

Although Howie was anxious to get back to the cities, he kept within the speed limit. He didn't want to take any chances being pulled over by a cop. Not now. It would be too difficult to explain why they had a person in the back seat with three F's finely cut upon his chest.

For the first forty-five minutes, Howie and Adam drove in silence, listening to the groans coming from the back seat. Every now and then, they glanced at each other and winced. By the time they reached the outskirts of Minneapolis, however, Mick was fully conscious and though groggy, was able to speak. Whatever Damien had drugged him with was wearing off. With some effort, he even managed to sit up. They had given him a bottle of pop when he complained his throat was parched.

"How're you feeling?" Adam asked after Mick finished taking a couple of sips.

"My chest feels like someone used it for a cutting board." Mick's voice was weak, and he paused every two or three words, taking a hard breath in-between. "It's like I've got one gigantic paper cut, and that baby really stings."

Howie glanced over at Adam. Mick was aware that he had been cut, but they hadn't said anything to him about what had been carved on his chest. Howie knew he had to be told and figured it was as good of a time as any to tell him.

"Say, Mick?"

"Yeah?"

"Your chest..." Howie swallowed hard. He didn't know how to say it except straight out. "Someone carved some letters on it."

"What!" Mick cried.

"Remember those letters we saw in the triangle on the sidewalk over at Maureen's?" Howie looked in the rearview mirror. Mick had turned on the flashlight and was examining his chest. "Well, somebody decided they'd look good on you too, except they didn't use a black marker."

"My God...why?"

"We'll find out whoever did it," Adam said in a tone that was controlled and tight.

"We'll find them, alright." Howie gripped the steering wheel so tightly that his knuckles turned white. *Nobody's going to do this to one of my partners and get away with it.* When he spoke again, it was through gritted teeth. "And when we do find them, we'll ask them real, polite-like, why they did it." *And then we'll punch their lights out.*

"I just wish I could remember what happened," Mick said.

Howie had no doubt that Damien was involved, and hoped that Mick had caught a look at his abductors. Without solid evidence, however, they would have a hard time connecting this to Damien. Knowing JD, he would need evidence. "Do you feel up to talking about it?"

"Sure, but I don't remember too much." There was a long pause. When the flashlight went on, Howie looked in the mirror. Mick was examining his chest again. "Do you think this will leave scars?"

"I don't know, but it's going to be pretty raw for awhile." Howie felt more than anger; he felt rage. If Mick was feeling those emotions, he wasn't showing it. That was Mick, though. Howie had always been amazed at how easygoing his friend was. He couldn't remember the last time he had seen Mick angry, even when he had good reason to be. "We'll clean off the blood when we get to my place."

"We should bring him to a doctor just to make sure," Adam said.

Howie nodded. "Yeah, I think--"

"No!" Mick cried.

"But--"

"Okay, whatever you say." Howie remembered the time back in high school when Mick once played an entire football game with a broken wrist. Only after the game, did he tell the coach that he was having some problems with his wrist.

"Everything's so hazy," Mick said. "It happened so fast." There was a pause and Howie figured that Mick was trying to reconstruct what had happened to him. "I was walking through the park and somebody jumped me...I sure remember that."

"Do you know how many there were?" Adam asked.

"No, but it was more than one. At least two, probably three. I struggled, but then I felt this sharp pain in my arm."

Howie shot a glance back at Mick. "What do you think that was?"

"I don't know. It could've been a needle. At least, that's what it felt like." Howie and Adam waited as their friend took a deep breath before continuing. "After that, everything got woozy. And it stayed that way for...hey, what day is it?"

"Tuesday," Howie said.

"Tuesday? That means all of this happened only in the past twenty-four hours?"

"That's right. Do you have any idea where you spent the night?"

"Not really."

"Do you remember anything about last night?" Howie recalled JD telling him that senses other than sight also gave important clues. "Did you remember hearing any sounds? Or smelling any odors?"

"I don't know. Let me think." They rode in silence while waiting for Mick's reply. "I vaguely remember something. I had this weird dream about angels singing, and there were bees. I think they were bees. They were talking about something."

Adam turned toward the back. "Do you recall what they were saying?"

"No. Maybe they were just buzzing and I thought they were talking."

"How about odors?" Howie asked. "Do you remember any?"

"Yeah, there was some kind of sweet smell. It seemed overpowering the more I smelled it. Like I could get sick from too much of it."

"You mean, like cheap perfume?" Adam asked.

"Something like that. Then I was in my bed and I couldn't breath. My mother had torn open my shirt and..."

Howie glanced in the mirror. "What's the matter?"

"That's when it happened, didn't it?" Howie could see Mick looking down at his chest. "I remember screaming at my mother that the stuff she was putting on my chest was hurting." He grew silent for a moment. "Only it wasn't my mother, was it?"

"By any chance, did you catch a glimpse of any faces?"

"No, I must've had that hood over my head all the time." Mick's speech grew groggier and he began stumbling over his words. "That's why in those dreams it was always pitch-black, and I wanted someone to turn on the lights."

Howie wanted to get back to the odor Mick had smelled. *Maybe it could've been the cologne of one of the guys that kidnapped him.* "Did the sweet smell come before or after you dreamt about your mother?"

"I don't know." Mick sounded tired. "I'm sorry, but everything's running together. I guess I'm still a little woozy."

"That's okay, don't worry." Howie knew they were pushing Mick with all the questions. "We'll talk more about it when you've had a good night's sleep."

EVEN THOUGH IT was late when they got back to Howie's, it was decided that Mick's parents ought to be called. After Howie finished relating to them an agreed-upon-story about their son staying at a friend's house last night, and was planning to stay at Howie's tonight, he put Mick on the phone. Howie had been evasive when Mick's parents asked what was going on, "He'll tell you. Just a minute." Mick told his parents that he had been tracking down leads on his own, and had forgotten to tell Howie or Adam. The reason he was staying at Howie's tonight was so they could piece together all the bits of evidence they had gathered. "It's going to be a late night, so I might as well sleep here." After Mick hung up, he said that his mother sounded a little skeptical but was relieved to hear he was okay. She knew he was working on some case, but had presumed it was still the one involving the missing cat. He also called Mary, using the same story he told his mother. Though relieved to hear from him, she sounded quite concerned. "Don't worry," he told her. "I'm fine. I'll see you tomorrow."

After they attended to Mick's chest, relieved that it wasn't as bad as it had originally appeared, they told him to soak in the tub for a while with Espon salts. He again declined seeing a doctor when they brought it up. Adam went home and returned with an old pair of sweatpants and shirt for him to wear. Howie said that tomorrow he would go with Mick to his house and get some of his other clothes.

"I've got to get home," Adam said. "I've got an eight o'clock class tomorrow, but then I don't have anything until early afternoon." He looked at Mick. "I'll drive back to see how everything is going."

"You don't have--"

"Don't worry, it's no problem. The school's only a half hour away. You guys will still be here in the morning, won't you?"

Howie yawned. "Yeah, I think tomorrow will be a day to take a little breather from this case."

"Okay. I'll see you tomorrow some time. Do you need any more help?"

"Naw, I can handle it from here."

Once Mick finished in the tub, he slipped into the sweatpants. He decided not to put the sweatshirt on, explaining that his chest was too sore. Howie helped him apply antiseptic ointment to his chest. "That should kill any germs and prevent infection," Howie said. "Are you ready to get some shut-eye?"

"Yeah, I'm zonked. Where am I going to sleep?"

"You take my bed."

"Where are you going to sleep?"

"The couch, and no arguments."

"I'm too tired to argue with you." Mick headed toward the bedroom. Howie had just lain down and was about to turn off the light when Mick came back. "We're going to get whoever did this, aren't we?"

"You bet we are."

"Do you think it will leave a scar?"

"I don't think so. Why don't you go to bed? We'll see how it is tomorrow."

This Angel Has No Wings

THE NEXT MORNING Howie got up, looked in upon Mick, and found him still sleeping. That didn't surprise him. He had heard him tossing during the night. He called Mick's school to let them know that Mick was sick in bed with a high fever and a chest rash. *Not exactly true but true enough.* Howie wanted to talk to Jodelle again, but it was still too early and he was too tired. He lay back down on the couch and fell asleep within minutes. It was mid-morning when he opened his eyes, finally focusing them on Mick who was lounging in his chair sporting a smirk on his face.

"I'm hungry. Are you going to feed me?"

Howie smiled mainly from relief. "You must be feeling better. I can't believe how tough of a cookie you are. Let me get dressed, and then I'll fix us both something."

After they had eaten and were about to have coffee, Adam came in. Howie was glad to see him because he was about to broach a subject with Mick that he had considered earlier. He was sure that Adam would support what he was about to suggest. "Maybe you want to stay off the case for awhile," he told Mick.

"What are you talking about?"

"I mean after everything you've been through, neither Adam or me would blame you if you decided to take it easy for awhile." Howie glanced over at Adam. "Would we?"

"Howie's right. You deserve some time off."

"Are you two kidding?" Mick set his cup on the table. "After what I've been through? No way. I'm on this case to the finish."

"Are you sure?" Howie asked.

"Yeah, I'm sure." Mick pointed to his chest. "I got a lot of myself invested in this case."

"Okay, it's your call."

"Guys, I've been thinking." Adam gnawed at his lip. "Don't you think it's about time to call JD?"

"And what are we going to tell him?" Howie asked. "That our partner was abducted and his chest carved up, but we don't know by who."

"Wait a minute," Adam said. "You and I know it was Damien."

"Yeah, but we have no hard evidence, and knowing JD, he's going ask me if we have any proof." Howie paused. "I'll call JD when I get a chance so he knows in general what we're working on, but I'm not turning this over to the cops."

"But why can't we just get some advice from them?"

"Because the word would get out that we aren't smart enough to handle our own cases." Howie intentionally controlled his tone. To argue amongst themselves would be playing right into Damien's hands. "And who would want to hire us after that?"

"Howie's right," Mick said.

"What?" Adam's eyes widened as he turned to Mick. "How can you say that after what happened to you?"

"It's because of what happened to me. We started this case and now I have more reason than ever to finished it ourselves. I don't have any problem using JD as a resource, but I want us to get the guy."

JODELLE HAMMOND DEBATED whether she should answer her phone. She was fearful that it could be Damien calling again. For the past three days, he had called. She didn't know how he had gotten her unlisted number. Ever since she had known him, though, he always seemed to have a way of finding out things. He had once told her that he had certain powers given him by the Prince of Darkness. His calling had unnerved her. The first time he had called, he acted like he was an old friend calling to renew a lost friendship. She told him they had nothing to talk about and had hung up before he could respond. The second time he called, as soon as she had answered, he had cautioned her not to hang up. He then warned her about the consequences of not returning the notebook. He didn't have to spell them out; she knew exactly what he was talking about. Yesterday, on Tuesday, when he called, he had mentioned her sister's name. "It's too bad that Maureen had to move." His tone was condescending and arrogant. "You wouldn't have her address, would you? I'd like to get in touch with her. I believe she has something that belongs to me. I'm sure she--" Jodelle had hung up, not wanting to hear his voice any longer.

Now, as the phone continued to ring, Jodelle decided to answer it. If it were Damien, she would simply hang up, and continue to hang up until his calls ceased.

"Hello," she said hesitantly.

"Jodelle, it's me."

"Oh, Maureen, I'm so glad to hear from you." Jodelle breathed a sigh of relief. "Are you okay?"

"Yes. I just called to tell you that I moved."

"Why did you move?"

"Because *he* was at my apartment."

"Oh, no!" Jodelle needed a cigarette. "Did he find it?"

"No."

"Thank God." She looked around for her pack of cigarettes. "Then you still have the notebook?"

"Yes."

Jodelle wrapped the telephone cord around her finger. "Maureen, it isn't safe to have that in your possession. You know what he's capable of." She squeezed the cord in her fist as her sister described the condition he had left her apartment. "I'm so sorry. Look, we need to talk. Can we meet?"

"When?"

"Today." Jodelle waited for a reply. "Maureen?"

"Is it that important?"

"Yes." As soon as she got off the phone, she needed to find her cigarettes. "Please, I beg you."

Several long seconds passed. "Okay, but where?"

"Do you remember that café by the community college we always stopped at for coffee after classes?"

"I remember it. What time do you want to meet?"

"Three o'clock." Jodelle squeezed the cord even tighter. "And please bring the notebook."

"I don't know if I should do that."

"Maureen, I beg you. It's vital that I have it to protect myself."

"What! What are you talking about?"

"I don't want to tell you over the phone. I'll explain when we meet." Jodelle bit her lip. "Will you bring it?" She became aware of the clock ticking the seconds off as she waited for an answer.

"I'll bring it," Maureen finally said.

"Thank you." Jodelle felt overcome with relief. "I can't tell you how much this means to me."

"I love you," Maureen said.

"I love you, too."

After hanging up Jodelle sat on the couch in front of the fireplace and lit up a cigarette. *Maureen sounded scared. That wasn't like her. She's the one who always took things in stride.* Jodelle remembered when, as young children, they were playing in the back yard. As the oldest, Jodelle had been told by their father to watch over her little sister. When a garter snake slithered from underneath the back porch, however, Jodelle had become hysterical. Maureen, on the other hand, calmly picked the snake up and brought it to the edge of their property and let it go. Maureen had been that way all her life. Nothing rattled her. Nothing, until now. The phone rang again, but Jodelle decided not to answer it. She was afraid of who it might be this time.

The cafe that Jodelle was to meet her sister catered to a nearby community college. Jodelle arrived ten minutes early, and had gotten a booth in the back. It was perfect. Away from the front windows where passerby's couldn't look in upon you, but yet, located where she had an unobstructed view of the entrance. She ordered a cup of coffee and then lit up a cigarette. As she waited, she thought about how she and her sister were so different. Both of them were adventurous, but Maureen always approached life with a common sense attitude. She, on the other hand, plunged right in without considering the consequences of her actions. They had horrible arguments after Maureen found out what kinds of things Jodelle was involved in with Damien. For months, Maureen had tried to convince her differently. *If only I would've listened. None of this would've happened.* Jodelle remembered the day she had come to her senses. The previous night she had been with Damien and the others as they inducted two young women into the coven. She had watched in horror as they were forced to do humiliating, degrading acts. What horrified her even more, though, was remembering that she had done similar things when she joined. That night she couldn't sleep. Early the next morning she told Maureen that she was leaving the coven. Maureen hugged her and said she would support her all the way. When Jodelle left, she had impulsively taken the notebook with her. She thought it would be something she could use against Damien if he ever threatened to make trouble. *How naive I was to think I could stand up against him.*

Jodelle looked at her watch. Five after three. The waitress stopped to ask if she was ready to order. "No, I'm still waiting for someone." No sooner had the waitress walked away, than Maureen walked in carrying a bag. Jodelle waved her over. The two of them hugged and then sat across from one another. She noted that Maureen kept the bag next to her on the seat.

"I'm sorry I'm late."

"I'm just so glad you came." Jodelle fought to retain her composure. "It's so good to see you. I've been so worried." She remembered her father's admonition about taking care of her little sister, and was determined to be strong. "I'm so sorry about your apartment. That had to have been scary."

"It was. It was just awful coming home and finding it that way." Maureen shuddered. "And then when I went into the bathroom and saw that...that drawing on the mirror, I knew I couldn't stay there. I knew he had been there."

The waitress stopped and refilled Jodelle's cup. Maureen ordered coffee. Neither of them wanted anything to eat.

"Why did you take the notebook?" Jodelle asked after the waitress brought Maureen's coffee.

"Because I was angry at you."

"Angry? But why?"

"Because I thought you had gotten back into that terrible group." When Maureen sighed, it was with a heaviness that matched the tone of her voice. "And I was afraid for you."

"I told you that when I left, it was for good; that I wasn't going back. What were you going to do with it?"

"At first, I thought about turning it over to the police but--"

"The police! Oh, my God!" Jodelle tried to control her emotions. She didn't want to think of what Damien might do. Her sister simply wasn't aware of the consequences of an act like that. "What stopped you?"

"I don't know. I guess I was concerned that you would be arrested, and I didn't want that to happen."

"How is it that he didn't find it in your apartment?"

Maureen offered a half smile; it softened the lines in her face. "I guess it was just luck. When I took it, I didn't want it in my apartment so I put it in a safe deposit box. Maybe I should have just burned the thing."

"I need to have it back."

"You told me that, but I don't understand. Why do you want it if you're not involved anymore?"

"Because he's threatened me. If I don't return it, he'll..."

"He'll do what?"

This Angel Has No Wings

"There are some pictures of me that he has." The only way to fully gain her sister's trust back was to tell her the truth. "Pictures that if others saw, it'd be terrible."

Maureen reached over and took Jodelle's hand. Her voice expressed love and tenderness.

"What kind of pictures?"

Jodelle looked away. She debated whether she should tell her, but she was scared what Maureen would think if she ever saw the pictures. "When they initiate you into a coven, they make you do things, and they take pictures of you." She could barely get the words out. "If these photos ever got out to the newspapers, the Hammond name in this city would be shamed for ever. I can't do that to the memory of our father. I can't do that to you."

"Do you know why that notebook is so important to him?"

Jodelle nodded. "I think so. And please believe me, it's for your own good that you don't know."

Charles Tindell

Chapter 17

FRIDAY MORNING CHAPEL services had just concluded and Adam was hoping to talk to Professor Lewis. Howie wanted him to ask about the notebook that Damien was so anxious to get back. He also wanted to find out if Lewis had ever run across anything like it, and if he had, what could he tell them about it. Adam also was curious, especially after being told that Jodelle had referred to it as *The Book of Shadows*.

After Adam and Howie found Mick late Tuesday night, it was Howie's suggestion that they should give themselves some time off from the case for a couple of days. "You guys need a breather," was the way he put it. Howie hadn't included himself, but Adam didn't argue since he had more than enough schoolwork to catch up on. Besides, both he and Howie figured that Mick needed time to heal. When Mick, however, announced that he was going back to teaching on Thursday, they tried to talk him out of it. Mick brushed them aside. "My chest is sore, but I can live with it." He also mentioned that after having gone through his experience he wanted to talk to Robby Davis. When asked who that was, he replied, "A kid who I feel is getting too close to this stuff on demons and Satanism." Adam had asked if JD had been called, but Howie said that he wanted to wait until they had hard evidence to connect Damien with what happened to Mick.

When Adam arrived at Professor Lewis' office, he found the door propped open and the professor hunched over his desk, making notations in a book. Adam rapped gently on the door.

Lewis looked up and smiled. "Adam, come in."

"Sorry for disturbing you, Professor Lewis, but if I could have a few minutes of your time, I'd appreciate it."

"Certainly, I always have time for students. That's what I'm here for." Professor Lewis closed his book, marking the page with a paper clip. "Sit down," he said and then discovered that he needed to clear off a stack of books from the chair. He picked up the stack, looked around for a moment, and found an empty spot in the corner. "Sorry for the clutter, but books are my life. Now, how may I help you?"

"I'd like to ask you about something." Adam glanced toward the open door. "It's in confidence."

This Angel Has No Wings

"You may ask, but I can't promise you I'll have the answer." Professor Lewis smiled. "And you may close the door if you'd like."

Adam closed the door and then sat back down. His professor probably suspected why he was there. Ever since Lewis had examined the chalice, he had reminded Adam that he was always available for consultations. "Have you ever heard of something called *The Book of Shadows*?" Adam asked.

Professor Lewis' smile faded and his eyes narrowed. "Yes, I have." He took off his glasses and laid them on the desk. "May I presume this is connected with what we have talked about before?"

Adam nodded.

"Do you possess such a book?"

"No." Adam knew that his professor would ask general questions without prying into the details of the case. He trusted that whatever was talked about would stay between the two of them. "I'm not even sure if I'd know one if I saw it. That's why I came to you. I thought you might know."

"I see." Professor Lewis shuffled through a stack of papers until he emerged with a spiral bound notebook, and held it before Adam. "I can assure you," he said, "it's not anything like this. It's much more elaborate. If you ever came across one, I think you'd recognize it as something highly unusual."

"How do you mean?"

"The paper that's used, for example." Professor Lewis fanned the pages of the notebook. "This is plain old notebook paper. *The Book of Shadows* is usually made up of parchment paper and the book itself often is bound in tooled leather." He set the notebook down. "The more fancy ones have carved wooden covers. They're quite elaborate and may take months to make."

"Wow, that's something. What exactly are in these books?"

"Leaders of covens use them to keep notes on such things as rituals, magical formulas, incantations, the use of tools, and other things."

"Tools? What do you mean, tools?"

"There are, for example, ritualistic knives, called athames." As soon as Lewis made the reference, Adam understood, but decided not to say anything about the one Jodelle had received. "The knife is an essential tool, used in invocations, evocations, and certain ceremonies. There are instructions--"

"Excuse me, but what's the difference between invocations and evocations? Don't we use invocations in chapel at the beginning of the service?"

"That is correct. An invocation is an appeal to a higher power. An evocation, on the other hand, is where you call upon spirits to actually attend the ritual." Professor Lewis peered over the top of his glasses. "I'm afraid I might be confusing you." He took off his glasses, and used the end of a stem for a pointer. "Let me give you an example. Someone can evoke, invite if you will, the demons of Satan to attend the ceremony."

"You mean they believe they'll come?"

123

"Oh, yes. That's why a circle is drawn. It's their belief that if you stand within the circle, you'll be protected from the very evil spirits you have called upon." Lewis slipped his glasses back on. "You might call it a safe zone."

"That's frightening." Adam wanted to know more, but he had interrupted his professor. "You were going to say something about some kind of instructions?"

Lewis shut his eyes for a few moments and scratched the side of his head. "Let's see. What was it? Oh, I remember. There are detailed instructions for doing all of these things, and they're recorded in this notebook. Losing *The Book of Shadows* would make it very difficult for one to do the rituals since the words for the incantations are very specific."

So that's why it's so important to Damien. He's lost his instruction manual. "But why is it called *The Book of Shadows*?"

"That has a very interesting history to it." Professor Lewis cleared his throat as if he was in front of a class and about to deliver a lecture. "When those who practiced witchcraft began to be persecuted, they had to go into hiding."

"You mean like when they burnt witches at the stake out in Salem in the 1600's?"

"Even before that. With the threat of persecution, they went into hiding, and as a result, started to lose touch with other members of their coven. They were afraid that their rituals would be lost, so they started writing them down. Since they had to meet in secret, 'in the shadows' as it were, their notebook became known as *The Book of Shadows*. It's also referred as a grimoire."

Adam was impressed by Lewis' knowledge. *The guy is incredible.* "Have you ever seen one of these books?"

Professor Lewis shook his head. "I've only talked to people who have had firsthand knowledge of such a book when they were members of a coven. Let me say this, however." He leaned forward and spoke in grave tones. "Whoever has this *Book of Shadows*, if they have taken it from the leader of a coven, warn them that they are in extreme danger."

HOWIE HAD TRIED to get hold of Jodelle all day on Thursday, but either she was out or she wasn't answering her phone. On Friday, he decided he would pay her a visit. He was just finishing up some notes and was about to leave when the phone rang. It was Jodelle. She had called to give him her new unlisted phone number and to find out if he had heard from Mick. She sounded genuinely relieved when Howie told her that Mick was back with them. When she asked what had happened, he told her that he preferred to talk about it in person. She had suggested that afternoon, but Howie said that wouldn't work, explaining that he would be with another client. He didn't tell her that he was going to Joey's school that afternoon to talk to Joey's class about being a detective. When Howie countered that they meet this morning, Jodelle agreed. *I'll meet with her this morning, and do the show and tell in the afternoon. The timing works out great.* Mick and Adam were coming over in the early evening to talk about the case. It would be a full day, but that was okay. He was anxious to find out if Mick had recalled anything further about his ordeal, and he wanted to hear what Professor Lewis had told Adam about the notebook.

WHEN HOWIE ARRIVED at Jodelle's, she greeted him and then led him into the den. It had turned chilly that day, and she had a fire going in the fireplace. The room felt cozy and secure. *No wonder her father liked it.* She offered him coffee, but he declined. When she asked to hear about Mick, he related the story, but left out the part about the letters carved on his chest. She didn't need to know at this time; she had been upset enough with everything else that had gone on. Besides, he suspected that the part about the eyes of the angel being chiseled out would be upsetting enough. He was right. After he told her about the angel, he waited while she lit a cigarette. "Tell me, do you have any idea why he did that to the eyes?"

Jodelle shifted in her chair and then crossed her legs, her right foot dangling, rapidly shaking back and forth. "It's a double warning."

"What do you mean by that?"

She puffed on her cigarette and exhaled the smoke along with a deep sigh. Her words came slowly and painfully, like a wisdom tooth that didn't want to be pulled. "If an angel has no eyes, then she can no longer see to protect you."

"Protect? What do you mean? Like a guardian angel?"

"Something like that. If an angel cannot see, then according to them--"

"Them? You mean Damien and his cronies?"

Jodelle nodded. "Without eyes, the angel is rendered powerless." She uncrossed her legs and then crossed them again, this time allowing her left foot to dangle. "Tell, me," she began, and then paused as she took another puff from her cigarette, "did it have wings?"

"Did it have what?"

"Wings? Did the statue of the angel have wings?"

"Yeah, why?"

"I remember one night, Damien spoke to the group about angels. He said that the demons of darkness had superior power. All that needed to be done was to gouge out the eyes of the enemy angels and to rip off their wings." Jodelle shuddered, and then glanced toward the fireplace before going on. "With no eyes, they cannot see to protect you. Without wings, they cannot return to heaven, and thus are rendered helpless, doomed forever to walk the earth."

"And you believed that?"

"No, but it scared me. The way he looked and talked. It didn't matter if I believed it, or if any one in the group did, Damien believed it."

"Didn't anybody question him about it?"

"No one would dare."

Charles Tindell

Howie wished Adam was with him; his partner knew more about angels and stuff like that, and could ask the right kind of questions. As far as Howie knew, it probably had some kind of biblical significance that might give them some clues. "You said the thing about the eyes had a double meaning. What's the other part?"

"Oh, my." Jodelle lowered her head and covered her eyes with her hand. She sat there breathing heavily. Finally, she looked up at him. "I'm sorry, but this is bringing up so many terrible memories. I don't know if I can."

"Don't forget about your sister." Howie spoke softly, trying to maintain a calm tone. He had to persuade her to continue without unduly upsetting her more. "This involves Maureen. You wouldn't want anything to happen to her that you could've prevented. You'd never forgive yourself for that."

"Yes, I know." Jodelle reached for her cigarettes. "Let me preface my remarks by saying that what I'm about to tell you I've never seen myself. I don't know if it's true." Her hand shook as she lit her cigarette. "One night, after we had finished and were about to close the circle, Damien informed us that he had something very special to share. As we stood there, he appeared almost ghost-like in the moonlight. He smiled that knowing smile of his and then told us that he had gotten a message from Belial." She stopped. "Do you know who Belial is?"

"Yeah, I've heard of the guy before," Howie said. "How did Damien supposedly get this message?"

"I don't know. He never told us."

"And nobody dared ask, right?"

Jodelle nodded. "Damien said that Belial told him that the ultimate ritual would call for that of a sacrificial victim, and..." Jodelle stopped and although she looked away, Howie could see that her face reflected the anguish he heard in her voice. "He said that before the sacrifice was consummated, the..." she hesitated, obviously struggling within herself, "the eyes of the victim would be gouged out."

"What!"

"I told you it was horrible."

"Do you really believe that ever happened?"

"I don't know what to believe. Maybe Damien was playing with our minds that night. He liked to do things like that."

Howie couldn't imagine someone's eyes being gouged out. "Is he really capable of doing such a terrible thing?"

"I don't know what to say. I don't think so, but he's changed so much since I first met him." She took a glance toward the fireplace. "This whole thing has become so awful. I feel so ashamed that I misled you."

"That's in the past, but you need to be straight with me now. I think you and your sister are in more danger than you realize."

"Does that mean you'll stay on the case to help?"

"Of course."

"About the fee. I'll double--"

"We'll talk about that later." Money had become a side issue now. Howie would have stayed on the case for nothing, and he was pretty sure Adam and Mick would as well, especially Mick.

"I want to show you something." Jodelle got up and went over to the desk. When she returned, she was carrying a beautifully bound black-leather book. Howie thought it was one that perhaps belonged to her father. "This is the notebook that Damien wants."

Howie first impulse was to jump up, grab it out of her hands and see for himself what was so important about it. "How did you get it?" he asked, keeping his tone calm.

Jodelle told him about her meeting with her sister, and why her sister took it in the first place. "That's why I made up the story about a cat. I needed to find out where my sister was so we could talk. I hoped that once that happened, everything would be okay. I didn't count on all the other things."

"May I take a look at it?" He wasn't sure what he would do if she refused. Perhaps, he would have to tell her what had happened to Mick. In any event, he wasn't leaving until he had a look.

Jodelle seemed hesitant at first, but then nodded. "Of course, you may. I'm afraid, though, you won't find it very understandable."

The paper was parchment. Howie flipped through the book. Nearly the entire notebook was filled. Jodelle was right, however. He had no idea what he was looking at. Nothing was written in English. *What is this; Egyptian hieroglyphics or something?* Strange symbols filled a number of the pages. One symbol looked like an upside down cross. Another was a circle with a five-pointed star drawn within it. When he turned to the next page, his body stiffened. In the center of the page was the symbol of the triangle with three F's inside of it.

"Look, if we're going to help you and Maureen, I need to talk to her again. And the sooner the better. Will you call her?"

"Now?"

Howie nodded.

"Okay, if that's what you feel. I need to go to my bedroom, though. I have her number there. If you excuse me, I'll be back in a few minutes."

As soon as Jodelle left, Howie rushed over to the desk. He figured that she wouldn't let him take the notebook, and he didn't know if she would allow him to copy anything from it. He searched through a couple of drawers until he found a sheet of paper. Sitting down, he opened the notebook to the last entry and began copying it. He was counting on Jodelle being gone for a while, figuring that she would have to convince her sister to come. Working as quickly as he could, he finished just as he heard footsteps coming toward the door. He made it back to the couch just as Jodelle opened the door.

"Maureen said she'd be here in twenty minutes," Jodelle said.

"How did she sound?"

"A little afraid. I'm sorry it took so long, but she had a number of questions, and I had to persuade her. I told her that I needed her help to get through this and that I trusted you. When I told her about Mick, that convinced her that you had a good reason to want to help."

"Will she come?"

Jodelle's eyes flickered. "I... believe she will."

For the next twenty minutes, they talked about things unrelated to the case. She talked about her love of the outdoors. He listened with interest as she told him about the camping trips she and her sister went on with their father. When asked about himself, he shared that he and his two partners had been friends since junior high. He also shared that his parents were both dead, and that he had neither sisters nor brothers. "I can't imagine having no brothers or sisters," Jodelle had replied. After a half hour passed, she became edgy again, and the conversation shifted back to the reality of the case.

"I don't understand where she is," Jodelle said. They had been waiting now for nearly forty minutes. "Maureen's always so punctual."

"Maybe she got tied up in traffic." It was a lame excuse, and Howie didn't believe it himself.

Another twenty minutes went by, and Howie lost track of the number of cigarettes Jodelle had gone through. The lingering smoke was giving him a headache and he needed to get some fresh air. When another ten minutes went by, Jodelle got up and went to the phone. "I'm going to call her again," she said, taking a slip of paper from her pocket and dialed a number. "I wrote her number down so I wouldn't forget." As she stood waiting for her sister to answer, her hand moved back and forth along the edge of the desk. When she hung up, her face registered her anxiety. "No answer."

Howie glanced at his watch. He hadn't planned on staying this long, and was afraid he was going to be late for his talk at Joey's school. "I need to leave for another appointment," he announced.

"What should I do about Maureen?"

"I'd suggest you stay home by the phone. I'll call later to check in. Okay?" He didn't like leaving her, but he had another client waiting.

Howie arrived at Joey's school ten minutes late. He rushed in and half-ran to Joey's classroom, feeling a little guilty for running in the hallway. Wanting to catch his breath and regain his composure, he paused at the classroom door. When he peeked through the glass, he saw a sad-faced Joey looking up at the clock. A chubby, freckled-face kid sitting across from Joey was pointing at Joey. Whatever the kid was saying to Joey, he was doing so with a smirk on his face. "Little rug rat," Howie murmured as he opened the door and walked in.

The young attractive brunette writing on the blackboard turned and smiled. "Sorry, I'm late," Howie said, and then glanced over at Joey and winked.

This Angel Has No Wings

"You must be Mr. Cummins." Joey's teacher extended her hand. No wedding ring, but an engagement ring. "I'm Miss Bracken. We're glad to have you here." She turned to her students. "Class, our guest is here." When the kids clapped, Howie felt himself blushing. Miss Bracken smiled at him and then turned her attention to the students to quiet them down. "Joey, do you wish to introduce your special guest?"

"Oh, boy, can I?"

"Of course. You're the one who invited him."

Joey bounced out of his seat and came flying up front. "This is Howie. He's a detective. He's going to find my cat, Midnight."

"Slow down, Joey," Miss Bracken said.

Joey looked over at his teacher and nodded. "Howie lives above a drugstore and has two partners named...ah, what's their names?" he asked as he looked up at his guest. Howie bent over and whispered into Joey's ear.

"Mick and Adam are his partners, but Howie's the boss. He tells them what to do." When Joey glanced at his teacher, she smiled.

"You did very well," Miss Bracken said. "Thank you. You may take your seat now."

Howie felt more nervous than he had expected. "Thanks, Joey, for that introduction." He looked out at the twenty-plus pairs of eyes glued on him. "Hello, everybody. I remember what it was like when I was a rug...ah, a kid in school." He cleared his throat. "We'd have someone come in and talk to us every now and then. The trouble was that they talked so much at the beginning, we never got a chance to ask questions. So I thought, we would begin by you asking questions. That way, I'll talk about things you want to hear about."

The first kid who raised his hand was the chubby freckled-face one. "Did Joey really hire you?"

"Yes, he and I have an agreement. He's one of my clients." As soon as Howie confirmed that Joey was a client, he noticed a number of the kids look over at Joey who was now sporting a grin that was too large for his face. The kid who asked the question slumped down in his seat; a sour look covered his face.

The next question came from a brown-haired girl with dimples sitting in the front row. "Do you really live above a drugstore?"

"I sure do." After Howie described his apartment and office, he told how he helped out at the drugstore's soda fountain every now and then.

A rosy-cheek boy with red-curly hair raised his hand, waving it back and forth frantically. "Can we see your gun?"

Miss Bracken spoke up. "I don't think it's necessary to see Mr. Cummins' gun." She turned to him. "You understand, don't you?"

Howie nodded. For the next twenty minutes, he answered questions about how he became a detective. Did he ever have a murder case? Can he eat all the ice cream he wants when he works? Does he have a badge? Was he ever scared? Does he have handcuffs? Why not? Does he think girls could be detectives? And so on. He was glad when Joey's teacher stood up and announced that there was only time for one more question.

Oh, no. The freckled-face rug rat again. The kid's tone of voice matched the sneer he had on his face. "Have you found Joey's cat yet?"

"No, but I'm working on it. It takes time." Howie hadn't said anything to Joey about his trip to the park. The fact that some kids there told him about seeing a man carrying a cat in a cage wasn't a good sign. Afraid that Joey's cat might have been taken and possibly sold for animal research, he had planned to check with the research facility at the university. He wanted to inquire how they obtained the animals they used in their research, but he hadn't had time. "What's your name?" he asked the freckled-face kid.

"Billy."

"Well, Billy, you have to understand that detective work takes a lot of time. It's not like what you see on television. Sometimes it can take weeks just to turn up one little clue." He looked over at Joey and smiled, hoping that he also heard what was being said.

"Thank you Mr. Cummins," Miss Bracken said. "Joey, is there anything you would like to say before your guest leaves?"

Joey stood up and glanced over at Billy before turning his big brown eyes toward Howie.

"You'll find my cat, won't you?"

Oh, man, don't do this to me. Howie looked around at the twenty-plus pairs of eyes watching and waiting. He forced himself to smile. "You bet, I will, Joey." *Now, let me get out of here before he asks me to promise and cross my heart in front of Miss Bracken.*

"I TELL YOU, it sounds just as weird as the rest of this whole thing." It was a little past seven on Friday evening, and Howie and his partners were in the office going over the case. Adam had just finished reporting what he had learned that morning from Professor Lewis about the notebook.

"So that's why it's called *The Book of Shadows*," Mick said. "I sure would like to see one of those things."

"I saw one this morning," Howie announced.

"What!" Mick exclaimed, his eyes doubling in size.

"Come on," Adam urged, "tell us."

Howie summarized his visit with Jodelle and how she had gotten the book from her sister. He went on to share her opinion what she thought the meaning could be of the angel's eyes being gouged out. When he related her account of Damien's vision, both Adam and Mick expressed their horror. They all agreed, though, that he was the type who could attempt such a thing.

"Why do you think Maureen never showed up?" Adam asked.

"I don't know. Maybe she had second thoughts." Howie had checked with Jodelle just before Mick and Adam arrived. She had worriedly told him that there was still no word from Maureen and that she would call him the minute she heard from her.

This Angel Has No Wings

"At least, Jodelle doesn't have to worry about the notebook," Adam said.

Mick agreed. "But I sure would like to see that thing. Are you positive Jodelle wouldn't let us have it for just a couple of days?"

"There's no way she was going to let that book leave her house."

"That's too bad," Adam said. "It might have provided us with some clues."

"It still can," Howie replied.

Mick glanced over at Adam and then gave Howie a puzzled look. "What do you mean?"

Howie opened the top drawer of his desk, pulled out a folded piece of paper, and carefully spread it flat on the desk. "Take a look at this."

Charles Tindell

Chapter 18

Howie rotated the sheet of paper so that Adam and Mick could see it right side up. "I don't know what you guys make of this, but this stuff looks like the kind of writing you'd see on the walls of pyramids." He leaned back in his chair and waited for them to examine what he had copied at Jodelle's.

Mick squinted at the markings on the paper and then scratched his head. "It doesn't matter which way I look at this thing, I still can't figure it out." He nudged Adam. "What do you think? You're the one who's taken Hebrew and Greek."

Adam moved the paper closer to him. "Some of these look like Greek letters." He pointed to one of the markings. "That looks like the Greek letter, Omega."

"And the other ones?"

"I'm really not sure. It's been a while since I've studied Greek." Adam looked up at Howie.

"Tell me, again. How did you get this?"

"When Jodelle went to make a phone call to her sister, she left the notebook with me. So I figured while I had the chance, I'd copy a page. This is the last entry in the notebook."

"Is this all you have?"

"Hey, with the time I had, I'm lucky I got this."

Mick picked up the paper. "Sure wish we had some idea what this means. Do you think Jodelle knows how to read this stuff?"

"I don't think so," Howie replied. "I got the impression that she might have had a general idea of what's in the book, but that's only because she heard Damien read from it at some of their gatherings."

"I think I know who might be able to decipher it," Adam said.

"Who's that?" Mick asked.

Howie had a good idea who Adam had in mind. "You're talking about your Professor Lewis, aren't you?"

"That's right, and I'm pretty sure he's got a background in ancient languages. Maybe he could translate this for us."

"It's worth a shot," Mick said as he looked over at Howie.

"I agree." Howie took the paper, studied the markings once more, and then handed the paper to Adam. "And while you're at school, make some copies for each of us. Okay?"

"Sure, no problem." Adam folded the paper and stuffed it in his shirt pocket. "What is Jodelle planning to do with the book, anyway? Doesn't Damien want it back?"

"You bet he does." Howie smiled at the thought of Damien having a temper tantrum. "He'd like to get his greedy little claws back on it."

"She's not going to give it back, is she?"

"I don't think so because in her way of thinking, it's her protection," Howie said and then added so that there would be no mistake at what the notebook meant to her. "She's using it to blackmail him."

"Blackmail?" Mick let out a low whistle. "Wow!"

"Wait a minute. Maybe that's too strong of a word." Howie remembered Jodelle telling him that she wished she had never gotten involved with Damien in the first place. "She just wants him to leave her alone."

"I don't blame her," Adam injected.

Howie nodded. "Neither do I. She's hoping now that she's got the notebook, he won't bother her because of fear of her going public with it."

"I just don't understand," Mick said. "What could be in that thing besides a bunch of mumble jumbo rituals for people who get their kicks meeting in cemeteries?"

Adam turned to Mick. "Professor Lewis said that if we are dealing with a hard core Satanist, there could be things in the book that he wouldn't want anybody to know about."

"Sure wish we could get our hands on that guy." Mick cracked his knuckles. "I'd soften him up a bit so he wouldn't be so hard core."

"I'm with you on that," Howie said. "What do you guys say that we get a good night's sleep and talk some more tomorrow?"

THE PHONE JOLTED Howie out of a sound sleep. "Hello," he mumbled and then blinked his eyes a couple of times as he tried to get a fix on the glowing hands of his alarm clock. He finally determined that it was a few minutes past midnight. The person identified himself but Howie was still too groggy to focus his attention. Besides, the caller spoke so softly that he barely could hear his voice. Howie laid his head back on the pillow and closed his eyes. "Who is this again?"

"Why, Howie, don't you recognize the voice of an old friend? You've hurt my feelings."

Howie's eyes popped open, the silky smooth voice could only belong to one person. "What do you want, Damien?" He tossed the covers aside, sat on the edge of the bed, and turned on the night lamp.

"We haven't visited for a long time and I miss you. I thought we could meet and have a chat." Damien's tone was arrogant, and Howie could visualize his sneering smile. "And I know just the place we could meet,"

Damien continued. "At a quaint little country cemetery. I think you're familiar with it. I know Mick is. Shall we say, tomorrow night at midnight?"

"You're out of your mind. Why should I--"

"Maureen for one reason."

The mentioning of Jodelle's sister sent a jolt through Howie. "What have you done with her?" he demanded.

"Howie, you shouldn't get so upset. That's not good for you." Damien's voice continued to be silky smooth. "Maureen wishes to express her apologies for not making the meeting with you and her sister this afternoon. She was…how shall I put it… unavoidably detained."

"What have--" When the sound of the dial tone cut short his words, he slammed the phone on the receiver and sat there, his breaths coming in short rapid waves. He ran his hand through his hair, wondering what he should do. As he sat listening to the ticking of the clock, trying to decide whether he should call Adam, the phone rang. "Hello." He half expected it to be Damien again, but was relieved and surprised to hear Mick's voice. "He did, huh? Adam, too? Yeah, well, he called me about ten minutes ago. No, we can't do anything about it now. We'll talk about it in the morning. Do me a favor, will you? Call Adam back. Tell him to come over tomorrow morning around eight."

MICK AND ADAM sat in Howie's kitchen having coffee, scrambled eggs and potatoes, and toast. Howie had just finished giving Mick a second helping. "Do you want any more?" he asked Adam. When Adam shook his head, he divided the rest between himself and Mick, poured himself his third cup of coffee, and sat down. He hadn't slept very well after the phone call from Damien.

"I don't get it," Mick said. "Why does the creep want to meet with us?"

"He told me that it had something to do with Maureen," Adam said.

"Yeah, I know, he told me the same thing." Mick pointed his fork at Adam. "But the question, is can we trust him? I don't think so."

"I don't think we can either." Adam glanced over at Howie. "Why don't you call JD?"

"That won't do any good. The first question he's going to ask is are we sure he has her?"

"She's missing. Isn't that proof enough?"

"Just because she didn't show up yesterday doesn't mean Damien has her." Howie could feel the tension between him and Adam rising on whether the police should be involved. "For all I know, she changed her mind about meeting with me."

"Why would Damien call us then?" Mick asked.

"Jodelle says that he likes to play mind games with people; he could be just trying to pull our chains."

"Okay, so we don't call JD," Adam said. "But I feel we still have to meet with Damien." He paused, waiting for Howie to answer. "Don't you agree?"

This Angel Has No Wings

"I guess so." Howie didn't like being put in the position that Damien had put them in. Damien was controlling it, and the guy knew it. *Knew it? He reveled in it.* The smug tone in his voice over the phone was evidence enough. "What other choice do we have? The only way we're going to find out anything is to meet with him. Right now, he's calling the shots." His mind went back to the phone call. "Did you guys hear any background noise when Damien called you?"

Mick shook his head. "I was too groggy. I had a hard time even concentrating on what he was saying."

"I heard something," Adam said. "It was some kind of music. I just figured it was his radio playing or maybe his stereo."

"That's what I thought, too." Howie took a sip of coffee, hoping it would help clear his head. "But there was something about the music that seemed familiar. I can't be sure, but it sounded to me like church music."

"Let me think." Adam closed his eyes for a few moments. "You know, now that you mentioned it, it could've been. I know it wasn't rock 'n' roll, or anything like that." He paused. "Say, you don't think this guy's a minister, do you?"

Howie shrugged. He didn't know what to think. "I doubt it, but I suppose it could be a possibility. In this crazy case, anything is a possibility. The question is how do we go about finding out?"

"It sure would be a whole lot easier if we had some idea of where Damien operated out of in the cities," Adam said.

"I agree," Howie said. "If we could only track his home base down, we might get a break in this case." For the next several minutes, only the sound of traffic from the street below could be heard as the three of them sat silently, each adrift in their own thoughts.

"I've got an idea how we might locate him," Mick finally offered.

"Let's hear it," Howie said.

"I just want you guys to know that I'm been giving this a lot of thought ever since that night." Mick paused for a moment as he rubbed his hand gently across his chest. He shared with them earlier that his chest must be healing because it wasn't as sore and was beginning to itch. He leaned forward in his chair. "Now, we know that Damien's about the same age as Jodelle, give or take a couple of years. Right?"

"Right." Howie wondered where Mick was going with this.

"Okay, so from the background information we have on Jodelle, we know that she graduated from high school in 1950. Isn't that right?"

Howie nodded.

"So I figured if I check the high school yearbooks for the years 1948 to 1952, there's a chance that I might run across a picture of Damien. If I do, then we'll have his real name. After that, I can check the school records and maybe get an address."

"Maybe he didn't graduate," Adam offered.

"Or maybe he did," Howie added, "but not from one of the city schools. Maybe he's not even from the area."

Charles Tindell

"I know it's a long shot, but what else have we got to go on?" Mick waited for any replies. Hearing none, he continued. "I think it's better than going around and checking all the churches because you thought you heard church music in the background when he called. Besides, there aren't as many high schools as there are churches in the area."

"You've got a point there," Adam said. "But I'm still going to follow up on the church angle. I'd find it hard to believe that Damien's a minister, but he could be working at a church in some other capacity."

"You mean like a janitor or something?" Howie asked.

"Yeah."

Howie thought that Adam's idea was a possibility, but he didn't want to dismiss Mick's theory, either. He was proud that his partners had invested so much of themselves in this case, and he valued their input. He didn't care what anybody said; they made a pretty good team. If they could crack this case without any help from JD, so much the better; it would help establish their reputation. "So how are you going to go about checking all the yearbooks?"

"I have a friend in the school administration building. I'll give him a call on Monday." Mick leaned back in his chair. "Who knows, maybe we'll get lucky and they'll have a library of yearbooks."

"And if they don't?"

"I guess I'll have to go to each individual school."

"That's going to take a long time."

"What choice do we have?"

Howie knew Mick was right. Besides, he didn't have anything better to suggest. "How are you going to recognize Damien? He could've changed quite a bit from high school."

"I know, but I'm hoping I'll be able to tell by the eyes. I remember reading someplace that the eyes are the windows to a person's soul."

Adam looked over at Mick. "That may be true in most cases, but I'm not sure if it is in this one."

"What do you mean?"

"If we were to talk to Professor Lewis, I think he'd point out that the person we're dealing with has no soul."

"As far as I'm concerned, your professor is right on target," Howie said. "Damien sold his soul to the Devil."

Adam agreed. "I think Lewis would say that there's more truth in what you just said than you realize."

"So, what time are we leaving tonight to meet this character?" Mick asked Howie. "I'm anxious to get a good look at him."

"He told us to meet him at midnight. That means we should leave here around ten. I'll drive." Howie thought about where the meeting was going to take place, and he wondered how Mick would react to revisiting the cemetery. "Are you sure you want to go?"

"I wouldn't miss this for the world. And remember, I've never seen this guy in person. Like I said, I'm anxious to get a first hand look at him, especially his eyes."

"You'll be okay, then?"

"If you're worried about me doing something out of line, don't," Mick said. "I'm not stupid. He's not worth it." His tone relaxed. "Besides, we don't know for sure if he's the one who carved me up."

HOWIE WAS ANXIOUS about getting to their meeting with Damien on time. He personally wouldn't have minded keeping him waiting, but was afraid that Damien's ego would be offended. If that happened, who knew what the guy would do. Besides, if Damien decided not to wait, and left, they wouldn't have accomplished anything. He also didn't want to be put in the position of having to wait until Damien decided to call again. That would give him too much control. "What time is it?" he asked.

Adam turned on the overhead light. "It's about twenty minutes to midnight. We should be there pretty soon."

The overcast night sky blanketed a countryside already devoid of lights. As he drove, Howie thought about the phone call he had made to Jodelle that afternoon. When he asked if she had heard from Maureen, she sounded terrified. "No, and I just know something has happened to her!" she cried. He tried to reassure her, but to no avail. He felt guilty not telling her about the phone call they had gotten from Damien, but he planned to be in touch with her again tomorrow. If necessary, he would tell her then.

"We're coming up to it," Adam announced. "It's just ahead."

In less than a minute, Howie drove up and parked the car outside the cemetery gates. He turned off the headlights. "Look's like we're here first."

"Maybe, but I don't think so," Mick said. "They're here. I can feel it."

"Where did they park, then?" Adam asked.

Howie looked around and saw nothing but the dark shapes of trees and bushes. "Maybe they flew here on their broomsticks," he joked, hoping that it would relieve the tension. It didn't. "What time is it?" he asked.

Adam looked at his watch. "Ten minutes to twelve."

"Let's wait for a few more minutes." Howie rolled down the car window, hoping he would hear something. The cool night air that drifted in felt good. Both Mick and Adam rolled their windows down as well. The three of them sat in silence, listening to the night sounds of the countryside. "Let's go," Howie finally said. "I've got the flashlight, just in case." He explained that he would bring the flashlight, but wouldn't turn it on. "We'd stick out like a sore thumb," he said. He hoped that they could find the statue of the angel without using the flashlight.

As they slowly made their way amongst the tombstones, Adam turned to Mick. "How're you feeling about this?"

"I'm not sure. I don't..." Mick looked off to his right.

Charles Tindell

"What?" Howie asked, looking in the direction Mick was staring, but saw nothing other than the dark shapes of what he hoped to be trees and tombstones. "What did you see?"

"I'm not sure." Mick continued to look straight ahead. "You know, your eyes can deceive you at night. I thought I saw something move."

Howie thought about turning on the flashlight, but didn't. If somebody was out there, it would be a dead give-a-way. "Let's go, then."

They made their way slowly, stopping every now and then to listen. It took them a good ten minutes before they reached the statue of the angel. Even in the dark, they could see the black holes where her eyes used to be.

"Maybe he's not going to show," Mick said. "He's--"

"Why, Mick, my friend, I would think that you of all people would not doubt me." The voice came from behind them.

Howie turned on the flashlight and pointed it in the direction of the voice. Damien! He was dressed in a dark robe with a hood covering his head.

"Please, let's be more considerate," Damien said. "If you wish for me to stay, I would advise you not to shine that on me."

Before Howie turned off the light, he noticed that Damien had a large medallion hanging from a silver chain around his neck. He couldn't be sure, but the medallion looked like it was a goat's head. "A little early to dress up for Halloween, isn't it," Howie said as he pointed the light toward the ground. "Your big night is not until next week. Being dressed up as a monk just doesn't seem to fit you."

Damien walked up to within five feet of them; his smile as arrogant as always. "I would be a little more respectful. After all, this is sacred ground." He looked at Adam. "Isn't that right?"

"I don't think you understand the word *sacred*," Adam said, his voice filled with contempt.

"We can discuss that later, but before we begin, I suggest that you look around." As soon as he uttered his words, Damien clapped twice. Within moments, a dozen or more hooded figures appeared seemingly out of nowhere. They closed in until they formed a tight circle around the four of them.

"Don't be alarmed; they won't harm you. I give you my word." Damien glanced around and then smiled. "Isn't this a beautiful setting? So peaceful and quiet. Of course, it would be nice if the stars were out. Then we--"

"Let's cut the crap," Howie said. "What do you want?"

"My, my, you sound so curt, tonight."

Mick took a step toward Damien. "I ought to--"

Howie grabbed Mick by the arm. "Don't; he's not worth it."

Damien rubbed his medallion. "Mick, by any chance, do you have something to tell me?" He held the medallion to his lips and kissed it. "What I mean is, as the saying goes, do you need to get something off your chest?"

This Angel Has No Wings

Howie held tight on to Mick. "Come on, let's get to it or else we're leaving."

"Oh, I don't think that would be advisable." Damien looked around at the circle. "They might not like it."

"So, what do you want?"

"What I want is for the three of you to leave Jodelle and myself to handle this matter ourselves. I suggested before that you stay off the case, but you didn't."

"We don't listen so well," Howie said.

"I was amused at your persistence, but now, quite frankly, I'm simply annoyed. So I tell you again to go and do your detective work for someone else."

"Jodelle hired us."

"Yes, and I'm sure she'll agree to my suggestion to relieve herself of your services. Of course, you may retain your fee." Damien smirked. "Perhaps, you could use the money to hire someone to think of a better name. After all, the MAC Detective Agency simply has no class." He paused. "What I'm saying is to get your experience with someone else."

"And what if Jodelle doesn't agree with you?"

"I have no doubt that she will agree."

Howie wondered why Damien sounded so confident. "And what makes you say that?"

"You give her these." Damien reached within his robe and brought forth two items. One, a gold bracelet. The other, a plastic bag. "The bracelet belongs to Maureen. I'm sure Jodelle will recognize it since she gave it to her for her twenty-first birthday. It is so touching how close the two of them are. As I understand it, Maureen promised Jodelle that she would always wear the bracelet."

"And what about this?" Howie asked as he looked at the plastic bag.

"There's a lock of Maureen's hair in it."

"So, you did take her!" Adam cried, taking a step forward.

"That's a safe assumption." Damien paused. "And I wouldn't come any closer, unless you want to deal with my friends here. They're here to protect me, you see. And although I gave my word that you'll be unharmed, I can't promise that if you should provoke them." He leaned forward and whispered. "And they would like for you to provoke them. They have come prepared." He smiled. "Now that I think of it, there is one final piece of business where I need to allow you to be of service to Jodelle."

"And what's that?" Howie asked.

"Since she has gotten a new phone number, I haven't been able to call her. If you would be so kind to tell her that I will contact her at your office Tuesday evening. Shall we say, eightish? And tell her that if she wants to see her sister again, she and I need to discuss a certain item she has of mine."

"You mean *The Book of Shadows*?"

"Howie, I underestimated you. Perhaps, you and your partners do have a chance in the detective business." Damien glanced at Mick and Adam. "I shall be leaving now. Make no attempt to follow, and especially don't try to leave the circle until they are ready to release you."

Damien turned and walked away. The circle parted and Damien disappeared into the night.

"Let's rush them," Mick whispered.

"No," Howie said, afraid that their actions might cause Damien to harm Maureen. "This isn't the time or place." He and his partners stood silently and waited. Several minutes went by before the circle opened, and they were allowed to leave.

This Angel Has No Wings

Chapter 19

MAUREEN HAMMOND STRUGGLED to free herself, but couldn't. Whoever had tied her feet and hands to the chair had done a good job. She wanted to yell for help, and would have, if it were not for the tape on her mouth. She hadn't been blindfolded, and she wondered why, fearful of what that might mean. Wherever she was being kept, however, it was too dark to see anything. She was fairly certain that she had to be in a large space since she didn't have an innate closed-in feeling. If she had been in a closet or a small room, she would have instinctively known it.

What happened to me? She searched her memory for answers. The last thing she could remember was entering the underground garage of the apartment building she had recently moved to. Fifteen minutes earlier, she had received a phone call from her sister. Jodelle had begged her to come immediately. She wanted her to meet with Howie Cummins, the detective. "It's urgent," Jodelle had cried. She finally agreed and was on her way to her car. The garage area was dimly lit as usual, and most of the other cars were gone. The sound of her own footsteps echoing on the cement only served to quicken her pace. *Let's see, now. I got to my car and was getting my keys out of my purse. Then it happened!* A blanket was thrown over her body, and powerful arms wrapped around her. She had struggled, even screamed, but it was useless. Everything went black soon after she felt a needle in her arm.

Stay calm, now, Maureen told herself as she sat in the darkness. Her words might have worked if the creaking noise from the ceiling hadn't startled her. The creaking came from directly above her and sounded like something very heavy being rolled across the floor. *Calm yourself. Try to get an awareness of where you are.* After taking a couple of deep breaths, she relaxed a little. It was then that she detected what seemed to be, at first, a sickly sweet odor. When she tried to place it, the only thing she could think of was when she was in high school biology class the day they had dissected a frog. She couldn't finish the dissection because she had gotten sick to her stomach. *Is that what I smell? Maybe.* Her breaths were coming rapidly now, and she feared that if she didn't get a hold of herself, she might start to hyperventilate. *Calm, stay calm. Use your head. Think.* She became aware of another odor mingled in with the first. It was sweet like-- A sound from above and off to her right got her attention. A shaft of light appeared from above, revealing a stairway. A door had been opened. *But leading where?* She could only see halfway up the stairway. Her breathing became more rapid as she heard voices at the top of the stairs. Two men. They were speaking softly, and she also heard music. It was an organ. She was sure of that. She kept her eyes glued on the stairs as she heard footsteps. *Some one's coming.* Whoever it was, he descended slowly, allowing each creaking step to announce his presence. She saw his shoes, the cuffs on his pants, the bottom part of a dark suit jacket, his hand on the railing, his--

"Are you going to be okay?" a voice at the top of the stairs asked. With the organ playing, he apparently felt no need to keep his voice low. "Are you sure you won't need any help?"

"Yes, I'm quite sure." The man who had paused on the stairs, chuckled. "I don't think our guest is in any position to cause any trouble."

"Okay, I'm going out front again. It sounds like the service is coming to an end."

There's got to be people up there who would help me. Please God, please. Maureen attempted to yell but only a muffled sound came out. She held her breath as the stairs began to creak again.

The man reached the bottom of the stairs and stood quietly. She couldn't see his face very clearly. With the light behind him, he appeared only as a silhouette form.

She let out another muffled cry for help.

"Now, Maureen, my dear, is that anyway to act upon seeing an old friend?"

Damien! The arrogant tone in his voice was the tip off.

"I would remove the tape if I knew for sure you wouldn't scream out." He walked closer. "Oh, it's not that anyone could hear you, because you see, this part of the place is nearly soundproof. But I wouldn't want you to scream for two reasons. The first is that I've had a rough day and have a headache. I don't need your ranting. Will you promise not to scream?"

Maureen glared at him.

"Oh, my, it doesn't seem like you want to promise me that. That's too bad. We could've had such an interesting chat about you and your sister, Jodelle." He turned to walk away, stopped and then came back. "Forgive me, I mentioned that there were two reasons I wouldn't want you to scream, didn't I? And I only gave you one. How inconsiderate of me. The second is behind you."

This Angel Has No Wings

Chapter 20

JODELLE SNUFFED OUT her cigarette in the ashtray on Howie's desk and then stole a glance at her watch. She crossed her legs and then folded her arms as though hugging herself; her body moving almost imperceptibly in a rocking motion. When she spoke, her voice was deceptively calm, like the eye of a hurricane. "What time did Damien say he would call?"

"Around eight." Howie looked over at the wall clock. They still had another ten minutes to wait. The time had gone agonizingly slow since Jodelle arrived twenty minutes ago. He, Jodelle, and Adam had waited in silence, each alone with their own thoughts.

Leaning back in his chair, rolling a pencil between his hands, Howie gave Adam a half smile. He was glad that Adam had met with Professor Lewis yesterday and had the chance to show him what had been copied from the notebook. Adam said that Lewis was very intrigued by what he had seen.

"Did he think he could translate it?" Howie asked.

Adam nodded. "He said that he thought so, but it might take a week or more, depending upon other projects."

Howie didn't think that was good enough. He wanted something sooner than that; he had a feeling that time was running out. After talking with Adam on Monday evening, he convinced him to see Lewis again. Adam agreed to see him the first thing on Tuesday morning. Howie told him to try and emphasize the need for the page to be translated as soon as possible. "But don't give away too many details of the case," he added.

Adam had arrived at Howie's office fifteen minutes earlier than Jodelle that Tuesday evening. "I've got good news," he announced as he sat down. "Lewis told me he'd give it his priority and try to have it translated within the next two or three days."

"Great." Howie was pleased and thanked Adam for his efforts. "Maybe this will give us the lead we need."

Now, as Howie sat watching Jodelle drum her fingers on the arm of her chair, he couldn't help but wonder what she would say if she knew he had copied a page from the notebook. He hoped that she would understand, but he wasn't prepared to tell her quite yet. He was worried that she would demand it back before it was translated, no doubt offering as an argument that it would give Damien all the more reason to exact revenge of some kind. *But if she doesn't know about the page, then Damien won't know either.* That was a good enough reason for not telling her.

Jodelle glanced at her watch again. "I can't stop thinking of Maureen and what he's done or going to do to her." Her tone was fearful, but harsh; it signaled that the eye of the hurricane had come and gone, and the anger was being unleashed. "If he's hurt her in any way, so help me, I'll make sure he pays if it's the last thing I ever do."

"We'll get her back," Adam said in a tone that was meant to be reassuring. Although Jodelle smiled and nodded, her eyes portrayed something else.

Howie felt sorry for Jodelle. On Sunday afternoon when he had showed her the bracelet, she recognized it immediately as her sister's. "Oh, no!" she had cried. "He must have stolen it from her." Howie shook his head. "I don't think so." She didn't want to face up to the reality that Damien had her sister. When she asked what the second item was, he was reluctant to show it, and only did so at her insistence. She had screamed and burst into tears when she saw the plastic bag containing the lock of hair. "Oh, Maureen, what has he done to you?" She grabbed the bag and held it tight against her chest. For a moment, Howie was worried that she might faint. It took three cigarettes and a cup of hot tea with a shot of brandy to calm her down. Only then did he tell her about the phone call coming from Damien on Tuesday evening. "But that's a couple of days away," she said. "Can't you find her before that?" He assured her that they were doing everything they could to locate her. He even shared Adam's hunch about Damien possibly working at a church, and also Mick's idea about checking the school yearbooks for his picture. When he told her that Mick was going to get on it first thing Monday morning, it calmed her down a little. "I'm sorry, but I just can't stand to think of my sister being in the hands of that monster. I know what he's capable of doing." Howie was glad she didn't ask what he thought about the likelihood of his partners finding out anything. If she had, he would have had to tell her that, at best, they were long shots. Now, as they waited for the phone call from Damien, he struggled, wondering if they really had that much time to give to long shots.

"Maybe you should go to the police." Howie secretly hoped she wouldn't, but had to give her the option. He and Adam had discussed it before she arrived. Even though Howie wanted to see this case to the end and to nail Damien on his own, with Maureen's apparent kidnapping now, Adam argued that the whole thing had been brought to another level. The truth was, and Howie hated to admit it, he had absolutely no idea where Maureen could be and he feared for her safety. In order to be fair to Jodelle, he felt he had to lay it out straight for her. *If she wants the cops, I'll get in touch with JD.* "Your sister could be in real danger, and right now," Howie hesitated, choosing his words carefully, "the leads we're looking into may take more time than we have."

Jodelle put her hand to her mouth, and looked first at Adam and then at Howie. It was a long time before she replied, and when she did, her voice shook with emotion. "You don't understand." She took a couple of deep breaths as though needing the strength to get her next words out. "I can't go to the police."

"What do you mean you can't?" Adam asked calmly.

"You don't know Damien like I do." She fumbled around in her purse, found a pack of cigarettes, lit one, and took a couple of puffs before continuing. "If he ever found out that I went to the police," she shook her head as if she didn't want to hear her next words, "he would make sure I would regret it for the rest of my life." Choking back a sob, she took another puff of her cigarette, the thin white smoke drifting toward the ceiling. "He would never let me nor my sister rest in peace. Never."

Adam touched Jodelle on the arm; his voice was soothing and gentle. "But if the police were involved, he'd have to leave you alone."

"That wouldn't stop him. He has ways."

"That may be true, but--"

"Please, I can't!" she cried. "I won't."

"I should tell you that he warned us that we should drop the case," Howie said, wondering what her reaction would be to that revelation.

"You're not going to, are you?" Jodelle bit her lip, her eyes were pleading. "You said you wouldn't."

"I know, but that was before Maureen was taken." Howie tried to follow Adam's example of keeping his voice calm, but he knew his partner was much better at it. "I just want to make sure that you're aware that Damien doesn't want us around." He gave her what he hoped she interpreted as a reassuring smile. "We'll stay if you want us to."

"Yes, I do. I need help and I can't go to the police. Please stay."

"Don't worry, we will; and we'll get to the bottom--" The ringing of the telephone stopped Howie short. He let it ring a couple of times and then took a deep breath before answering. "Mac Detective Agency." He put his hand over the receiver, "It's him." Jodelle took one last puff of her cigarette, and tried to compose herself. "Yeah, she's here. Just a minute." He handed her the phone.

"Is my sister alright?" Howie was amazed at how calm Jodelle sounded. "Can I speak to her? But why--" Her eyes flickered nervously. "Yes, of course, I know the place. You'll bring the photos?" When she mentioned photos, Howie and Adam looked at each other and shrugged. "Please, let me talk to--hello, hello." Jodelle closed her eyes and hung her head for a moment before slowly putting the receiver down. "He hung up."

"He has a nasty habit of doing that." Howie wished he could get his hands around Damien's neck right then and there. He considered himself a non-violent person, but there was something about Damien's smugness that triggered a desire to take him and pound him into the ground.

Adam turned toward Jodelle. "What did he have to say?"

"That I should meet him at the Lakewood Cemetery in an hour."

"Is that the big one just south of downtown?"

"Yes, and he said that I should come alone. I'm to meet him by the main mausoleum. When I get there, I should wait."

Howie wondered what Damien was up to now. "Wait? How long?"

"He didn't say, but he warned me that if he sees anyone with me at the mausoleum or near it, he won't come. Once we meet, I'm to give him the notebook and he'll tell me where I can find Maureen."

"So what's this about photos?" Howie asked.

"There are some pictures he has that I want back."

"Are they of you?" It was a guess, but Howie was sure his hunch was right.

Jodelle nodded. "If they were released and other people saw them, they would ruin the family name. I can't allow that to happen."

"What's in those photos?"

"I'm too ashamed to tell you." Jodelle paused to wet her lips. "They are pictures of me with others doing...unspeakable things." She closed her eyes as though afraid to see the reaction on Howie or Adam's face. "Things that decent people would find disgusting." She opened her eyes and looked at them. Her face and voice begged for them to believe her. "It's a part of my life that I want to forget. Can you understand that?"

"Yeah, I can understand."

"So can I," Adam added.

"Thank you." Jodelle wiped a tear from the corner of her eye. "I can't begin to tell you how much that means to me."

"But I don't trust Damien," Adam said. "I don't like the idea of you meeting with him alone."

"And neither do I," Howie said, and then looked at Adam, "but what else can we do?" He turned his attention back to Jodelle. "We're going with you but don't worry, we'll stay out of sight."

"But how--"

"We'll talk about it on the way. As I said, don't worry, we won't jeopardize you getting your sister back."

Jodelle looked at her watch. "Don't you think we better go?"

"We'll take my car," Howie said.

"What about Mick?" Adam asked.

"I don't know." Howie took out a pad and pencil. "He said he'd be back by eight. It's already eight-fifteen, and we can't wait any longer. We're just going to have to leave without him. I'll write him a note. He'll understand."

IT WAS NEARLY eight o'clock and Mick had been at the school administration building for almost four hours going through stacks of yearbooks. It could have been worse he told himself. *I could've had to go to each individual school. That would have taken forever.* Luck, however, had been on his side. On Monday, he had inquired at the administration office as to whether they kept an archive of yearbooks for all the schools. "It's not our policy nor in our budget to do that," the secretary to the vice president had told him, and then added, "but Mr. Williams, one of the assistants, has taken it upon himself to collect them." She glanced around and then whispered, "He's rather eccentric. Around here, we call him, Wild Bill." When she didn't get a reaction, she explained, "Bill is a nickname for William. You get it, now?" After Mick smiled and nodded, she informed him that her boss decided that they would allow Wild Bill to keep his collection in one of the small storage rooms downstairs. "He benefits having rent-free space," she said with a smile, "and we have the benefit of access to his books."

For the next two nights, Mick also had the benefit of access to Wild Bill's collection. The storage room was stuffy and poorly lit, and the detective work had been more mentally demanding than he had anticipated. The books had to be gone through slowly as he methodically studied each page of pictures. On Monday night, he had spent nearly five hours going through the yearbooks. He would have stayed longer but the security guard came to tell him that he needed to leave. "Sorry, but we have to lock up the building. You can come back tomorrow." A couple of pictures that night had caught his interest, and one in particular, he thought was promising. He took the time to track down the name, but learned that the young man had been killed while driving home from the senior prom. When Mick had gotten home that night, he called Howie to tell him that he hadn't had any luck thus far. "How many more do you have to go through?" Howie had asked. "I'm not even half way done." Howie had encouraged him not to give up. "I'm not planning on it," Mick said. Although Mick wanted to sound upbeat, he felt discouraged.

Mick leaned back in his chair, rubbed his eyes, and stretched. Every forty-five minutes or so, he found that he needed to take a break to rest his eyes. He had planned to be at Howie's when the phone call came in from Damien, but he had lost track of time. When he discovered what time it was, he thought about calling but decided not to for fear of tying up Howie's phone. He would be filled in later.

It was nearly nine when Mick found what he was looking for in a yearbook from one of the south suburban schools. "That's got to be him!" he cried, and then slammed his fist on the table in triumph. What first drew attention to the picture were not the eyes, however, but the arrogant smile. As Mick studied the eyes, he was sure it was Damien. The name under the picture was Allan Dresmore. He turned to the back of the book to see if the kid was listed in any activities. The only activity listed was the Chess Club. Mick decided not to waste any time. He knew Mrs. Benning, a Social Studies teacher who had taught at that school. He ran up the stairs and asked if he could use the phone. "And I need to use a directory if you've got one."

His luck was still holding. Mrs. Benning answered on the second ring. Mick introduced himself as a fellow teacher who was doing some work with a detective agency. He went on to explain that he was calling to do a job reference check on Allan Dresmore, and asked if she remembered him. "Yes, I do. Mainly, because he was such a loner." When he asked if she ever had any trouble with him, she said, "No." He was trying to figure out what to ask next when she suggested that he might want to talk with the school counselor since she believed that he had seen the Dresmore boy. "What's the counselor's name?" he asked. "Michael Walker? Thanks so much. I certainly will talk to him."

This time, the phone was answered on the first ring. "Hello, may I speak to Michael Walker?" Mick waited as he heard the woman say, "It's for you, dear." Mick decided to be up front. He told Walker that he was investigating Dresmore on a kidnapping charge and that it was vitally important to find him before he harms his victim. After assuring the former counselor that in cases of life or death, he needn't worry about any confidentiality concerns; the court would overlook such sharing of information. Whether that was true, Mick didn't know. Walker hesitated and then told him that Allan was a loner and never got involved with any school groups. "Did you ever counsel with him?" Mick took notes as Walker told him of one particular time when Allan was brought to his attention. Allan's class had been given the assignment to write on their favorite hero. "Whom did he write on?" Walker's reply did not surprise him. Allan had not only chosen to write on Satan, but also, when he was brought in to see Walker, he acted as if it was no big deal. According to Walker, Allan's parents were not very supportive and neither one of them wanted to get involved. When Mick commented that he was thinking about calling the parents, the response he got told him that his luck had run out. Allan's family had put their house up for sale a month before graduation. The house was sold and the family moved out east two days after Allan Dresmore graduated.

THE DRIVE TO LAKEWOOD Cemetery took less than a half hour. Howie parked just outside the main entrance. Adam had suggested that they drive in and park by the office, but Jodelle wouldn't have it. She didn't want to take any chances of Damien seeing them. "The mausoleum isn't that far, it won't take me long to walk from here."

Howie took hold of Jodelle's arm just as she turned to open her door. "Are you sure we shouldn't go with you?" He hoped she heard the concern in his voice. "We'd keep out of the way, and watch from a safe distance. Damien would never see us."

"He's right," Adam said from the back seat. "He wouldn't even know we're around. We just don't want anything to happen to you."

"Thank you, both of you, but I'll be okay." Jodelle took a deep breath. "I just want to get this thing over with so I can see my sister again."

"I understand," Howie said, "but if you're not back in a half hour, we're coming in. You be careful now."

This Angel Has No Wings

Jodelle sat for a moment before opening the car door and took another deep breath before getting out. Adam and Howie watched her walk across the street toward the main gate.

"Don't you think we should follow her?" Adam asked. "Like I said before, I don't trust that guy."

"I don't either, but we better do as she says. Who knows what would happen if we were seen. We don't want to jeopardize any chances she has of getting her sister back." *If she even can get her back.*

WITHIN TEN MINUTES' time, Jodelle was standing, waiting on the steps leading up to the mausoleum. Although the day had been pleasantly mild, with the setting of the sun, it had cooled down considerably. She buttoned her coat, wishing she had brought a warmer one. Being at this cemetery brought back memories. She knew that meeting here was intentional on Damien's part. *He's playing mind games, again.* The night she had been initiated into the coven, the ritual was held here at Lakewood. It was cool that night and partly cloudy, with the moon going in and out of the clouds. "A perfect night for you to become one with us," Damien said. Jodelle recalled being both excited and scared. She wasn't sure what she was getting into but she trusted Damien. He told her he would take care of her. Around midnight, they broke the padlock on one of the cemetery's several entrances and sneaked in. She had been to the cemetery only once before; that was at her father's funeral. He was buried in a family plot near the west end of the cemetery. Damien had known about it, and told her she need not worry; they would be at the other end of the cemetery. "It's a big place. There's room enough for all of us," he remarked with a smile. Still, she felt guilty knowing that her father was there, and would undoubtedly highly disapprove of her involvement with such a group. Her initiation was held on a hill overlooking the mausoleum. It started innocently enough until-- "Stop it," she told herself. She wanted to push it out of her mind, but the sound of a barking dog off in the distance brought back further memories of that horrible night. The group formed their circle as usual and Damien read from the notebook. Another member of the group walked up and handed him a mongrel dog, not much bigger than a puppy. It was whimpering, and she felt sorry for it. Damien stroked it like it was his favorite pet. And then in one swift motion he laid the dog down, took a knife--

"Good evening, Jodelle, it's nice to see you again."

She jumped at the sound of Damien's voice. When she turned, he was standing less than ten feet away. It sent shivers down her spine knowing that he could have come that close without her hearing him. He looked the same but she was surprised to see him dressed in a three-piece suit and tie; something she had never seen him wear before. He had always dressed casually, often times in slacks and shirt, occasionally, even a sport coat.

"I didn't have time to change," Damien said, obviously aware of her surprise at seeing him dressed as he was.

"Where's my sister?"

"Come now, is that anyway to greet an old friend, especially after all the things we have been through together." He moved closer. She saw him glance at the bag she was clutching. His smile turned arrogant. "I see you have something for me."

"Where's Maureen?"

"Tsk, tsk, such impatience." Damien folded his arms as though posing for a photograph. "Don't you know that patience is a virtue?"

"How would you know anything about virtues?"

"My, you have such a sharp tongue, but I would guess that you're not quite yourself these days. You've been under so much stress."

"No thanks to you."

"Well, you'll soon be done with me." He glanced at the package she was holding. She wasn't afraid of him grabbing it and running. That wasn't his style. He would take great delight in having her hand it over. "That's for me, I presume."

"Yes, but I want the photos and the negatives, and then I want my sister."

"Oh, you're so demanding." He reached inside his coat. "I have everything right here." When Jodelle reached for the envelope, Damien pulled it back. "You shall have them but first I have a question."

Jodelle stared at him, and for the first time in her life, she realized what it meant to hate someone.

"Would you like to come back into our little group?"

"What? You must be out of your mind to think that I--"

"But, I miss you. We had such great times together. Do you remember the evening we shared a cup of...what shall I say...nectar together?"

"I don't even want to think about that. I'll never come back. Never! You're one sick person. You're nothing but--"

"Now, be careful what you say, you may regret it." Although his smile remained, the tone had turned harsh. Jodelle knew from experience that she had come close to crossing the line with him. "Here are the photos and the negatives as you requested." He handed them to her and took the notebook.

"Don't you want to check it?" Jodelle asked as she looked in the envelope to make sure it contained both pictures and negatives.

"My dear, I trust you. Apparently, more than you trust me. Besides, if you deceived me, I believe you know what the consequences would be."

"Where's Maureen?" Jodelle cried, glancing toward the hill overlooking the mausoleum.

"Oh, please, give me a little more credit. She's not up there." Damien's tone had become ingratiating. "I know your detective friends are in the car waiting for you."

"How did--"

"I've told you that I have been given a gift by Belial. What must I do to convince you of that?" Damien paused as though waiting for her to acknowledge his gift. "Besides, you should know me better than that. Do you actually think I would chance bringing Maureen here in case those fools you hired decided to set me up?" He looked in the direction of the main gate. "They're such amateurs. I warned them to stay off the case, but I think you should tell them to stay. It might prove amusing." He reached into his pocket, pulled out a piece of paper, and handed it to her.

Jodelle glanced at the paper. "What's this?"

"The directions on how you shall find your sister. I was even so kind as to draw a map for you. It's not too bad if I have to say so myself. But if you find it difficult to follow, your friends out in the car would be helpful. They're familiar with the place, especially, Mick."

His arrogant attitude was unnerving Jodelle, and she needed a cigarette.

"I see you have taken up that nasty habit again," Damien said as he watched her get a cigarette. "My dear, don't you know that those things will kill you?"

Jodelle didn't reply as she searched her purse for matches.

"Here, allow me." Damien reached in his pocket and pulled out a book of matches. After he lit her cigarette, he gave the matches to her. "Keep them. It appears as though you may need them."

"Is my sister--"

"I'm sorry, but I'm afraid I need to go. I have other things I must attend to." He turned to walk away, but stopped. "Oh, one more thing. Please wait for ten minutes to let me be on my way. I have other eyes watching. If they see you move or try to follow me, you may never find your sister." He sneered. "Now, you wouldn't want that on your conscience, would you?" Without giving her a chance to reply, he walked away.

"How long has she been gone?" Adam asked.

"About a half hour." Howie was second-guessing the decision not to have followed her. *What if Damien decided to take Jodelle as well?* That was a possibility that he hadn't thought of until now.

"Do you think we should go in?"

"Not yet." Howie leaned his forehead on the steering wheel and closed his eyes. His head was pounding. He felt exhausted. "We'll wait for a couple more minutes."

"Okay, but-- hey, here she comes."

Howie was relieved to see her, but she was alone. *What is he up to now?*

By the time Jodelle got to the car, both Howie and Adam had gotten out. "Where's your sister?" Adam asked.

"He didn't bring her but he gave me directions and a map showing where we can find her. From what I can tell, the place is somewhere south of the cities." She gave Howie the hand-drawn map. "He knew the two of you were here."

Adam gave her a puzzled look. "How in the world did he know that?"

"I don't know but he knew." She pointed to a spot on the map. It was marked with an upside-down cross. "He said you would know this place."

Howie showed it to Adam. "Look familiar to you?"

"Yeah, that's the same place where we found Mick."

"You mean the cemetery?" Jodelle exclaimed.

Howie put the map in his pocket; he didn't need it to find the place. "Damien seems to have a thing for cemeteries." He couldn't help but think of when they found Mick and what had been carved on his chest. *Damien wouldn't do that to Maureen, would he?* Howie hoped the answer was no, but he had an uneasy feeling. Jodelle was wrong; he did know what Damien was capable of doing. "I see you've made the exchange," he said, noticing the brown envelope she was carrying.

"Yes, at least that part's over with." She looked back in the direction from which she came. "Can we get out of here and go get my sister?"

Howie opened the door for her. "Let's go."

While Howie drove, Jodelle recounted the conversation she had with Damien. "He was so calm and cool, like he didn't fear anything." She buried her face in her hands for a moment. "I'm so sorry about everything that's happen. I was so stupid to get involved with him."

"That's over with now," Howie said.

"It's not over with until I get my sister back."

IT WAS WELL after midnight when they drove up to the iron rod gates of the cemetery.

"Just a minute," Howie said as the three of them got out of the car. "I'll get my flashlight from the trunk." He led Jodelle and Adam in the direction where they had found Mick. Brittle leaves crunched under their feet.

"Is that an owl I hear?" Adam asked. When they shined the light in that direction, they heard the flapping of wings, but saw nothing.

"How much further?" Jodelle asked.

"Not much." Howie had the uneasy feeling that Maureen wouldn't be there.

"Where is she?" Jodelle cried as Howie scanned the area with the flashlight. "He said she would be here. He promised me. He--"

"Over here!" Adam yelled.

Howie shined the light in Adam's direction. His partner was standing by the statue of the angel. When they got there, the beam from the flashlight illuminated the angel.

"Oh, my God!" Jodelle cried.

The right wing of the angel was gone, its pieces scattered on the ground. "Some one must have used a sledgehammer to do that kind of damage," Howie muttered.

"That's Damien's way of saying he was here," Adam said.

Howie shined the light at the partially damaged left wing. "It looks like he didn't have enough time to finish the job."

"He'll finish," Jodelle said. "He often bragged about always finishing what he sets out to accomplish. It's his..."

"What's the matter?" Howie asked.

"Shine that light down here," she said, pointing at the statue's base.

Adam moved closer and then knelt down to get a better look. "What in the world is that?" He looked up at Howie. "See that? It looks something like a crescent moon and an X."

Jodelle screamed as she sank to her knees and buried her face in her hands. "Oh, please, no!"

Howie knelt besides Jodelle and put his arm around her. "That's some kind of satanic marking, isn't it?" He waited, but no response came. Her body trembled against his. "Come on, you need to tell us."

Jodelle mumbled something that he couldn't make out.

"I'm sorry, but I didn't hear that. What did you say?"

"It's a symbol."

"Symbol of what?"

Her breaths were coming rapidly now. "For a blood sacrifice."

Howie shined the light on the markings again. "What's Damien telling us with this?" When she didn't reply, he knew they couldn't waste any more time. "Look, your sister's in trouble. We need to know as much about this as you can tell us if we're going to track her down and help her."

Jodelle took a couple of deep breaths. "It means that Damien's planning to offer a sacrifice, and he's telling us it's going to be my sister."

"What!" Adam exclaimed. "Why, that dirty..." he turned away for a moment. When he turned back, his voice was calmer. "Do you have any idea where this might take place?"

"No," Jodelle sobbed, "but I know it's going to happen soon."

Howie helped Jodelle to her feet. "What makes you say that?"

"Because of Samhain."

"What's that?"

"Damien always considered it as holy day for Satanists; the start of the Celtic New Year. Halloween."

When Adam looked at him, Howie knew exactly what was going through his mind. *Halloween's only two days away!*

Chapter 21

When Maureen had turned her head, she caught a glimpse of a shape from the corner of her eye, but couldn't make out what Damien had referred to as to his second reason for not wanting her to scream.

"Let me help you." Damien grabbed her head and twisted it until she winced in pain. She was afraid that her neck would snap. When she focused, she forgot about her pain; for sitting in a chair in the corner was an older woman. There was just enough light to see her face. Her eyes were closed and something about her waxy complexion was unnerving.

"Let me introduce you to Mrs. Grimswell. She just had her hair done. Doesn't she look nice?" He paused. "I think so, too. She'll look so natural for her revival tomorrow evening, and she needs her rest."

Maureen's horror came out in muffled cries.

"Now, now, I told you that she wouldn't like it if you started screaming," Damien chided. "After all, you wouldn't want to wake the dead, would you?"

Her breaths came rapidly now. Damien just laughed and then turned, and walked away. When he got to the top of the stairs, he closed the door, and Maureen found herself alone in the darkness with Mrs. Grimswell.

This Angel Has No Wings

Chapter 22

Right 24. Left 36. Right 7. Nothing! Hurry up. Try it again. Right 24. Left 36. Right 7. Nothing! Howie pounded on the tombstone. *What's wrong? Why doesn't it open?* Droplets of sweat ran down his temples. His hands were clammy. His mouth, dry. *How long had he been at it? Hours? Days? Whatever. Time was running out. The clues to finding Damien were sealed inside that tombstone. Once he found Damien, he would find Maureen. If he could only find the right combination.* He took a deep breath. *Just relax. Stay cool. I've got to get this open. Try something different. Yeah, that's it! Something different. Come on, come on, open!* He banged his fists against the granite. *Why can't I figure this out?*

Howie massaged his aching hands, raw now from pounding at the stone. He leaned forward to try a new set of numbers when suddenly the hairs of his neck prickled. *Somebody's watching me.* He looked up. To his right, five or six tombstones away stood a lone figure. Dressed in a monk's robe the person stood silently, watching. *Who are you? Listen, mister, I presume you're a mister, why don't you take that mask off; it's not Halloween…yet.* Howie waited. *You're not going to talk, huh? Well, suit yourself; I've got work to do.* He turned to concentrate on the lock. *Let's try this again. Just stay cool.* His fingers ached as he tried the combination. He yanked and yanked at the lock, but it wouldn't budge. *Why can't I get it?* The ringing of a bell startled him. It was the monk; he had a large bell in his hand and swung it back and forth. *What's he's doing? Forget about it. Makes no difference. Don't get shook. Try it again. Time's running out.* Howie wiped his sweaty palms on his jeans and then went back to work on the lock. *Come on, what's wrong with you!* He banged his fists against the tombstone again. *Stop ringing that bell!* he cried and then watched as the person slowly removed his mask.

HOWIE AWOKE WITH a start and blinked his eyes a couple of times. His breathing was rapid and heavy, like he had just run up a steep hill. *Why is that bell still ringing?* It took him a couple of moments to orient himself. When he realized he was in his own bedroom, his breathing slowed to a more normal rhythm. He rubbed his eyes, shook his head to clear his mind, glanced over at the nightstand, and only then reached for the telephone. "Hello." It was Mick. Howie threw the covers back and sat on the edge of the bed. His tee shirt, damp from perspiration, clung to his skin. "Wait a minute, speak slower, will you? I didn't get much sleep." He fought to keep his eyelids from closing. "Yeah, yeah. What!" His eyes popped open. "Say that again. No kidding!" A jolt of adrenaline surged through his body as Mick told him that he had found Damien's high school picture. "That's great. I knew you could do it." Howie managed to slip off his tee shirt, and then used the sheet to dry off his chest. "So his name's Allan Dresmore? Do you know where he lives?" Howie glanced at the clock. Ten after seven. He could be dressed and out the door within fifteen minutes. It would be his pleasure to give Dresmore a personal wake-up call. "No address, huh? That's too bad. At least, we've got his name." Howie nestled the phone between his chin and shoulder as he stretched his arms out in front of him. "You do? And he's a friend of Dresmore's? Good. Hope he's there. Sure, I'll let Adam know. He's coming over before going to school. Let me fill you in on some things, now." He brought Mick up to date on the events of last night: Damien's phone call, Jodelle's rendezvous with Damien by the mausoleum at Lakewood Cemetery, the subsequent late drive to the country cemetery, the angel whose one wing had been hammered off, and the Satanic symbol forewarning of a blood sacrifice. He explained what Jodelle had said about the upcoming celebration of Samhain. "Yeah, I know we don't have much time. You do what you can, okay? I hope you come up with something. Sure. Keep in touch." Mick hadn't been surprised that Maureen was still missing. He, like Adam, also didn't trust Damien. Although Mick sounded excited about his lead, Howie heard the concern in his voice as they talked about how time was running out.

After Howie hung up, he lay back on the bed. He closed his eyes, but when the face of Maureen Hammond flashed through his mind, he couldn't sleep knowing Damien still had her. He dragged himself out of bed, washed, and got dressed. He was sitting at his desk thinking about his dream and having his second cup of coffee when Adam came in.

Adam plopped down in a chair, stretched out his legs, and let out a long sigh. "Are you as tired as I am?"

"Yeah." Howie leaned back, raised his arms toward the ceiling, and yawned. "Do you want a cup of coffee?"

"I've already had a cup. So, have you heard anything from Mick?"

"I sure have. While he was checking the archives at the school administration building, he found a picture of Damien in a 1951 year book."

"Really?" Adam sat up straight. "What school."

"West High." He took out his notepad and reviewed his notes. "We know now that Damien's real name is Allan Dresmore. Mick tried to get an address, but found out that Dresmore's family moved out east right after graduation."

"No forwarding address at all?"

"Apparently not, but Mick got the name of a classmate who used to hang around with Dresmore. It's some guy by the name of Leonard Merrick. By any chance, does that ring a bell with you?"

"Nope."

"Me, either. The school counselor told Mick that this Merrick and Dresmore were pretty chummy through their senior year."

"Do we know where this guy is?"

"That's the one break we got. Mick called Merrick's house on the chance he was still living there. He wasn't, but his parents still are. His mother said she and her husband kicked their son out a couple of years ago. She didn't know where he was living now, but gave Mick the name of the place he was working at the time."

"Where is this place?"

"By the capital in St. Paul. It's called *Groovy Records* or something like that. Mick's hoping he's still working there. He's going over after he's done with school today." Howie leaned back in his chair. "It's not much of a lead, but it's about the only real lead we've got right now."

"At least, that's something. How's Jodelle doing?"

"She's resting at home. When I brought her up to her door last night--"

"You mean early this morning."

Howie nodded. "Well, anyway, I told her she needed to get some sleep. She said she'd try, but wanted to be kept updated. She's coming over here around six. That's a good time. Mick said he should be able to make it by then also. Can you make it?"

"I wouldn't miss it. This case is too important." Adam paused. "You know I wouldn't be going to school if there was something I could be working on right now."

"I know what you mean." The dream Howie had flashed through his mind. "I only wish I had something to give you to check out."

"Just how much time do we have?"

"Jodelle said that this thing would take place at midnight tomorrow night." Howie looked at the clock. "So that means we've got about forty hours."

"Man!" Adam shook his head. "Do you think Damien would really..." he hesitated, "I mean, would he really do that to Maureen?"

"I don't know. There's a part of me that says the guy's bluffing. Like Jodelle told us, Damien likes to play mind games." Howie rubbed his forehead; he wasn't sure if his headache was from lack of sleep or tension. Probably both.

"And what's the other part of you say?"

Howie looked up. "That he's going to do exactly what he said. And right now, I don't have a clue as to how we can stop him. I don't know where he is. I don't know where he's keeping Maureen. And I don't have any idea where it's going to take place." He put his elbows on the desk, and buried his face in the cradle formed by his hands for several moments. "All I know is that we have until midnight tomorrow night."

Adam ran his hand through his hair. The expression on his face told Howie that he also was feeling the weight of the case. "I know what Jodelle said about the police, but she's not thinking right. You've gotta call JD."

Howie opened his mouth to argue, but instead picked up the phone. Adam was right. They were stymied and a person's life may be at stake. As he waited for JD to answer, he thought about what he could have done differently. Maybe if he hadn't been so stubborn in wanting to solve the case himself. Maybe-- "Hello, JD, it's Howe. I'm calling because I, ah, need some advice on a case we're working on."

"Go ahead. I'm listening."

"We have a client whose sister is missing." Howie paused. "Listen, this has to be off the record, and just between you and me. The police cannot be officially involved."

"Okay, I'll go with that for now. What's this woman's name?"

Maureen Hammond. I'm not going to go into the whole story now, but we believe she's in the hands of a character by the name of Damien. We just found out that his real name is Allan Dresmore. This guy is into Satan worship. I have a feeling that he's planning to do something terrible to her on Halloween night."

"Like what?"

Howie thought about what happened to Mick and wondered if Damien would take it a step further. "Mutilate or...kill her. We need to locate him and fast."

"What do you need?"

"First of all, if you could run Dresmore through your files and see if you can come up with an address or something."

"You've got it. What else?"

"Mick is going to check out a lead this afternoon, but I don't think it will go very far. Adam thinks the guy might work in a church."

"You mean as a preacher?"

"Could be, but he could be a custodian or a music director. We don't know."

"That's a long shot; there are a lot of churches." JD paused. "If I find an address on this guy, I'll check out the churches in the area he lives. Anything else?"

Howie glanced at Adam, and then cleared his throat. "Do you have any other suggestions?"

"Not right at this minute. It sounds like you're doing everything you can with what you have. You know as well as I do that a missing person's case isn't easy. Just keep dogging it. Sometimes a clue will open up when you least expect it."

"I hear you." Howie appreciated JD's support. "We'll be in touch." He hung up the phone and shared with Adam what JD said.

"That makes me feel better that we have him involved."

"Look," Howie began, "I'm sorry I got you guys involved in this whole thing."

"Don't be so hard on yourself," Adam said. "We're in this together. I just know that something has got to turn up." He paused. "I'm going to talk to Professor Lewis about that page you copied. Even if he's only got it partially translated, that might help."

"Let's hope so. We need all the leads we can get." Howie offered Adam a half smile; he appreciated his friend's never-give-up attitude. It was something he needed right now. "Thanks."

"For what?"

"Just thanks." Howie checked his notepad. "I'm going down to West High myself. Maybe there's somebody else who remembers Dresmore. I know it's not much, but as JD said, we got to hope that something will turn up. I'll see you later."

Adam stood, walked over to the door, and then stopped. He pointed to the movie poster. "Why don't you take Bogie with you? He might bring you some good luck."

"Thanks I will, and let's hope that your Professor Lewis has something for us. I'd like to have some encouraging news to give to Jodelle for a change."

After Adam left, Howie scrupulously went over his notes beginning from the day Jodelle Hammond first walked into his office. Just as he had expected, however, there were no new insights. He called Mick's school, leaving word to have Mick call him immediately. When the person asked if this was an emergency, he did not hesitate. "Yes, it is." Mick called back within ten minutes. "What happened?" he exclaimed. "Everybody okay?"

"Yeah, I just wanted to tell you that I'm going down to Dresmore's old school."

"For what?"

"To check with the cooks, custodians, other teachers, the school nurse, and anybody else who was working there when he was a student." It was a long shot, but Howie was desperate.

As soon as morning chapel was over, Adam rushed to Professor Lewis' office. He hadn't seen the professor in the chapel and that concerned him. Lewis never missed chapel unless he was sick. When Adam arrived at his office, he was relieved to see the door open and Professor Lewis working at his desk. Lewis looked up and gestured for him to come in.

"Ah, Adam, I was just about to go looking for you." Professor Lewis cleared several books off a chair and motioned for his visitor to sit. After Adam sat down, Lewis peered at him through wired-rimmed glasses for a few moments. "You look tired."

"I guess I am a little." Adam didn't want to waste any time with small talk. He needed to get as much information about the markings as he could. Maybe they held a clue as to where Damien might have taken Maureen. "I've got a question about the page I gave you; was that written in some form of ancient Greek?"

"Oh, no, some of the letters may have been similar to the Greek alphabet, but what you gave me was a combination of the Runic and Enochian alphabets."

Charles Tindell

"The what?"

Lewis smiled, and then repeated what he had said.

"I'm sorry, but I guess I've never heard of those."

"Don't concern yourself. Most people haven't. Those who have are ancient old professors such as myself."

Adam wondered if they held any clues for the case. "What can you tell me about these alphabets?"

"A lot, but I sense that you're pressed for time, aren't you?"

Adam nodded, amazed again at his professor's power of observation.

"I thought so. In that case, I'll just give you a short summary. The Runic alphabets, and there are several of them, were used by the Germanic peoples from about the third to the thirteenth centuries."

"So they're not used anymore?"

"Interestingly enough, in the twentieth century, they were popular among those emphasizing the neo-Nazi belief system." Lewis' eyebrows rose. "I could say more, but we'll save that for another time." He cleared his throat. "The other alphabet, the Enochian, has a very fascinating history. According to some, it was the language spoken on the lost continent of Atlantis."

"Why do you think the person used these alphabets?"

"My guess would be that they wanted an alphabet that isn't well known. And the reason for that is that it would be in keeping with the ceremonies and rituals they're practicing. They're very secretive and wouldn't like others to know about them. The term *rune*, itself, actually means secret or mystery." Professor Lewis paused. "Do you understand how using these alphabets might connect with *The Book of Shadows*?"

Adam knew that Lewis had slipped into playing the part of professor and was challenging him to use his deductive powers of reasoning, but he was too tired to think, and he didn't want to take the time to reflect. Under different circumstances, he would have enjoyed engaging his professor in a discussion. For this time, however, he merely shook his head.

"Let me explain, then. You see, *The Book of Shadows* is like a personal diary. As I told you before, the person writes in it his formulas, instructions for making the tools of his trade, and also the things that he and the members of the coven may have tried. All of which he wants to keep secret."

"When you say *tried*, you sound like you're talking about experiments."

"I suppose one could think of it in that way. On that basis alone, there could be some highly incriminating stuff within it. That's why the book is so guarded, and also why its owner would do anything to get it back."

"Speaking about the book, I suppose it's going to take you longer than you said to translate that page." Adam hoped that Lewis had perhaps translated a couple of lines by now. At this point, with the clock running, he would take anything. The thought of someone like Damien experimenting on Maureen was horrifying.

This Angel Has No Wings

Professor Lewis leaned back in his chair, and smiled. "The reason I was about to go looking for you when you appeared at my door was to tell you that I've finished the project. The page has been translated."

"It has!" Adam could hardly wait to tell Howie and Mick. "That's just great. How did you do it so quickly?"

"It took the better part of two days, staying up most of the night. I even skipped chapel this morning to review it. I had to make a couple of minor changes, but it's ready for you."

"That's terrific. I'm just sorry you lost sleep over--"

Lewis waved his hand back and forth. "No, no, don't apologize. I enjoyed it. It was a challenge." He took off his glasses and laid them on the desk. "Besides, an old man like myself doesn't need as much sleep as some might think." He looked toward the door and then put his finger up to his lips. "And as far as chapel this morning, I knew Professor Johanson was preaching. He always uses the same sermon every year. I know it by heart." Lewis picked up his glasses and put them back on. "Enough about that. I suppose you're anxious to see it?"

Adam leaned forward. "I sure am."

Professor Lewis opened the top drawer of his desk. "Here it is." He handed Adam the paper. Underneath Howie's printing, was Lewis' translation:

> *My Lord Satan and Master Lucifer I acknowledge you as my God and praise and promise to serve and obey you while I live. I renounce the other God. I promise to do as much evil as I can and draw all others to evil. If I fail to serve you and adore you I give you my life and I shall burn in Hell. I shall soon honor you. We shall drink the life force and you my Lord Satan shall partake of a soul.*

"Wow, this is really something!" Adam exclaimed. "Thanks a lot for doing it."

"You're most welcome. As I said, it was my pleasure." Lewis pointed to the paper. "I should tell you that since there were no punctuation marks with the markings, I took it upon myself to put the periods in where I thought they should be."

"Thanks." Adam quickly read it again. "I do have one question. What's it talking about when it refers to this life force?"

Professor Lewis' eyebrows knotted as his face took on a grim expression. "That's a veiled reference to blood. According to ancient magical thinking, the life force of anyone is their blood. To drink of the life force means that whoever wrote this is planning a sacrificial ritual where the blood will be consumed."

"What!" Adam cried. "Are you serious?"

"Oh, yes, quite serious. Blood is considered to be the vehicle of the animal's life energy. To consume its blood is to grasp its spirit." Lewis leaned forward, peering over his glasses. "I have a deep seeded foreboding, however, that whoever wrote this isn't talking about the blood of an animal."

Lewis' words only managed to reaffirm Adam's deepest fears. He noticed the time on the clock above his professor's desk. In approximately thirty-six hours, Maureen would become the victim; her life force would be... "Professor Lewis, do you know anything about a witches' celebration called Samhain?"

"Only that in addition to it being what we celebrate as Halloween, it's also the beginning of the Celtic New Year." Lewis tugged at his earlobe for a moment. "And if I'm not mistaken, there's also the belief among some that the Devil and other spirits of the dead will be moving about. During the night of Samhain, they're at the height of their power, especially at the stroke of twelve."

Adam glanced at the clock again. His neck muscles ached. Howie had told him not to give away too much of the case, but he felt he had to risk it. Without mentioning the part about Maureen being missing, he told Lewis about the angel at the cemetery whose eyes had been chiseled out, and her one wing broken off. "Do you have any ideas as to what that means?"

"Whoever did those things was sending a message that the forces of evil were moving to position themselves to gain control and power. The struggle between good and evil has always been, in my opinion, a struggle about power."

Hearing Lewis talk about power made sense to Adam. Damien was exactly the kind of person who needed and wanted power. For Damien, power was his way of manipulating others to do his will. "Do you think just sending the message was enough for the person?"

"I don't think so." Lewis' tone grew solemn. "Whoever sent that message also wanted to let you know that they're going to perform some act of evil that will prove they have power over good."

"Doesn't that tie in with what you translated?"

"Oh, yes. When someone takes a life, they're proclaiming that they have usurped the power of God. As you know from your studies, the biblical understanding is that since only God has given the life force, only God has the power to take it."

"How do you stand up against someone like that?"

"You cannot back down from the power he claims, and you must show that he has no power over you." Lewis reached over and took hold of Adam's arm, surprising him with the strength of his grip. "You have to remember, the power they have over you is your fear of them. If you do not fear them, they become powerless."

Adam nodded; he appreciated the advice, but felt drained. He needed to share this with Howie and Mick. Perhaps, with the three of them working on it, they would come up with an idea as to where to search for Maureen. After thanking Lewis, he stood up to leave. He had grown fond of Lewis and deeply respected him. Lewis would be exactly the right person to help him deal with his personal struggles about the ministry. "I wish I could stay longer, but I've got to go."

"I know you do." Professor Lewis glanced up at the clock. "And you don't have much time, do you?"

MICK LEFT SCHOOL shortly after he finished teaching his sixth-hour class. Upon receiving the phone call from Howie that morning, he had stopped to see Waite, the principal. "I need to leave right after my last class today. Is that okay?" After Waite said that he saw no problem with that as long as it didn't become a habit, Mick added, "And I need to take tomorrow off because of a family crisis." This time Waite was reluctant and asked what was the problem. "It's a private matter, but it involves my sister." Mick surprised himself how easily he could lie with a straight face. When Waite commented he didn't know he even had a sister, Mick replied, "Her name is Maureen." He was glad that Waite asked no other questions. That entire day dragged and Mick found it difficult to concentrate on his teaching duties. He declared in each of his classes that the time would be devoted to "catching up on your reading assignments." While his students read, he sat at his desk jotting down notes about the case. By the time his last class of the day ended, he was so anxious to follow up on his lead that he bolted out the door along with the students.

It was nearly four when Mick arrived at Leonard Merrick's place of work; an offbeat record store located on Seventh Street in St. Paul. The store was squeezed between a used furniture place and a pawnshop. The window of the record shop displayed psychedelic posters of music groups that Mick had never heard of before. As he walked in, he immediately became aware of the strong smell of incense permeating the store. A teenage boy sorting through records peered warily at him; the acne-faced kid wore a tie-dye tee shirt and blue jeans. A chain with a small padlock on it hung around his neck. When Mick greeted him with a nod, he simply turned away with a look of indifference. *Probably wondering what a guy with a shirt and tie is doing in a place like this. Well, kid, so am I.*

Mick walked up to the cash register. A heavyset, bald-headed man had just finished giving change to a girl Mick guessed to be in her mid-teens. She was wearing black lipstick, and sporting a hairstyle that he would be hard pressed to describe. The bald-headed guy wore a necklace with silver crossbones on it that stood out against his black tee shirt. The guy's left forearm displayed a fire-breathing dragon. "Hi, I'm looking for a guy named Leonard Merrick." Mick said. "I was told that he works here. Is he around by any chance?"

"What do you want him for?"

"It's a private matter."

"Okay, he's in the back, I'll get him for you."

As Mick waited, he noticed in the back of the store a display of tee shirts advertising rock bands. Under the glass counters by the cash register were a display of long-stemmed pipes, and necklaces of various sorts. Under another section was an assortment of skeleton keys. Next to the keys were an assortment of cigarette lighters and cases whose covers displayed dragons, crossbones, and a variety of other inscriptions. He was looking to see if any of them had a triangle with the letter's F inside of it when he heard a squeaky voice.

"You looking for me?"

The squeaky voice belonged to a redheaded guy wearing a sequined tee shirt, jeans, and a necklace with a skeleton key attached to it. "Are you Leonard Merrick?"

"Yeah, but call me Lenny. Why do you ask?"

"I'm looking for a friend of yours. His name is Allan Dresmore."

"I wouldn't say he's a friend of mine, but I know him." Lenny's eyes flickered back and forth, like a mouse on the lookout for a cat. "We hung around together for a while a few years back."

"It's very important that I find him."

"I don't know where he is, but I tell you this, when you run across him, you're going to find him to be one weird character." Lenny noticed Mick smile and glance over at the bald-headed guy with the tattoo. "Don't let that guy fool you," he said. "He's married and has three kids. He lives in the suburbs and goes to church every Sunday. See that tattoo on his arm?"

"How can I miss it?"

"It's not real. It's only for show. He dresses like that for the customers. This place is a gold mine. A gold mine, I tell you!"

"I bet it is." The entrance door opened, and a group of kids walked in, each wearing clothes that Mick knew wouldn't be allowed at his school.

"Here comes some more bread," Lenny said as he pointed to the kids who had just entered. He shot a glance over at his boss. "Man, do you know what his mark up is on the records and the other stuff? It's fabulous. I tell you, I--"

"Hey, look, I'm sorry but I don't have time to talk about your boss' gold mine. What can you tell me about Allan Dresmore?"

"When he got too weird for me, I had to split."

Mick suppressed a smile. He found it hard to believe that anything would be too weird for Lenny. "What do you mean? Too weird?"

"Like spooky-weird, you know. He started talking about demons and Satan, and wanted to party in graveyards at night. I went to one, but man, that whole scene freaked me out."

"Why? Did they do a lot of drinking at these parties?"

Lenny shook his head. "That's another thing that was freaky about him. He didn't allow booze or drugs. I couldn't even bring my weed." He paused and grinned at Mick. "Do you know what I'm talking about, man?"

"I know you're not talking about dandelions."

Lenny snickered. "Hey, man, you're hip. We just have to get you out of that neck choker and--"

"Do you know what happened to Dresmore?"

"I know he's in the cities someplace, but I never see him anymore. Man, when he talked about dead bodies and graveyards, that's when I had to split. I told him to get a job as a grave digger or something."

"What did he say to that?"

Lenny shrugged. "Nothing. He just laughed."

Mick asked a few more questions but it was obvious that Lenny didn't have any other information than what he had given. He thanked Lenny for his time, declined his invitation to a party in South Minneapolis at a house rented by beautiful chicks, and told him that he may want to talk to him again.

"Hey, man, is Allan in trouble or something?"

"Here's a number you can call." Mick handed him a business card. "If you should happen to see him or hear from him in the next twenty-four hours, call it. There's twenty bucks in it for you."

"MAC Detective Agency? Hey, man, that's far out. No wonder you dress the way you do." Lenny slipped the card in his pocket. "You sure you don't want to come tonight? Those chicks would flip knowing that you're a detective. We could put your handcuffs to good use."

"Maybe next time," Mick replied, anxious to leave. The smell of incense was giving him a headache. As he walked out, the bald-headed man with the fake tattoo smiled at him and told him to come again. When the guy gave him the peace sign, Mick couldn't help but notice his diamond studded wedding band.

As soon as Mick left the store he hunted down a phone booth and called Howie. "Hi, are you going to be in the office for awhile?"

"Yeah. Why?"

"Is Adam there, too?"

"He's sitting in front of my desk right now and Jodelle's coming in a half hour. What's going on?"

"Listen, when she gets there, the three of you just stay put. Okay? I'll be in rush hour traffic, but I'll be there as soon as I can."

"What's going on?" Howie asked again.

"I've gotten us a lead."

"That's great. What is it?"

"This guy, Lenny, said that Damien could be working as a gravedigger at some cemetery."

"What?"

"Look. I've got to go so I don't get tied up in traffic."

"Well, get a move on it. We don't have much time left."

"I know. That's why I want all of you there. "I'll explain more when I see you."

Charles Tindell

Chapter 23

Maureen had no idea how much time had passed since Damien had first come down. After he had left, she again found herself alone in the dark with a corpse. She had to fight the tricks her mind played on her concerning the cadaver sitting in the chair behind her. *How had Damien referred to her? Mrs. Grimswell; that's right.* At one point, she was sure she heard Mrs. Grimswell breathing. Maureen tried to calm herself. *Breath slowly through your nose. In...out. In... out. In...out. That's it. Remember what Father would say.* "Get control of yourself and the situation." *In...out. In...out.* When she calmed down, she realized that what she had thought was the breathing of Mrs. Grimswell had actually been the sound of her own breathing. At another point, she panicked again when she heard footsteps. These were not imaginary, however. *Oh, my, God. She's coming toward me.* Maureen anticipated with horror Mrs. Grimswell's icy fingertips touching the nape of her neck. It was only when she realized that the footsteps were coming from above and that somebody was walking across the floor was she able to calm down. Afterwards, she had dozed, but it had been a fitful sleep. She had dreamt that there were chairs encircling her. In each chair sat a corpse, and they were all reaching out for her. Some were even inching their chairs closer to her. When she awoke, if it had not been for the tape on her mouth, she would have been screaming. *I can't do this to myself. It's going to drive me insane. Maybe that's what Damien wants to happen.* The very idea of that both terrified her as well as making her more determined not to let it happen. *What would father advise?* "Get control of the situation; don't let the situation get control of you." *Easier said than done, Father.* Maureen closed her eyes to concentrate. Then an idea came to her so quickly, it surprised her. She was sure that her father had somehow communicated it to her. The very thought of connecting the idea with her father gave her a moment of peace. *It's crazy but it's worth a try.* Others would consider carrying on an imaginary conversation with Mrs. Grimswell as her cracking under the strain, but she hoped that it might be a way of controlling her fear. She closed her eyes and imagined herself walking up to Mrs. Grimswell.

Hello, my name's Maureen Hammond.

That's a pretty first name.

166

This Angel Has No Wings

Thank you, and may I ask your name?

Certainly, my dear. My name is Matilda Grimswell, but everybody calls me Tilly.

At first, Maureen had to force herself to continue the imaginary conversation, but over time, she became more comfortable with it. Making up a family history and stories about Tilly provided the opportunity to push her fears aside. She shared with Tilly about how she and her sister, *Her name is Jodelle,* had always been close.

Some day we want to travel throughout Europe together. It's been something we've talked about since we were kids. We went with Father a couple of times, but never by ourselves.

Oh, that sounds wonderful. I've never been to Europe; the farthest I've ever been is Niagara Falls.

Why don't you come along? We'd love to have you.

That sure would be fun. I'd love to see—

Maureen first heard the door open at the top of the stairs, and then the creaking of the steps announcing someone coming down. Voices. Two men. *Please, God, please, let it be someone who's coming to free me.* She held her breath as she concentrated on the voices. It sounded like they were about halfway down.

"Hey!" a voice yelled from the top of the stairs, "do you need my help?"

"No, the two of us should be able to handle it."

Maureen didn't recognize the voice that had asked the question, but there was no mistaking whose voice it was that had answered. *Damien! My God, what are they planning to do? What do they need help for? Me? Why? For what?*

The stairs began to creak again. As the two men came down, she heard them laugh. When they got to the bottom, they stood quietly, peering at her. Both were dressed in dark suits and ties.

"Oh, I see you're awake," Damien said. "I trust that you've had a chance to rest. We came for Mrs. Grimswell. Her revival is in a couple of hours and we have to take her upstairs." He turned and looked up the stairs. "Turn on the lights!" he ordered.

The entire room lit up so bright that Maureen had to shut her eyes for a few moments. She tried to speak, to plead with him to let her go, but only muffled sounds came out.

"What's that you say?" Damien looked at his partner. "I think she's wondering how we're going to get Mrs. Grimswell upstairs."

Maureen wished they would take the tape off her mouth so that she could talk. If they did, she would try and strike a bargain. *My sister and I would pay you whatever you want. And we wouldn't say anything to the police.*

"Since Mrs. Grimswell is not able to walk up, we'll use the elevator." Damien smiled. "I'm afraid you'll be alone tonight."

Maureen watched as the other man whispered something to Damien.

"Is that so?" Damien arched an eyebrow. "John thinks you might have need for another potty break." He stood in front of her with his arms folded as though trying to decide what to do. "But I don't think so. You see, the first several days you were with us, you were pretty much out of it. We could give you water and let you have your potty breaks without worry."

Not wishing to look at Damien's smug smile, Maureen turned her head and closed her eyes, hoping that he would get the message.

"You may want to know that it's Wednesday already," Damien said. "You've been with us since last Friday."

Oh, no; six days! Maureen opened her eyes and glared at Damien.

"How time flies when you're having fun." Damien's smile faded. "Now that you're more alert, I don't think I want to take any chances with you. You're just going to have to hold it. If you can't, and you do have... an accident, don't worry. We'll clean you up for the party tomorrow night. We have a special room here where you can lay down and relax as we cleanse and purify you."

"The prep room?" the other man asked with a note of concern in his voice. "I don't think we--"

"Let me do the thinking," Damien said curtly, and then turned his attention to Maureen again. "As I was about to say, the table where you'll be bathed is stainless steel and may be uncomfortable, but it will do." He walked away, stopped, and then came back. "I'll be back to check on you later." A thin smile crossed his lips. "Just to make sure that you're not in need of anything. I'll even bring you a sip of water. After all, I wouldn't want our main attraction to become dehydrated."

Maureen listened as the two of them struggled to put the body on what she guessed was some kind of rolling cart. She heard the elevator door open, then close. Damien's friend walked by and touched her on the cheek. When he did, she noticed that part of his index finger was missing. She looked into his eyes and thought she saw a sense of dread. *He feels sorry for me!* She wanted to scream out that he could help her. He didn't have to do whatever Damien was forcing him to do. *Help. Please.* He turned, however, and walked away. When he got up to the top of the stairs, he switched off the lights and closed the door. She was in darkness again. *The next time they come, it'll be for me.* She felt so totally alone and scared that she now wished that Mrs. Grimswell was still with her.

This Angel Has No Wings

Chapter 24

MICK RUSHED INTO Howie's office, uttered a quick hello to Adam and Jodelle, and then turned his attention to Howie. "I'm sorry, I'm late, but traffic was terrible."

Howie leaned back in his chair and glanced up at the clock. Half past six. Considering that Mick had been in downtown St. Paul only forty-five minutes ago, he had made good time. "That's okay, don't worry about it." He paused. "You didn't get a speeding ticket, did you?"

"No! Why would I--"

Howie winked, and when he grinned, it was obvious that it was his way of settling his partner down.

Looking sheepishly at the other two, Mick nodded and then smiled. He took a deep breath, letting it out slowly. "Okay, I got the message. I guess I'm a little wound up."

"Hey, no problem, you'd do the same for me." Howie was concerned; his friend looked exhausted. "Do you want to sit down? I can get a chair from the kitchen."

"No, don't bother." Mick went over to the window ledge and used it to sit upon. He rubbed his eyes a couple of times, and then ran his hand back through his hair a couple of times. "While I catch my breath, fill me in on what you found out over at Damien's former high school."

Howie had already chastised himself for having spent too much time on what had turned out to be a dead end. "I didn't find out much. I struck out."

"You mean nobody else over there remembered him?"

"A couple of the teachers vaguely recalled him, but only when I showed them his picture." Howie noticed Jodelle glancing at the clock *Twenty-nine hours left.* "Tell us about what you found out."

Mick stood up, moved away from the window, and leaned against the wall. For the next few minutes he recounted the conversation he had with Lenny Merrick. As Mick talked, Howie glanced over at Jodelle a couple of times. The first time, she was tugging at her earring. The next time, she was chewing on her lip while repeatedly looking up at the clock. When Mick mentioned that Lenny thought Damien had a thing for dead bodies, Jodelle gasped. She quickly fumbled in her purse and pulled out a pack of cigarettes. Her hands shook so much that she barely was able to get one lit.

Mick waited until Jodelle exhaled. "I'm sorry, but that's what he said. I didn't mean to upset you."

Jodelle tossed the burnt match into the ashtray, and took another puff of her cigarette. "You don't have to apologize. What you're saying shouldn't surprise any of us." She looked from Adam to Howie. "I only wish that I hadn't gotten Maureen into this whole mess. She doesn't deserve it."

"You're right," Howie said. "She doesn't." He turned his attention back to Mick. "Did this Lenny guy have anything else to say?"

"Yeah, he said that Damien asked him if he wanted to steal some embalming fluid."

"Some what?" Howie wasn't sure he heard right.

"Embalming fluid. Lenny thought he was joking, but by the look Damien had on his face, he knew he was dead serious. That was one of the things that spooked him about Damien."

Adam gave Mick a puzzled look. "What in the world was he going to do with embalming fluid?"

"Do you have any idea what he'd do with it?" Howie asked Jodelle.

"Not exactly." She looked just as shocked as Adam. "I've only heard that some people use it in making drugs."

"Drugs!" Adam let out a puff of air. "Don't tell me that he's a drug freak."

Jodelle shook her head. "He's many things, but he's not that." She flicked the end of her cigarette into the ashtray. "The only thing I can think of is that he could sell it at a good price."

Howie wouldn't be surprise if Damien sold the stuff on the side. That was another aspect of the case they didn't have time to deal with now. They had to find Maureen, and fast. He wanted to know why Mick had sounded so excited over the phone. "Okay, where do you think your talk with Lenny is going to lead us?"

"Cemeteries."

"What are you talking about?" Adam asked.

"This might be the break we've been looking for," Mick said.

"I think I know what you're getting at," Howie said, "but why don't you explain."

"If what Lenny said about Damien having a thing for dead bodies is true, then he just may be working at one of the cemeteries in the area. Lenny had even suggested to Damien that he should become a grave digger."

Jodelle snuffed out her cigarette. "I know he always liked having our gatherings in those places." Her voice and eyes reflected a measure of hopeful excitement. "Now that I think about it, he was quite knowledgeable about cemeteries in the Twin Cities area."

Mick moved over and stood by the edge of Howie's desk. "That's good to know. I figure that we could call the cemeteries to see if they have someone working for them that fit Damien's description."

"I don't know," Adam said, "this whole things sounds like a mighty big long shot."

"I know that, but we don't have much else to go on at this point," Mick said with a note of irritability. "Did you ever follow up on your theory about him working at some church?" he asked Adam.

"I made phone calls most of the afternoon today, but no luck." Howie could hear the disappointment in Adam's voice. "And I know I barely scratched the surface of the number of churches in the area. Your idea sounds more plausible, but what if he doesn't work at a cemetery anymore?"

"Then we just have to hope that we find someone who remembers him. If we do, then maybe we can get an address."

Howie had hoped that Mick had come up with a more promising lead. Personally, he favored Adam's theory, but with the time they had left, they could never contact all the churches in the area. "Just how do you propose in doing this?" he asked.

"We can divide up the cemeteries and each of us calls."

"I want to help, too," Jodelle said.

Mick looked over at her, "You don't need to--"

"She's my sister, and I want to help." Jodelle shot a look at the clock. "We have less than thirty hours. So, please don't any of you argue with me."

"We're not going to," Howie said. "You have every right to be in on this."

"I agree," Adam said. "So let's get going. Just how many cemeteries are there?"

Mick shrugged. "I don't know, but I'm counting that there can't be too many."

Howie stood up. "Let me go get a telephone book." By the time he came back, Jodelle had lit another cigarette. "I suppose we just look up cemeteries." He opened the book, found the C's, and turned to the heading marked, Cemeteries. "Here we go." He ran his finger down the page, flipped the page over, and ran his finger down again. "Looks like there's about twenty or so. I'm not sure if all of these are cemeteries. Some of them look like they could be associations of some kind."

"We'll call them all," Mick said.

"Sounds good to me. We'll divide these up between us. That would give us each about five or six."

"That doesn't seem to be so bad," Jodelle said.

If only it was that simple, Howie thought. "At this time of evening, many of these places are probably closed."

"What do we do then?" Adam asked.

"Then we have to go out to the cemetery and find someone who works there."

Charles Tindell

"But couldn't that take a long time?" Jodelle glanced at the clock again.

"I'm afraid we don't have any other choice." Howie waited to see if anyone offered another option. "Okay, here's the plan. Since I only have one phone line, we can't afford to waste time waiting around while one of us is using it. I suggest that we all go home and get on the phone." He saw the frustration on their faces. "Sorry, but that's the only plan I've got, and unless someone has a better idea, I suggest we get going."

Adam looked at the other two, and shrugged. "Let's do it. How are we going to divide them up?"

Mick gestured toward Jodelle. "Since you live south, why don't you take those that are in your area. That might save us some driving time."

"Good idea," Howie said. He took out a notepad and began writing the names and phone numbers out. He wrote out Mick's list first. "Here you go."

Mick grabbed the list and was headed for the door when Howie called out. "Wait a minute."

"What?"

"I think we should all meet here tomorrow by noon."

"Noon," Jodelle cried. "That would only leave us twelve hours."

"I know, but we may need the time to check these out." Howie's head was spinning. Though he felt bone tired, he had to think straight. "Let's do this. When you're done with your list, come to the office. With any luck, we'll all be done before noon. And if by any chance, we hit on something still this evening, we make an effort to contact the others."

"Sounds good to me," Mick said. "See you tomorrow if not before."

"We have to find her," Jodelle said as Howie handed her a list. He saw the tears forming in her eyes.

"Maybe Damien won't go through with it," Adam said.

Jodelle brushed aside her tears. "Oh yes he will, and for two reasons. The first is that it's a way of getting back at me." She shut her eyes for a moment, and shook her head as if she couldn't believe this was happening. After taking a deep breath, she continued. "And secondly, he wants the power. He thinks he can do anything and get away with it. Once he starts something, he's determined to finish it. It's like an obsession with him. He's always been like that."

Howie stood up and looked Jodelle straight in the eyes. He spoke with such conviction that it even surprised himself. "This is one thing that he's not going to finish. Not if I can help it." He softened his tone. "Go home and make those phone calls. None of us are going to give up until we find her."

Jodelle smiled, but Howie felt it was just a brave front on her part. "I'll see you tomorrow," she said. "Be sure to call me if you find out anything. I don't care what time it is, call me."

As soon as she left, Adam turned to Howie. "Have you heard from JD?"

Howie exhaled deeply. "Yeah. He called earlier."

172

"And?"

"Nothing, but he's still working on it. What can I say?" Howie resumed writing out a list of cemeteries for Adam. "Here you go."

"Let's hope our luck changes," Adam said as he took the list from Howie. He was about to leave when he pointed to the chair Jodelle had been sitting in. "She left her cigarettes and matches here."

"Just put them on the desk. She'll pick them up tomorrow."

"What if we come up with zero on this?" Adam asked as he looked at his list.

"Let's not even think about that."

MAUREEN JOINED IN *the laughter with Jodelle and Tilly as they strolled down Piccadilly Circus in London. The English weather had blessed them with a gorgeous fall day. Pleasantly warm, and not a cloud in the sky. She was particularly pleased that Tilly had decided to accept her invitation to come with her and Jodelle on their trip. Tilly was having a marvelous time. Not wanting to miss a thing, she stopped and explored every shop along the street. Both Maureen and Jodelle were amazed at how much energy she had for a woman her age.*

"Thank you so much for inviting me," Tilly said as they walked the crowded streets. "I would never have dreamed that I'd ever have dared to do something like this. How can I ever repay you?"

"We're just so glad you decided to come along on our adventure." Maureen nudged her sister. "Aren't we?"

"Oh, yes, we sure are. When Maureen told me about you and how much fun you were, I just knew you had to join us." Jodelle gave Tilly a hug. "You're every bit of fun that my sister described you to be."

"Thank you." Tilly's blue eyes grew large as she looked around. "I just love London. I wish I could stay here forever. It's a dream come true."

Maureen was about to suggest that they hop on one of the two-decker buses and take a ride to Trafalgar Square when a wave of uneasiness came over her. Someone's looking at us. Looking? More like staring. *The thought that someone was watching them made her apprehensive.* Who could it be? And why? *She stopped and looked around. Although she couldn't spot anyone, she still had the unnerving feeling that they were being observed. She peered up at the buildings, thinking that perhaps someone was looking at them from a window.* Who are you? Where are you? I know you're there. I can feel your eyes on me. *She turned to tell Jodelle and Tilly, but they were gone. The crowds had disappeared. The streets were deserted.* Where has everybody gone? *A chill came over her, and she wondered if the sun had gone behind a cloud. When she looked up, dark stormy clouds now blanketed the sky. She turned in every direction looking for her sister and Tilly. She kept turning around and around. She couldn't stop. Everything became a kaleidoscope of various shades of gray. She spun faster and faster until she--*

Maureen opened her eyes, blinking them a couple of times. Sitting on a chair no more than ten feet away was a person. Damien! With his elbow resting on the arm of the chair, his chin was nestled in the wedge formed by his forefinger and thumb. He sat there, smirking. *How long has he been there?*

The very thought of him staring at her when she had been sleeping sent chills through her.

"I'm glad you're finally awake. I trust you were able to get some rest." He looked at his watch. "It's five minutes after the bewitching hour. My favorite time of the night." She wondered how he could keep that smirk at the same time he was talking. "You should know that I was very concerned about you."

Maureen shook her head. *I don't care what you do to me, but you're not going to sit there and lie to me, and expect me to believe it.*

A shadow of a frown drifted across his face for an instant and then the smile reappeared. "I came down because I thought you could use a drink of water." He picked up a cup from the floor and held it in front of him, moving it slowly in her direction. Instinctively, she moved her head back. "Now, now, you mustn't mistrust me." He tipped the cup slightly, allowing the liquid to splatter on the floor. "See, it's only water. Would you like some?"

She was going to refuse, but her tongue felt like a stick of dry wood. As she was trying to decide what to do, her eyes moved to his other hand. He was holding what looked like some kind of knife.

"Don't be alarmed about this." Damien held the knife up for her to see. "You're probably wondering what I'm going to use it for, aren't you?"

Maureen stared at him, hoping he could see the loathing in her eyes. *Don't let him play mind games with you. Control your fear.*

Damien stood up and walked over to her. When he got to within a couple of feet, he showed her the knife. "If you're thinking this is a scalpel, you're right. Actually, it's a very valuable one. A collector's piece." He set the cup down and held the scalpel in front of her. "Just look at this pearl handle. It's six inches long and fits my hand perfectly. And the blade is just the right length, four inches. It's one of my most prized possessions."

My God, is he going to kill me? Her thoughts went to Jodelle and it terrified her to think that she may never see her sister again. *Dear, Lord, no!* Maureen tried to yell but her screams only came out muffled.

"Don't get so upset," Damien chided. "You needn't worry. I'm not going to harm you." His words dripped with smugness. "You should be ashamed of yourself. Just what kind of monster do you think I am?"

If you'd only take this tape off my mouth, I'd tell you.

"I'm going to cut a little slit in the tape so that you can drink your water through a straw." She watched as he took a straw from his suit pocket. "I thought about taking the tape off, but decided that you might do something foolish like screaming. I couldn't allow that." Damien touched her cheek with the scalpel's blade. "Feel how sharp it is? If I was you, I'd hold my head very steady so I can make a nice clean cut." He touched the corner of her mouth with the blade. "Oh, before I begin, I forgot to tell you. In case you're wondering, I did clean it after I used it on Mrs. Grimswell in the prep room."

This Angel Has No Wings

Maureen shut her eyes. *Get hold of yourself. Keep calm. Keep calm. Keep calm.* She could smell Damien's cologne. It was the same as what her father had used. Old Spice. His fingertips, smooth and soft, now touched her cheek. The sound of his heavy breathing flooded her ears, his warm breath brushed against her face. The blade moved slowly, slicing through the tape. *Oooh! Stop! Stop!* The pain was intense, sharp. Her eyes flew open. Damien was grinning.

"How clumsy of me. It seems like I may have miscalculated and sliced your lip. Sorry." He held up the cup and inserted the straw into the slit.

As she sipped, she could taste her blood. *Don't think about it. Drink. Keep yourself strong; alert. Wait your chance. It will come. It's got to come. Please, God, please.*

When Maureen finished, Damien slid his finger across the opening in the tape. He showed her the blood, and sneered as he licked it off.

Charles Tindell

Chapter 25

HER LIP STUNG and felt swollen, but Maureen no longer had the taste of blood in her mouth. She had hoped that Damien would do something to stop the bleeding, but he made no effort. She didn't know how long he had stayed, but it seemed like hours. He had simply moved his chair closer and began talking about how he had come to work at the funeral home. She was not surprised when he said that the funeral home had been the perfect cover for him. *It fits you to a tee, you creep!*

"John, that's the fellow who was down here earlier, owns this place." Damien paused and then grinned. "But I own him. He's such a weak individual that he lets me do anything I want around here. Of course, it could be because he's afraid of me." Damien's grin had turned into a sneer. "Don't you want to know why he's afraid?"

When she had not responded, Damien picked up the scalpel and began looking at the pearl handle. "I didn't hear your answer. Let me ask you again. Don't you want to know why he's afraid of me?"

Don't give him cause to do something more. Play along with him. Act like you're scared. She nodded, pretending to blink back tears.

"Ah, that's more like it." Damien set the scalpel down, crossed his legs, and leaned forward. When he spoke, it was in hushed tones. "He's fearful that some pictures I took of him might turn up in his wife's hands. He knows that would be most unfortunate for him."

All the while Damien talked, Maureen's thoughts focused on when he and his friend would come to get her. She had prayed that Jodelle would have found her by now. *Maybe the detectives she hired will find me.* She had kept that hope before her as Damien continued talking.

When Damien had finished his story, he looked at his watch. "I'm afraid I have to get to bed." He stood up and stretched. "It's going to a big day for all of us. Get some rest."

After Damien left, Maureen made up her mind that, if at all possible, she wasn't going to let him get away with this. *Even if something happens to*

This Angel Has No Wings

me, I have to let people know I was here. She thought about trying to tear off a piece of her blouse with her teeth. *No, bad idea. That would be too obvious.*

As she sat there, she tapped her fingers on the wooden arm of the chair. *That's it! The chair!* It brought back memories of when she sat in her father's chair at his desk. As a little girl, she had scratched her initials into the arm of the chair with a paper clip. Her father had scolded her and sent her to her room. The next evening as he was working at his desk and she was reading on the couch in front of the fireplace, he asked her to come over. At first, she thought she was going to be scolded again. Instead, he set her on his lap and pointed to her initials. "Those will always remind me of you." He smiled and kissed her on the forehead.

Maureen didn't have any paper clip, but she could move her fingers and that gave her an idea. *Maybe just maybe, it will work. It has to.*

Charles Tindell

Chapter 26

Howie sat at his desk staring at a cup of coffee he had poured himself a half hour earlier. Between last night and that cup of coffee, he had contacted all the cemeteries on his list. Not one led to a single lead. *Not one lousy lead!* Mick had called an hour earlier and said that he was driving out to a cemetery in Northeast Minneapolis. "This might be what we're looking for," he had said excitedly. "The supervisor I spoke to says they have someone working there who fits Damien's description." Mick had talked so fast that Howie had to ask him to slow down. "If I turn up anything, I'll give you guys a call. Wish me luck."

"Yeah, good luck," Howie had said, and after hanging up, muttered, "Hope you have better luck than I did."

It was nearly eleven now, and Howie anxiously waited for Jodelle and Adam. *Maybe they've tried to call.* A couple of times he had picked up the phone to check if it had a dial tone. Once, he had even gone to the door because he was sure he had heard the downstairs entrance door open and bang close. *You're hearing things, buddy. Steady yourself down. Don't go losing it, now.*

Sitting in his chair, Howie looked over at the movie poster of *The Maltese Falcon*. *Bogie, I'm afraid I might have blown this case and it's going to cost someone her life.* "Come on, don't think that way," he told himself. He picked up his notepad and began paging through it. After only a few pages, however, he hurled it across the room. "Nothing!" he cried. "Just nothing!" Standing up abruptly, nearly tipping over his chair, he stormed over to the poster. He stood in front of it for a few moments and then yanked it down. *Who do I think I am pretending that I'm a detective?* He felt like putting his foot through the poster, but he couldn't do that to Bogie. *He's not the one who deserves it.* Howie set the poster against the wall, and went back and sat down. He folded his arms on the desk, put his head down, and closed his eyes. If there had been a closet in the room, he would have gone in and shut the door behind him.

This Angel Has No Wings

The ringing of the phone jolted Howie back to reality as he grabbed for the receiver, nearly knocking over his coffee in the process. "MAC Detective Agency," he answered as he took his handkerchief out and wiped up the coffee he had spilled. *Let's hope this is the lead we need.* As soon as he heard the voice, he knew it wasn't. He took a breath and tried to sound as cheerful as he could. "Hi, Joey. How're you doing?" He listened as Joey excitedly shared how the other kids in class now think he's so cool because he's hired a detective. *Kid, if they only knew the loser you hired.* Howie waited with dread for the anticipated question. It came early in the conversation. "Sorry, but I'm afraid I haven't found Midnight, yet." *Why don't you tell the kid the truth? You're a lousy detective and his cat is probably a victim of road kill.* "Joey, I have to tell you something." Howie paused, wishing his head would stop pounding. He couldn't remember the last time he'd had a good night's sleep. "What's that? I didn't hear you. Say that again." He listened as Joey told him that he thought that he was the bestest detective in the whole wide world, and that he just knows his cat will be found. "Thanks for having so much confidence in me, but listen now..." Howie hesitated. He could picture Joey's brown eyes and innocent smile. He glanced over at the movie poster sitting against the wall. "Joey, I...I just want you to know that I haven't given up. Yeah, I will. Thanks for calling." After he hung up, Howie sat for a long time staring at his cup of coffee. Finally, he got up, went over and picked up his notepad, and then walked over and hung the poster back on the wall. After straightening out the framed poster, he sat back down at his desk. He took a deep breath and then glanced up at the clock. Eleven-thirty. *Twelve and a half hours left.* He opened his notepad and resumed reviewing his notes.

"IT'S TIME FOR you to get ready for your trip," Damien said. He and another man that Maureen had never seen before had just come down the stairs. The other man stood off to one side; he had thinning hair and a pasty-gray complexion. He was shorter than Damien by a good three inches, and quite a bit older. Both of them were dressed in dark suits and ties. At another time and place, and under different circumstances, Maureen would have taken one look at the two of them and quipped, "They sure look like undertakers!"

Damien looked at his watch and then spoke to the other man. "We need to be on the road by two." The older man nodded, not saying a word. "That gives us a little more than a couple of hours to do all the necessary preparations."

"With you helping me, that shouldn't be a problem," the other man replied in a quiet voice. "What time are we going to get up there?"

"We should be up there by around seven. That will even allow us time to stop for a bite to eat along the way."

"Will getting there at seven give us enough time?"

"It should." Damien smiled as he turned to Maureen. "You see, my dear, there's a great deal of preparation to be done once we arrive up north.

The altar has to be constructed; the circle drawn, wood to be gathered, robes--"

"Can I get the fires started?"

Damien glowered at the man who cowered under his piercing stare. "I told you already, you could!" he said sharply, and then pointed his finger at him. "Now, don't you ever interrupt me again. Do you understand?"

Maureen felt her body stiffen at the harsh tone of Damien's voice. *Stay calm. Don't panic. Breathe easy. Don't let that mad man see any fear in your eyes.*

"You have to excuse Alfred," Damien said. "He doesn't have very good manners at times." He glanced in Alfred's direction. "Do you?"

Maureen felt sorry for the man whose tiny black eyes reflected his terror. She couldn't be sure, but she thought he was trembling.

"Do you?" Damien snarled again, not looking at Alfred. "I didn't hear your answer! Don't make me ask again!"

"Yes," came the meek reply.

Damien smiled at Maureen as he motioned toward Alfred. "See, even he agrees with my assessment of his manners. I'm a pretty good judge of character."

You're crazy. You're absolutely nuts. Maureen was sure Damien had to have some kind of personality disorder. *The guy's like Dr. Jeckle and Mr. Hyde.*

"It's going to be such a glorious night. And I have especially good news for you." Damien paused as if waiting for a reaction from her.

Let me go. That's the only good news I want to hear from you. That and your promise I'd never see you again.

"Ah, I can see that you're anxiously awaiting to hear what the good news might be." Damien shot a glance at Alfred. "Don't you agree?" he asked cheerfully. "I mean, doesn't she look like she's full of anticipation?"

Alfred nodded. When he looked at her, he avoided making eye contact.

I don't think he wants to go along with this. Maureen felt a twinge of hope. *If only I could be alone with him for a couple of minutes. Maybe, just maybe, I could get him on my side. He'd help me. I know he would.*

"We won't keep you waiting any longer," Damien said. "Here's the good news. The weather tonight will be mild and clear. Isn't that wonderful?"

You can stick that weather in your ear. Maureen looked at Alfred. *Why don't you help me? You can do it. Don't be afraid of him.*

"The weather man said that it will be warmer than usual and promised that the kids will have their best Halloween in years. And I agree. It truly will be a Halloween to remember. I do believe it will be perfect for any outdoor activities."

If Damien would only take the tape off her mouth, she would warn him not to go through with whatever he was planning. When she tried to speak, however, it came out as muffled noise.

"What's that you're saying?" Damien turned to Alfred. "I think she's wondering what kind of traveling arrangements we've made for her."

This Angel Has No Wings

Let me go, you arrogant creep! Maureen felt both fear and anger. *Concentrate on the anger. Don't let the fear get the best of you. Let the anger work for you.*

Damien walked over and squatted down in front of her. He was so close that she noticed the beginning of a sty in the corner of his left eye. "Did you know that you're going to be riding in style? First class. Nothing but the best for you." He stood up and nodded at Alfred. "Why don't you tell our guest how she'll be traveling?"

Alfred looked in her direction, but didn't make eye contact. He hung his head as if he was about to confess something he had done very wrong. "I don't..." he began, and then turned to Damien. "Why don't you--"

"Tell her!"

Maureen winced as Alfred jump back and then glanced around as though looking for some place to hide. *Poor man. Why does he put up with that? What does Damien have on him?* She thought of her sister's ordeal. *Pictures? I bet that's it. That seems to be Damien's thing.* She waited as Alfred inched closer. When he looked at her this time, he briefly made eye contact.

"We'll be taking our new funeral coach."

"Isn't that splendid!" Damien exclaimed. "And I must tell you that the scenery on the way will be outstanding. Many of the trees up north are already losing their leaves and taking on skeleton shapes; it will be a feast for the eyes."

What's he up to now? Be careful, he's got that arrogant tone in his voice. Don't be fooled by that phony smile.

Damien smiled at Alfred. "Of course, she won't be in a position to take in the sights, will she?"

What's he talking about?

"Why don't you go get it so she can see it."

Maureen watched Alfred as he scurried away. Within moments, she heard the elevator door open and then close. *Where's he going?*

"Don't worry, he'll be right back." Damien stepped in front of her and turned from side to side as though modeling some new fashion. "Do you think this suit is me?" He brushed something off his jacket sleeve. "To tell you the truth, I don't think I'm the type to be wearing suits and ties. It doesn't fit my personality."

A strait jacket would be the only thing that fits your personality! When they untied her, she would put up a fight. *You may take me but I'm not going easy.* Her plan was to have the element of surprise on her side. If she could knock Damien down, it just might give her enough time to run up the stairs and out the door. *Maybe there would even be some people up there that would help me.* She wasn't worried about Alfred. *He'd run and hide.* While she was still working out her plan, a rumbling from above caught her attention. It was the same noise she had heard before; something heavy being rolled across the floor.

"Don't worry about that, that's only Alfred. He can be so noisy at times." Damien buttoned his suit coat. "As I was asking, do you think I'm the suit type?"

This guy is full of himself. He's absolutely mad.

"You don't think I am, either, do you? I agree. Tonight, I'll be wearing my robe. It's so much more comfortable." His eyes swept over her. "I think you women have the answer in wearing dresses. Dresses give a person such freedom of movement."

If I had the freedom of movement now, I'd kick you right in the-- The opening of the elevator doors behind Maureen got her attention.

"May I please have some help?"

Damien's smile disappeared as he glanced toward the elevator. "I'll be right there." He shook his head and then whispered, "He's such a wimp. I don't know why I put up with him."

Maureen heard what sounded like a cart being rolled out of the elevator and then the sound of it rolling toward her. She turned her head, and out of the corner of her eye, she saw it. *Oh, my God.* She watched as the two of them moved the wood casket in front of her.

"Isn't it a splendid work of craftsmanship?" Damien patted the top of it. "It's solid oak, has brass railings, and can be hermetically sealed."

Don't let him get to you. Don't let him get to you. Stay calm. Breath. In...out. In...out. In...out.

"Don't look so alarmed." Damien spoke in a reassuring tone of voice. "I personally picked this out. It has the softest cushions you have ever laid on." He chuckled. "Oh, I suppose I spoke too soon. I can't imagine that you have laid in too many caskets, have you?"

Don't panic. Get a hold of yourself. Think straight. They're going to have to untie me. Get ready. She stared at the base of the casket, not wanting to make eye contact with Damien for fear of him becoming suspicious of her plan.

"This is such a clever idea of mine." Damien stroked the side of the casket. "Even if people were looking for you, who would ever think of stopping a hearse?"

Stay calm. He's coming.

Damien walked passed Maureen to the back of the casket, and began to push it past her. *What's he doing? What's going--* Maureen heard another cart being rolled in her direction. When Alfred pushed the stainless steel gurney in front of her, she stared at it in horror.

"I'm afraid Alfred insists that before we put you in his new casket, he wants you cleaned up. So that's what we shall do now. We'll take you to the prep room, clean you up, and put a nice new virgin-white robe on you." Damien's face twisted into a question mark as he asked mockingly, "You are a virgin, aren't you?"

She kept her eyes on Damien as he moved to the right of her. *Get ready. You can do it. You have to try.*

This Angel Has No Wings

When she felt something touching her left arm, she turned just in time to see Alfred plunging a syringe needle into her arm. The room began to spin, and she could barely keep her eyes open. *Stay awake. You got to...*

ADAM AND JODELLE arrived at Howie's office within a half hour of each other. Jodelle was the first to arrive. As soon as she came in, he could tell she hadn't had any luck with her list. Besides looking as though she hadn't slept all night, she had the appearance of someone who was in short supply of hope. When Adam came ten minutes later, she leaped up and looked at him with anxious anticipation. "Sorry," he said and just shook his head. With those words, she fell back into the chair. It wasn't long before she opened up her purse and took out a pack of cigarettes.

Jodelle eyes darted back and forth between the Adam and Howie. "What are we going to do, now?" She sounded desperate. "There's nothing left to go on."

"We're still waiting on Mick." Howie tried to sound hopeful. He heard the helpless feeling in Jodelle's voice, but had no answer for it. He was glad that she couldn't read minds. If she could read his mind, she would discover that he was feeling the same sense of helplessness. That time was running out was more than a cliché, it was becoming a nightmarish reality.

"When did you say Mick thought he'd show up?" Adam asked.

Howie looked at the clock; it was a few minutes past noon. "It's been a couple of hours since he's called me. He's got one last lead to track down. He should be here any minute." He hoped the phone would ring and that it would be Mick calling to tell them that he had located Damien.

"I wish he'd hurry up and get here." Jodelle began drumming on the arm of her chair.

"Would you like a cup of coffee or something to eat?" Howie asked, wondering when she ate last.

"Yeah," Adam added. "I can run out and get you something."

"No, thank you. I'm too upset to eat." Jodelle took a puff of her cigarette. "I keep thinking about my poor sister and..." she glanced at the clock, "we just have to find her."

"You told me that Maureen could take care of herself." Howie wanted to try and divert Jodelle from spending all her time thinking about what might happen to her sister. He was afraid she might go off the deep end. He had witnessed that before and didn't have the time or energy to deal with that now. "Didn't you tell me that she was a tower of strength?"

"Yes, even though she's younger, she was always the stronger one." A trace of a smile appeared on Jodelle's face. "She takes after our father in that respect. He was a man who could handle himself in any situation. Many people respected him for that."

When Adam spoke, it was with tenderness. "From what you've told us about your father, he sounds like a man who was blessed with many outstanding attributes."

"Oh, he was. That's why I wish he were here right now. He'd know what to do."

"You miss him, don't you?"

"I do. When he died, I was devastated. I didn't know what to do with myself. Maureen would've given me support, but I was ashamed to ask for it. Being the older sister, I should've been watching out for her." Jodelle took a puff off her cigarette and then put it out in the ashtray. "I think I got involved with Damien as a way of escaping my grief." Having made that self-disclosure, she leaned her head back against the chair and closed her eyes.

As they waited, Howie racked his brain trying to think of any clues they might have missed. He agreed with Jodelle; they just couldn't sit around doing nothing while waiting for Mick to show up. "Look, what do you say that we think of some options just in case Mick's lead fizzles?" He hoped Jodelle would be strong like her father, now. "We need to think about the different locations Damien might have taken your sister."

"But that could be any number of places."

"It could," Adam said, "but Howie's right. We have to narrow it down to--" He looked at Howie. "What would you say? Three or four places?" After Howie nodded, Adam continued. "That way, at least, we're doing something."

Howie knew Adam understood what he had in mind. Now, if they could convince Jodelle, it might give her some hope. "If we can narrow it down to say a couple of places, we can divide them up and check those out."

"That's a great idea," Adam said. "Do you have any suggestions?"

"Just one. There's an outside chance that this thing could happen at the cemetery where we found Mick." Howie was glad to see that Jodelle was listening with interest. "Is there any chance that he'd go to the cemetery where you had your meeting with him?"

"I don't know, maybe."

"That's two places. Let's put some other options on paper. When Mick comes, we can look at them and then decide. It's a gamble, but it's one we're going to have to take."

For the next fifteen minutes the three of them considered possible locations. Jodelle suggested two other cemeteries within the city limits that Damien had talked about during their meetings. They ruled out the smaller cemeteries in the area on the basis that gatherings would be too easy to spot from the road.

Howie was just going over the list of eight possible sites when the door opened and Mick walked in. "Did you find him?" Howie asked.

Mick shook his head. "Sorry, but it was a bust."

"Oh no!" Jodelle cried.

"So what happened?" Adam asked.

This Angel Has No Wings

"When I got over there and showed the supervisor the picture of Damien, he still wasn't sure. That gave me some hope, but the more we talked, I realized we weren't talking about the same person."

"What gave it away?" Howie asked.

"As it turns out, this guy who looked like Damien has a limp from some accident he was in a couple of years ago." Mick slammed his fist into his palm. "If that supervisor had only told me that over the phone, I wouldn't have wasted all this time."

"Don't be too hard on yourself," Howie said, "we know the feeling. All of us struck out as well."

Mick went over and sat on the window ledge. "Where does this put us now?"

It was a question Howie didn't want to hear. Although they had made up a list of possible places where Damien might have taken Maureen, he had a gut feeling that none of them would pan out. *I should call JD, but what could I tell him? That I had blown this case? That I should have called him in right at the very beginning? That my stubborn pride is going to get a woman killed?*

"I need another cigarette." Jodelle opened her purse. When she got her cigarettes out, the package was empty. "I have to get some more."

"Just a minute," Howie said as he opened one of his desk drawers. "You left these here yesterday." He handed her the pack of cigarettes and the book of matches.

Jodelle reached for them but dropped the matches on the floor. "Oh, I'm sorry. I'm just so nervous."

"Let me get them for you." Mick was about to hand her the matches when he glanced at the cover. "Where did you get these?"

"I don't know. Why?"

Mick tossed the matches to Howie. "Look at the cover and see if it brings anything to mind."

Adam stood up and looked on as Howie examined the matchbook cover. "What are you getting at?" Adam asked Mick.

"Just read the advertisement and think about some of the phone calls we received. And how about that music? We just assumed it was coming from a church organ."

After reading the cover, Howie knew what Mick was questioning. Now, if Jodelle would only supply the missing piece. "Think. Where did you get these?"

Jodelle's eyes flickered for a few moments. "I think it was when I met Damien in the cemetery. Yes, I'm sure of that. I needed a cigarette. He lit it for me and told me to keep the matches." She looked perplexed. "Why are you asking?"

"Because of what's on the back of the cover. It's an advertisement for Johnson Funeral Home. I think this finally is our break."

"What?"

Mick spoke up. "Lenny said that Damien liked to be around dead people?"

Jodelle's mouth dropped open. "Is this where you think he's working?"

"That explains the music," Adam said.

"Let's pay this place a visit." Howie said.

"Where is it?" Adam asked.

Mick looked at the match cover. "It's over in South St. Paul. It should take us forty-five minutes to get there."

"I'm driving," Howie said. "We'll make it in thirty."

"I'm going with you," Jodelle said.

Howie's first inclination was to say, no, but the look in her eyes told him that she was determined. "Okay, let's go." He looked at the clock. It was already two-fifteen. He thought about calling JD, but there was no time to waste.

Chapter 27

THE CAR SCREECHED to a halt just as the light turned red. "We almost made it!" Howie exclaimed to Mick.

Mick had both hands on the dashboard, still bracing himself. He raised his eyebrows and gave Howie a tight smile. "My foot almost went through the floor board," he said through gritted teeth.

"Hey, I'm just trying to beat the clock." Howie glanced in the rear view mirror. "You guys okay, back there?"

"I'm fine," Jodelle said.

Adam brushed back a shock of hair, leaned forward, and tapped Mick on the shoulder. "Will you tell our driver to cool it? And tell him that we're just as anxious as he is to get to that funeral home, but not as customers."

Howie had pushed his luck. He had run the last two lights as they were turning red. The second one was debatable as to whether it was still yellow when the car entered the intersection. A horn blared and a dark-blue sedan squealed to a stop; its driver had started into the intersection as soon as his light had turned green. As they zipped past the irate man, he shook a fist at them. "Sorry, but we're in a hurry," Howie muttered.

As Howie waited for the light to change, he drummed his fingers on the steering wheel. *Come on, come on.*

"How much farther is it?" Jodelle asked.

"It should be only a couple of more blocks." Howie glanced at his watch. Ten minutes till three. They had made good time. He felt hopeful about this lead. His instincts told him that they were on the right track this time. The light turned green and he floored it. At the next intersection, Mick braced himself again, but the light stayed in their favor.

"There it is," Jodelle cried.

"Where?" Howie asked.

"Up ahead on the right," Mick said.

Howie had to think fast. In less than a minute they would be there, and he had not yet formulated a plan. *Think, man, think.* He berated himself for not having had the foresight to talk it over with his partners on the way over. *Too late now even to ask for suggestions. No time.* When the idea came so quickly, it even surprised him. It was a simple plan, but it was the best he could come up with, and he thought it had a good chance of working. It has to work he told himself. He quickly shared it with the others.

"Are you going to be able to pull that off?" Adam asked.

"Of course, he is," Mick said, and then looked over at Howie. "Aren't you?"

"You always said I was a born actor. Hopefully, this will prove it." Howie slowed the car and then made a right hand turn into the parking lot of Johnson's Funeral Home. The shape of the white stucco building reminded him of a White Castle hamburger joint, only this was classier and six times as spread out.

"It's kind of strange looking for a funeral home," Mick said.

This whole case has been strange. "It looks like there's only one car here." Howie pointed to a black Buick parked by the side entrance. That means that only one person is working. He could handle that. Even if there were two people inside, he figured his plan would still work. If there were more than two, that could present a problem since he didn't have a plan B. He shut off the engine, and then turned to Mick. "You and Adam take the side and back entrances. I'll go in the front."

Adam opened his car door. "Where should we meet?"

"They must have some kind of lobby area. Meet me there. Remember what I told you, I'll keep them busy while you two search the place."

Howie felt a hand on his shoulder. "What about me?" Jodelle asked. "I'm not staying here knowing that Maureen may be in there."

"Look, I need you to stay and be the look-out just in case someone sneaks out of the building while we're in there." Howie didn't know what they were getting into, but he didn't want to take the chance of Jodelle being caught in the middle of something. "If you see anyone leaving, lay on that horn."

Jodelle looked as though she was about to protest, but then nodded. "When you find her, you let me know right away, won't you? You won't forget me out here, will you?"

You mean if we find her. "Don't worry, we'll let you know," Howie said. He got out and opened Jodelle's door. "You get in the front seat," he told her. "I'll leave you the keys. If anyone comes out, give us a blast on that horn."

"What if they get into that car and take off? Should I follow them?"

"No." Howie hadn't thought about that possibility and he couldn't afford to leave either Mick or Adam out in the car. If there was a chase, and there could be, he didn't want to be left behind. "You start the car. When you see me come out, I'll be moving. So, just open the door, slide over, and I'll take the wheel."

"What about us?" Mick asked.

"Somebody's got to search the place. We'll come back for you guys." Howie's mind felt like it was riding a merry-go-round that had spun out of control; there were too many factors to content with. He turned to Jodelle. "Just make sure you remember in what direction that car heads out. Okay?"

Howie waited until Mick and Adam got to the side of the building before he started for the main entrance. With him coming in the front, and his partners coming in the side and back entrances, nobody could leave without being seen. As he approached the main door, Howie had to give Damien credit for having such a clever cover. *This is right up his alley. The creep!* Just before he opened the door, he took a deep breath to compose himself. He soon found himself in a carpeted lobby with high back Victorian chairs and couches covered in red velvet, round marble coffee tables, and brass floor lamps with pleated ivory colored light shades. The furnishings along with crystal chandeliers suspended from a ten-foot ceiling made him feel as though he had stepped into a turn-of-the-century hotel lobby. From the lobby area, a wide hallway, led straight ahead to a back entrance. Branching out from the main hallway, were two other hallways. One angled off to Howie's left and the other, to his right. He waited until Mick and Adam joined him. "Did you guys see anyone?"

"No," Mick said. "The place is deserted."

"Do you hear that?" Adam asked. Organ music played softly over a sound system. "Do you think that's what we heard over the phone?"

"I can't tell, but it sounds like it," Howie said. "What about you?" he asked Mick. "What do you think?"

"I don't know, it could be"

Adam glanced around. "Do you think she's here someplace?"

"I hope so," Howie replied, "but we better--"

"May I help you?" The voice came from a tall, lanky man dressed in a dark suit who seemed to have appeared out of nowhere. He stepped into the lobby from the hallway to their left. He wore a smile that looked as if it was held in place with hair spray.

Howie cleared his throat. "Ah, yes, my uncle died. I'd like to talk to someone about making arrangements."

"Of course, and your name, please?"

"My name?" Howie didn't want to give his real name for fear the guy with the plastic smile was connected with Damien. If that was the case, Howie was sure that he would recognize his last name. "My name is Howard," he cleared his throat again while noticing a couch in the corner. "Howard Davenport."

"Well, Mr. Davenport, you have my deepest sympathy. The death of a loved one is always difficult. My name is John Bones. I'm the owner."

"Bones?" Besides being amused at the name, Howie was also curious. "I thought this was the Johnson Funeral Home."

"Mr. Johnson died five years ago." Mr. Bones replied, still retaining his fixed smile. "When I purchased the home from his family, they gave me permission to keep the name, Johnson Funeral Home. This place has been in the neighborhood for nearly fifty years. It had a good reputation already so I thought it best not to change the name. I'm sure you understand."

"Of course." Howie wondered if the guy slept with that phony smile. "Are you the person who makes the arrangements, or is there someone else?"

"You may talk to me. I would be happy to be at your service. I know this must be a very difficult time for you." He turned toward Mick and Adam. "Are you members of the family as well?"

"No, they're friends," Howie quickly said. "They came along to give me support. Why don't you guys wait out here while Mr. Bones and I talk."

"It must be nice to have such good friends. They are certainly welcome to come in and join us if they so desire."

"We'd rather not," Mick said. "Thank you, anyway."

Howie took the funeral director aside. "I think you and I need to talk privately about the arrangements." He lowered his voice. "There are some things that are quite unusual. You see my Uncle Hubert was quite eccentric."

"Certainly. I understand."

Adam made himself comfortable in one of the high back chairs. "Take all the time you need. We'll wait out here for you."

Howie walked into the office, making sure the door was shut behind him.

"Have a chair, Mr. Davenport."

"Thanks." Howie watched as Bones sat down behind his desk, opened a drawer, and took out several forms.

"Before we get to the details of the actual service itself, there are some questions that I need to ask for our records." His smile had not left him. "As I said, I know this must be hard for you, but this is a necessary part of the process."

"Go ahead and ask your questions. I'll do my best to answer them, but you'll have to be patient and give me time."

As soon as the door closed behind Howie, Mick and Adam jumped up from their chairs. "You take the left hallway," Mick said, "I'll take the other one. Be sure to try every door."

"What if we run into someone?"

"Just tell him that you're looking for a bathroom or something."

"And if we run into Damien?"

Mick's eyes narrowed. "I hope we do." He gave Adam a pat on the arm. "Just be careful. I'll meet you back here."

Adam watched Mick move down the hallway, open a door and disappear behind it. "Well, you better get going," he told himself. Partway down the hall he came upon some double doors. Cautiously, he opened one and peeked in. An oak casket rested on a stand near the far right end of the room. The smell of funeral sprays permeated the space. The casket was open, but from where Adam stood, he couldn't see who was in it. He closed the door, but then stopped. He opened the door again and slowly approached the casket. When he got close enough to view the body, he was relieved to see that it was an elderly gentleman. "Sorry, I didn't mean to disturb you," Adam whispered, and then felt foolish in doing so. There were doors to the right and left of the casket, leading out of the room. He took the left door. It led into a hallway. The next two doors he tried opened into sitting rooms. Although the next two doors were restrooms, he checked both out to be thorough. Empty. He came to a T in the hallway. To his right, the hallway had a couple of doors on each side, and then branched off again. To his left, the hallway came to an end, but there was a door halfway down.. He quickly walked to the door and opened it. The room had no windows; it's only source of light at the moment came from the hallway. From what he could tell, the room was some kind of storage space. The sound of movement startled him, causing him to jump back. Although he couldn't be sure, he thought the noise came from the far corner of the room. It was too dark to see. "Maureen?" he whispered. The sound of rattling paper unnerved him. He felt for the light switch, found it, took a deep breath, and flipped the switch. "What in the world?" he cried.

"Before we go any further, Mr. Davenport, I think it might be a good time for me to show you our selection room."

"Selection room? What's that?"

"It's like a showroom where we have a display of caskets." Howie couldn't believe how the guy could be talking about caskets and smiling at the same time. "I'll show you the various models, answer any questions you may have, and then leave you to yourself." Bones leaned forward slightly and folded his hands on his desk. "The selection of a casket for one's loved one is one of the most intimate decisions a family member can make, and therefore, I strongly believe that it should be a private affair."

"Oh, I'm...I'm...not up to that yet," Howie stammered. "I just...just..." he paused as he bit his lip and sniffled. "I'm sorry, I don't mean to go on like this, but he was my favorite cousin."

"Cousin?" Bones set his pen down. "I thought you said he was your uncle?"

"I did? I mean, that's right, he is." Howie buried his face in his hands for a moment. "Forgive me, but I'm just not myself."

"That's quite alright. I understand." He handed Howie a box of tissues.

"Thank you." Howie took the box, got a couple of tissues, and loudly blew his nose. "May I have just a few moments to compose myself?"

"Of course." Bones stood up. "I'll just step out and check to see if your friends are in need of anything."

"Oh, that's not necessary." Howie quickly put the tissues back on the desk, and smiled "I'm ready now. It doesn't take me long to work through my emotions." Although Bones still had his plastic smile, Howie wondered what was going through his mind.

"You were saying that your uncle was eccentric," Bones said as he sat down. "In what way might that affect his service?"

Charles Tindell

"I'm not sure how this is going to sound." Howie leaned forward. "You see, my Uncle Hubert was an admirer of King Arthur and the Knights of the Round Table."

"I'm not sure I understand what that has to do with the services we provide." Bones wrote something down on a sheet of paper. "But let me assure you, that whatever your wishes, we will do our best to accommodate them."

Howie took another tissue and blew his nose again. "That's comforting to know because Uncle Hubert wants to be buried in a suit."

"That is certainly a standard practice. I don't see how--"

"You don't understand." Howie gave him a weak smile. "Uncle Hubert requested that he be buried in a suit of armor."

"In what?" The smile flickered for a moment.

"A suit of armor," Howie repeated. "That's not against the law, is it?"

"Ah, I don't believe it is." Bones cleared his throat. "I must say, though, this is a most unusual request."

Howie moved his chair closer to the desk. "Let me tell you the story behind it. It all started when Uncle Hubert took a trip to England as a young man..."

MICK FELT SICK to his stomach. He had just come from what he figured to be the preparation room. It reminded him of a surgical operating room. A long stainless steel table stood in the center of the room. In several of the drawers he found an assortment of scalpels and other instruments whose use he didn't want to venture a guess. He was glad to get out of there, but now he had entered into a room full of caskets. While he was sure he wouldn't find anything, he walked around checking every casket. Several of the caskets were closed, and he opened them cautiously. With the first one he opened, he had his eyes shut, and only peeked once he had raised the lid. After he finished checking all of the caskets, he looked at his watch. Howie had been in the office for nearly a half hour now. Mick stepped out into the corridor and moved to another door. It led to the garage. A funeral hearse and two black Cadillacs took three of the four stalls. He checked out each of the vehicles. Nothing. As he came back into the corridor, a door at the far end was opening. "Oh, oh," he muttered and ducked back into the garage. He left the door open a crack, and then breathed a sigh of relief when he saw it was Adam.

"Hi, buddy," Mick said as he rushed unannounced into the corridor, startling Adam, causing him to jump back.

"Hey, don't do that to me." Adam leaned against the wall; his heart pounding. "Have you found anything of Maureen?" he asked Mick.

"No, have you?"

Adam shook his head. "What do you say, we check down that way." The first door they tried led into a small storage area. When they opened the other door, they came upon a wooden stairway leading down into the basement.

"It's pretty dark down there," Adam said. "Can you see anything?"

"No, but here's a light switch." Mick flipped the switch. "We better go down and check it out, don't you think?"

"Let's do it." Adam followed Mick. "They should oil these steps or something," he whispered as they slowly moved down the stairs.

When they were about halfway down, Mick stopped. "Do you smell that?"

"Yeah, smells like flowers. Why?"

"I'm not sure but there's something familiar about that smell." Mick closed his eyes and sniffed the air. "I have a feeling that I've been here before."

"You mean when they kidnapped you?" Adam noticed beads of sweat running down his friend's forehead.

"Yeah, maybe." Mick wiped his brow with a shirtsleeve. "There's something about this place that makes my flesh crawl."

"Take a gander at that," Adam said when they reached the bottom. He pointed to a high back wooded chair shoved up against a floor-to-ceiling pillar. *It's an odd place for a chair.* He glanced around the room. At the far end, he noticed elevator doors.

Mick and Adam moved closer to the chair. "What's that on the arm?" Mick asked.

"It looks like someone's initials." Adam bent over to get a closer look. The letters were barely visible. "Looks like HW."

"Wait a minute." Mick sat in the chair. "I bet somebody sat here and scratched their initials." He leaned forward to examine them. "When you see them from this side..." he looked up at Adam. "MH."

"Let's go find Howie," Adam said as he rushed toward the stairs.

THE FUNERAL DIRECTOR was showing Howie a catalogue depicting grave vaults when Mick and Adam barged in. Bones looked up so quickly that his glasses slipped to the edge of his nose. He pushed them up, regained his composure, and resumed his smile. "If you just give us a few more minutes, Mr. Davenport and I will--"

"We got something!" Adam blurted out.

Mick shut the door. "She's been here!"

"What are you gentleman talking about?"

Howie leaned over and grabbed Bones by his tie, pulling him across the desk toward him. "We're talking about Maureen Hammond. Where is she?"

"What are you doing? Have you gone mad? Stop, you're hurting me."

"Mick, stand guard outside the door," Howie said. "Be on the watch just in case the place gets a late afternoon visitor."

"If somebody comes in, what should I tell them?"

"Tell them the place is closed for the rest of the day." Howie waited until Mick shut the door behind him. "Okay, Bones, where is she?"

"I have no idea who you're--"

Howie yanked down hard on Bone's tie with one hand as his other hand pushed the back of his head; his face slammed into the desk. "Oh, my nose!" Bones cried out.

"I asked, where is she?"

"I don't--"

Howie yanked again on the tie. The nosepiece of Bones' glasses broke, sending both halves flying in different directions. "Don't give me any more of that 'I don't know stuff.'" Howie stood up, moved around the desk until he was positioned beyond the chair Bones was sitting in. He jerked the funeral director's head back, strangling him with his own tie. Bones clawed at the silk rope around his neck, but to no avail. His face turned the color of a beet. "If you don't come clean, we'll make sure you are charged with accessory to murder."

"Murder!" Bones gasped. Blood dripped from his nose. "It wasn't my idea. I told him that she shouldn't be here." Even though he could barely get his words out, Howie wouldn't give him any slack. "He told me he wasn't going to harm her." Bones struggled to free himself but was no match for Howie. His eyes bulged as he cried, "I don't want to get involved with any murder."

"Where did he take her?" Howie pulled harder.

"Better watch it," Adam said, looking at Howie with concern. "He looks like he could pass out. If he does, that's not going to do us any good."

Still hanging on to the tie, Howie moved back around and sat down. He pulled Bones toward him, squashing his face against the desk. "Okay, I'm giving you some slack." He loosened his grip. "But if you don't give us the information we want, and fast, so help me, God, I'm going to bounce your face on this desk until you do."

Bones wheezed until he was able to take a couple of deep breaths. "He...he took her up north."

"Where up north?"

"Some place outside of Ely."

"Ely!" Adam exclaimed. He gave Howie a worried look. "That's four hours away."

"What time did they leave?" Howie asked.

"A...a...few minutes after two."

Howie looked at the wall clock behind the desk. Four-fifteen. "Okay, now tell us where they went."

"It's a place he found some time ago. He uses it for special gatherings."

"A cemetery?"

"No, I think it's an abandoned farm house."

"What do you mean, you think?" Adam asked. "Haven't you ever been there?"

Bones shook his head. "I was going there tonight for the first time."

"If you've never been there, how would you know where to go?"

"He drew me a map."

Howie looked over at Adam and smiled. "Well, that's considerate of him. Where's this map?" When Bones didn't answer, he gave a yank on his tie.

"No, no. Wait. It's in my desk. Top right hand drawer. In the back."

"Take a look," Howie told Adam.

Adam opened the drawer. "Here it is. I got it."

"Good. Call Mick in."

If Mick was surprised to see the funeral director with his face squashed down on his desk, he didn't show it. After Howie filled Mick in, he turned his attention back to Bones. "Okay, what else did he tell you about the place?"

"All I know is that once you go thirty miles past Ely, you take the first gravel road to the right." He reached for the box of tissues, pulled out a couple, and held them to his nose. "I'm not sure how far you go on that road. He told me that if I came up tonight, I would know which turn off to take from the fire sign."

"Fire sign? What are you talking about?"

"Years ago, people who lived out in the country had signs with numbers on them." Bones took several more tissues. "When they called to report a fire, the fire department would know where they were located by their fire number."

"You mean to tell me you don't know which sign to turn at?" Howie asked.

"That's right."

"You're lying."

"I swear to you, I'm not. He was very secretive about that area." Bones looked at each of them as he dabbed at his nose with the tissues. "The sign must have some kind of symbol on it. I don't know what symbol, though."

"We better get moving," Howie said. "We can't waste anymore time here. Any suggestions what we do with him?"

"I know just the place," Mick said. "Come on, Mr. Bones, there's a chair downstairs that's just waiting for you."

They took Bones down to the basement. Mick found some rope in a drawer and tied his feet and arms to the chair.

"What do you know," Adam said, "here's some Duct tape to put over his mouth." He tore off a strip and handed it to Howie.

"Keep smiling," Howie said as he slapped the tape over his mouth. "Let's go now."

At the top of the stairs, Mick flipped the lights off, and yelled down, "Sweet dreams, Bones. We'll be back for you...maybe."

"Okay," Howie said, "did you find anything else here that might be a clue. Anything out of the ordinary?"

"I found a cat," Adam said.

"A what?"

"A black cat. The poor thing was in a wire cage in one of the storage rooms."

Charles Tindell

Howie's mind raced. "Did you see any white markings on it?"

"I didn't look that close."

"I want to take a quick look before we leave. I have a feeling I know who it belongs to."

This Angel Has No Wings

Chapter 28

"Do I have to drive the whole way?" Alfred asked.

Damien kept his eyes shut and continued to lean his head back against the headrest, choosing to ignore Alfred. His thoughts were of later that night, and of those within the coven. There had been movement in the group against him. *I'll solidify my power over them. After tonight, they still may not like me but they'll fear me like they have never before. When I--*

"Are you awake?"

"Yes." Damien didn't move. *How can I sleep with you whining?*

"I asked if--"

"I heard what you asked, and yes, you have to drive."

"But why?"

"Because I said so." Damien looked at his watch. "We'll stop for a bite to eat around five. After that, I'll drive."

"But that's still a half hour away."

"Just drive." *If you don't stop your whimpering, I'm going to cut your tongue out.* That thought intrigued Damien. He had read about such things being done in earlier times. *That could prove interesting. Perhaps, I should threaten to do that to any within the group who chose to ignore my leadership.*

"Do you think there's any chance of her suffocating?"

Damien opened his eyes. *Why didn't I leave him back at the funeral home?* "She's got plenty of air."

"So, you didn't seal the casket?"

"No. Now, don't worry about her. She's resting comfortably." *Probably getting more rest than I am. At least, she doesn't have to listen to your incessant chatter.* Less than five minutes went by when Alfred spoke up again.

"How long before that shot wears off?"

"Why?"

"I wouldn't want her to wake up while she's in that casket, would you? That would be awful for her."

"We'll be there long before that stuff wears off." *Hmmm, waking up in a coffin. And knowing it!* Damien turned around and looked through the glass window at the casket. *Imagine the fear one would have realizing where they were.*

197

The idea excited him. He turned back around. "After it wears off, she'll only be groggy for about an hour. That will be perfect timing." Damien smiled. "After all, we wouldn't want a lifeless body, would we? That wouldn't be much fun, now would it?"

Alfred shot a glance at him. "We're just going to scare her, aren't we? I mean, we're not going to do anything more than that?"

Damien shut his eyes and leaned his head back. "Just drive, will you."

This Angel Has No Wings

Chapter 29

Howie glanced in the rearview mirror at Jodelle and Adam in the back seat. Adam had his eyes closed, his head resting against the back of the seat. Jodelle was staring out the window. He could only guess what was going through her mind, and didn't like the images the flashing through his. When he glanced in the mirror again, Jodelle noticed him and smiled.

"How're you doing?" he asked.

"Not so good. I just hope that we'll find her in time."

"We will, don't worry." He smiled back at her. Jodelle had more courage than she gave herself credit for, and he would tell her that once this was all over. Now, if they would only find Maureen, and find her alive.

Mick touched him on the arm. "Do you want me to drive?"

"No, that's okay." Howie preferred driving; it gave him something to do. They had been on the road for nearly four hours, and had just turned off the highway. The sign read, Ely - 27 miles. They would get there around nine, which didn't give them a lot of time. Pushing the gas pedal, he inched up the speedometer. He would have driven faster if it had not been for the unfamiliar winding road and how pitch-black it was traveling through the sparsely settled forest area without the benefit of streetlights. As it was, he was driving over the speed limit. Mick had cautioned him, however, to be careful for deer crossing the highway. He hadn't paid any attention to the warning until three deer had run across the road some twenty yards ahead and he had to hit the breaks. After that, he slowed back down to the speed limit.

"I still can't believe how lucky we were in finding Joey's cat," Mick said.

Howie was glad that Mick brought up Joey and his cat; talking about it might lessen the tension they were all feeling. "Yeah, I'm looking forward to seeing his face when I tell him." Howie was ecstatic when he discovered that the black cat in the cage had white markings identical to what Joey had described for Midnight. For a few minutes, he had struggled as to whether he should leave the cat at the funeral home. Having found Midnight, he didn't want to let Joey's pet out of his sight. "We don't have room to take it with us," Mick had argued, "and we don't have time to bring it back to the office. It'll be okay where it is for now; it looks healthy." Howie reluctantly agreed. "Okay, but we're coming back and getting that cat no matter what time of night it is." As an after thought, he added, "Besides, we should check on that funeral director, Bones."

Mick pointed to a sign, Ely - 21 miles. "It won't be long now."

Howie relaxed his grip on the steering wheel. These past several hours had been like an eternity. "The sooner we get there, the better." Earlier, outside of the funeral home in St. Paul, the four of them had briefly discussed the options they had. Howie had tried to reach JD, but the police sergeant who answered said that Davidson was on a case. When the sergeant asked if he could help, Howie hung up; he didn't have the time to waste trying to get the city police involved now. He suggested that they stop at the police station in Ely to enlist their help.

"How big of a town is Ely?" Jodelle asked, having offered no objection to getting the police involved now.

"I don't know, but they have got to have a police department," Howie said. "Once they hear what Damien is planning, they'll come with us."

"I'm glad we're doing this," Mick said.

"So am I," Adam said from the back seat. "We'll need all the help we can get."

THEY ARRIVED IN Ely shortly after nine, found a gas station, and asked directions to the police station. When they got there, the dispatcher told them that the chief and his two deputies were out serving a summons. There were no other officers available.

"What time will they get back?" Howie asked.

"I'm not sure. It could be an hour or two."

"What!" Adam exclaimed. "How come so long?"

"Because the guy getting the summons lives out in the woods about ten miles out of town," the dispatcher replied. "He's an ornery cuss. That's why the Chief brought the others with him. He was expecting trouble, and he said he'd get back when he got back."

Jodelle tugged at Howie's sleeve. "What are we going to do?"

"We can't wait around." Howie turned to Mick. "Here's the deal. You and Jodelle stay here and convince the Chief when he comes back to come up to that farmhouse. Meanwhile, Adam and I will take off." He handed the map to Mick. "Here, I'll leave you this."

"Won't you need it?"

"I have it memorized."

Mick glanced at Adam and then back at Howie. "I don't know if just the two of you going is such a good idea."

"Look, I don't have time to argue," Howie said.

"What are you going to do when you find them?"

"We'll figure that out on the way."

"Has she come to yet?" Damien asked as Alfred walked up to him.

"Yes, and she wants to talk to you."

"Is that so? Well, I feel honored." Damien walked over to where Maureen was bound to a tree. Her hands had been tied in front of her with one end of a rope, and then the rope slung over a tree branch. He had instructed Alfred to pull on the rope until her arms were raised over her head. Once that was accomplished, he told Alfred to tie the rope to the trunk. As Damien approached Maureen, he could see that she had both a look of fear and defiance in her eyes. He liked that. He liked that a lot. "I understand you wish to speak to me." He stood before her and smiled. "First, allow me to pay you a compliment. You look so elegant in your nice new white robe. It almost looks like a choir robe, doesn't it? I almost expect you to start singing any minute. Do you know any appropriate hymns?"

"What did you do with my clothes?"

"My, my, such a nasty tone of voice. You shouldn't sound so harsh. If I didn't know you better, I might think you were angry at me." He chuckled. "If looks could only kill, I'd be the one dead by now." He checked the rope to make sure it was tied securely to the tree. "As far as your clothes, we disposed of them. They were smelly and soiled. We bathed you and got you a new outfit. I have to tell you, that robe has never been worn before."

"If you want money, I'll give it to you."

Damien scoffed. "Do you think I want your money when I have you. You of all people should know that money isn't everything. Didn't your father ever tell you that money is the root of all evil?"

"You're not going to get away with it. My sister--"

"Your sister?" Damien laughed. "Did she ever show you the pictures I took of her? They are quite lovely and very..." he paused and stroked his chin. "Hmmm, how should I describe them? I know. Provocative. They are quite provocative."

"Why are you doing this?"

"Because it's Halloween. It's trick or treats. I played a trick on your sister and you're going to be the treat." He pointed toward several people off to her right. "Do you see what they're doing? They're preparing the altar. I've got to say it's very ingenuous the way we're constructing it. Would you like to know how we're doing it?"

Maureen shook her head.

"Oh, don't be like that. You'll spoil all the fun." He pointed toward the group again. "They're using an old barn door for the altar. It'll be set upon some cinder blocks we found in back of the barn. Don't worry about slivers from the door. We'll drape it with a black cloth. With your white robe and blond hair against the black, it will be a perfect backdrop." He smiled. "Of course, it's a little stark." He glanced over at the altar. "I know. To offset the starkness, we should have another color. Perhaps, red. Blood-red."

"You're sick. You should be locked up."

"What a terrible thing to say to someone who has gone to so much trouble in planning this celebration for you." Damien put his hand to his heart as if her statement had hurt him. "I'll just pretend that I didn't hear you say that," he added, and then walked away.

ADAM ROLLED DOWN the car window. "It's so dark out there, I can't see a thing." He turned on Howie's flashlight and shined it toward the side of the road. "How far have we gone?"

Howie looked at the odometer. "Just about thirty miles." It was already after ten, and he was worried. He had promised Jodelle that they would find her sister in time, and he was determined to keep that promise. "Keep watching for that road."

"I have been. We've seen lots of dirt roads in the past few miles going off one way or another. Who would want to live out in these boondocks, anyway?"

"I don't know, but this dirt road is supposed to go off to the right." Howie slowed the car for fear of missing the turnoff.

"Better slow down some more," Adam said. "It's really tough to-- hey, I bet that's it up ahead."

"Okay, I see it." Howie stepped on the gas. When he turned the corner, he almost lost control of the car as the rear end fishtailed. "Whoa!" he cried, and then glanced over at Adam who was hanging on to the dashboard. "Hey, I can't help it, I don't have any experience driving on these kind of roads."

"You're getting it now."

Howie couldn't believe how much darker it had become. The forest was like black curtains on both sides of the road. "Now, all we have to do is to find this fire sign."

"We don't know what exactly we're looking for, do we?"

"That's right. We're on our own now. Damien told Bones the sign would be obvious." Howie was getting a headache, and his neck muscles felt tight. Take it easy, relax, he told himself as he loosened his grip on the steering wheel. "See any yet?"

"What are they suppose to look like?"

"I'm not sure but I think they're the size of a car license. They got numbers on them, and are staked several feet off the ground. Also, look for a driveway leading off into the woods."

"What did that funeral director say about the farmhouse?"

"That we wouldn't be able to see it from the road. It's tucked away in the woods someplace." Howie wished he had something to take for his throbbing headache.

"Why would anyone do something like this?" Adam shot a glance over at Howie. "What's wrong with Damien, anyway?"

"Who knows? Jodelle told me that he likes the power that comes from being in charge. The more power he has, the more he has control. He gets his kicks from having control over the lives of people."

"I suppose you're right. He thinks…hey, wait a minute. Stop!"

Howie slammed on the brakes.

"Back up."

"Did you see something?" Howie put the car in reverse and backed up until Adam told him to stop. "What is it?" He leaned over and saw what Adam was beaming the flashlight on. The sign, barely visible, stood among over grown weeds.

"I can't see the numbers," Adam said. "I'm going to have to get out."

Howie watched as Adam ran to the sign, brush the weeds aside, and then rushed back to the car. "What number was it?" he asked as Adam got in.

"115. That doesn't say anything to me. Does it to you?"

"No, that can't be it. It'd be too easy to have it be the first one." Howie checked the speedometer. They had gone barely a mile since they had made the turn. He would have to slow down even further for fear of missing any signs. "Let's go on and hope that whatever one it is, we'll know it."

"HERE COMES CHIEF LEADBECK now," the dispatcher said. Mick and Jodelle jumped up from their chairs. "He's the one carrying the clipboard."

Mick with Jodelle following rushed toward the tall man whose full walrus mustache had more hair than his head. He was engaged in an animated conversation with the two other officers.

"We need to talk," Mick said

"Son, can you wait a few minutes? I need to do a debriefing with my officers. We just came from a tough situation." He walked past Mick.

"It's a very urgent matter."

"I know, I know, everything is urgent," the Chief muttered without looking back.

"He's going to kill my sister!" Jodelle screamed.

Chief Leadbeck stopped, turned around, and came back. He looked at both of them, sizing them up. "Let's talk in my office. Henry?"

"Yeah, Chief?"

"You and Jim finish that report." He eyed his two visitors. "And stick around for awhile, will ya?"

Leadbeck led them into his office, offered them chairs, and then sat down behind his desk. "Now, why don't you tell me what's going on?"

Chapter 30

ADAM CONTINUED TO hang out the car window, shining the flashlight into the heavy brush as they drove slowly along the edge of the road. Beyond the brush lay an impenetrable dark wall of trees. Occasionally, the beam from the flashlight would fall upon a section of forest from which glowing amber eyes stared back at them. The first time Howie saw the eyes, he thought it was a person, maybe even Damien. Every thirty feet or so as they moved down the road, Adam would glance over at Howie. "Nothing. Keep moving."

"Okay, but when you see another one, tell me." Howie was glad that Adam had such a keen eye for spotting the fire signs.

"What time is it, now?" Adam asked.

"Just about eleven." Howie wiped the perspiration from his forehead. He had his window open, but the cool air didn't keep him from sweating. They had only found and checked out two signs in three miles. It had taken them nearly a half hour to do so. They almost missed the last sign because of the overgrown brush. He didn't dare drive over twenty miles per hour for fear of missing a sign. Although he hated the feeling, he was scared that they weren't going to find Maureen in time. *How could I ever face Jodelle if something happened to her sister?* He forced the thought out of his mind. Even though Adam didn't say anything, Howie sensed that he also feared the worst by the anxious tone in his voice and the worried look in his eyes.

"I hope we took the right road." Adam sounded like he was beginning to question his own judgment.

"According to the map Damien drew, we did."

"What if that funeral director pulled a fast one on us? Maybe that map is a just a ploy to throw us off."

"I don't think so," Howie said. A rabbit dashed across the road ten feet in front of them. "Bones was pretty shook up. He wasn't too happy with Damien using his place to keep Maureen." He glanced at the spot where the rabbit disappeared. "He's going to have to answer to the police when we get back. It's my guess that he'll probably--"

"Hang on. I think I see another one."

This Angel Has No Wings

Howie slowed the car to a crawl as his partner shined the light on a sign sticking out above the tall weeds. "Can you make out those numbers?" he asked.

"Looks like 133." Adam leaned further out the window. "No, that last number is a five. It's 135." He settled back in his seat. "I don't think that's it."

"Are you sure?"

"Not completely, but something tells me to move on." Adam shined the flashlight on the brush up ahead. "Let's go."

Howie was counting on Adam because of the conversations he had with Professor Lewis. If the fire sign had any number or symbol that was anti-religious, Adam would know. At least, Howie hoped he would. "I've got an idea to save us some time," he offered.

"Yeah, what's that?"

"The last three signs have been spaced more than a mile apart. I'm guessing the next one will be at least a mile from here." Howie stepped on the gas. He was taking a chance but the odds were in his favor. "Once we've gone a mile, I'll slow down again. It's a risk, but it's one we have to take. The clock is running against us."

"Okay, I'm with you but I'm still going to watch for them."

After they had gone another mile, Howie slowed the car down. They hadn't traveled more than another quarter of a mile when Adam shouted, "Here comes another one!"

Howie brought the car to a stop once they came up to the sign. "Looks like somebody marked that one up with black paint." He squinted but couldn't make it out. "Can you see those numbers?"

Adam turned off the flashlight and tossed it on the seat. "This is it!"

"Are you positive?"

"Oh, yes. That number is 666. It comes from the Book of Revelation."

"So what does it refer to?"

"It's the mark of the Beast."

THE DOOR FROM Chief Leadbeck's office flew open. "Where are Henry and Jim?" The dispatcher pointed to the conference room. The Chief stormed over and opened the door. "Come on, let's go!"

"What's up, Chief?" Henry asked, setting down his cup of coffee.

"Looks like we may have a problem. I'll fill you in on the way out to the squads. Bring the shotguns."

"The shotguns?" Jim glanced over at the other officer.

"You heard me. Let's get moving." He pointed to Mick and Jodelle. "They're coming with me. You two follow. And no sirens."

"WE'LL LEAVE THE car here and walk in," Howie said as he pulled the car to the side of the road. He turned off the headlights but kept the parking lights on.

"What are you doing? Aren't you going to turn them off?"

Charles Tindell

Howie shook his head. "When Mick and Jodelle come with the police, they'll be able to spot the car easier with them on." He looked down the road from the direction he and Adam had come from, hoping to see flashing red lights. "I sure hope that they're able to convince the cops."

"If anybody can do it, Mick can," Adam said as he picked up the flashlight.

"Better not turn that on." Howie opened the door. "That would be a dead give-a-way that we're coming."

"I know, but it may come in handy." Adam got out and met Howie in front of the car. They moved along the edge of the road until they came upon the driveway leading back into the woods.

"Looks like we can follow this," Howie said.

The two of them moved quickly for several minutes. "How far back is this place, anyway?" Howie whispered.

Adam motioned. "There's something up ahead." As they moved further, at a slower pace now, the silhouette of a building stood out against the night. "That must be the old farmhouse he told us about."

The place reminded Howie of a haunted house that he and Mick took their dates to a couple of years ago one Halloween night. They had paid two bucks a piece to get in. "It sure looks deserted," he whispered as they walked up to it. As they moved passed the house, they came upon the barn. One of the doors was missing and they saw a vehicle inside. They moved closer for a look.

"That's a hearse in there!" Howie exclaimed, positive that it had to have come from the Johnson Funeral Home.

"And there's a casket in the back," Adam said as he looked in the rear window. "You don't suppose?"

"We better take a look just to make sure." As Adam stood guard, Howie opened the back of the hearse, climbed in, and slowly lifted the lid of the casket. "Nothing here," he said as he closed it, and then wiped the sweat running down his forehead. "They've got to be around here someplace. Let's check in back." The two detectives made their way to the back of the barn.

"Over here." Adam pointed to a pathway leading back into the woods. "This may be what we're looking for."

They hadn't gone more than a couple hundred yards when they saw a soft reddish glow through the trees. "What's that?" Howie asked.

"Looks like it could be bonfires."

They moved rapidly, covering another hundred yards. As they drew nearer, they saw the clearing in the woods.

"Let's get as close as we can," Howie said. The two of them inched forward until they were nearly to the edge of the clearing. They took cover behind a large evergreen.

Adam moved a branch to look out into the clearing. "I don't suppose you brought a gun?"

"Gun? What are you talking about? You know I don't carry one."

"I know, but I was sort of hoping you got one for this."

"And you're going to be a peace-loving preacher?" Howie glanced at the ground around the trunks of the trees.

"What are you looking for?"

"Something we could use as a club."

Adam showed him the flashlight. "I told you that this might come in handy. When my heart's pounding as hard as it is now, I'm not as peace loving as you might think. I figure I could clobber a few of them with this before they got me." He looked out into the clearing again.

"Do you see her?"

"Not yet," Adam replied. "Wait a minute, there she is."

"Where?"

"Off to the right. She's tied to the tree."

Howie moved a branch. "Look at the way she's strung up," he said, feeling the anger rise in him. In the center of the clearing he counted eight people in robes. The eight had formed a circle around another robed figure. He had a good idea who that was. "That's got to be Damien in the middle of that circle. I wonder what he's doing?"

"I don't know, but he's holding something up in the air." Adam cocked his head. "I can't make out what he's saying. Can you?"

"No." Howie watched as the circle parted and Damien walked toward the bonfire located near Maureen. It was then that Howie noticed the homemade altar. Damien placed the object on the altar.

MICK TRIED TO present an outward calm appearance as he looked at the speedometer. Seventy-five and climbing. Even though he figured that Chief Leadbeck knew all the dips and curves in the road, he still felt uneasy. His stomach felt like he was on some thrill ride at the State Fair. "How much further until we get to that turn off?"

"It'll be another fifteen minutes even at this speed." The Chief had told him that he had a pretty good idea which dirt road the map was referring to. He had been on it a couple of times. "I hope your friends were smart enough to leave their car in sight because there are just too many fire signs to check out on that road."

"What time is it?" Jodelle asked.

"Eleven thirty," Mick said.

ADAM TOUCHED Howie on the arm. "Did you see that silver thing Damien placed on the right side of the altar?"

"Yeah, what is it?"

"It's a chalice, and I've a feeling it's pretty similar to the one he sent us." Adam's breaths were coming quick and heavy. "And you know what he used that one for."

"You don't think he'd..."

The chanting began again, sounding like giant insects humming in the night. There was no mistake as to what Damien held above his head this time. The blade of the knife caught the reflection of the fire. The circle parted and Damien walked over to the altar and laid the knife down. Howie watched as he walked over to Maureen. "What's he saying to her? He better not--"

"No!" Maureen screamed.

Howie jumped up but Adam grabbed him. "Wait a minute, are you crazy? You can't just go charging in there."

Howie clinched his fists. "If I know this guy, he'll do her exactly at midnight." His temples pounded as he glanced at his watch. "We got less than twenty minutes left."

Adam moved a branch and looked out toward the clearing again. He wet his lips and swallowed hard as he turned to Howie. "I've got an idea."

This Angel Has No Wings

Chapter 31

CHIEF LEADBECK slowed the car to sixty. "We should be coming up on that dirt road in a few minutes. I hope your friends waited for us."

"I've a feeling they didn't," Mick said. Howie could be impulsive at times, and Mick was glad Adam was with him to provide a balance. "Howie's not the type to sit around and do nothing."

Leadbeck grunted as he gave Mick a questioning glance. "How long have you guys had this detective agency?"

Mick hesitated, aware that Jodelle was listening to their conversation from the back seat. He didn't want to give her or Leadbeck the wrong impression. "Adam and I became part of it this summer. We work on a part-time basis. I'm a teacher. Adam's going to school; he's going to be a minister."

"Is that right?" Leadbeck didn't sound overly impressed. "How about the other guy?"

"He's been at it longer and works at it full time." Mick was stretching the truth and hoped Leadbeck didn't ask him how much longer. Three weeks would have seemed laughably inexperienced to a grizzly old cop like him. He had learned from talking with the dispatcher back at the station that Leadbeck has served as Chief for over twenty years.

"Does he carry a gun?"

"What?"

"Does he have a license to carry a gun?"

"No, why?"

Leadbeck shook his head. "Because he could be getting into a kettle full of boiling water with this...what's his name?"

"Damien."

"The guy sounds like a loony, but a dangerous one. And if he's up there with his group, your friends are going to run into more than they can handle." Leadbeck paused before directing his attention to Jodelle. "How did your sister ever get involved with this Damien?"

"It's a long story, but she was trying to protect me."

"Well, you're going to have to fill me in later; there's the road we turn on." Leadbeck slowed the car and made the turn with ease. He flashed a half grin over at Mick. "I hope you weren't expecting me to make that corner like you see cops do on television."

"No, sir." Mick was relieved to know that Leadbeck couldn't see his hand gripping the edge of his seat.

"It shouldn't be too long, now," Leadbeck said.

"What time is it?" Jodelle asked.

Mick glanced at his watch. "A quarter to twelve."

"So, what do you think about the plan; good idea?" Adam asked.

Howie shook his head. "I don't know. It sounds awful risky." He glanced toward the group of robed figures. "What if Damien doesn't fall for it?"

"I'm all ears if you've got a better idea."

Howie stared at Adam for a moment. "Okay, we'll go with it." He looked out at the clearing again. The group was quiet as Damien read from a notebook. *That's got to be The Book of Shadows. I'd love to get my hands on that.* "Give me about five minutes to get into position." He took a deep breath and let it out slowly. "Wish me luck."

"Hey, remember that albino squirrel we saw at Jodelle's place?" Adam asked.

"Yeah, why?"

"We said it's suppose to bring us good luck."

"It better, or else he's one dead squirrel."

"Take care of yourself," Adam whispered, and then watched Howie backtrack before circling around to where Maureen was tied to the tree. As Adam waited, he looked up through the treetops. The blue-black sky was filled with tiny specks of sparkling lights. He closed his eyes for a moment; the smell of the evergreen reminded him of the time he had lit a stick of incense in Howie's office. "It smells like a Christmas tree lot in here," Howie had complained. They had laughed when Mick made the same comment when he came in. It took three days before the office was clear of the smell. Adam glanced at his watch. *Two more minutes.* The odor of burning wood drifted past him, reminding him of the time he roasted marshmallows at camp. He looked out at the clearing and then over at Maureen. He wished he had some water; his mouth was so dry he could barely swallow. *One minute to go.* He looked in the direction where he thought Howie would be by now, but couldn't see any movement. "Here goes nothing," he muttered as he came out slowly from behind the tree and started walking toward the circle. Even though Damien had his back to him, Adam was surprised that the others didn't notice him. *What's the matter, guys? Too busy with your mumble jumbo?* It wasn't until he had gotten to within fifty feet of the group that one of the hooded figures pointed in his direction.

"An intruder!"

The circle collapsed upon itself as Damien stepped to the front of the group. Several of the others began moving toward Adam, but stopped when Damien held up his hand.

Adam moved to within twenty feet of the group, and then stopped. "Hello, Damien. I see you've got yourself a party going on."

"Yes, and it's a private one." The light from the bonfire reflected off Damien's face, giving him a grotesque appearance. "I don't recall you being invited." He looked past Adam as if trying to see if there was anyone else. "But since you're here, you certainly can stay." His eyes narrowed as he sneered. "In fact, you'll have to stay."

"I don't think so; the party's over." Adam's eyes shifted back and forth; he wanted to be prepared in case someone decided to rush him. If that happened, his whole plan could fail. "Do you think I'd be stupid enough to walk out here by myself? You can't see them but my partners are in the woods with the police. They're just waiting for me to give them a signal."

Several of the hooded figures began murmuring, turning to one another and pointing to the woods behind Adam. "Silence!" Damien snarled, and then directed his attention back to Adam. "The police you say?" he asked in a mocking tone of voice. "If they're here, why would they send you out alone?"

"Because I told them I'd try to talk some sense into you and your cronies." Adam didn't expect that Damien would believe him but he was counting on his arrogance. "That you'd surrender peacefully with no trouble."

"You offend me by assuming I'm so naive." Damien handed *The Book of Shadows* to one of the others. "If it is as you say, call forth your forces of goodness. Tell them to speak to me. Have them show themselves." He held out his arms, wrists together, as if he was preparing to be handcuffed.

Adam swallowed. His heart was beating so fast that he could feel it against his shirt. "Okay, you've got me, but I didn't come up here all by myself. My friends are back in Ely and they're bringing the police."

"I rather doubt that. And even if it were so, they'll be delayed. I've made sure that the Chief and his two officers would be kept busy for awhile so they wouldn't disturb our party." When Damien laughed, some of the others laughed as well. "You see, I've thought of everything."

Adam stole a quick glance at Maureen. "I guess you're as clever as Professor Lewis said you'd be."

Damien's eyebrows rose. Several moments passed before he spoke. "Really, and who is this enlightened person that you refer to? Anyone I know?"

"He's a professor at the seminary."

"I see; a professor of theology. I'm impressed. It's so nice to get a compliment like that from the *other* side. You must tell him that I am pleased." Damien smirked "Of course, that is, if you get a chance to see him again."

"Lewis also said that he thought you were quite clever."

"Really? How so?"

"In that you were familiar with some of the ancient languages. He wondered where you might've studied them."

"Too bad he's not here tonight. We could've had an interesting discussion about..."

Howie was glad that Adam still had the attention of Damien and the others. It had taken him longer than he had expected to circle around behind them. A couple of times, he had to rest for a moment to catch his breath. Tromping through the woods, being swatted in the face with low hanging branches was not his idea of having fun. While Adam worked his part of the plan, Howie crept up to the altar. When Maureen saw him, he put his fingers to his lips. He grabbed the knife, slipped over to where she was, and cut through the ropes that bound her. He motioned to her to follow him, and they disappeared into the woods.

"Can you run?" he whispered. She had bare feet, but there was no other choice.

"I can try."

"Good, let's go. We'll get away as far as possible, find a hiding place, and then stay there until the police come." They hadn't gone very far when Maureen screamed and fell to the ground, nearly pulling him with her.

"What's the matter?"

"My foot," Maureen cried in pain.

As soon as Adam heard Maureen's scream he took off running back toward the trail he and Howie had come from.

"After him, you fools!" Damien shouted.

Adam didn't have to look back to see if anybody was coming; he heard them crashing through the brush, and their angry shouts. He wasn't that far ahead so he couldn't simply slip off and hide. *If I can only get to the car, I can get in and take off.* That thought was comforting until he realized that Howie had the keys.

"Get him! Don't let him get away!" The shouts came from further back now. Adam was thankful that he was in such good shape. In high school, Mick had tried to encourage him to go out for tight end. "With your speed, you'll make the team easy." All he wanted right now was to make it to the car. His plan was to jump in, lock the doors, and hope for the police to get there soon. A branch hit in the face, cutting his lip. He hoped Howie and Maureen had gotten away. *What was that scream all about?* He risked a look back and saw that one of them was gaining. *How can he run so fast with that robe on?* At the rate the guy was gaining, Adam realized that he'd never make it to the car in time.

Maureen's scream had jolted Howie. He didn't know what happened. "Are you okay?" he asked as he knelt down beside her.

"No," she groaned. "I stepped on something sharp. It hurts bad."

Howie could see a branch-like stick imbedded into the bottom of her right foot. "You can't run with that thing." His mind was racing as he knew something had to be done, and done fast. "I'm going to have to pull it out."

"Do it," she said. "I--"

"Shhhh. Someone's coming." Howie could see two figures; one was carrying a flashlight. It would be only a matter of time until they found them. If he had to, he would carry Maureen. "Come on, we--"

The beam illuminated them, hitting them in the faces. "There they are!" a voice shouted. No sooner had the person shouted, then he turned off the light. Howie moved closer to Maureen as he heard twigs snapping to the side of them. "One of them is circling behind us," he whispered.

ADAM TRIPPED AND fell, hitting the ground hard. Dazed, he struggled to get up; his right shoulder throbbed. Keeping going, he told himself. He had just taken a few steps when he was tackled from behind. He hit the ground again. The pain in his shoulder was so intense that he thought he'd pass out. He groaned as he was yanked him up by his right arm. "Okay, we're going back to join the rest."

"You're not going anywhere!"

The voice came from behind them. When they turned, Adam could distinguish three police officers. Two of them had shotguns pointing at them; the other had his revolver out. Behind and to the side of the officers were two other people.

"Hey, buddy, you okay?"

Adam recognized Mick's voice. "Yeah, I think so. Tell your friends that I'm the good guy. This clown dressed up for Halloween is the one they want." He winced in pain. "And there's more coming any second."

The officer with the revolver spoke. "Okay, son. I'm Chief Leadbeck. Your friends here have told me the whole story. How many more are coming?"

"There were nine of them altogether. I don't know how many came after me. Some of them probably took off after my friend."

"Where's my sister?" Jodelle asked.

"We don't have time for that now," the Chief said. It was evident that he was used to giving commands to people and expecting them to obey. "Here's what we're going to do. Little red riding hood here is going to shout back to his friends that he's got you."

"I ain't going to--"

Leadbeck grabbed the guy by the neck, nearly lifting him off the ground. "Listen, I haven't got time for any arguments."

"Okay," the man gasped as Leadbeck released his grip.

"Do it now!"

"I got him! Hurry up!"

"Okay." Leadbeck pointed to Adam. "You lay down, and let this clown act as if he's holding you. We'll hide in the tree line. When they all get here, we'll just round them up like a herd of cows."

"You touch my shoulder once more," Adam whispered as the guy knelt down beside him, "I'm going to personally make sure you never walk again."

In less than a minute, other robed figures came running up. They stood around Adam, panting, holding their sides, gasping for breath. One of them kicked him in the side.

"Do that again," the Chief yelled, "and you'll be called hop-a-long." He and his two officers came forward with shotguns pointed at the group. Mick and Jodelle rushed over to Adam.

"Are you okay?" Mick asked, helping Adam up.

"I'll live."

"Where's my sister?" Jodelle asked excitedly.

"I don't know. She and Howie took off into the woods." Adam walked up to those who had chased him. He borrowed a flashlight and shined it in their faces. "There's seven here, and Damien's not among them. He and the other guy must've taken off after Howie and Maureen." He handed the flashlight back to the officers. "They're going to need your help."

Chief Leadbeck ordered Damien's group to lie down, spread-eagled, on the ground. When one of them complained, he growled, "Shut up." After handcuffing the seven of them together, he told his officers to watch them. "I'm going after the other two."

"I'm going with you," Mick said. One look from Leadbeck, however, told him that that wasn't going to happen.

"Why aren't they rushing us?" Maureen whispered.

"I don't know. Maybe they're just playing with us."

"I'm so glad you..." she stopped as they heard a movement behind them.

"Not very quiet, are they?" Howie said.

"What are we going to do?"

"We're not going to wait here like rabbits caught in a snare. We need to move. Can you walk if you lean on me?"

"I can hop. It hurts, but I'm not worried about the pain right now."

"You're a pretty brave lady."

Howie had Maureen put an arm around his neck and they started moving away from the sounds. They hadn't gone more than five yards when someone rushed them, knocking both of them down. Maureen screamed. Howie bounced back on his feet but was hit again. The guy was powerful, but Howie managed to ram him against a tree. He waited for the guy to get up, but he just lay there. Howie turned to check on Maureen only to be hit over the head. He fell to the ground. Somebody was on top of him. Although Howie fought hard, he knew the other person had the upper hand, and then he saw the glint of the knife.

"Oh, my God, no!" Maureen cried.

This Angel Has No Wings

Chapter 32

WITHIN MOMENTS AFTER Maureen cried out, a beam from a flashlight struck Howie and his assailant, and a gunshot echoed throughout the woods. The man on top of Howie gasped as though the air had been knocked out of him, and then fell to one side, writhing on the ground. Howie laid there for a second, trying to catch his breath, and figure out what had happened. He sat up and looked around, trying to get his bearings. The man lying beside him moaned. Whoever had fired that shot was coming toward them; Howie could see the beam from the flashlight bouncing up and down. "Maureen, where are you?" Howie whispered.

"Over here." The voice came from behind him.

She sounded frightened, and he didn't blame her. His heart was pounding as he kept his eyes on the beam of light coming toward them. "Are you okay?"

"I think so. Are you?"

"Yeah."

"Who is that coming?"

"I don't know. We'll find out in a second." As the beam of light came closer, Howie caught a glimpse of the gun the person held in his other hand. *Maybe that shot had been meant for me. What if this guy is one of Damien's group?* He felt around for the knife.

"Police officer!" a deep male voice called out. The officer shined his flashlight first on Howie and then on Maureen. After that, the beam of light stayed fixed on the man who had been shot. "Are you two alright?"

"Yeah, I think so." Howie said. "Who are you?"

"I'm Chief Leadbeck from Ely. Your friends, Mick and Jodelle talked to me." He kept his gun pointed on the wounded man. "I didn't want to shoot but he gave me no choice. It looked like he was about to get you with that knife."

Howie watched as Leadbeck checked the man, making sure he kicked the knife away. "How badly is he hurt?"

"Not bad. It's just a shoulder wound. He'll live. It could've been worst. He can count his lucky stars that I'm a good shot."

"Help me," the guy moaned.

"Shut up," Leadbeck said, "You'll get help."

Howie scrambled to his feet, remembering that there had been two people after them. "There's another guy around here some place." He glanced around. "He's over in that direction. I slammed him up against a tree. He might be knocked out."

Leadbeck shined his flashlight in the direction Howie pointed. "Well, there's nobody there, now." He turned around slowly, shining the light at the trees and bushes surrounding them. Not a trace of anyone. "Maybe we can get some answers from this fellow." He shined the flashlight into the man's face.

As soon as Howie saw the guy, he realized it wasn't Damien. He knelt down beside the wounded man. "Where is he?" he demanded.

"I don't know who you're talking about."

"Don't give me that!" Howie yelled.

The guy looked up at the police chief. "Get me to a doctor, will you? I'm going to bleed to death."

"You'll be okay." Leadbeck motioned for him to stand. "Come on, get up. We're going to rejoin your friends."

Howie went over to Maureen. "Can you make it?"

"I think so."

"How's the foot?"

"I managed to get the stick out. It hurts, but I can walk if I lean on you." She slowly got up with Howie's help.

Chief Leadbeck joined them with his prisoner. "How is she?"

"She can make it back, but we'll have to take it slow."

"That's no problem. This guy isn't in any shape to move very fast, himself."

Howie glanced around. "What about Damien?"

"Can't worry about him now."

"But--"

"Listen, son, he's probably a long ways off by now. You're just fortunate that I found you in these woods. If it hadn't been for her scream, I might not have made it in time."

When they finally made it back to the others, Jodelle ran up and hugged her sister. After bandaging up Maureen's foot with material torn from one of the hooded robes, they started toward the farmhouse. On the way back, Adam shared with Leadbeck what their plan had been.

"That's a pretty bold thing you did, walking into that clearing by yourself."

"Thanks, but I sure wish Damien hadn't gotten away."

"Don't worry about it. We parked our squads by the old farmhouse. When we get there, we'll radio for more help. He can't have gone too far on foot. We'll search these woods until we find him."

"I don't think that's going to happen," Adam said as they walked up to the barn.

"What makes you think that?"

"Look, the hearse is gone. He must've circled around us and taken it."

"Chief, quick, come over here!" one of the officers yelled. He was shining his flashlight at the squad cars.

"I'll be a..."

"What is it?" Adam asked.

Leadbeck muttered something under his breath that Adam didn't hear. "He took time to smash our car radios, and slashed a couple of tires on each car."

Howie and Mick came running up. "What are you going to do?" Howie asked Leadbeck.

"I guess we'll just have to combine the tires and spares we have to get one car running."

"Our car's out on the road," Adam said.

"Son, you can go ahead and check on it, but I've a feeling that you'll find your tires in the same shape as these."

Adam had a sinking feeling that Leadbeck was right. "That means by the time we get back, he'll be well on his way."

"Maybe so, but I don't think he'll get too far in that hearse. It should be easy to spot him."

"So now what?"

The Chief stroked his mustache. "Well, after we fix up one of our squads with four good tires, I'll have my two officers drive into town with three of the prisoners including the fellow who was shot. Once they lock them up and get the other guy over to the hospital, they'll come back with some more tires."

IT WAS NEARLY two hours before they all got back to Ely. After the Chief took care of his prisoners, he told one of his deputies to go over to the hospital to keep guard over the wounded prisoner. "He should be out of surgery by now. And don't be talking to Mabel about it." Leadbeck noticed Howie and his friends listening. "Mabel's the night nurse," he explained. "She's one of the best, but she's too curious for her own good."

"What are you going to do about Damien?" Howie asked, wondering how far he had gotten by now.

"I'll put out a call to the police departments between here and the Cities." He turned to the dispatcher. "Put out an alert for a 1965 black hearse. Tell them to approach with caution." He turned and smiled. "The boys will have fun with that one."

An hour later, Chief Leadbeck came in to where they were sitting and having coffee. "They found the hearse. It was abandoned in St. Cloud three blocks away from the bus depot."

"What about Damien?" Jodelle asked.

Leadbeck shook his head. "Nothing."

Charles Tindell

Chapter 33

HOWIE OFFERED MORE coffee to Mick and Adam as they waited in Howie's office for Jodelle to arrive.

"Just a warm up," Mick said. "I want to sleep tonight."

Adam held his cup up. "About half, okay."

After pouring their coffee, Howie poured himself another cup. It was the end of the second pot, and it looked black as ink. His partners were tired. He was tired. None of them had gotten more than three hours sleep. They had arrived back from Ely around ten that morning. Before taking Jodelle and Maureen back to Jodelle's house, they agreed to meet that evening; it was at Jodelle's request.

Once they dropped off the two sisters, they drove over to the Johnson Funeral Home. From there they called the police. Chief Leadbeck had contacted the St. Paul police while they were with him in Ely. One of the Captains was a friend of his; they had worked together as rookie patrolmen years ago. The Chief gave his friend an overview of the case and told him that he should expect a phone call. He informed the Captain they had probable cause to take the owner of the funeral home, Mr. Bones, into custody for questioning. "One of the guys from the MAC Detective Agency will be calling you." He had paused, looked over at Howie, and winked. "When you meet them, they look pretty young, but they're okay. Yeah, I'll vouch for them."

BEFORE HOWIE MADE the phone call from the funeral home, he made sure they found Joey's cat and brought him out to the car. "I don't want the cops taking the cat as evidence," he explained. The police arrived within minutes after Howie called them. They took Bones in for questioning, telling Howie that he and his partners along with Maureen and Jodelle would have to come down to the station the next day to make statements.

Howie dropped Adam and Mick at home around two, and then drove over to Joey's. He had to wait for Joey to get home from school, but it was worth it just to hear the kid yell, "Midnight, it's you" and to see his brown eyes get as big as full moons. "I knew you'd find him. I knew it. You're the bestest detective in the whole wide world." Howie declined the ice cream and cake Joey's mother wanted to serve him as a celebration. Although he wanted to, he was too tired to decline the two dollars in nickels, dimes, and pennies Joey gave him as his fee. He would use the money to buy Midnight a coming-home present. Some catnip, maybe, or a rubber mouse. It was nearly four-thirty when he got back to the office. He collapsed in his chair, planning to jot some notes down on an idea he had about finding Damien, but instead, laid his head on the desk and fell asleep. It was not until Mick and Adam walked in an hour later that he woke up, surprisingly, feeling quite refreshed.

Mick sat down, leaned back in the chair, and stretched his legs out. "At least, Damien's group is broken up. Jodelle and Maureen should be happy about that."

"I would think so," Adam said, and then yawned. "Man, I'm exhausted. I need to get to bed early tonight." He put his head back on the chair, and closed his eyes. "Wake me up when she gets here."

"What time is she coming over?" Mick asked.

Howie looked at the clock. "It's six now. She should be here any minute." He heard the downstairs entrance door open and close. "That's probably her."

Mick stretched his arms in front of him, and groaned. "Ah, that feels good. You know, that Chief Leadbeck is a pretty neat guy. I had to laugh when he said that Damien's group won't be practicing their mumbo jumbo for awhile."

"Yeah, that's for sure," Howie replied. "He told me that three of the eight were wanted on priors, and two were on parole. The other three were thinking about testifying." The door opened and Jodelle came in. Howie was hoping that their meeting wouldn't take too much time. He had something he needed to talk over with Mick and Adam. "Come on in, I'll get another chair."

Mick got up. "Here, take mine. I've got to stand up for awhile or else I'm going to fall asleep. That chair's too comfortable." He went over and stood by the window.

"Thank you." Jodelle sat down. Although she looked tired, Howie thought her face seemed more relaxed. "I wanted to make sure I gave you this." She reached in her purse, pulled out a white envelope, and handed it to Howie. "There's two thousand dollars in there in hundred dollar bills."

Howie had to consciously keep his mouth from dropping open. He noticed the startled looks on his partner's faces. If they were like him, they had seen but never owned a hundred dollar bill. "That's very generous, but I think we agreed on only--"

"I know what we agreed upon, but you and your partners deserve it." She looked around and smiled. "You earned every penny of it. I only wish we would have gotten Damien."

"The police have an all-points bulletin on him," Howie said. "Besides kidnapping your sister, they'd like to question him about a number of other things. I also called my police detective friend and filled him in on everything. He'll be on the lookout for Damien as well. If the police get him, and I think they will, he'll do some jail time."

"I hope so."

"He will if we have something to say about it," Adam said as he glanced over at Mick. "Isn't that right?"

Mick nodded. "You bet. I personally would like to meet up with the guy just one more time, and on my terms this time."

Howie gave Mick a knowing smile. You just might get that chance. "What are your plans for the future?" he asked Jodelle.

"That's one of the reasons I wanted to meet with all of you. I wish to share my good news. My sister and I are going on a month long trip to Europe as soon as we can." She paused for a moment. "You know, just to get away from everything."

"That's great," Adam said.

"Sure is," Mick added.

"Thank you. We thought it'd be a great chance to reacquaint ourselves." For the next several minutes, Howie and his friends listened to Jodelle as she talked about revisiting some of the places that her father had taken them years ago. She thanked them again and left.

"Well, I have to go, too," Adam said as he got up from the chair. Mick echoed the same sentiment and started for the door.

"Wait a minute," Howie said. "Don't you two go anywhere. I have a hunch where we can find Damien."

This Angel Has No Wings

Chapter 34

DAMIEN PARKED THE car, rolled down the window, and sat, listening. It was quiet, peaceful. That's why he liked cemeteries. Years ago, he had seen a photograph of a cemetery in England. The cemetery dated back to the seventeenth century. Over its entrance hung a sign for all those who were visiting to read and ponder: *What thou art, we once were. What we are now, thou wilt become.* He liked those words. Death had always intrigued him. He didn't fear it because he was the master of it. He had witnessed the moment of death in animals. *Curiously fascinating.* And he had hoped he would have been able to witness it of a person. To be there at that exact moment. To witness the final breath being taken; the spirit departing the body. It would be gloriously exciting. What happened up north was a disappointment, but he wasn't defeated. There'd always be another time. Another place. Another candidate. Other coven members.

After he finished what he had come to do this night, he would start new in another part of the country. Perhaps, out west. There was no reason to go back to the Cities; everything he needed was in the car. The money he had taken from the funeral home would be more than enough to get him started. He would take over another coven or start his own. Either way, it wouldn't be difficult. There are always fools who are easily persuaded. Once he had a group, the members could be molded into anything he wanted them to be. They would do whatever he willed them to do. *Why? Out of fear of me.* He chuckled. *And if they didn't fear me, they soon would.*

He glanced at his watch. *Nearly midnight. Time to go.* He got out, went to the back of his car and opened the trunk. The black satchel was tucked in the corner. He struggled getting it out. After setting the bag down, he took a deep breath, and gazed into the star-filled sky. The night was clear but it had turned cool. On the way down, the radio announcer warned of possible frost. He was glad that he had worn a jacket but knew that once he started, he would work up a sweat, and soon discard it. Closing the trunk, he looked around just to make sure he was alone before he started into the cemetery. As he walked through the main entrance, he felt serene. He liked walking among the dead; it gave him a feeling of invincibility.

A couple of times, Damien had to set the satchel down and rest. It was heavier than he had remembered. He hadn't needed to carry it for some time since he always had one of the others carry it for him. *Fools. They would do anything for me.*

When Damien arrived at the statue of the angel, he was pleased to see that it hadn't yet been repaired. Pieces of the wing still lay scattered upon the ground. "What's the matter, doesn't anybody care about you?" He placed the satchel near the statue, unzipped it, and took out several hammers and chisels, and a small sledgehammer. "How do you like these?" He paused, looked around at the surrounding tombstones and spoke as if he was addressing the inhabitants beneath them. "I forgot, she can no longer see." He snickered. "Well, my dear angel, I've come to finish the job. You shouldn't be surprised at that, for I always finish what I begin. What's that you're asking?" He cocked his head. "So, you want to know what I plan to do?" He held up a hammer and one of the chisels. "Once I relieve you of your other wing, I shall leave my mark on you." He cocked his head again. "It will be a triangle with the letter, D, in its center. I'm going to place it right here." He touched the left side of the angel's chest. "Oh, dear, your heart is beating so rapidly. You're not frightened, are you?" He smiled, pleased that the idea about leaving his mark came to him on the drive down. "Don't you see? It'll be a monument to me. Even if others removed it, many will still come to this spot." He paused and looked around. "This will be a sacred place to the followers of Belial. And you will be powerless to do anything about it." He placed the end of the chisel in what he considered to be a good spot to begin, and raised the hammer. "It's time."

"Hello, Damien." Howie stepped out from behind a monument to the right of him. "Pardon me for interrupting."

"You! How--"

"Let's just say I knew you had an aversion to angels."

Damien smiled. "Well, I must confess that I may have underestimated you."

"We can't all be perfect, can we?"

"You knew I'd come back to finish this, didn't you?"

"I had a hunch you would."

"So what happens now?" Damien tightened his grip on the hammer as Howie moved closer.

"I think you and I should take a trip back to the Cities." Howie was now less then ten feet away. "I have a police detective friend who would love to have a cup of coffee with you and get to know you better."

"You have nothing on me."

"Yeah, what about what you did to Mick? He wasn't too happy about that. And what about those packages you sent us?"

"What packages? I'm not aware of any packages." Damien shrugged. *The fool has no concrete proof of my involvement.* "And as far as what happened to your friend, I wouldn't know. Tell me. Was he hurt or something?"

"Okay, wise guy, there's still the business about Maureen."

"Yes, that was an error in judgment. What started off as a Halloween prank became, what shall I say," Damien paused. "I think a good word might be *overzealous*. Keeping her in the funeral home was not called for. And I admit that bringing her up north was carrying the prank too far. She didn't really think I was going to harm her, did she?"

"If you think anybody is going to buy that, you're crazy."

"It doesn't matter what you think." Damien's smile had turned into a sneer and his body tightened with anger that his plans were being disrupted. "I'm not going anywhere with you." He dropped the chisel and then turned the hammer around, its claws pointing toward Howie. "And I don't think you can take me. You tried that once." He held the hammer up for Howie to see.

"How about if I help?" Adam stepped out from behind a tree to the left of Damien. "I'd like to be in on this party as well."

"Don't forget about me." Damien turned around and saw Mick.

"Well, what do you know," Howie said. "You're still in the circle. I suppose it's more like a triangle. If you were an angel, we could say we've just clipped your wings."

"He never had wings in the first place," Adam said.

"It worked just like you said it would," Mick said to Howie. "I waited until he went in, and then I pulled the car in right next to his." He moved closer to Damien. "Where you're going, you're going to have to turn in your robe for new garments."

Damien thought about trying to make a break for it, but he knew it would be useless. The hammer would prove to be an effective weapon, but he didn't think he could take all three. No matter. He would take his chances with the police and the courts. He had talked his way out of other charges in the past; he was confident he could do it with most of these as well. Other than Maureen, they had no real charges against him, and he was confident that others in his group would not testify against him. He tossed the hammer on the ground. "Okay, if you insist; I'll go with you for now. Shall we take my car or yours?"

"Check that duffel bag before we go," Howie said.

Adam knelt down, opened it, and then looked up and smiled. "Guess what I found?" He stood up and handed it to Howie.

"Well, we finally have the illusive *Book of Shadows*. I--"

"I believe that belongs to me." The voice came from the left of them. A man, pointing a gun at them, slowly stepped from the shadows into full view.

"Professor Lewis!" Adam cried.

Chapter 35

"Hello, Adam. I'm sorry you had to find out this way." Professor Lewis peered through his glasses at the others. "You're Howie, aren't you. I remember you from the lecture I gave. And you, I haven't met you before, but you must be Mick. Adam has spoken very highly of both of you."

Damien tore away from Mick's grip and moved in Lewis' direction. "You came just in time. I--"

Lewis pointed the gun at Damien. "Stay where you are, please."

"But--"

"You weren't going to give it back, were you?"

"I swear to you, I was. I just needed it this one last time. After I finished with the angel, I was going to--"

"Enough," Lewis said quietly, but forcefully. "You're very good at lying and deceiving others," he paused, and then slowly shook his head, "but you should know that you can't do that with me. I'm here to take back what is mine."

"What are you talking about?" Adam asked.

"It could be only one thing," Howie said. "*The Book of Shadows.* Am I right, Professor?"

Lewis nodded. "A splendid deduction. I would have been honored to have had you in class."

"Count me out. I don't think I'd want to be one of your students."

Adam felt like he was in a bad dream. One of his best friends was smarting off to a professor Adam had come to admire and respect. Not only that, but there was some connection between Professor Lewis and Damien. He looked at Lewis, not wanting to believe what his instincts were telling him. "I don't understand. Why are you involved with all of this?"

"It's a long story, and I don't have time to go into all of it now. Suffice it to say that when my wife died of cancer, my faith in the power of goodness died with her."

"So that's when you started playing around with the other side," Howie offered.

"Yes, only I didn't play at it. I studied and worked hard at understanding the powers of darkness. I never intended to use what I learned to harm anyone."

Mick pointed to Damien. "Yeah, you should've told that to this creep."

"I realize that now."

"How did Damien force you into this?" Adam asked, still not wanting to believe what was unfolding before his eyes.

Damien chuckled, but quickly stopped when Lewis glanced at him. "I'm afraid it was I who got him involved. He wanted to learn, and I was willing to teach. He was such a promising student." Lewis sighed. "Except, he took it further than I had anticipated."

"*The Book of Shadows*, then? It's yours?"

Lewis nodded. "It contains years of work."

"How did--"

"I'm sorry," Lewis said. He pointed the gun in the direction of the cemetery's entrance, and motioned to Adam and his partners. "No more questions. It's time to leave. Damien and I have something to discuss."

"We're not leaving," Howie said.

Lewis peered over his glasses at Adam. "Please, convince your friend to go. I would not like to use this gun, but I will."

Adam and his professor locked eyes. No one spoke. The only sounds were of the wind moving through the trees and of leaves scurrying amongst the tombstones. "I think we better do as he says," Adam finally said.

"That's a wise decision," Lewis said. "Now, I want you to go to your car. Rev the engine a couple of times so I know you're there. After you do that, leave." He looked at Howie. "And please, don't try and trick me by one of you doubling back. Remember, I do have the gun, and I will use it if necessary."

"What about Damien?" Mick asked.

"He won't be coming with you."

Chapter 36

"WHAT DO YOU think Lewis is going to do with Damien?" Mick asked as they approached their car.

"I don't know." Howie said.

"He wouldn't shoot him, would he?"

Mick's question brought them to a halt just as they reached the car. "Professor Lewis wouldn't do anything like that," Adam said. "He couldn't."

Howie looked back in the direction from which they came. "We can't be sure of what he'll do. It sounded like that *Book of Shadows* was mighty important to him. He wasn't too happy with Damien trying to run off with it."

A pained expression swept over Adam's face. "Yeah, but killing him?"

"I find that hard to believe, myself," Howie admitted. "But Damien double-crossed him. Who knows what--"

The sound of a gunshot reverberated through he night. Adam looked toward the cemetery. "I'm going back."

"Are you crazy," Mick said. "If he shot Damien, he'll shoot you, too."

"No, he won't."

"Mick's right," Howie said. "We--"

"I don't care what you guys think, Lewis is a sick man and needs help. I'm going and you're not going to stop me."

"Okay, but you're not going alone. We'll go with you. Your professor may be sick, but remember, he's got a gun."

They moved quickly among the tombstones, stopping every so often to listen. When they came to a spot from which they could make out the figure of the angel, they stopped again. "Do you see Lewis?" Howie whispered.

"I don't see anybody," Adam replied. "Maybe he took off. Lets get closer."

They slowly moved to the area where they had first confronted Damien. "Over there!" Mick cried, pointing to a person lying near the base of the statue. All three rushed to the body.

"Oh, no," Adam said. "It's Professor Lewis."

This Angel Has No Wings

Howie knelt down, placed his hand on the side of Lewis' neck. "He's dead."

"Oh, man," Mick muttered.

The sound of two gunshots startled them, causing them to instinctively duck as though the shots had been fired in their direction.

"I think they came from the direction of the car," Adam said.

"Damien must be up to his old tricks, again," Howie said. "Let's go find out, but we better go slow." They hadn't gotten far when they heard the revving of a car engine.

"What's he doing?" Mick asked.

"The creep is telling us good-bye," Howie said.

"Come on," Mick urged, "maybe we can catch him."

"I don't think that's going to happen."

"Why not?"

Howie cursed under his breathe. "Those two gun shots. If I know him, he was shooting out the tires of our car."

Charles Tindell

Chapter 37

HOWIE LEANED BACK in his chair. It had been two weeks since the night Professor Lewis had been killed. Damien had disappeared without a trace.

"Any more news from the police?" Mick asked Howie.

"JD called me this morning; he talked to a detective friend of his who works out of the St. Paul department. He said that they're speculating that Damien's left the state, possibly even the country by now. They're confident they'll eventually get him, but it may take some time." Howie paused. "He also told me that he thought we did a pretty decent job on this case, considering that it was our first one." JD had also chided him for waiting so long before getting him involved, but Howie decided to keep that to himself.

"How are Jodelle and Maureen doing?"

"Not too good. I talked to Jodelle a couple of days ago. After their trip, they may decide to relocate. They're not sure yet." Howie looked at Adam. "How are things over at the seminary?"

"Everybody's still in shock. I still can't believe it myself."

"Yeah, I know what you mean." Howie took a deep breath, wondering how Adam was doing. Lewis' involvement in Satanism had shaken his partner. Adam seemed more confused than ever about becoming a minister. He made a mental note to ask Kass to have a talk with him. The case had been hard on all of them, and he needed to check something out. "Say, I've been meaning to ask you guys something for a couple of days, now."

"Oh, yeah," Mick said. "What's that?"

"I know that this has been a pretty rough case." Howie cleared his throat. "Do you guys want to continue working with me? I mean if you decide that you've had enough of the detective business, I'll understand."

"Are you kidding?" Mick looked at Adam. "Tell me he's kidding."

"Look," Adam began, "we gave it our best shot. Maybe not everything worked out the way we wanted to, but Damien's group was broken up and that crooked funeral director is going out of business. Mick and I have talked it over. We want to continue."

Mick offered Howie a half smile. "Didn't you promise that you would bring some excitement into our otherwise dull and boring lives?"

"I know, but--"

"No buts about it. We're with you."

"Thanks. It's good to have you." Howie took a deep breath. "What do you say that you go home and get some rest? Who knows what kind of cases we'll get next."

"That sounds good to me," Adam said. "I've got some thinking to do about school. I need to reassess some things."

Mick said. "Mary and I are going out to dinner tonight and just relax. And when I go to school tomorrow, I'm planning to have a nice long talk with Robby Davis."

"Who's that?" Howie asked.

"He's the kid I told you about who thinks demons and witches are cool."

"Good luck. If you need--"

"I think someone's knocking." Adam looked toward the door.

"Come on in," Howie yelled. The door opened slowly. It was Joey and another kid. "Hi, Joey, who's your friend?"

"Patrick."

Patrick's reddish-brown hair matched his freckles. He was a couple of inches shorter than Joey, and although he had brown eyes, they were not nearly as large as Joey's. He seemed unsure of coming in and with one hand clung to Joey's shirt.

"Hello, Patrick, My name is Howie. These are my partners, Mick and Adam."

Patrick nodded and then whispered in Joey's ear while pointing at Howie.

"Yeah, he's the one I told you about. He's the bestest. And see that chair?" When Patrick tilted his head to look around Howie, Howie got up and stepped aside. "That used to be a dentist chair," Joey said. "You know, when you go and they do things to your teeth." Joey held his finger to Patrick's mouth and made a sound like a dentist drill. Patrick's mouth dropped open as he looked from the chair to Howie and back to the chair.

Mick tapped Adam on the arm and then pointed at Howie. "Did you know that about him being the bestest? I bet he--"

"Don't push it," Howie said through clinched teeth. He smiled as he turned his attention to Joey and his friend. "Well, what can I do for you?" He figured that Joey had come to show Patrick what a detective's office was like. *I suppose he's going to ask me if I carry a gun or--*

"Patrick wants to hire you to find Freddie."

Oh, no. "I'm sorry, but I've gotten out of the cat finding business. I suggest--"

"Freddie's not a cat," Joey said.

"He isn't?"

"No, he's Patrick's favoritest pet turtle."

Mick got up. "Well, I've got to go. I got some school papers to correct."

"I'm going, too," Adam said.

Charles Tindell

"Wait a minute, guys," Howie pleaded. "Don't leave."

"Hey," Mick said, "you can handle it."

"Yeah," Adam agreed. "After all, you're the bestest."

After his partners left, Howie took out his notepad. "Okay, Patrick, let's start from the beginning. When was the last time you saw Freddie?"

Charles Tindell's writing career began one hot July day in 1995 while sitting in a canoe in the Boundary Waters Canoe Area in northern Minnesota. His first book *Seeing Beyond the Wrinkles* is the recipient of the National Mature Media's coveted GOLD AWARD designating it among "The Best in Educational Material for Older Adults." His second book *The Enduring Human Spirit* has recently been published.

He and his wife, Carol, have three sons and four grandchildren. Oil painting, ventriloquism, baking bread, canoeing, and writing are among his interests. He serves as a volunteer police chaplain for his community. He has spoken around the country on the subject Spirituality and Aging.

This Angel Has No Wings is his first mystery and the initial offering in the MAC Detective Series featuring Howie Cummins and his partners, Adam Trexler and Mick Brunner. He is currently working on the second mystery, *This Angel Doesn't Like Chocolate.*

Printed in the United States
22350LVS00005B/1-60